CONFESSIONS

OF A

CELEBRITY
BODYGUARD

THOMAS FITZSIMMONS

ALSO BY THOMAS FITZSIMMONS:

Fiction

Confessions of a Catholic Cop
Confessions of a Suicidal Policewoman
Rockers—Stories

Although inspired by real-life characters and actual events, *Confessions of a Celebrity Bodyguard* is a work of fiction. Names, characters, places, and incidents are either the products of the author's imagination or are used fictitiously. Any resemblance to actual persons, living or dead, events, or locales are entirely coincidental.

ISBN: 978-0-9789762-6-2

Manufactured in the United States of America

www.thomasfitzsimmons.com

For Wendy, of course, and the denizens of Yorkville
who supply me with endless inspiration....

Celebrities sleep peaceably in their beds at night only because rough men stand ready to do violence on their behalf.

CONFESSIONS

OF A

CELEBRITY
BODYGUARD

GRAMMY AWARD–WINNING SINGING sensation and international sex symbol Audra Gardner expired on September 15 at approximately 12:05 a.m. Her two bodyguards, a retired New York City police lieutenant, Shamus Beckett, and his son, moonlighting off-duty police officer Michael Beckett, discovered Audra naked in the bedroom of her lavish twenty-million-dollar Manhattan town house, lying facedown in a pool of her own vomit. A hypodermic needle containing heroin laced with fentanyl—a powerful opiate usually found in patches given to cancer patients—was still stuck in her slender arm. The twenty-one-year old, multitalented superstar who was adored by millions, had died utterly alone.

Although she had received thinly veiled death threats—e-mails, texts, and phone calls—from a mysterious individual claiming to be a divine messenger calling himself the Angel of Death—the police found no evidence of foul play. Besides the lack of real motive or other physical evidence, tracing the source of the easily available heroin had proven futile. And so the medical examiner ruled, over the vehement objections of her dogged senior bodyguard, that Audra's passing was an "accidental combined drug-intoxication overdose." The superstar's recent, well-publicized booze- and drug-fueled public meltdowns, arrests, and stints in various rehabilitation centers left them no choice.

Which was exactly what the Angel of Death had anticipated.

He had attended Audra's rain-soaked funeral at Westchester County's Sleepy Hollow Cemetery. Hidden under an umbrella in a sea of umbrellas at the back of the crowd, standing beside the famous New York socialite Brooke Astor's tomb. Watching as a cherubic-faced minster delivered a canned graveside eulogy while, off to his right, he overheard Shamus Beckett telling a skeptical journalist that Audra had been murdered by the Angel of Death. All of this took place while Shamus's son Michael—*A heroically handsome Irish-American possessed of quick fists and a .38- caliber temperament,* according to one gushing female crime reporter— lurked menacingly on the fringes of the interment, scrutinizing the attendees.

Although Shamus continued to investigate Audra's death for months, he died never knowing that her slaying was a divine act of His love. That the Angel of Death was, in actuality, an Angel of Mercy. For he had saved Audra from further earthly suffering and, most importantly, the loss of her immortal soul. Saved her from becoming just another sad, drug-addicted has-been, a faded star to be pitied and forgotten. The Angel of Death would not allow that to happen. In death, the world would always remember Audra as a great talent and beauty. In death, she'd be immortal.

That was the Angel of Death's gift to Audra Gardner.

His gift to them all.

CHAPTER 1

EVEN UNDER THE cover of darkness, amid the chaos of Lincoln Center traffic, we knew at once that we were being followed—the battered, blue Chevy passenger van, two car lengths back. But we were careful not to alarm our client; the short, chunky, nineteen-year-old star of the mind-numbing reality TV show, *Jersey Shore Confidential*. Francine "Tata" Andolini, the self-proclaimed Queen of the Guidettes, was sitting in the dark in the rear of our armored SUV, chain-smoking—I hated breathing in secondhand smoke—and jabbering with what sounded like her boyfriend.

"Oh, yeah?" Tata shrieked. "Ya keep it up, Nicky, and I'll cut ya balls off. Ya hear me, Nicky? Ya piece a shit." She flicked her cigarette out the window into the night.

Destiny Jones, my former partner in the NYPD and estranged honey bunny, was driving, her eyes constantly flickering to the rearview mirror. She ran different tests. Eased up on the accelerator. The battered blue van hung back. She hit the gas. The van sped up. She changed lanes. The van followed.

"Think he's a stalker?" Destiny said, excited at the prospect.

"Could be." I powered down my window, letting out the last of the secondhand smoke, and letting in vehicle- exhaust fumes; I didn't know which was worse. I looked into the passenger-side mirror. Checked out the rusting, rattle-bang Chevy van that, in the dim light, looked like it had been hand-painted by a pre-schooler. "That's the worst paint job I've ever seen."

"Ugly color too," Destiny said. "Metallic blue?"

"This from someone who drives a cherry-red sports car."

"It's scarlet, you dolt."

I bit back a smile. The van wove in and out of my mirror. "I can't make out the license-plate number. You?"

"He's got his brights on—smart." Destiny and I had used the very same trick to blind suspects we followed when we worked anticrime together in Fort Apache, the Bronx's high-crime 41st Precinct.

"Thanks for taking me along today for the advance work," Destiny said. "I had no idea there was so much involved."

"You want to be a bodyguard, you have to learn this stuff."

Destiny and I had begun our day's advance work by traveling the exact route that we were now taking, alert for construction, street closures, or anything else that could delay Tata's arrival at the MTV Rap Music Awards. We had arrived at the Beacon at 10:00 a.m. sharp and met with the theater's head of security, an ex-cop we both knew. Together we conducted a walk-through of the facility. Planned Tata's entrance and exit, chose her seat in the VIP section. We discussed emergency plans in case of fire, don-nybrook, or bomb threat. Verified that all emergency exits were accessible and unobstructed.

We were both startled by the sudden blare of sirens, ear-piercing horns.

A rush of fire engines, police cars, and ambulances came rac-ing off West Sixty-sixth Street onto Broadway and roared north, compelling all vehicles to pull over. Seeing the Chevy van was now stuck at a red light, one lane to the left and parallel to our SUV, I did my best to peer into the van's illegally dark-tinted windows. Saw a small white skull hanging from the van's rearview mirror. Bony fingers gripped the steering wheel.

"Screw this," Destiny said. She jammed the SUV into *park*.

"I'm gonna find out who's in that van." She placed her hand the butt of her Ladies' Glock 19 and started to get out.

I grabbed her arm. "Don't." I couldn't help but notice that her skirt had ridden up—way up—exposing yummy thighs.

"I'm just gonna find out why he's following us."

But the light turned green and the blue van tore off, made an illegal left turn, and disappeared behind a conga line of charter buses.

"That's that," I commented. Destiny settled back, relaxed her gun hand, and readjusted her navy-blue skirt. Even though we were no longer a couple, I took that moment to admire her. A first-class hottie, Destiny was one of those women who was always manicured and, whether she wore sweats or a cocktail dress, perfectly coiffed; she groomed herself like a cat. Which was one of the reasons that most men, and some women, were wildly attracted to her. Another was her cynically sensual, in-your-face personality.

"Everything, like, all right, Ms. Jones?" Tata said from the backseat.

"Call me Destiny."

Tata snorted. "Like in Destiny's Child?"

"Something funny?"

"No," Tata sniggered.

Impatient horns blasted behind us. Destiny shifted into gear, stepped on the gas.

Hearing a rustle, I glanced at the backseat as the puzzlingly popular and utterly talentless D-list reality star used a tiny spoon to scoop cocaine out of a small vial, place it under her surgically enhanced nose, and snort. Even though we'd bodyguarded her before, the dumpy, faux-tanned little twit had no idea that Destiny and I were retired New York City cops. I took a deep breath, told myself to relax. Whatever drugs a client snorted, shot up, smoked or ingested was none of our business. Yet it took all the self-control I could muster to stop from snatching the vial and pouring the coke out the window.

"So, Francine," Destiny said, "why do they call you Tata?"

Tata executed an exaggerated eye roll, screwed the cap back on the coke vial, dropped it in her black Chanel-style clutch purse. "It's because I show everyone my tatas, silly—see?" Tata pulled down the front of her Valentino-style dress, unholstered and jiggled her ample, orange-hued breasts. "And they're real," she gushed. "I love them!"

I couldn't believe my eyes.

"Great," Destiny said, irritated. "Good luck with those."

Turning around, I used a thumb and forefinger to massage away the headache that was forming behind my eyes; this was going to be a long night.

As Destiny stopped at another red light, I spotted a car full of "stalkerazzi" directly behind us in a Honda with New York press license plates. I groaned, tired of these photographers who aggressively stalked and harassed celebrities. For that reason I did not pay attention to the black Harley-Davidson motorcycle that was three car lengths to the rear, zigzagging in the heavy traffic.

Destiny tapped the gas, swerved around a row of double-parked charter buses. We could see the sweeping spotlights and crowds that jammed the sidewalks in front of the Beacon Theatre from three blocks away. As we crossed Seventy-second Street, I noted the line of black SUVs that were double-parked in a queue, lined up along Broadway, waiting to drop off clients.

My Droid vibrated. Tata's press agent, Sid Schulsky, was calling—he was the one who had actually hired us. Sid was outside the Beacon Theatre, waiting for Tata to arrive.

"She coked up?" he asked.

I lowered my voice. "Does Howdy Doody have wooden balls?"

"Shit," Sid groaned. "Limos are gridlocked. Take your time." He hung up.

"Sid wants us to take our time," I said over my shoulder.

"I have time for a cigarette?" Tata said.

I hesitated before I said, "Sure," and made sure that my window was still down.

Tata fired up another smoke.

"Should I drive around the block?" Destiny said.

"No," I said, worried that driving around the block in this traffic could take twenty minutes, or more. "Pull over."

Destiny steered to the curb alongside a fire hydrant. She dropped the sun visor and checked herself in the mirror. As per instructions from Gaetano "Sweet Tommy" Lisi—former Mafioso and current sole owner of Lisi & Beckett Protective Services, Inc. (my police- lieutenant father, Shamus, now deceased, had been his business partner)—she had done her best to play down her striking good looks. Good luck with that.

Destiny's lustrous, long black hair was tied up in a rather conservative bun. The brand-new navy-blue business suit she wore was traditional business attire, the female version of the Hickey Freeman I wore; it did little to disguise her womanly curves. The minimal makeup she'd applied served to mute her full lips and large, smoldering eyes. However, there was nothing—and I mean *nothing*—she could do to mask her personal magnetism.

Sweet Tommy Lisi had lectured Destiny: "Lissena me. Even D-list celebrities don't like to be upstaged by the fuckin' help—pardon my French." And Lisi should know. The former bodyguard to La Cosa Nostra's *capo di tutti capi* (boss of bosses) was the subject of a made-for-TV movie; he'd once been a D-list celebrity himself.

Destiny fiddled with her hair as I eyeballed a dozen rotund tourists who reminded me of a family of hippos. They were standing at the curb, stuffing their fat faces with a street vendor's dirty-water hot dogs and gaping at the SUV, trying to figure out which celebrity was sitting behind the tinted windows.

"Oh my god!" Tata said from the backseat. "I hate it!"

Startled, I turned around. "Anything wrong?"

Tata's eyes were glued to her iPhone. "Justin Bieber just posted a photo of his new haircut on Instagram—uh, like gross."

"No!" Destiny whipped out her own iPhone, toggled to the photo. "It's a different color too—he's still a cutie, though." The two women giggled.

I made a face at the female bonding. Destiny's social- networking addiction, along with her fascination, bordering on obsession, with celebrities—she checked Internet feeds incessantly—had always bugged me. Destiny maintained almost 5,000 Facebook "friends," a Twitter, Instagram, Snapshot, Kik, and who knows how many other accounts, which she used to follow and "correspond" with dozens of friends and celebrities.

My Droid vibrated. I checked the screen. *Now* texted the press agent, Sid Schulsky.

"Ready, Tata?"

Tata exhaled a lungful of smoke, tossed her cigarette, and smiled wonderfully. "Sure." Giggle. "What the fuck." A faux-diamond necklace and matching earrings sparkled even in the SUV's dim light.

Showtime.

I poked Destiny. "Drive, sugar britches."

"Call me that again," Destiny pulled from the curb, "and I'll shoot you."

CHAPTER 2

THE EXTERIOR OF the Beacon Theatre was lit up with strobes and vintage searchlights (World War II–era) that swept the night sky. Gigantic banners announced *The MTV Rap Music Awards*. Members of the local, national, and international entertainment press, their video cameras and microphones at the ready, were agitating behind metal police barricades that lined the entire length of the red carpet, which ran from Seventy-fourth Street to the theater entrance. A procession of rap-world luminaries—the more fashionable attired in garish pimp costumes—were stopping at intervals along the red carpet, being interviewed by *Entertainment Tonight, Access Hollywood, Extra, People* magazine, etc.

Destiny inched the SUV to the curb. An attendant accepted the keys from her as we sprang from the vehicle. I placed my hand on the rear-door handle and waited for the signal from Tata that she was ready to alight. I took that pause to scan the area.

The red-carpet photos and interviews were progressing smoothly. Faces from the rap world—Jay Z, Dr. Dre, Nicki Minaj, Birdman, Lil Wayne, Wiz Khalifa, Ludacris, Pitbull—as well as other A-listers—Jennifer Lawrence, Ben Affleck, Taylor Swift, and the "it" girl of the moment, superstar Victoria Carrington, were posing their way through interviews.

I glanced south, where a thousand raucous fans and fifty

or so stalkerazzi were jam-packed behind the police barricades at Seventy-fourth Street. A half-dozen tubby female police officers—of the five-foot, two-inch-tall variety—were standing guard. I knew that if things got hinky, there was no way those cops could control the crowd. I checked to see how many event security guards were on duty. Not counting the dozen or so celebrity bodyguards that we knew (one retired detective was a tabloid rat who regularly betrayed celebrities' confidences, another was bedding his Grammy Award–winning client), I saw only eight Beacon Theatre security guards. When we'd conducted our advance, we'd been assured by the event producers that they would provide at least fifteen men on duty outside for the red carpet. And another fifteen inside the theater.

"Hello, Detective Stone."

Hearing the barely audible female voice behind me, I turned to see who'd spoken—surprised, flattered that someone, *anyone* remembered that for two seasons, I'd moonlighted from the NYPD, played a recurring acting role as Detective Eric Stone on *Law & Order*.

"You're looking well," she added.

"Solana?" I'd finally placed the voice of my former live-in lover; we'd been involved while Destiny was my police partner. The silken beauty in a short black cocktail dress and catch-me fuck-me shoes strode toward us. I took in her long, shimmering ink-black hair, pouty lips, brazenly seductive eyes, tiny waist, and the rich, firm swell of goodies above and below.

"It's been awhile," Solana said.

"Yes, it has," I said lamely.

Destiny moved up beside me, instinctively protective.

"Oh, hello, Destiny," Solana said, no liking or warmth in her voice. "You look…er…nice."

Destiny eye-strafed Solana, looking her over from head to toe. "Thanks."

"And I love your new no-makeup look," Solana said.

"Although, if you don't mind me saying—." She plucked a red lipstick from her purse, offered it to Destiny. "You could use some color."

"No, thanks," Destiny said, rising easily to the challenge. "I'm allergic to the drugstore brands."

"So," I said, stepping between my two exes before things got ugly. "Here for the concert?"

Solana glared at Destiny, put away the lipstick. She fingered a press pass hanging from a chain around her neck. "Covering it for the *New York Post*. Their online edition." She glanced at the SUV. "Who're you bodyguarding?"

"Tata Andolini," I said.

"No. Really."

"Tata Andolini."

"Oh." Solana snickered. "Well, nice seeing you, Michael." She nodded curtly at Destiny, then put on a show sashaying back toward the red carpet.

"God, how I hate that woman," Destiny muttered.

Tata cracked the SUV's rear door open. "I'm ready."

I pulled the door fully open, offered Tata my hand.

"Hold it." Destiny fingered a packet of tissues from her knockoff designer purse and handed it to Tata. "Your nose," Destiny said, unable to mask the disapproval in her voice.

Tata sat back, checked herself in the SUV's overhead makeup mirror. Saw the cocaine residue on her nostrils and upper lip. She giggled, pulled a tissue from the pack, and wiped. "Now, how do I look?"

"Like butter." Destiny gave her the thumbs-up.

Again I offered Tata my hand, and positioned myself to momentarily obscure the cameras just in case the Valentino dress rode up—it was a well-publicized fact that Tata never wore underwear. She placed her hand in mine, then slid ever so gracefully—even in six-inch Gucci heels—from the SUV.

There was an explosion of flashbulbs. A roar from the crowd.

Tata stopped and waved. Waved to the red-carpet press. Waved to the fans and paparazzi. Worked them into a frenzy by blowing them kisses.

The press agent, Sid Schulsky, clad in a loud, plaid polyester sport jacket and mismatched polyester tie, rushed over, air-kissed Tata. He whispered something into her ear. Tata smiled and nodded. And then they did the unexpected, the unthinkable. She and Sid walked away from Destiny and me, away from the safety of the red carpet, toward the fans to sign autographs.

Fuck! Destiny and I scrambled to position ourselves at Tata's side.

"Tata!" a professional autograph hound shouted from behind a barricade. He produced three 8-by-10 publicity shots of Tata for her to sign. Professional autograph hounds sold the photos to dealers who auctioned them on the Internet. Tata obliged, then edged along the barricade, scribbling her autograph on everything and anything that the fans thrust at her.

"Keep your eyes on their hands," I whispered urgently to Destiny. "Never mind their eyes or words. Watch their hands."

"Yo! Tata! Tata! Take a picture with me?" A gushing teenage guido held a digital camera in his hands. "'Ey! Yo! C'mon! Please, Tata. Ey! Yo!"

"I want a picture too," a preteen girl pleaded.

"Me too," a beanpole-thin guy attired from head to toe in black said as he adjusted a black fedora hat. "You should take a picture with me. I'm your biggest fan!" His voice sounded like a garbage disposal trying to digest a spoon.

"I'm, like, sorry," Tata said sweetly, signing autographs in quick succession. "I take a photo with you"—giggle, sniffle, giggle— "I'll have to take one with, like, everybody. I'll never get into the theater."

"Please. Please. Please," the preteen girl wheedled.

"All right," Sid Schulsky said. "One photo."

I wanted to strangle the PR agent. "That's not a good idea,

Sid," I said, one eye on the guy wearing the black hat. I didn't like his loony half-smile or his wound-tight posture. "Really, it isn't."

"It'll be all right," Sid said. His ridiculous comb-over hair had become slightly lopsided. "Trust me." He took the preteen girl's cell phone, aimed it at the girl and Tata. "Smile," he said and snapped the photo.

That ignited a sudden surge of the crowd. Barricades fell.

The female cops thrust up their hands, screamed that everyone should stop where they were. No one paid any attention.

"Get her into the theater," I said urgently to Destiny, standing between Tata and the swarming crowd. "Now!" The mob poured over the fallen barricades, overwhelming me and the policewomen, trampling anyone who fell in their way.

Destiny guided Tata quickly along the sidewalk. Several kamikaze stalkerazzi tried to block Tata's path. Destiny shoved one guy back, elbowed another, sent him careening into Sid Schulsky, who stumbled and was engulfed by the mob. A half-dozen brassy, screeching Jersey girls rushed Tata, begging for autographs. Destiny plowed through them.

The beanpole wearing the black hat came from behind. Grabbed Tata. Pulled her between two media trucks. "Take a picture with me," he said. "Quick." He wrapped his right arm around Tata's waist, pulled her close, held tight, extended his cell-phone camera with his left arm, ready for a selfie. "Smile."

"No!" Tata flailed her arms and struggled to break free. "Get offa me!"

"Let her go," Destiny said.

"Fuck you," the guy in the hat said.

I came up from behind. Used both hands to box the guy's ears. Thwack! The guy's hat flew off. He yelped in pain, released Tata. Threw a sudden blind mule kick that caught me on the right shoulder. I staggered back. The guy spun. Charged. I sidestepped. Grabbed his arm. Flung him face-first into a media truck. He bounced off. Turned. Threw a wild punch. I countered with a hard right that landed square on his nose and knocked him to the ground.

I laced my arms around both women. Ushered them out into the standstill Broadway traffic, skirted the red carpet, press, and stampeding mob, and entered the Beacon Theatre though the main lobby.

"You ladies all right?" I asked once safely inside.

"What the fuck?" Tata said, catching her breath, tears in her eyes.

"That sort of thing happen often?" Destiny asked her.

Tata shook her head, clueless about the role she'd played in starting all the drama. "Not in a while."

"Hey, look." Destiny gestured out the glass doors.

The guy wearing the black hat was staggering along the street, glaring into the theater lobby, pressing a filthy handkerchief to a bloody nose. He stepped into the metallic-blue Chevy van.

"He's the son of a bitch who followed us," Destiny said.

"You're right," I said as the van sped off. "He is."

CHAPTER 3

"**N**O PRESS!" A battered, tear-streaked Tata said to Sid Schulsky, who was himself disheveled; his comb-over looked like a razzed squirrel's nest. He'd lost one shoe and a jacket sleeve.

"But the entertainment press is waiting for you," Sid said. "They love you!"

"Hey, dick-wad." Tata flipped stands of tangled hair off her orange-bronzed face, and pulled off an askew false eyelash. "No press. Go look for your shoe and leave me alone."

Sid walked dejectedly away.

I wondered why a person with Sid's resume—years ago he had been the East Coast head of publicity for a major film-distribution company—would put up with the likes of Tata, whose only claim to fame was as a barely literate whack-a-doodle on an inane reality TV show.

"I need to freshen up," Tata sniffled, "before I go to my seat."

Destiny escorted her to the ladies' room. I returned to the main theater entrance to see if order had been restored outside. Ambulances were arriving and assisting the police in attending to the trampled. At least one woman appeared to be seriously hurt. I found a quiet corner of the lobby and used the downtime to check my phone for messages.

An e-mail from the NYPD pension bureau informed me that

I would be receiving my first direct-deposit pension check next month. Another e-mail was from a cop who wanted to know if I was planning on selling any of my uniforms, accessories, or guns. Another cop pal asked if I was throwing myself a retirement party—I had no interest in a party. The last e-mail message was from an ex-cop real-estate agent who wanted to sell me a condo in Pompano Beach, Florida.

"Testing. Testing. One, two, three. Testing," a booming voice said.

I pocketed my phone, walked over to the center auditorium door, and gazed down the aisle to the lit stage. I knew several of the stagehands, members of Teamsters Local 321, from working past bodyguard gigs. The Teamsters were fiddling with microphones, conducting a sound check on the elaborately decorated, neon-drenched stage. I spotted a familiar face among a group working on cable connections. It took me a moment to place the guy: Sean Keating. My lips curled sourly. Destiny had once arrested the violent, red-bearded, twentysomething. Responding to a radio call of a domestic dispute, Destiny had entered a tenement hallway and stumbled upon a drug deal in progress. Keating had pulled his weapon and Destiny cracked him across the face with her Glock, knocked out several of his teeth. Charged him with possessing crack cocaine, carrying a loaded gun, and resisting arrest. I was wondering how that thug had finagled his way out of prison, and landed a much sought-after union job.

Then I remembered that the 321 had long been a haven for criminals of Irish ancestry. The Westies, a murderous Hell's Kitchen Irish-American gang and close associates of the Mafia, had once lorded over 321. Although the United States attorney had destroyed the Westies back in the nineties, rumors persisted that elements of organized crime still controlled the union.

"Sorry about what happened out there," Sid Schulsky said as he came up beside me. He was now wearing two shoes and holding his ripped jacket sleeve in his hand. His comb-over, which was parted just above his left ear, was back in its stiff-sprayed place. "It's a miracle none of us were hurt."

"No worries, Sid." I slapped the press agent on the back. "Let me ask you something. How many polyesters did it take to make that jacket?"

"Very funny." Sid scowled.

I had first been introduced to Sid Schulsky eight years ago while moonlighting for my father and Lisi's bodyguard agency. A straitlaced family man and diehard police buff, Sid was one of Lisi & Beckett's first and most loyal clients. Not only hiring them, but also referring them to other press agents. That was a huge boon, because busy entertainment press agents could make or break a security company.

"I told them a hundred times, they needed more security," Sid complained. "Hell, they need metal detectors. Especially for a show like this." He checked his wristwatch and announced, "The red carpet's a bust, so I'm done."

"You taking off?"

Sid nodded. "My youngest daughter has a piano recital tonight."

Destiny and Tata, looking none the worse for wear, came strolling out of the ladies' room. Sid told Tata he was leaving, that he'd call her in the morning, and headed for the exit.

Destiny and I escorted Tata into the auditorium. We moved down the long, sloping center aisle. I ushered Tata into the VIP section and sat her among the rap- world luminaries and several of her reality-show peers. She had hardly sat down when the general-admission doors opened and several thousand enthusiastic ticket holders streamed into the three-tiered theater.

Destiny and I, along with the other celebrity bodyguards, remained standing in the aisles until almost everyone was seated. Then we took our posts in a side aisle where we could keep an eye on our clients. As I glanced absently around the crowd, I found myself searching for my ex, Solana Ortiz. Thought I'd spotted her twice, once up on the balcony. The next time I could have sworn I saw her standing in the aisle directly across from us.

I'd been smitten with Solana, a former writer on *Law & Order*, from the moment I laid eyes on her at my audition. Although at first she treated me with cool indifference, she eventually sought my professional help when a serial arsonist struck the very South Bronx neighborhood where she lived and I worked—a long story. That life-and-death experience had thrown us together and we wound up falling in love and moving in together. The relationship stopped working after a year—Solana began to accuse me of being "involved" with Destiny, which was not true at the time. But she used that as an excuse to have an affair. I figured that she was looking for a way out.

Not that I could lay all the blame on her.

The suicide of a close friend and former police partner had had a lingering psychological effect, causing me to brood, become withdrawn. But worse was to come after my sister Shannon died from a drug overdose.

I had always been a lousy big brother and therefore felt guilty about her death. With the help of the NYPD narcotics unit, I'd embarked on a three-month-long crusade, determined to locate and punish whoever sold my sister the drugs that killed her. I kicked down doors. Cracked heads. Upset the balance of power in the Bronx drug world. In retaliation, the drug dealers arranged for heroin to be planted, and discovered by Internal Affairs, in my personal car. I was suspended but later cleared of all criminal charges. Still, I was buried in the NYPD building maintenance division, no longer a threat to the drug trade. That is, until I formed a team of Rockers—a secret society of vigilante cops and ex-cops who, among other things, waged a clandestine war against drug dealers—for a price.

My Rockers and I resumed kicking down doors and cracking heads with a vengeance. As a result, I spent more and more time with my best friends: Destiny and ex-cops Thomas McKee and

Ernie Serria, among others. I neglected everyone else in my life, including Solana. But in the end I had to admit that the breakup was for the better. With Destiny's support, I came to realize that my relationship with Solana was always about Solana. There was never really an "us." Still, I sometimes found myself wondering what would have happened if we had toughed it out.

"Isn't that Sean Keating?" Destiny said above the theater noise, pointing at the red-bearded thug she'd once arrested, standing in the wings of the stage. "What's he doing out of prison?"

"I was wondering the same thing," I said, and we exchanged a frown. "By the way, you did well out there tonight."

"Bullshit," Destiny said. "I was in over my head. If you hadn't shown up, that guy wearing the hat would've decked me."

The Beacon Theatre's house lights grew dim. The crowd cheered. The stage lights came up as bone-rattling rap music blared and choreographed dancers two-stepped, stanky-legged onto the stage. I handed Destiny a set of earplugs—I'd attended these events before—then inserted a pair in my own ears.

The MTV Rap Music Award Show lived up to its dubious reputation. About halfway through the performances, strutting fans wearing the latest gangsta fashions, some sporting gang colors, tats, and gold-capped front teeth, began to roam the aisles. They loudly taunted, threatened, and cursed one another. Soon a full-blown gang fight erupted in the second-tier balcony. People were standing in the aisles, on top of seats, exchanging punches, piling atop one another. I couldn't believe my eyes when a woman was suddenly hoisted into the air and literally tossed off the balcony. I cringed as she landed on the heads and backs of audience members below. Miraculously, she and the people she'd crashed-landed on appeared to be unhurt.

Ten rows behind the VIP section, a Snoop Dog look-alike slapped a woman in the face, then brandished a chrome-plated automatic handgun. I dashed into the aisle to shield Tata from the gunman just as a rival gang-banger knocked Snoop Dog to the ground, than kicked and stomped him. A dozen baton-wielding event security guards overwhelmed the combatants, disarmed Snoop, and dragged the combatants away.

Not five minutes later, another gang fight broke out in the rear of the theater. And then another brawl started not five rows from where I was standing. I was beginning to fear that we would be caught in the middle of a riot when a linebacker-large homeboy came barreling menacingly down the aisle. I stepped forward to block his path. Pulled out my earplugs. Shouted to be heard.

"Help you?" I said.

The homeboy, wearing an ornate sweat suit and designer sunglasses in the darkened theater, stunk of booze. He smirked, looked down at me, then over my head. "How comes I don't see no niggahs in your VIP section, muthafucka?"

Since the VIP section was occupied by well over 90 percent people of color, I didn't know what he meant. "Please return to your seat."

But the homeboy grabbed me by my suit-jacket lapels. The rancid smells of stale booze, cigarettes, and spittle sprayed my face. Destiny raced up from behind and threw a punch to the guy's kidneys. He grunted. Used me like a rag doll, hauled me around and slammed me into Destiny. Knocked her on top of a row of fans. I smashed both my forearms down on the guy's wrists, broke his grip. Punched him in the face. The homeboy merely smiled, revealing a mouthful of gold grill-covered teeth. He whipped out a combat knife and stepped into the same warrior knifing-fighting stance that I was taught in the military: uh-oh. The homeboy turned suddenly and slashed at Destiny, who leaped back out of range. Then he faced me.

I was about to pull my weapon and shoot the son of a bitch when the guy attacked, executing expert vertical and reverse slashes. I backpedaled. Kept my eyes on the knife, judged the guy's alcohol-impaired pace and rhythm. As he lunged in a sloppy vertical thrust, I feinted to my right, used my left to knock the knife away. Stepped in and kicked him in the groin.

One of the other celebrity bodyguards, the media rat, appeared from behind and cracked the guy, hard, on the head with a sap. The guy went down and stayed down. I glanced around at the riotous crowd in case the guy had backup, and realized that he was alone. Absolutely no one had paid any attention to the altercation. I thanked the other bodyguard for backup, then turned to Destiny. "We've gotta get Tata out of here," I said. "Go get the SUV."

With some difficulty I made my way to Tata, told her she should leave, that I couldn't ensure her safety. Tata, still shaken from the incident outside with the guy with the black hat, didn't argue. I ushered her and her reality- TV-show love interest, a skinny, greaser kid with spiked hair who called himself Nicky Bada-bing, out the side entrance. I paused briefly, glanced back into the theater looking for Solana just as another fight broke out. I hoped she would be safe.

"Where to, Tata?" Destiny said, as we all settled into the SUV.

"Le Bain," Nicky Bada-bing said.

Tata giggled.

The site of the Rap Music Awards' after-party, Le Bain was a trendy nightclub with fog machines, a pretty good DJ, and killer Hudson River views located in the Standard Hotel, in the heart of the Meatpacking District. Once the district had been an odoriferous no-man's-land, home to over two hundred slaughterhouses and meatpacking plants. By the 1980s, it had become a notorious high-crime area: a center for drug dealing, a BDSM subculture, and transsexual prostitution. Beginning in the late 1990s, the neighborhood went through an almost miraculous transformation. High-end boutiques and nightclubs catering to young professionals and hipsters opened. Celebrity-endorsed restaurants soon followed. In 2004, *New York* magazine called the Meatpacking District "New York's most fashionable neighborhood."

Destiny steered onto Broadway, turned left on Seventy-fifth, then a left on West End Avenue. I called Le Bain's general manager on my cell phone and arranged for Tata and the boy-greaser's early-VIP arrival. Then Destiny and I sat in resigned silence as Tata and Nicky snorted coke, drank tequila from a bottle, and—to our horror—preformed slurping sex acts upon one another in the backseat.

Destiny stopped at a light on Fourteenth Street. "We're almost there," she called, a signal that the two D-listers should pull themselves together. Three minutes later, we stopped in front of the Standard Hotel on Washington Street.

Destiny parked in a hotel loading zone and placed an official NYPD plaque on the dashboard. A big guy dressed head to toe in black leather, blond hair spilling out from under his black motorcycle helmet, steered a black Harley-Davidson onto the street, and parked vertically between two cars. At the time, I didn't think anything of it.

Destiny and I escorted Tata and Nicky to the head of a long line. Several cheering fans begged in vain for their autographs. Others squawked loudly that they were cutting the line. We ushered the two D-listers past the fans and velvet rope to the parting doors of a waiting elevator.

Le Bain, with its sleek black-on-black color scheme, was fairly crowded with good-looking young people that time of night. Destiny and I ignored the undercover narcs we spotted—we had to assume they were working—as we escorted Tata and Nicky into Le Bain's lounge, past the floor-to-ceiling windows, through the fog, strobe lights, and throbbing dance music. Checking the place out, Tata and Nicky wandered over to the indoor pool and then upstairs to the Vegas-style rooftop bar. It was covered in lush (albeit artificial) grass and dotted with pink water beds—straight and gay couples, some obviously underage, were snorting coke and all but copulating on the beds. I spotted a slick twentysomething black guy I knew to be a drug dealer making the rounds, glad-handing people, slipping them small envelopes—now I knew why the undercover narcs were there.

Tata and Nicky finally settled on a couch behind the roped-off VIP section, which was reserved for the Rap Music Awards' after-party.

"Two double shots a' tequila, the Gran Patrón Platinum," Nicky told an attractive waitress, smiling into her eyes. "Don't fuhgeddabout the salt and limes. And keep 'em coming."

A gawking crowd of curiosity seekers began to gather outside the VIP section.

"Please. Keep moving, please," Destiny told them.

I noticed a tall, blond, Fabio-type guy dressed in black leather, a black motorcycle helmet under his arm, being escorted by management across the room and into the VIP section. Figured he was the biker I'd seen outside on the black Harley-Davidson—every woman in the club turned to look at him. The biker moseyed over to Tata and Nicky. Tata jumped up, gave Fabio a big hug.

"Now, there's a handsome man for you," Destiny noted as Fabio took a seat alongside Tata. "You know, if you like tall, blond, blue-eyed, cleft-chinned hunks."

Fabio noticed Destiny's gaze and smiled at her. Destiny smiled right back.

"A guy wears his hair that long, he's probably gay."

"Take my word for it," Destiny said. "He's not gay."

I decided right there and then that I hated that guy.

The waitress brought the tequila. Tata and Nicky threw their shots back, licked some salt, sucked on limes. Tata slammed her glass down on the coffee table, hard, and screamed: "Ohhfahhh!" She shot to her feet, practically leaped atop the table, and began to gyrate suggestively and twerk to the music. The crowd stopped to watch, cheered her on, and as a head-banging rap song began to play, Tata flashed her tatas.

"My god," Destiny gaped. "Someone should throw a net over her."

An hour later, Tata was still dancing on a table and flashing her tatas. The VIP section was beginning to fill up with the Rap Music Awards' producers, performers, agents, managers, and guests.

"There's the punk," Destiny said. Sure enough, Sean Keating and a couple of other 321 Teamsters had joined the crowd, and were dancing with a pair of garishly attired, female-rapper types. "I'll bet he's dirty."

"Ain't our business anymore," I said.

"Didn't you tell me that 'crew' and 'talent' don't socialize?"

"Rarely."

"Keating's a Teamster," Destiny said. "That's considered crew, right?

"Right."

"So what's he doing here?" Destiny said.

"Good question." I thought for a moment about tipping off the undercover narcs. But then decided against it. I didn't wish to blow their cover.

Keating looked our way. If he recognized Destiny, he didn't show it. Not that I expected him to. Destiny was not in uniform, wore her hair differently, and was dressed like a businessperson.

"Yo, peeps!" Tata waved as her *Jersey Shore Confidential* costars came be-bopping across the dance floor, and entered the VIP section. Tata stopped dancing, covered her tatas, stepped off of the table, and called out: "Yo, Monkey Man. Yo, Hood Rat. Yo, Big Gina. Yo, Sleepy Joe. Wassup?" Tata air-kissed everyone. Threw back another shot of tequila. More salt and lime. "Ohhfahhh!" She grabbed Nicky, jumped on his lap, and sucked face.

"Please, tell me all these kids are putting on an act," Destiny said in astonishment. "That they're not for real."

"They're putting on an act," I said, straight-faced. "They're not for real."

"Hey, Big Gina!" Tata yelled to her castmate, who was fawning over Fabio. Gina was a big, wide-bodied brunette wearing a tight crotch-length cocktail dress, sporting humongous fake boobs, tattoos, and way too much makeup. "You stay away from Nicky. You hear me, Gina? You cunt!"

"Hey, Tata." Gina flipped her the bird. "You blow dead mice."

Tata threw a slice of lime in Gina's face. "You fuckin' skank."

"Whore!"

The two women sprang to their feet, charged each other, crashed over the table, and tumbled to the floor; boobs flopped, skirts rode up around their waists. Nicky and the crowd on the dance floor began cheering, applauding, and egging the women on. I dove into the melee and managed to extract Tata as Destiny fought to restrain Big Gina. But Big Gina wasn't about to quit. She screamed a sting of curses, broke free from Destiny, and made a clawing lunge for Tata. Destiny snatched a handful of Big Gina's hair from behind, yanked her back, and flung her onto a couch.

"Stay there, bitch," Destiny said into Big Gina's face. "Or I'll slap your tits together." Big Gina eyeballed Destiny for an angry moment. Then she sat back, pulled down her skirt, and raised her hands in surrender.

I noticed Fabio making a hasty exit: good riddance.

Destiny turned to Tata. "Let's get you to the ladies' room." She helped the snarling Tata hold her torn dress together, preventing it from completely falling off.

"Nicky!" Tata hollered. "Get your ass oveaheah!"

Nicky hustled to Tata's side, grinned smugly, apparently happy to have two women fighting over him. "That's Gina's a crazy bitch," Nicky said. "Ya know?"

Tata wiped her snotty nose with the back of her hand, then stuck an orange finger in Nicky's oily face. "I'm gonna cut ya balls off, Nicky."

"For what?" Nicky said, all innocent. "Aw, c'mon, Tata." He put his arm around her. "I didn't do nothin'—I swear."

"Don't you touch me." Tata shoved Nicky away. "You fuckin' her, Nicky? Hah? You fuckin' that skank?"

"Hey! I ain't never laid a hand on her. Honest."

"I ever find out you did?" Tata said, the threat left hanging.

"I swear on my mutha's grave," Nicky said. "I never touched her."

"Ya mutha ain't dead, Nicky."

"I'm just sayin'," Nicky said.

CHAPTER 4

"I WASN'T ANY GOOD tonight. Was I?" Destiny spun the steering wheel left. Played chicken with a discourteous woman driver. Cut her off. "Hey, bitch," Destiny screamed. "Go suck a bag of dicks!" and rounded a corner on two wheels.

I braced myself, terrified we'd crash. My hands were gripping the door handle and console, feet planted and legs pushing down on the floorboard as hard as possible. Destiny straightened us out and raced north on Park Avenue.

"You did great," I said, my voice cracking. "Really."

"Bullshit," she said.

We had just dumped a legless Tata Andolini and her love muffin, Nicky Bada-bing, into the lap of a Four Seasons Hotel doorman. Lisi had informed us that although Tata lived with her father down in Little Italy, the *Jersey Shore Confidential* production company, in order to keep the cast of wackos under control, was paying for their rooms for one night.

Destiny slowed, then ran a red light. We were on our way to the Yorkville garage where Sweet Tommy Lisi kept two armored SUVs and one four-door Jaguar sedan. The crooner Bobby Caldwell's "My Flame" was playing on the SUV's radio.

"Hey," I said, "you did fine." I raised my right hand. "Scott's honor."

"Uh-huh." Destiny smirked. "First I did 'great.' Two seconds later, I did 'fine.' Next you'll tell me I did okay, for a woman."

Oh, boy.

I kept my mouth shut—an acquired discipline if one is to continue a harmonious relationship of any kind with Destiny. Out my window, a leggy socialite stepped out of a chauffeur-driven Rolls-Royce and sashayed into a grand Park Avenue co-op.

"You're ignoring me now, that it?" Destiny said. "I want to talk and you zone out." She shook her head. "You're never going to change."

"Look, Destiny. I've met dozens of bodyguards over the years. Given a choice, I'd chose to work with you any day, hands down. And you wanna know why? 'Cause I trust you. I trusted you when you were a cop. I trust you now. You're the same person you were before the shooting."

Which was a total lie.

"I feel like I've lost the edge." Destiny turned right on East Ninetieth Street.

I heaved a resigned sigh; here we go again. "It takes time to come back," I said. "After what you've been through? I mean, you survived a gunshot wound *and* brain cancer. What do you expect?"

She stopped for a red light at Lexington Avenue. "It's been over three years."

"So?" I said. "There are no hard-and-fast rules. Some people bounce back quicker than others. Don't be so hard on yourself." I reached and switched off the radio. "What we both need is a drink."

"I'm going home. I'm tired."

Huh? Destiny turning down an after-work cocktail? I didn't like the sound of that. And not because she might very well have a man waiting for her at her apartment, which was supposedly none of my business but would drive me crazy if it were, in fact, the case. My concern was the painkiller addiction she'd acquired while recuperating from her surgeries. It had destroyed our romantic relationship and nearly ended our friendship. My gaze slid to the woman I still loved, alert for signs that she was relapsing: fidgeting, motormouth, constricted pupils.

Destiny drove across First Avenue, slowed, turned into the garage driveway, and stopped at a closed steel security gate. Although the five-floor former carriage house was open twenty-four hours, because of numerous armed robberies of the lone overnight attendant, management chose to lower the gate and turn off the lights around midnight. I stepped out of the vehicle, peeked through the gate into the interior, searching for the attendant; I couldn't see much in the dimly-lit gloom. I rang the attendant's bell, which was loud enough to hurt my ears and wake up the neighbors. The overhead fluorescents sparked on, and the gate slowly rattled up. The usual overnight attendant, a blushing knucklehead who had a crush on Destiny, appeared. She pulled into the garage and handed over the keys and her parking stub—a no-charge swap for her personal vehicle. The attendant ran off to fetch her car, a panting puppy fetching a bone.

The attendant's footfalls faded and the garage was all at once quiet, save the steady hum of an ancient vending machine.

"You have any dollar bills?" Destiny gestured to the machine.

I took out my wallet, handed her two singles. She fed them in, pushed a button. The machine's gears made a racket as it selected her purchase. A bottle of Avian dropped noisily into the well. Destiny claimed the water, fingered out the change from the coin dispenser, handed it to me.

The attendant returned with her red—sorry—"scarlet" Mazda MX-5 convertible sports car. I held Destiny's door open as she stepped in and placed the Avian in a center-console cup holder.

Destiny buckled her seat belt. "Go straight home, you reprobate."

I couldn't help but notice how her skirt rode up. She saw me looking and promptly pulled it down. Although we'd been broken up for over a year, we'd had drunken sex only a couple of months ago—a mistake Destiny said would never happen again.

"You get some rest." I closed her car door. "We'll talk tomorrow."

Destiny sat there for a moment. Revved the engine. "Did you know Solana was going to be at the Beacon Theatre tonight?"

"I had no idea."

Destiny's expression was skeptical.

"I swear." I rose my right hand.

"Okay." She tapped the gas, pulled out of the garage.

I stepped out onto Ninetieth Street as she made the left turn onto York Avenue. "What was that all about?"

CHAPTER 5

DESTINY SAW BECKETT watching her in her rearview mirror as she turned north onto York Avenue. Like most men, Beckett was clueless when it came to women. He had no idea that Solana Ortiz had probably orchestrated their "chance" meeting tonight at the Beacon Theatre. But to what end? "What do you want, Solana, you crazy bitch?" she murmured in the darkness.

Destiny stepped on the gas and merged easily onto the nearly deserted northbound FDR Drive at East Ninety-sixth Street. She cracked open the bottle of Avian, reached into her jacket pocket, fingered out two 750 Vicodin—time to get high. She popped both pills into her mouth and washed them down.

The headache had struck predictably during the brain-shredding Rap Music Awards, but there was no way she'd ingest prescription painkillers around Beckett; he'd flip out. Okay, two 750s might be overdoing it a bit, but her head *did* hurt, so why not enjoy the drug-induced euphoria she craved? Regardless, Beckett would never understand.

Beckett was there by design the evening she was gunned down in the line of duty; he shot and killed her would-be assassin. Beckett then picked up her seemingly lifeless body, raced to the hospital, carried her into the emergency room. He had remained at the hospital throughout the long and risky operation during which a bullet, as well as a deadly brain tumor, was removed from the base of her skull.

He had spent the ensuing days and nights at her side; he rarely left the hospital. Upon her discharge he moved, albeit temporally, into her Hastings-on-Hudson one-bedroom apartment, and assumed the role of full-time caretaker; he cooked, cleaned, and saw to all her personal needs. He cheered her on during her slow and painful convalesce. That is, until she became a full-blown substance abuser. That was when Beckett became suspicious, argumentative, hard.

"I lost my only sister to drugs," he had fumed. "I'm not going to lose you."

"You don't understand what I'm going through," Destiny had told him. Not that she understood herself. Unlike TV, where bullet wounds were no worse than bee stings, being shot actually traumatized a person's entire central nervous system. Posttraumatic stress—lethargy, nightmares, depression, and panic attacks—all of which Destiny now suffered, were the results.

"I want you to come stay with me in the city for a while," Beckett had told her. "Get you out of this rut. And I want you to get professional help. Maybe enter rehab."

Destiny had agreed to stay at Beckett's place, but said absolutely no to seeing a drug counselor or entering rehab. She would not admit that she had a drug problem, mainly because she couldn't deal with the embarrassment of entering "the farm" along with the other drunks and druggies. Besides, cops don't ask anyone for help.

Destiny spent the ensuing days in Beckett's twenty-fifth-floor Yorkville apartment bingeing on ice cream and her favorite TV program, *Antiques Roadshow*. As usual, Beckett was supportive. He took her for long walks in Central Park, to Broadway plays, concerts, museums, lunches, dinners, and antiquing in upstate New York, doing his level best to keep her occupied. And Destiny succeeded in going cold turkey. She even started going to the gym in Beckett's building, joined a yoga class. But then she found a box of photos he had hidden in his bedroom closet, on a high shelf above his rack of dress shirts and 150-plus ties. Photos of him and his ex-girlfriends.

"I didn't hide those," Beckett said when she confronted him. "It's where I keep them."

Destiny was holding the stack of photos in her hand, flipping through them, reading the names off like she was dealing a deck of cards. "Diane. Gail. Cindy. Melody. Constance. Djuna. Sheila. Enia. Enia. Enia. Solana. Solana. Solana. Solana. Solana." Destiny looked at Beckett. "And one of me."

"Yeah. So?"

"Why so many photos of Enia and Solana? Explain that!"

"They liked to have their pictures taken."

Destiny flung the photos in exasperation, scattering them across the room.

"You're making something out of nothing."

"I don't get it," she fumed. "Why do you keep pictures of ex-girlfriends in the first place? I mean, why is that?"

"Why wouldn't I?" Beckett said, kneeling on the gleaming parquet floor, picking up the photographs. "I'm still friends with most of them."

"Well, I don't like it." Destiny stomped around the room. "Makes me think you still have feelings for them. Do you?"

"Not the way you mean."

"Good. I want you to throw out those pictures."

"No," Beckett said, offended. "My past relationships are none of your business."

Destiny had stormed out of Beckett's apartment and straight to a notorious Dr. Feel-Good's office, where she procured a prescription for Vicodin. But Beckett, suspicious as always, had followed her. When she left the doctor's office, Beckett confronted the doctor, threatened him with arrest if he ever prescribed painkillers to Destiny again. Next, he alerted Destiny's primary-care physician, her oncologist Dr. Goldsamp, as well as every pharmacy within miles that she was abusing painkillers; no one would touch her after that.

"How dare you?" Destiny was outraged. "You're not my father!"

"You're going to rehab," Beckett told her.

"Don't tell me what to do," was her reply. "Get out of my life."

To her surprise, he did.

Destiny flicked on the Mazda's right-directional signal, crossed the Willis Avenue Bridge, merged left onto Interstate 87 North. Not five minutes later, she steered off at Exit 12 toward the Henry Hudson/Saw Mill River Parkway. She settled into the center lane and recalled that Beckett had indeed gotten out of her life—for all of a month. But when she failed to answer any of his phone calls, texts or e-mails, he showed up at her apartment. Convinced her building superintendent that something was wrong. Beckett and the super found her passed out on the kitchen floor, an empty bottle of booze on the table and a handful of Vicodin scattered around the linoleum floor. Beckett had called an ambulance, accompanied her to the emergency room, where they pumped her stomach. The next day Beckett didn't say a word about the nearly fatal accidental overdose. He didn't have to. Even she knew she'd hit bottom. And so she allowed Beckett to drive her to a lower Manhattan rehab center.

Once again, the most decent, steadfast, and loyal human being she had ever known had saved her life. And she was grateful. But the incident had forced her to finally confront her wavering emotions. She realized that she felt differently about the man who'd once been her everything. They'd become impossibly close. Which was why she didn't think she was *in* love with him anymore. And was why she'd had a heart-to-heart talk with him last year and ended their romantic relationship. Although she knew she had hurt him, to his credit Beckett seemed to understand.

"We can always be friends," was all he said.

They had remained friends, the best of friends, even weathering a recent drunken sexual indiscretion that was as much her fault as his. She had been feeling lost and lonely and Beckett was there for her, as always. Which was why she would always watch his back; that conniving bitch Solana Ortiz was up to something. Not that it would do her any good. Destiny was fairly confident that, since Solana had cheated on Beckett, walked out on him, there was no way he'd rekindle that toxic relationship. Then again, experience had taught her that men follow their peckers into places they wouldn't go with machine guns.

Destiny switched on the radio and sang along to a 1950s oldie, a favorite of her mother's, which reminded her that she'd yet to mail her octogenarian parents the money she sent monthly, money they needed desperately to pay for their lifesaving prescription medications. She made a mental note to FedEx the cash—always cash—early tomorrow morning.

Destiny turned left on Farragut Parkway, then turned onto her block, and spotted exhaust fumes emitting from an idling car that was parked across the street from her apartment building. The plain black Ford Crown Victoria was a favorite of law enforcement. Instead of pulling into her underground garage she drove around the corner, killed her headlights before turning onto her block and pulling to the curb. She opened her glove compartment, lifted out the pair of cheap but pretty good binoculars left over from her days of doing surveillance, and peered through the eyepieces. Saw two white men in dark suits.

CHAPTER 6

THE YORKVILLE STREETS were eerily quiet at that time of night. A cool, salty breeze whipped off the East River. I took a deep breath. The air smelled clean—well, clean for a big city. I shrugged up my suit-jacket collar, stuck my hands in my pockets, and headed toward my Third Avenue apartment.

I walked west, past tenements built in the late 1800s and early 1900s, when Yorkville was known as Germantown because of its large German-born immigrant population. East Eighty-sixth Street, a main artery, was the heart of Germantown and, because of its dozens of German restaurants, butcher shops, dance halls, pastry shops, beer gardens, social clubs, bakeries, delicatessens, and confectioners, was often called Sauerkraut Boulevard. Some of the street's more colorful establishments played up the Bavarian kitsch with oompah bands, waiters in lederhosen and barmaids in dirndls. Sadly, because of gentrification and rising rents, the German businesses had closed. Only one restaurant, the Heidelberg, and one delicatessen, Schaller & Weber, remained. The yuppies had moved in, and Germantown was now well on its way to becoming another characterless, high-income, high-rise Manhattan neighborhood.

Glass breaking.

I froze. Cocked an ear. Checked for movement on the street ahead in the murky darkness. I didn't see anyone, didn't hear anything else unusual. I placed my hand on the butt of my Smith & Wesson snub-nose .38, continued down the block glancing into the dark recessed areas of the old tenements, alert for lurking assailants.

I heard music and drunken laughter coming from an open window off to my right. A dog barked. A TV blared one of those obnoxious late-night infomercials. A man and woman cursed one another. Ahead, a tractor trailer shifted gears as it raced down Second Avenue. A lone police siren wailed in the distance. I smelled cigarette smoke, heard footsteps. I spun and pointed the .38.

"Don't shoot," Sweet Tommy Lisi said, his voice a cigarette-stained bark. He raised his hands in mock surrender. "You kill me, fucko, you'll never get paid."

"You asshole." I lowered my weapon. "You looking to get killed?"

"Hey…" Lisi dropped his hands. "I'm sittin' onna fucking stoop, in my own fucking neighborhood, minding my own fucking business." The former wiseguy was talking around an unfiltered Lucky Strike. "That a crime?"

My heart raced. My hands trembled; I'd almost shot my father's childhood friend and former business partner. I holstered my weapon.

"Where you coming from?" I said, noticing Lisi was attired in a threadbare designer suit, rumpled white shirt, and stained silk Charvet tie. Having weathered a battery of physical problems and actually coming back from death—he'd been shot and clinically dead for fifteen minutes—plus the loss of his beloved wife of thirty-five years, Lisi looked every bit his seventy-plus years old.

"Brad and Angelina're in town," Lisi said by way of explanation. The insinuation being that the former "bodyguard to the stars" was once again working for Hollywood royalty. I doubted that was the case.

"How *are* Brad and Angelina doing?" I said, being a wiseass.

"They're young. Rich. Beautiful. Fuck you think they're doin'?" Lisi dumped his smoke. "Got time for a drink?"

"Is a grizzly bear Catholic? Does the pope shit in the woods?"

"Whatever," Lisi said as we continued toward Second Avenue. "So, how'd it go tonight?" He used a battered Cartier lighter to light another cigarette.

"Guess who I ran into outside the Beacon Theatre?" I glanced around, still paying close attention to our surroundings—some habits never die. "Solana."

Lisi puffed his smoke, morphed into a pretty good Bogie imitation. "Of alla the gin joints in alla the towns in alla the world, she walks inta mine."

"She's working at the *Post*."

"I know," Lisi said. "She's what we usta call a cub reporter."

"You know this, how?"

Lisi tapped off some ashes. "Saw her a few weeks ago at P.J. Clarke's. She went inta Rathbones last week too. She was asking about you."

"Really?" I thought about that. "Why the hell didn't you tell me?"

"I forgot." Lisi shrugged. "Destiny see her?"

"Oh yeah."

"*Marrone.*"

"You can say that again."

Lisi chuckled. "How'd the Tata gig go? She's a piece a' work. Right?"

I told him about the near riot outside the Beacon Theatre, about the character who had followed us in the derelict blue van from Tata's hotel. That he later laid hands on her. "I had to punch his lights out," I said. "Tall, skinny guy; dresses in black, wears a black fedora. Stunk of cigarettes and booze. Looks like he needs a bath."

"Oh, fuck," Lisi said.

"You know him?"

"Matt the Hat." Lisi took out his smart phone, opened a picture file, held a photo up, a mug shot. "Lookit."

"That's him," I said.

"Name's Matthew Gluck." He put his phone away. "He useta to be a big-shot art director for a some high-end advertising firm. That's where he met the singer Audra Gardner."

That was the A-list superstar my father and I had been body-guarding when she died from a drug overdose. My father, who died shortly thereafter in a horrific car accident, and I were the ones who had discovered her body.

"She was endorsing a perfume or some such shit that The Hat was working on. He met her onna photo shoot. He became obsessed. Went offa the deep end. She had him arrested for stalk-ing. The DA offered to let him plead to a D-felony, no jail time, but he wouldn't take it—unfuckingbelievable."

"I think I remember the case," I said.

Lisi puffed his cigarette. "Claimed he wasn't stalking the Gardner woman. Said he was stalking a guy was stalking her. Said he was protecting her. Got himself convicted a' stalking. Sentenced to eighteen months inna can."

We skittered around a steaming pile of fresh dog shit—so much for the pooper-scooper laws.

"I'll check with the Bureau a' Prisons in the morning," Lisi said. "See if The Hat's on parole. If he is, and he's stalking Tata, I'll advise her to press charges."

We stepped aside to allow an angry-looking drunk guy to stagger past.

"Ya did the right thing, fucko," Lisi said. "Someone lays hands onna client, you do whatcha gotta do. *Capeesh?*"

"Got it."

"Do anything after the Beacon?" Lisi wanted to know.

"We took Tata and some greaser kid, Nicky, to a club."

"Nicholas Genovese. Calls himself Nicky Bada-bing," Lisi said, faintly annoyed. "He's her boyfriend onna show—a pathological liar. Brags about how rich he is. Claims to be heir to the old Genovese drugstore chain. But he's completely fulla shit, a cheapskate con man. Hasn't got a pot ta piss in. How'd that go?"

"Not well—what the hell's wrong with Tata?"

"Spoiled," Lisi said. "She's the youngest and only daughter. Her father thinks the sun rises and sets on her."

"You know her family?"

"Her father. He owns an Italian restaurant down in Little Italy. A cash-only business. Owns the building. Place is a gold mine."

"What's his story?"

"A hardworking immigrant. Devoted family man."

"Yeah? Well, his daughter acts like she was raised by wolves."

"She didn't piss off Destiny, did she?" Lisi said. "God forbid."

"No." I shook my head. "Tata loved her."

"So, Destiny's her old self?"

"Getting there."

In contrast to the barren side street, Second Avenue was like Mardi Gras. The streets were alive with revelers. The bars and restaurants were overflowing.

A gang of rollicking jocks stumbled out of the Auction House on Ninetieth Street, and lined up in a queue to enter Genesis Irish pub. A Tourette's-syndrome vagrant, dressed in rags, was squatting in a tenement doorway, yelling obscenities. A taxi dropped off a squabbling older couple who entered a teeming Mexican restaurant. An enormous sixteen-wheeler grinded gears and belched exhaust as it rumbled south.

Lisi glanced into the Irish pub. "The donkey joint's packed." He pointed his cigarette at the pub next door. "Rathbones okay with you?"

I had killed the deranged gunman who'd shot Destiny in front of Rathbones pub. Put my gun to the assassin's head. Shot him once in the left temple, point-blank range. Left him to bleed out on the sidewalk—his blood had long since washed away. "No problem," I said.

Lisi took a last puff on his cigarette, flicked it into the street. The Tourette's-syndrome vagrant bolted from the doorway, knocked aside a couple of jocks, claimed the discarded butt, and puffed it to life.

The Lady Gaga music and the raucous laughter hit me like conflicting winds as we stepped into the crowded bar. Six off-duty 23rd Precinct cops sat at a table off to the left. Several of them gave me a thumbs-up, another waved; one beer-grinning joker flipped me off.

Most of the other tables were taken up by a youngish preppy crowd enjoying the music and ten-cent buffalo wings.

We made our way to the center of the long bar. Shook hands with a pack of regulars. Took a few minutes to catch up on the latest neighborhood gossip. At the center was a debonair former racketeer known as Bobby G. A racketeer is someone involved in various nonviolent, illegal activities but not necessarily a member of La Cosa Nostra. As usual, I noticed that something unspoken passed between Bobby G and Lisi—a subtle nod, eye contact an instant longer than normal. Lisi once told me that when he'd had his heart attack, Bobby G and I were the only ones who called him daily, brought him groceries, took him to his doctor appointments, ran his errands, etc.

"Me and Beckett got a little business to discuss," Lisi said after a few minutes. "We'll see youse all later."

"Not if we see youse first," Bobby G said.

Lisi feinted a punch to Bobby G's midsection as we headed to our usual spot at the head of the bar. I glanced across the avenue to where the world-famous Elaine's restaurant had stood for nearly fifty years. Like many regulars, I never gave much thought to the lovingly seedy little Second Avenue saloon someday closing; I'd taken the place for granted. But when the cantankerous owner, Elaine Kaufman, died, the restaurant died with her. And now I really missed the crowd of regulars, the bartenders, the drama; there was always drama at Elaine's.

Rathbones bartender, Charlie, a retired firefighter, greeted us with handshakes and a warm smile. He handed me a frosty bottle of Coors Light, a vodka on the rocks with a twist for Lisi.

"Hey, Lisi," Charlie said with a smile. "How was the Italian food?"

"It was good—how'd you know what I had for dinner?"

"It's on your tie." Charlie pointed at a large tomato- sauce stain, then marched to the other end of the bar to fill orders for a harried waitress.

"Nobody likes a wiseass, Charlie." Lisi picked up his drink. Looked at me. Toasted. "*Salud.*"

"First today," I said and took a long pull on my beer. "God, that's good."

Lisi sipped his vodka, put the glass down. "Gotta talk to you about something."

I nearly groaned. Lisi had been after me for years to take my father's place at the once-thriving Lisi & Beckett Protective Services, Inc. But the company had been losing A-list clients for years, thanks to my father's touch of dementia and then sudden death. Lisi's advancing age and assortment of health issues didn't help matters—thus the D-list Tata Andolini gig.

Another issue was that I had only just retired from the NYPD and didn't know if being a full-time, career bodyguard was my thing. Not to mention that I wasn't exactly comfortable going into business with a former member of La Cosa Nostra. Over the years that lifelong association had caused my father multiple problems, like being passed for key NYPD assignments. Not that he ever complained or confided in me about it. My father and I were never close, and maintained a distant, rather businesslike relationship—typical Irish. "Okay, Tommy," I said. "I'm listening."

Lisi hunched over the bar, lowered his voice. "I gotta client. Says she's being stalked."

"Stalked?" I felt a wave of relief.

"You know, threatening e-mails. Texts. Cell-phone calls."

"So you know who the stalker is?"

Lisi nodded. "He calls himself the Angel a' Death."

I nearly spit up some beer. "Not again."

"Yeah. That guy." Lisi drank his drink. "At least we know he's for real, not like the guy who's supposedly stalking Tata."

"Tata has a stalker?" I said.

"She claims to be getting threatening voice mails, e-mails, text messages. But when I ask her to produce them, she don't. She keeps shining me on, coming up with excuses—believe me, she's fulla gahbidge."

"Why? What's the point?"

"You ain't a genuine celebrity unless you got a stalker." Lisi shrugged. "Don't ask me to explain it."

I drank some more beer. "The clients do drugs?"

"Of course."

That fact gave me pause. The Angel of Death had stalked numerous celebrities over the past ten years, including our client Audra Gardner. Six, who were drug- addicted, had died from a heroin dose spiked with fentanyl, a powerful, potentially deadly opiate. There were those, like my father, who did not believe in coincidence, and thought the Angel of Death was responsible for all six overdose deaths. That the serial stalker was, in actuality, a serial killer. But the NYPD, while acknowledging the Angel of Death connection, thought that the serial-killer theory was far-fetched. Heroin was readily available, and junkies were always attempting to "spike" the high. Plus, celebrities weren't the only ones dying from overdoses. Over 10,000 individuals die from an "accidental drug intoxication overdose" in the United States each year.

"Your client file a complaint with the PD?" I asked.

Lisi shook his head. "She don't want the publicity. I mean, when she's in town, the stalkerazzi actually sleep in cars outside her town house. Follow her everywhere."

"So she wants it handled on the QT," I said. "I get it."

"You know how it is: Once they file an official complaint, some clerk at the precinct'll call the tabloids, sell the information—"

"And the media feeding frenzy begins."

"They wanna to avoid that," Lisi said.

"They?"

"Her mother runs things."

"What can I do?"

"I want you should bodyguard the client. You start tomorrow. I can getcha the usual. One hundred an hour."

"All right." I swallowed more beer.

"A' course," Lisi said, "you'd earn a full partner's share if you'd take your father's place. I mean, the firm already has your name on it. We won't even hafta change the stationery."

"I appreciate it, Tommy." I patted my father's old pal on the back. "Really. But I'm still not ready."

"Okay, fucko," he said. "I get it. When you're ready."

Charlie the bartender served us two more drinks.

"Okay," I said to Lisi. "Who's the client?"

Lisi waited until Charlie was out of earshot. "Victoria Carrington."

I did a double take, remembered that I'd seen the young, incredibly beautiful A-list superstar last evening, walking the rap-music awards red carpet. "What's her story?"

"She's been in and out rehab and mental institutions for years," Lisi said. "She's a tri-sexual and proud of it."

I tried to get my mind around that idea. "A tri-sexual?"

"A free sprit. Does anything with anyone, or anything for attention. Makes the Kardashians look like wilting violets. But nunna that means anything to us. *Capeesh?*"

"Okay." I drank the fresh beer. "How'd the job come about?"

"Meg Dvoretz," Lisi said.

I knew Meg. She was an old-time press agent, a sometime associate of Tata's press agent Sid Schulsky. Thanks to Sid's endorsement, Meg was also a longtime Lisi & Beckett client.

"Back to the A-list," I said. "I'm impressed, Tommy."

"Lissena me, don't go ordering champagne yet," Lisi said. "Meg just landed the account. Says we got Victoria only when she's in town, which ain't that often. Besides," Lisi hung his head, "we got the job because no one else wants it. She's that wild."

"Hey, it's a beginning," I said. "Who're you teaming me up with?"

Lisi told me.

"Retired Secret Service," I said. "I know him. Good man—what about Destiny?"

"What about her?"

"Let Destiny work the Carrington gig with me."

Lisi made a face. "Might not be a good idea."

"Why's that?"

"You know how she is," Lisi said. "Destiny takes shit from no one—not that I don't admire that quality. But I don't need her getting inta Victoria Carrington's mother's face, telling her off."

"The mother difficult?"

"Lynn Carrington's the stage mother from hell," Lisi said.

"That tabloid gossip?" I asked. "Or truth?"

Lisi shrugged.

"Well, is she crazy? Evil? Psychotic, or what?"

"Hey, if she was, I'd tell you."

"Relax. Okay. I've got it. She's the stage mother from hell."

"And maybe a little psychotic." Lisi drank more vodka. "But inna good way."

"Look," I said. "I'll make sure Destiny knows she's dealing with a nut job. Tell her to make allowances, keep her mouth shut. Speak only when spoken to. She needs to work, Tommy, to keep her mind occupied."

"Know what?" Lisi put his glass down. "I'm gonna leave it up to you. Way I see it, you're gonna be my partner someday anyway. You might as well start putting together your own team."

"So, you'll let Destiny work the Carrington gig?"

"Hey, fucko," Lisi said. "I just told ya. It's up to youse."

CHAPTER 7

LISI HAD JUST ordered us another round when my cell phone vibrated. I checked the caller ID: Destiny was calling. "Be right back." I took my phone outside to the relative quiet of the street. "Speak of the devil and she shall appear," I said into the phone.

"Say what?" Destiny asked.

"Never mind," I said. "Lisi just booked us. You and me for tomorrow."

"Good. Look, something's going on."

The panic was subtle, but I picked up on it right away. I pressed the phone closer to my ear. "What's that mean?"

"Someone staking out my building. Looks like feds."

"So?"

"Believe me, no one in my building's worth the trouble."

I heard a commotion to my right. A couple of drunken jocks were cursing each other, squaring off on the sidewalk outside the Irish bar. The guy with Tourette's syndrome was watching the altercation with avid interest.

"So what do you think is going on?" I said.

"Just stay on the line with me."

"Okay." I could hear her Mazda slip into gear.

"All right," Destiny said. "I'm driving by the feds now—I swear, they're eyeballing me."

"So? Let them."

"I'm pulling into my garage," Destiny said. "Going down the ramp. Now I'm parking. Turning off the engine. Getting out. Okay. Two white guys in dark suits are coming down the ramp—told you so."

"Don't hang up," I said. "Can you video stream them?"

"I'll try."

I keyed my smart phone and booted up Skype. A moment later I was seeing the inside of Destiny's underground garage. I heard a man's voice say: "Destiny Jones?"

"Who wants to know?" she said.

"Woo, take it easy with that gun," the voice said. I knew that Destiny had pulled her weapon; I held my breath. If either of those two men did anything stupid, she wouldn't hesitate to shoot.

"We're federal agents," a voice said.

"Sure you are," Destiny said. "Let's see some ID. You, fat man, you first."

Two men walked into the frame, their hands raised. The streaming picture was not very clear or steady, but I could determine that one guy was older. Heavyset. The other was young. Tall. Blond.

"I'm Special Agent Sobel." The older one reached into his suit-jacket breast pocket, pulled out an ID case, flipped it open, held it out at arm's length.

"Okay," Destiny said. "Now you, blondie. Slowly."

"I'm Special Agent Englund." Englund produced his ID.

"What the hell's wrong with you two?" Destiny said, and the agents lowered their hands. "Ambushing a woman, at night, in an underground garage."

"You are Destiny Jones?" Sobel said.

"Yes."

I saw sweeping headlights in the background; another car must have pulled into the garage. I heard car doors open and close. Heard snippets of passing conversation. Two people walked in and out of the background. Then another car pulled into the garage, its headlights swept over the smart-phone screen.

"Isn't there somewhere private we could talk?" Sobel said.

"Look, Agent—what was it? Sobel?" Destiny said. "I've had a long day. I'm tired. Tell me what you want."

"All right." Sobel slipped his ID back into his jacket pocket. "Were you ever a member of, or do you know anyone who has ever been associated, in any way with crews of vigilante cops called Rockers?"

I felt the hair on my arms prickle.

"Vigilante cops?" Destiny said.

"Rockers," Sobel said. "Were you ever a Rocker?"

"I don't know what you're talking about," Destiny said flatly.

"As a former police officer," Sobel said, "you know that lying to federal authorities is a felony. Now, I repeat: Were you ever a Rocker?"

"I don't like your tone, Agent Sobel."

"What's my tone have to do with anything?"

Englund said, "What do you know about the German Hotel explosion?"

"In Yorkville?" Destiny said. "Only what was in the papers. That it was a gas leak. That a lot of people died."

"You know dammed well it wasn't a gas leak," Sobel said.

"Oh?" Destiny said. "What was it?"

"We know for a fact that Michael Beckett and his Rockers were paid by the owners of the German Hotel to evict a drug dealer, Lochlainn O'Brian," Englund said.

"Which they did," Sobel said.

"We know that O'Brian later blew up the hotel in retaliation," Englund said, "and planted his ID on someone else in order to fake his own death."

"Which he almost got away with," Sobel said, "until Beckett found out."

"We know Beckett gunned down O'Brian," Englund said.

"Really," Destiny said. "From what I read in the papers, Lochlainn O'Brian was a drug-dealing murderer, a terrorist. He must have had lots of enemies. You investigating terrorists or—what did you call them? Rockheads? Rockballs?"

"Being evasive," Sobel said, "leads us to believe you have something to hide. Do you have something to hide, Destiny?"

"You know, I just love it when a stranger calls me by my first name."

"Just answer the question, Ms. Jones," Sobel said.

"I'm not answering any questions," Destiny said, "but I'll tell you one thing. You *ever* ambush me again, you'd better be wearing bulletproof vests."

"Threatening a federal officer is a felony," Englund said.

"And trying to bully an armed female is dangerous," Destiny said. "Good night."

Destiny must have turned and walked away, because I was suddenly looking at cars, concrete walls, and then the inside of an elevator.

"Holy shit," Destiny said. "You get all that?"

"Yeah," I said. "I sure as hell did."

CHAPTER 8

I ENTERED THE 19TH Precinct station house on East Sixty-seventh Street the following morning half expecting to be swarmed by federal agents and arrested.

I had stayed up most of the night, agonizing over what had transpired in Destiny's underground garage. I wondered what the two agents, Sobel and Englund, actually knew. Figured that if they could prove anything, I'd already be in handcuffs. Regardless, if the feds were in fact investigating me—and not just fishing—someone at my former command might know.

I threaded through cops and civilians and reached the desk. A roly-poly sergeant named O'Hara was on duty. His focus was not on the incessantly ringing phones, but the sausage McMuffin that he was stuffing into his fleshy face.

"Hey, fatso."

O'Hara looked up; muffin crumbs and egg yolk clung to his chin. "Oh. Hey, Beckett. What're you doing here?"

I held up an empty black-leather satchel. "Cleaning out my locker."

"Been putting it off, huh?" O'Hara said, chewed, and took another bite.

"Something like that."

"A lot of guys do."

I glanced at the muster room, then at the captain's office,

the clerical office, and property room. I didn't see anyone who didn't belong. Nothing was out of the ordinary. "Anyone looking for me?"

O'Hara crumbled the McMuffin wrapper, dropped it into a bulging McDonald's bag, pulled out another sandwich, and unwrapped it. "Like who?"

"Gwyneth Paltrow."

"In your dreams." O'Hara bit into the sandwich.

"Later," I said, and headed to the stairs.

I shook hands with a couple of plainclothes cops as I entered the locker room. They congratulated me on my retirement and wished me well. Talked about how smart I was to be getting out, what with a loony left-wing, anti-cop Mayor Bill de Blasio (aka, Mayor Putz) in office. Of course, some said the pathologically lying, tax-dodging con man and race-baiter, Reverend Al Dullard, was actually running the city.

I walked down the aisle to my locker, placed the satchel on a long wooden bench. I dialed the master lock's combination, which I'd been dialing for twenty years. I opened the tin locker, saw the 8-by-10 photo of myself posing with the cast of *Law & Order* affixed to the inside of the door. I peeled the photo off, studied it. I wished my father had been alive when I landed the part on the show. I wondered if he would have been proud. Not that he would ever tell me. I placed the photo into the satchel and recalled the excitement of working on an acclaimed TV show.

I'd seen the open call in a local newspaper requesting actors to audition for *Law & Order*. Having no acting experience of any kind, I auditioned on a lark and was flabbergasted when I landed the role. The short-lived, part-time acting gig had opened up a whole new world to me, and I thought seriously about resigning from the NYPD and pursuing an acting career. But in the end I came to terms with the fact that landing the role was a once-in-a-lifetime fluke. And that the NYPD, being a cop, was in my blood.

I peered into my locker. As always, my uniforms were cleaned and pressed. Shoes spit-shined. My polished but worn gun belt hung on a hook in back. I lifted the gun belt, strapped it on over my blue jeans, pulled the Browning 9mm Hi-Power, and studied it: a sexy weapon, thick handle, long barrel, blue steel.

I'd spent eighteen years in the 41st Precinct in the South Bronx—those were the best years of my life. I spent the last three years assigned to the desirable 19th Precinct "Fort Hook"—a reward for killing the psycho who'd gunned down Destiny. There was talk about downtown assigning me to the detective division. But my record of multiple suspensions, coupled with my constant "attitude problems," encouraged the powers that be to change their minds. Not that I gave a shit. As an adrenaline junkie addicted to the action of the front lines, I was never attracted to the dull, tedious life of a detective—not that I couldn't have used the additional pay.

But like many cops, I loved being in uniform, loved the action, loved the independence of working my own sector with little or no supervision. Knowing the residents and their families, business owners and their employees firsthand. Knowing who to offer a helping hand to, who to "discipline," and who to run out of the neighborhood. My father had spent thirty-five years in uniform, as had two of my uncles. Guess you could say that being in uniform was part of a Beckett's DNA. There'd never been a detective in the family. Although, ironically, I'd played one on *Law & Order*—a wildly successful and cartoonish portrayal of the NYPD where detectives are venerated and street cops are fawning incompetents. In the real world, street cops conduct all initial investigations, and then hand off what they can't solve on the spot to the detective division—but not always. Destiny, one of the best natural investigators I'd ever known, had broken up both a prolific burglary ring and a child-pornography ring while in uniform with no help from the detective division.

I slipped the Browning back into the holster. Pulled it quick-draw style like I'd done countless times on the street. Re-holstered it. Pulled it again. I took a bead on a horsefly racing up a wall, and my mind wandered.

I'd seen too much death during my time on the job. Stood by helplessly as accident victims, innocent crime victims, as well as criminals, perished. I'd seen cops slain in the line of duty. Lost one of my partners to suicide. And I'd taken lives. None that I regretted.

I holstered the Browning, unstrapped the belt, and placed the whole unit in the satchel. I took out my uniforms, folded them neatly, placed them on top of the gun belt. I reached to the top shelf, moved aside a stack of files, picked up a black-leather five-bar citation shield holder. Among the various colorful citations bars was a solid green bar representing the Combat Cross. Awarded to: *Members who have successfully and intelligently performed an act of extraordinary heroism, while engaged in personal combat with an armed adversary under circumstances of imminent personal hazard to life.* I had placed the original medal—a gold Maltese cross with the seal of New York City set in the center— on my deceased (from suicide) partner's coffin, and buried it with him. I dropped the citation-bar holder into the satchel.

I took down a stack of old case files, started to flip through them—these were my most memorable cases—a murder for hire, a youth-gang extortion scheme, a serial pedophile—the stories I'd write about if I ever found the time and discipline to pen a memoir. But the process of reviewing the files began to depress me. I laid them on the bench, organized them by date, placed them in the satchel. I removed my combination lock from the locker door, dropped it into the satchel, zipped it up.

I looked around the locker room, trying to come to terms with what I was feeling—a deep sense of loss. I never thought leaving the NYPD would be this difficult. But it was time for me to go. I was old school. A dinosaur. I didn't fit in anymore. I walked out of the locker room for the very last time.

I stopped to shake hands with a couple of uniformed Hairbags (old-timers) on the way down the precinct stairs. We razzed each other for a few minutes, then made plans to get together for a few beers later in the week. I broke away, waved to a couple of detectives, and entered the roll-call office.

"Yo, Beckett," the roll-call man said. "What're you doing here? Retirement doesn't agree with you, or what?"

I plopped down behind an unoccupied desk. "You need anything from me?"

Roll Call shook his head. "Nope. Paperwork came in from the pension section weeks ago. You're officially a low-life civilian. Congratulations."

"Yeah." I tried to smile. "Hey. Anything unusual going on?"

"In this place?" Roll Call snickered. "Define *unusual*."

"Seen any feds hanging around?"

"Sure." Roll Call stopped typing. "Ever since the papers blew the whistle on 'the jobs' little numbers game, they've been poking around, looking for someone to crucify."

"They looking at anyone in particular?"

"Not yet." Roll Call went back to his computer.

The "numbers game," the manipulating of crime reports—the downgrading of crimes to lesser offenses and/or discouraging victims from filing complaints to make crime statistics look better—had long been part of the culture of the NYPD. Assault becomes harassment, robbery becomes grand larceny, burglary becomes criminal trespass. In the past I had myself been ordered to downgrade the charges against dirtbag criminals on more than one occasion. I didn't agree with the practice—why the hell give the dirtbag criminal a break?—but I followed orders.

"You know, there was something," Roll Call said. He leaned back in his chair, flipped a toothpick onto his lips. "A civilian came into the station house—a tall, skinny guy, unshaven, dressed all in black. Claimed he was assaulted last night at the Beacon Theatre by a plainclothes cop."

Bells went off in my head. "Wore a black fedora?"

"Yeah," Roll Call said. "That's him."

"He file a complaint?"

"He tried. The guy had his load on. The desk officer schmoozed him, told him we'd look into it, sent him on his way."

Which meant that the desk officer had played down the assault and did not file a UF 61 (complaint report)—a classic case of the aforementioned crime-statistic manipulation which, in this case, had worked in my favor.

"Well, I'm outta here," I said.

Roll Call got to his feet, shook my hand. "Good luck, Beckett."

"Thanks." I slapped him on the shoulder. "Gonna miss your ugly face."

"No," Roll Call said. "You're not."

My cell-phone alarm chirped, reminding me that the Victoria Carrington bodyguard gig started in two hours—I had to hurry. I needed to drop off my gear at my apartment, put on a business suit before meeting Destiny at Tommy Lisi's Ninetieth Street garage. I shouldered the satchel and headed downstairs.

I waved to the desk officer, Sergeant O'Hara, on my way out. He waved a half-eaten sandwich at me and belched a good-bye. I alighted from the precinct, stopped at the top step, glanced around East Sixty-seventh Street. Police cars were parked every which way, up and down the block. Uniform officers came and went. I waved to a couple of firefighters I knew, members of Ladder Company 16, Engine Company 39, who were loitering outside the firehouse next door, watching the girls go by.

A police car came racing down the block and screeched to a stop. Two officers I knew sprang out, removed two hard-looking male prisoners from the backseat, and marched them inside the station house. I took a deep breath and realized that I felt empty inside. I was barely retired from the NYPD and I already missed being a New York City cop.

CHAPTER 9

"**L**ISI'S BLACK SUV," Destiny was telling the manager of the Ninetieth Street garage just as I entered. "The new one." The manager spoke into an intercom, directing whomever was on the second floor to bring down the vehicle. His loud, static-edged voice echoed throughout the cavernous structure.

Destiny turned to me. "Serria and McKee called."

"When?"

"A few minutes ago."

"Shit."

As I mentioned earlier, ex-cops Ernie Serria, Thomas McKee, and Destiny had been part of my Rocker team. Four years ago we'd spent time evicting a dozen violent drug gangs from residential buildings and boutique hotels in the Bronx and Manhattan. We seized all of the cash, guns, drugs, and even a cache of C-4 explosives; flushed the drugs, dumped the guns and the C-4 in the East River and divided the cash—around $175,000 apiece by the time we disbanded. We'd busted heads, survived a couple of gun battles.

"What'd they say?"

"The feds who surprised me in my garage, Sobel and Englund, showed up at McKee's house on Silver Beach," Destiny said. "He told them to get the hell off his property. McKee called and warned Serria. When they showed up at Serria's, they couldn't get past his two pit bulls."

Lisi's SUV came rolling down the ramp and stopped near the exit. Out stepped a six-foot, in-shape, clean-cut, dark-skinned black guy I'd never seen before. The guy nodded a greeting to us and headed across the garage to the office.

"Who's the new guy?" I said.

"No idea."

"Timely coincidence." I eyeballed the new hire. "Wouldn't you say?"

"I would."

I checked where the garage security cameras were located; at least two were pointing our way. I gestured for Destiny to follow me to a corner of the garage as far away from the attendants and cameras as possible. The feds were known to employ listening devices and lip- readers.

"You look tired," Destiny said.

I took another long look at the new garage attendant. He and two regular attendants were jockeying cars around the garage, arranging them for pickups. Something about the new guy didn't feel right.

"How the hell do the feds know about me, Serria, and McKee?" Destiny said. "We all wore ski masks. There was no way anyone could identify our Rocker team."

"Someone talked," I said.

"Yeah, but who?"

The new garage attendant walked back to the office, spoke to the supervisor, and began matching keys with parking stubs. I noticed that he was using the office door's glass as a mirror to observe us—not that that was necessarily unusual. Destiny rated second and third looks everywhere she went.

"Am I nuts," I said, "or is he watching you?"

"He's watching us," Destiny said. "Check his ankle."

There was a bulge on the attendant's right ankle.

"He's either an inmate out on bail," I said, "wearing a GPS device—"

"Or he's wearing an ankle holster," Destiny said.

"Or the guy's got fat ankles and we're being paranoid."

A van pulled in and blocked the new attendant's view.

"We need to set up a meeting with Serria and McKee," I said. "Figure out what the feds know. How they know it." I checked my wristwatch. "C'mon. We gotta go meet Lisi."

Destiny drove to a car wash, then to a gas station, where I purchased four difficult-to-trace prepaid cell phones. We had to assume that, since the feds were investigating us, that all of our home and cell-phone communications would be monitored. I handed one of the prepaids to Destiny, pocketed one; I'd give the other two to Serria and McKee when we met. Then I checked the SUV thoroughly for bugs and tracking devices; didn't find any.

We entered the FDR Drive going south at Ninety-second Street. I looked over my shoulder, then used the rearview mirror, searching for a tail, didn't see anyone. I heard noise overhead, glanced at the clear blue sky, saw several helicopters crisscrossing above, any one of which could be manned by federal agents.

"Any interest in who we're bodyguarding?" I said, my eyes now on a 55-foot NYPD Harbor Unit craft that was running parallel to us on the East River.

Destiny flicked on her directional, eased into the left lane, and hit the gas. "I assumed it was Tata again. No?"

I shook my head. "Victoria Carrington."

"No way!"

"Way," I said.

"Former Mouseketeer? Grammy Award winner? Emmy Award winner? *People* magazine's sexiest woman alive?"

"Don't forget, certified loony tune."

"That's amazing," Destiny said. "I follow her on Twitter."

"Wow. Amazing."

"How'd you like five fingers shoved up your nose?"

I laughed. Destiny really was slowly returning to normal. Above us, the Roosevelt Island aerial tram swung in the wind as it made its lumbering accent up its cables and across the East River.

"Victoria Carrington is being stalked by someone calling himself the Angel of Death," I said. "I'm assuming it's the same Angel of Death my father swore stalked and murdered Audra Gardner. Anyway, Victoria's mother's the one hired us."

"Lynn," Destiny said.

"What?"

Destiny pulled to the center lane to pass a slow driver. "That's her mother's name. Lynn. Her father's Colin, a wannabe rock star. He gave his daughter her first hit of coke when she was eleven years old—she's twenty-one now. Injected her with heroin when she was fifteen."

"Nice guy."

"He and Lynn have been divorced for years."

"Hard to believe." I cracked my window, let some air in. "What else you know about Lynn?"

"She was Miss South Carolina twenty-years ago," Destiny said. "She's one-quarter American Indian, but denies it. She's a frustrated entertainer. Jealous of her daughter. According to the tabloids, she pimped Victoria out to record producers and casting directors of both sexes when she was fourteen years old—allegations Lynn denies. She's known as the stage mother from hell."

"So I heard," I said. "That reminds me: Lisi wants you to take it easy on Lynn. Cut her some slack. Apparently she has all sorts of issues."

"A woman with issues," Destiny said. "Go figure."

Her sarcasm was so rich that I couldn't help pointing out, "Now, see, if I said that, you'd rip my face off."

"Yes," Destiny said. "I would."

We hit almost no traffic as we raced down the Drive. Although I usually thoroughly enjoy the snaking East River views, I was focused on the traffic behind us. A yellow cab caught my attention, then a minivan, and then a black Harley-Davidson. Its rider's blond hair spilled from under his helmet and whipped in the wind.

"Where do we get off?" Destiny said.

"Next exit."

Destiny waited until the last second before she eased down on the brakes, cut perilously and skillfully across two lanes of traffic, and exited at Twenty-third Street.

"Stay on Twenty-third," I said, keeping my eyes on the traffic behind us. As far as I could tell, no one exited after when we did.

Destiny put the pedal to the metal. Wove in and out of traffic. Had to slam on the brakes twice. Once to avoid striking a delivery guy on a bike who'd run a red light. And then, as we crossed Sixth Avenue, she rolled down her window and cursed a clueless old woman who exited a taxi on the street side. At least she didn't tell the old broad to go suck a bag of dicks.

"Make a left on Seventh Avenue," I said. "A right on Charles Street."

Three minutes later we slowed at a stop sign and entered the quiet, narrow, tree-lined, utterly charming residential block that was Charles Street.

"Where to?"

I gestured ahead. "Head for the stalkerazzi."

A dozen of the shutterbugs were staked out on the street and sidewalk directly in front of Victoria Carrington's West Village town house. A group of thirty young female fans were sitting on the town-house steps. Photos of Victoria, along with marker pens, were posed in their hands.

Radio Man, an infamous, schizophrenic movie buff, sometime bit actor, and autograph seeker—whom the actor George Clooney had flown first-class to the 2008 Academy Awards, all expenses paid—was sitting on the sidewalk, off to the side, dressed in moldy rags. An ever- present battery-operated radio hung from a wire coat hanger slung around his neck. His battered Schwinn truck bike leaned against Victoria's wrought-iron fence.

Destiny rolled down the street, parked at the fire hydrant in front of the town house. Our arrival was the signal that the superstar was about to come out. The stalkerazzi stirred from slumber, the fans began to chatter excitedly. Radio Man got to his feet and waved to me. I waved back.

Inside the town house a large dog began to bark. The stalkerazzi snapped to, pointed their cameras like firing- squad rifles. At the top of a long flight of perilously steep concrete steps, the town-house door opened. Sweet Tommy Lisi, a Rottweiler nipping at his heals, came scurrying out, followed by two fashionable young men carrying what I recognized as hair and makeup kits. The stalkerazzi grumbled and lowered their cameras: false alarm. Lisi, wearing the same rumpled suit he wore last night, legged carefully down the steep steps and opened the SUV's rear door and climbed in back.

"That fuckin' Rottweiler scares the living shit outta me—pardon my French." Lisi wiped perspiration from his brow. Reached into his suit-jacket pocket, took out two documents, and handed one to me, one to Destiny.

"Confidentiality agreements," Lisi said. "Sign them."

"Already signed one," Destiny said.

"For Tata Andolini," Lisi said. "Youse gotta sign a separate agreement for each client." We signed and handed them back. Lisi checked the signature, put the agreements away.

"Now, Destiny," Lisi said. "Lissen'a me. Since this is your first A-list gig, we gotta go over Lisi's Rules."

Destiny looked at me. "He kidding?"

I shook my head.

"Rule number one," Lisi said. "You don't speak to the client unless spoken to. Ever. Don't make comments, small talk. Don't offer your opinion about nothing. Celebrities don't wanna be your friend. They don't give a rat's ass how you feel, what kinda day you're having, what your sign is, what your thoughts are about anything or anyone. *Capeesh?*"

"I get it," Destiny said. "Rule number two?"

"Repeat rule number one." Lisi reached inside his jacket pocket and pulled out a pack of Lucky Strikes. "Oh, and another thing. Be careful if you find yourself dealing with Victoria's employees. Ya know—maids, stylists, hair or makeup people, assistants, agents, PR people—whoever. Take it from me, most of them are brown-nosing, backstabbing rats looking to curry favor with the celebrity. So watch what you say. Always." He stuck a cigarette in his mouth, powered down the window before lighting it. "Keep in mind, celebrities don't live inna real world. They're insulated by ass-kissing yes-men. A lot of them are clueless. They don't know their own phone numbers. Zip codes. I know a few couldn't use an ATM card if you gave them written instructions. *Capeesh?*"

"*Capisco*," Destiny said.

"Now, lissena me, botha yuhs." Lisi took a drag, blew the smoke out the window. "We got a problem. The client's been drinking—no surprise there. But she's fighting with her mother. I wouldn't be surprised if she didn't make the show."

"Show?" I said.

Lisi said that Victoria was scheduled to leave in five minutes to appear on the Jimmy Fallon show. The purpose was for her to promote her first movie, a mega-budget romantic comedy, *Double Date*. After Jimmy Fallon, Destiny and I were scheduled to drive Victoria back home. Then, at 7:30, escort she and her mother to the billionaire Ron Langlois's East Side town house for drinks—the very same Ron Langlois that I had once body-guarded—another long story—and who I despised. After cock-tails, Victoria and Lynn were attending an event honoring Jack Nicholson at the Plaza Hotel.

"Tomorrow morning," Lisi continued, "youse're taking

Victoria to *CBS This Morning*, then *The View*, then to lunch at Le Bernardin."

A car pulled up and several more stalkerazzi piled out. A group of tourists strolled down the street. We could hear one of them ask a stalkerazzi what was going on, which celebrity they were waiting for. To his credit, the stalkerazzi refused to tell them. But the tourists whipped out their cell-phone cameras and waited just the same.

Lisi checked his battered Rolex. "Youse two better get ready."

The three of us alighted from the vehicle.

"Destiny," Lisi said. "Clear the steps. Beckett, move those fucking rat-bastards away from the front a' the house."

"Make a hole, gentlemen, please," I said to the stalkerazzi. "We've gotta give Victoria some room." I herded the shutterbugs to the left of the stairs, where they stood in a squirming cluster.

"Let's move off the steps, people," Destiny said to the young female fans. "Please. We need the steps cleared." The fans grumbled as they straggled off the steps and formed a line that ran from the town-house fence to the SUV, all but blocking the sidewalk.

"When Victoria comes out," Lisi said to us, "we'll form a sorta wedge. Beckett, you take point. Once we get her locked inna car, youse will tear-ass to Jimmy Fallon." Lisi's cell phone vibrated. He checked the caller ID. "Hello, Meg. No, we ain't onnaway. We're still at the town house."

I figured that had to be Meg Dvoretz, Victoria's press agent.

"'Cause she hasn't come out yet," Lisi said. "Yes, she's finished with hair and makeup. No, I ain't gonna knock on her door and tell her to hurry—it ain't my place. Yeah, I know traffic's a nightmare. Relax. We'll get there. I'll call you when they're onnaway."

Again the Carrington Rottweiler began to bark. The stalkerazzi aimed their cameras at the town-house front door and waited. There were the usual "practice" cameras clicks and flashes. The fans also got ready, held the Victoria Carrington photos and pens for easy signing. Radio Man got to his feet, looking as scary as ever with his dirt-layered, greasy face and wild, crusty hair. He took a position by the curb, several photos of Victoria and pen in hand.

The Carrington front door swung open and the Rottweiler tried to dash out. Victoria grabbed the dog's collar, handed him over to an Hispanic housekeeper, who yanked him back inside. Victoria eased out and closed the door behind her—amid a fusillade of camera clicks, a barrage of flashing lights.

"Victoria!" the stalkerazzi called out. "Look this way!"

Twenty-one-year-old Victoria Carrington, looking every bit the sexiest woman alive in my opinion, paused at the top of the stairs and surveyed the pack of fans and stalkerazzi before her. She took her time. Slipped on a pair of D&G Elite sunglasses. Zipped up her custom Testoni alligator jacket, which matched her crotch-length skirt. She took out a cigarette and lit it with a Dunhill Rollagas solid-gold lighter. She glanced at the stalkerazzi and broke into a Chiclets-white smile that caused her fans to clap and shriek with joy. Cameras clicked and video whirled.

"We love you, Victoria!" a fan screamed.

"Iwoveyou!" Victoria slurred. "Iwoveyouall!"

"*Marrone*," Lisi whispered. "She's fuckin' trashed."

"We're gonna let her go to Jimmy Fallon like that?" Destiny said.

"Ain't our business what she does," Lisi said. "We're the hired help. We ain't her friends. Remember that."

Victoria took a long, last pull on her cigarette, dropped it on the stoop, crushed it out with her six-inch alligator shoes. She shrugged up her jacket collar. The fans screamed and swooned. Victoria stepped down onto the first step.

I realized right away that she was having difficulty. Her one hand was on a wrought-iron railing, her other reached out for balance, like a tightrope walker. Her legs were stiff, like stilts. She made it to the third step. On the fourth, her heel caught. Her feet got tangled. She let go of the railing. Pitched forward in a dive. Struck a stair. Crumbled upon impact. Bounced. Went ass-over- teakettle. Careened painfully down the remaining stairs like a B-movie stuntwoman. By the time Victoria hit the sidewalk, blood was seeping onto her face.

Fans screamed in horror. Radio Man burst into tears. The stalkerazzi swarmed, snapping away rapid-fire; this was their money shot, the one they prayed all their lives for. The picture that made all those endless hours of tracking and pestering celebrities in all kinds of weather, worthwhile.

I knelt down and turned Victoria over. She was pretty banged up. I slipped off my suit jacket and covered her exposed legs and crotch—thank goodness she wore underwear. "Victoria? You okay?"

She looked at me cross-eyed. "Who... ?"

"I'm Michael, one of your bodyguards."

She took a moment to process that, reached out and squeezed my hand. "Think we can still make Jimmy Fallon?"

"You're shittin' me," Lisi said over my shoulder.

"I shit you not," Victoria said and promptly passed out.

CHAPTER 10

"**V**ICTORIA?" I SAID. "Talk to me. Victoria?" I was pressing my white handkerchief to the laceration on our A-list client's head in an attempt to stanch the flow of blood. The stalkerazzi penned us in. Cameras flashed. Video whirled.

"Destiny!" Lisi said. "Get these fucking mooks outta heah, for Christ sake!"

Lisi took out his cell and dialed 911.

"You heard the man," Destiny said to the stalkerazzi. "Get back, guys. C'mon, give us a break. Give us some room." She herded the grumbling shutterbugs away, but the fans, tourists, and curiosity-seekers continued to take cell-phone photos. Neighbors had thrown open their windows. A few had come out of their homes. Cars blocked the narrow West Village street. Horns honked. Drivers cursed.

A police car pulled onto the block and blasted their siren, forcing the rubbernecking drivers to move on. Destiny identified herself to the two old-time uniformed cops as they alighted from their radio car. The two Hairbags were only too happy to assist with crowd control.

Moments later an ambulance, lights pulsing, sirens screaming, came racing down Charles Street. Two EMTs, one male, one female, medical kits in hand, stepped from the vehicle. I got to my feet, allowing them access to Victoria.

"What happened?" the female EMT asked.

"She fell down the stairs," I said.

As the male EMT removed my bloody handkerchief and then pressed sterile gauze to Victoria's head wound, the female snapped something under Victoria's nose—her eyes popped wide open. Her arms flailed. She tried to sit up. "Whoa."

"Don't move," the female EMT said, her hands pressing gently down on Victoria's shoulders. "Please be still."

"What happened?" Victoria said.

"Just lie back—holy shit," the male EMT said. "You're Victoria Carrington!"

"That's me," Victoria said, like a dazed child.

"I'm your biggest fan," the male gushed, and produced a cell phone. "Take a picture with me?"

"No," Lisi screamed. "No pictures, ya fuckin' mook."

Grudgingly, the EMT put his cell phone away.

Lisi's own phone rang. "No, Meg, we ain't onna way. 'Cause Victoria fell down the town-house stairs. Yeah, she's hurt. Fuck ya think? No. There's no way she's gonna make it to Fallon. And she ain't gonna make it tonight to Langlois's, or the Jack Nicholson event. *Capeesh?*" He ended the call, put his phone away.

Radio Man pushed through the clot of fans, who held their noses at his smelly approach and fell over each other giving him room. "Tell her mother," Radio Man shouted. "Someone should tell her mother."

"Good idea, Radio," Lisi said. "Destiny. You go tell her. But try to convince her to stay inside. She comes out, we'll have a real zoo on our hands."

Destiny pushed past the stalkerazzi, cleaved through the frenzied fans, and climbed the town-house stairs, thoroughly excited about seeing the inside of a superstar's residence for the first time. She took a deep breath, rang the Carrington doorbell. The Hispanic housekeeper answered.

"Yes? How may I help you?"

"Victoria hurt herself," Destiny said, and motioned toward the sidewalk.

"*Dios mio!*" The housekeeper blessed herself.

"I need to speak to her mother."

"Ms. Lynn upstairs, in office."

"Where's the dog?"

"Dalton upstairs with Ms. Lynn." She stepped aside and pointed across an elegant foyer to a set of sweeping stairs. Destiny thanked the maid, entered the ornately furnished town house, breathed in the scent of expensive furnishings. She walked slowly across a gleaming white marble foyer floor, then across a large—could it be an ultraexpensive Persian Ardebil carpet? What looked like an antique Tufft pier table—one was appraised for over three million on *Antiques Roadshow*—was at the bottom of the staircase. On it sat what appeared to be a Ming Dynasty vase—those could be worth up to ten million. A print of *The Birth of Venus* by Sandro Botticelli—it had to be a print!—hung on a wall. A magnificent what looked like a Schonbek chandelier was suspended overhead; she'd read somewhere that Schonbeks graced Buckingham Palace and the White House.

Destiny started up the thickly carpeted stairs and heard a growl. She stopped. Dalton was poised at the top of the stairs. He barked, bared his teeth. "Dalton." Destiny froze. "Good boy."

"Dalton!" a voice she assumed was Lynn Carrington said. "Shut the fuck up!"

"Hello? I'm Destiny. Tommy Lisi sent me."

Dalton stopped growling, eyeballed Destiny, tilted his big head as if sizing up how to attack.

"Dalton! Down!" Lynn said. "Gawd, I hate that slobbering mutt."

The Rottweiler sat down and thumped his stubby tail ominously.

"In here," Lynn commanded.

Destiny stopped to allow Dalton to sniff her fist. She scratched him behind the ear, patted his head, then moved down a long hall. "Hello?" She stepped through an open door, into a brightly-lit, well-equipped home gym. The room was lined with floor-to-ceiling mirrors. Several adjustable weight-training benches were set in front of a two-tiered rack of dumbbells. Two elliptical cardio machines faced a large wall-mounted flat-screen TV. Dalton entered the gym, lay on the floor, bored once again.

Destiny saw her manicured feet first. Lynn Carrington was standing on her head on an exercise matt, in a *salamba sirsasana* yoga position in the center of the room.

Naked.

"Oh, sorry," Destiny said and turned to leave.

"What is it you want, sugar?"

Destiny stopped by the door, stared at the dumbbells. "Well…er…Victoria fell. She fell down the stairs. An ambulance is here."

"Oh, my God." Lynn lowered herself to her feet, grabbed a short, black silk robe, slipped it on. As she dashed down the hall, parted the curtains, and peered down at the street, Destiny couldn't help but notice how different she looked from her daughter. Victoria was tall, thin, blond-haired, amber-eyed, and flashy. Whereas her mother was short, curvy, dark-complexioned, and sexy—her American Indian blood?

"Doesn't she understand…" Lynn let go of the curtain, stepped away from the window. "Every public meltdown! Every failed relationship! Every screw-up is a reflection on *me*?"

Wow, Destiny said to herself. There it was: the notorious self-absorption that all of the tabloids wrote about.

"I'd better get down there," Lynn said.

"Tommy Lisi asked that you stay in the house," Destiny said. "What with all the paparazzi."

Lynn began to object, but then opened a bureau drawer, lifted out a hand mirror, and checked her reflection. "Good thinking. I'm not camera-ready anyway." She walked out of the room. "Come with me, sugar."

They entered a beautifully furnished home office. Lynn sat at a highly polished mahogany Chippendale desk and appeared to check a calendar.

"We've hair and makeup coming at five-thirty," she said. "Drinks with Ron Langlois. Then the Jack Nicholson event at the Plaza." She turned to look at Destiny. "Victoria is supposed to present Jack with an award. Realistically, do you think she'll be able to attend?"

"Tommy Lisi says no."

"I'm not going without Victoria—I mean, what's the point?" She hit the speed dial. "Meg?"

Destiny figured she was talking to the press agent, Meg Dvoretz.

"Yes. I know all about it, sweet pea," Lynn said. "Listen, cancel hair and makeup. Contact Langlois's assistant, send regrets. Same with the producers of the Nicholson event. And you'd better see about rescheduling *CBS This Morning* and *The View*. Then I want you to meet Victoria—hold on." She addressed Destiny. "Where are you taking her?"

"NYU Langone is closest," Destiny said. "Thirty-third and First Avenue."

"You hear that, sweet pea?" Lynn said. "Call me from there and let me know how she is. All right, then." She hung up, then addressed Destiny:

"Do me a favor, will you, sugar?"

"Sure."

Lynn gestured for Destiny to follow. They left the office and walked back to the gym. She pointed at Dalton. "Take that fucking mutt downstairs with you?" Lynn dropped her robe, squatted down on the exercise matt, and flipped back into a nude headstand.

I was squatting on the sidewalk, holding Victoria's hand, telling her she was going to be fine, when Destiny exited the town house. One of the EMTs secured a thick brace around Victoria's neck.

"Don't leave me, Michael," Victoria said in a frightened little girl's voice. She squeezing my hand. "Promise?"

I ignored the strange fixation on me, the first person she'd laid eyes on after blacking out. "I won't leave," I said. "I promise."

An EMT pulled a long spine board—designed to provide rigid support during movement of a patient with suspected spinal or limb injuries—from the ambulance. They lifted Victoria onto the board, then onto a gurney. Rolled her to the ambulance and loaded her into the rear.

"Stay with me?" Victoria pleaded.

I climbed in, sat beside her, held her hand. I wasn't sure about the psychology involved, what our client was thinking, but I knew how to comfort a young damsel in distress.

An EMT closed the doors.

Five minutes later, the ambulance pulled into the Thirty-third Street Langone Medical Center emergency- room entrance. The rear doors flew open. The attendant pulled out the gurney and pushed through a set of wide swinging doors.

I was walking alongside Victoria, holding her hand, when a trauma team set upon us. I followed as they wheeled her into a corner cubicle. A doctor stepped in front of me. "Sir, you have to step out. Please."

"No!" Victoria said in a panic.

"It's okay, Victoria," I said. "I'm not going anywhere."

I backed out and the doctor pulled a curtain closed in my face.

"Looks like our client's found a new friend." Lisi was standing behind me.

"More like a big brother," I said.

"She could do worse," Destiny said, one of her underhanded compliments.

"I don't get it," I said. "She hasn't asked for her mother, or anybody."

"'Cause there ain't nobody," Lisi said. "Her mother don't give a rat's ass, and she knows it. You're the closest person inna the whole wide world to her for the moment. But don't let it go to your head. Remember you're an employee. She's a celebrity. She'll use you until she don't need you anymore."

Langone Medical Center's director of security, Mark Chin, another ex-cop Destiny and I knew, approached us not two minutes later. Once apprised of the patient's identity, he agreed to pull guards from around the hospital to deal with the media circus and general chaos that was sure to follow.

"Tommy Lisi!" Meg Dvoretz, Victoria's PR agent, came racing across the emergency room.

"How you doin', Meg?" Lisi and she embraced. "You know everyone?"

"Hello, Michael. Destiny." The diminutive fifty-year-old raked her fingers through her short, kinky red hair. "Where's Victoria?"

Lisi gestured to a closed curtain. "With doctors."

"Anyone witness her take the fall?" Meg said, eyes wide with anticipation. "Please. Tell me there were no witnesses."

"Thirty or so stalkerazzi," Lisi said. "It's all on film."

"Shit." Meg threw her hands up. "So all I can do is damage control." She sighed deeply. "After all I've done for that little bitch." Meg took out her cell phone, dialed, and barked orders at whoever answered her call.

I'd heard other press agents like Sid Schulsky grouse about the celebrity clients that they represented. How a PR agent functioned as a punching bag, enabler, procurer, and fabricator.

That in the end, no matter how hard they worked, no matter how good they were at their job, the celebrities took it all for granted. There was no appreciation, and certainly no loyalty.

Mark Chin reappeared. "You guys better look at this." He held up a large-screen tablet for everyone to see. The tabloid Web ssites were already posting photos of Victoria's drunken disaster. We watched a montage of her tumbling down the stairs, of her lying bleeding on the sidewalk, of her being carried into the clearly marked Langone Medical Center emergency room.

"My god." A gaping Meg Dvoretz was looking over our shoulders. "She could have been killed."

"This is going to be worse than we thought," Chin said. "The hospital is short of manpower. You guys'd better bring in some extra bodies."

Lisi looked at Meg. "You inna position to authorize me hiring more security?"

"Do it," Meg said. "Just do it."

As predicted, the hospital was soon overwhelmed. Lisi's reinforcements—two retired cops and two Secret Service agents—arrived within the hour and helped repel reporters and stalkerazzi. But the starstruck, obsessed fans, some faking sickness or injuries, who flooded the halls, were a different kind of problem. They offered us favors: money, sex—*anything* to get close to Victoria Carrington. All were escorted out. The obnoxious ones were forcibly ejected.

"Can I help you?" Destiny said, stepping into the path of a furtive-eyed female, dressed in a doctor's smock as she was about to enter the examining area where Victoria was being treated.

"I'm seeing a patient," she said, eyes on a clipboard in her hand.

Destiny glanced at the hospital ID affixed to the woman's smock. "That photo doesn't look like you."

Lisi stepped forward. "Whatta we got heah?" He fingered a

thin strap that hung around the "doctor's" neck; a tiny Minox digital camera was attached. "You got any real ID?"

Reluctantly, the woman produced press ID from the *National Enquirer.* In a low voice she said, "I'm authorized to offer you twenty-five thousand dollars if you'll let me get a photo of Victoria."

"Get her outta heah," Lisi said.

"Thirty thousand?" the reporter said. "Forty? Fifty thousand?"

Destiny seized the tabloid reporter's arm and pulled her toward the exit.

My cell phone rang. "Beckett."

"Michael? It's Solana. Look to your left. Down the hall."

I saw Solana a hundred feet away, standing at a nurses' station amid a group of emergency-room orderlies and nurses. She waved to me. I waved back.

"I need to speak to you," Solana said. "In private."

"Sure." I put my phone away. "Be right back," I said to Lisi. Walked down the corridor, wove through the emergency-room workers, past the nurses' station, and followed Solana into a stairwell. "What's up?"

"I need a favor, Michael," Solana said. "I want to interview Victoria Carrington."

"Not gonna happen."

"Let me take a photo then?"

I shook my head, faintly disappointed but not surprised that she only wanted me for a favor. "No can do."

"You don't understand," Solana said. "I really need this job."

"I hear you, but Victoria would fire Lisi. Maybe blackball him in the industry. There's no way—"

"How about this?" Solana pressed. "Let me know when she leaves the hospital? You don't even have to tell me where you're taking her. I'll follow. No one can blame Lisi for that."

This was the deceitful Solana I had broken up with. "I can't."

She stepped back and her expression became hard. She folded

her arms across her chest. "The FBI contacted me. They want to talk. About you."

I hadn't seen that coming. But it made perfect sense. I was living with Solana when I formed my Rocker team—not that I was concerned about what Solana knew. I'd made it a point not to discuss my Rocking activities with anyone outside my team. "I'm sorry they're involving you."

"Being sorry doesn't help me keep my job."

"Hey, Solana," I said, finally getting exasperated. "We're not together anymore. Remember? You're the one who took a hike. I'm sorry, but this isn't my problem."

"Oh, but it *is* your problem."

"What's that mean?"

"You help me, I'll help you."

"How," I said, "will you help me?"

"By not telling the FBI what I know."

"What do you think you know?"

Solana shrugged. "More than you think."

"Wow." I glared at the woman who had once looked at me with adoring eyes. Who had referred to me as her knight in shining armor after I'd saved her from a serial arsonist and murder.

Solana was destitute after she'd been burned out of her Bronx apartment; everything she had owned went up in smoke. I moved her in with me, supported her both financially and emotionally. Things were great for a few months and then the adoring looks vanished—I guess familiarity really does breed contempt—and Solana fell into what became a chronic depression.

"What's wrong?" I'd ask her time and again, thinking it was me, that I was doing something wrong, still naive enough to think I could make a woman happy. "Tell me what I need to do."

"You wouldn't understand."

"Try me."

"I can't compete with Manhattan women."

"Compete?" I was baffled. "What are you talking about?"

"I don't have the clothes, jewelry…"

"You have plenty of clothes. What about the fur coat I gave you for Christmas?"

"I didn't ask you for it," Solana said, sulking.

I was stunned. "What the hell does that have to do with anything?"

"The coat was all about you showing off to your friends."

A light went off in my head. I realized that I didn't know the woman I was living with. I began to withdraw from her. And then I became preoccupied with my Rockers, putting drug dealers out of business, finding whoever was responsible for my sister's death. Which was when Solana had her affair, then left me for the other guy.

A booming hospital intercom voice brought me back to the present. I glanced down the hall. Destiny had returned from tossing out the *National Enquirer* reporter.

"Tell the feds whatever you want, Solana." I turned and exited the stairwell.

Destiny was speaking to Lisi as I came down the hall. "Would the *National Enquirer* really pay fifty-thousand dollars for a photo?"

Lisi shook his head. "She's fulla shit. We let her take the picture. The *Enquirer* would say she ain't authorized to make a deal—they'd stiff you."

Meg Dvoretz came down the hall. "The doctors want to keep Victoria for twenty-four-hour observation," she said to Lisi. "I've booked a private suite."

"What's the, whatchamacallit, prognosis?" Lisi said.

"She bruised some ribs," Meg said, a catch in her voice. "The head wound is superficial. Other than that, she's okay."

Two male orderlies arrived, entered the examination area, pulled back the curtain. Victoria was sitting up in bed, wearing a white hospital gown. There was a small bandage on the top of her head but, as Meg had said, other than that she looked okay. Actually, she looked better than okay. She looked beautiful.

As we approached, a doctor was telling Victoria how lucky she was that she was doing well and he'd see her in the morning. He handed a clipboard to the orderlies, smiled politely at us, and walked away.

Victoria saw us standing there and smiled weakly. "I'm ready."

The orderlies transferred her to a transportation gurney. Then we—that is, Lisi and our entire team—escorted her into a waiting elevator. I couldn't help but notice that as we rose to the fifth floor, Victoria spent the whole time staring at me. "How you feeling?" I said.

She didn't answer, but she sure didn't seem sick anymore.

We exited the elevator and rolled the gurney down a hallway. Meg and the orderlies entered a suite while the rest of us waited outside.

"Now, lissena me," Lisi addressed the four reinforcement bodyguards. "No one gets inta Victoria's room except her mother, Meg Dvoretz, and necessary medical staff. Make sure you check everyone's ID. I want two of youse on duty at all times. Whack it up anyway you like. *Capeesh?*"

"What about us?" I asked.

"Botha yuhs come with me," Lisi said. "We gotta talk."

"Hold it," Meg said to Lisi. She held the door open as the orderlies rolled out the now-empty gurney and pushed it down the hall. "She wants him."

"Who him?" Lisi said.

"Him," Meg said. "Beckett. C'mon, Michael. Chop, chop."

I looked at Lisi, not sure how to react in a situation like this. Lisi shrugged. "Go."

And so I entered the room, wondering what this was all about.

Meg stepped aside and allowed me to enter. "Here he is."

"Leave us," Victoria told Meg. "And I don't wish to be disturbed."

Meg made a face, stepped out of the room, and closed the door behind her.

Victoria and I were alone.

The suite was small and reminded me of a hotel room in a Hilton. The furnishings were the same, except for the hospital bed, which was off to my right. Victoria was sitting up.

"Come in," she said, her voice low, weak. "Sit. Please."

I advanced across the room, claimed a chair, and pulled it alongside her bed.

"Michael—" Victoria began, then winced from pain.

"Your ribs?" I said.

She nodded, took a slow, deep breath. "My neck's stiff too."

"Take your time."

Which she did. A full minute of deep breathing went by before she said, "You know about the Angel of Death?"

"Yes," I said. "Lisi filled us in."

"I want you to be my bodyguard."

"That's what we're here for."

"No." Victoria shook her head ever so slightly. "I want you. Personally."

"I don't understand."

She closed her eyes, like she was fading out. I figured that she was still a bit drunk, or perhaps stoned on painkillers. Would the doctors prescribe narcotics to a known substance abuser?

"I don't mean to be politically incorrect," Victoria said. "I know all about Mr. Lisi's reputation. I'm sure he was quite formidable once, but now, frankly—well, he's too old. And the woman…"

"Destiny," I said.

"She's no match for a man, especially some crazy—"

"You'd be surprised."

"You, on the other hand…" It took some effort for Victoria to look me up and down. "Meg tells me, if her own mother needed a bodyguard, you'd be her first choice."

"That's nice of Meg to say."

"Mr. Lisi told her you're probably the best, most natural bodyguard he's ever seen. You certainly look the part."

"I do my best," I said, well aware that Lisi told every client that every one of his bodyguards were the best, most natural he'd ever seen. It was his standard pitch.

"Will you be my bodyguard?" Victoria said in that little-girl way again. There was a hint of desperation in her voice. She reached out a shaky hand and I noticed that her lips were quivering. "Please? Will you?"

Whether she was acting or not, I took her hand, held it. "Of course."

"Promise?" She broke into a sob. "Promise you won't let him kill me."

"What? Hey, no one's going to kill you." I felt a surging urge to comfort her. I stood, put my arms around her, held her as she cried into my chest. After a few moments she seemed to regain control. She stopped crying, looked up at me—she had amazing amber eyes—and kissed me squarely, passionately on the lips.

I pulled back. "Victoria—"

"Shush." She wouldn't let me go, held me at arm's length, her amber orbs boring into mine. "Say it." The scent of her expensive perfume was intoxicating. "Say you promise you won't let him kill me."

"Promise," I said, still tasting her. "I won't let him kill you."

She smiled ever so slightly, pulled me close, love-bit my lower lip—ouch!—and then kissed me again—deeper this time, with even more passion. I couldn't fight her. I kissed her back; our lips crushing together, our tongues finding each other, my mind awash with the reality that the *People* magazine's sexiest woman alive was in my arms. We groaned, fondled, and groped each other and then fell back onto her bed.

Afterward, I rocked her in my arms, repeated that I wouldn't allow anyone to hurt her, and, for whatever reason, wondered if my father had made a similar promise to Audra Gardner.

CHAPTER 11

"**W**HAT VICTORIA HAVE ta say?" Lisi lit a smoke as we left the hospital and sucked in a long, hungry lungful. We pushed through the media ranks, which had swollen to include the legitimate press, if there even is such a distinction anymore. The sky was clear and a chill frosted the air. As usual, First Avenue was jammed with bumper-to-bumper traffic.

"She wants me to bodyguard her full-time," I said, happy I'd taken the time to freshen up after our tryst, especially to tend to my love-bit lip. "Seven days a week. She wants me to move into her town house."

"That's great," Lisi said, nearly rubbing his hands in greed. "We're talking ten grand a week for you, plus support staff."

"You going to do it?" Destiny said.

"I don't know," I said, trying to keep my face turned away from her.

"What're you, nuts?" Destiny said.

"She's neurotic, paranoid."

"Hey, fucko," Lisi said. "Haven't you learned anything? She's the client. If she's crazy, that's her business. It ain't our place to psychoanalyze her. Besides, you don't take the gig, she'll find someone else who ain't as good as you. What if something happened to her then? It would be your fault."

"All she has to do is stop shooting dope," I said. "She doesn't need twenty-four-hour-security. I'd only be feeding her paranoia."

"Yeah? Well, maybe she ain't as paranoid as you think."

"Meaning?"

"Let's talk over a drink."

We walked a few blocks north and then west, paused outside a stately town house. An elegant bronze crest hung from the building's ground-floor window, under which were the words *Bocca al Lupo Ristorante*.

"Let's go in heah." Lisi dropped his cigarette, crushed it with his foot.

We descended a short set of stairs, and as we entered the restaurant, I paused to scan behind us for an FBI tail. Didn't see anyone.

A distinguished, tuxedo-clad maître d' rushed across the warm, cozy room to greet us. "Welcome," he said, smiling. "Will you be dining with us this evening?"

"Maybe," Lisi said. His eyes were fixed on five sharkskin-suited, central-casting wiseguys sitting in a rear booth with a group of flashy, hard-looking blondes. The wiseguys noticed Lisi. Several nodded and Lisi nodded back. Off to the right, a half-dozen thugs in leather jackets were perched at a polished mahogany bar alongside a large vase, which contained an impressive bouquet of fresh flowers. I noticed the telltale gun bulges under the thugs' jackets, figured they were the wiseguys' bodyguards. If Destiny and I were still active duty, we'd roust them just for the hell of it and check for gun licenses.

"Youse two get a table," Lisi said, then gestured to the wiseguys. "I gotta go pay my respects."

"This way," the maître d' said.

Destiny and I followed him across the dining room, past several well-dressed patrons, to a corner table. The maître d' pulled Destiny's chair out for her, then handed me a thick, leather-bound wine list. We sat alongside one another, our backs to a brick wall, and watched Lisi as he embraced and kissed the wiseguys.

"Isn't that 'Ice Pick' Martucci," Destiny said, "sitting in the middle?"

"That's him." I opened the wine list. "Gambino crime-family capo. Suspect in at least twenty-six mob hits—the ones we know of. Uses an ice pick to the brain. And I'll bet the blondes are their *goumada*."

"Their what?"

"Mafia mistresses. Should we order a bottle of red?"

"Thought Lisi was out of that life."

"He is," I murmured, not really paying attention. "The Chianti looks reasonable."

"How do you know Lisi's out of the life?"

A formally attired sommelier appeared and I did order a bottle of Chianti. The sommelier gestured his approval, and moved off just as a waiter set down a basket of hot garlic bread—the aroma was mouthwatering—bread sticks, a plate of butter, a small bowl containing oil-cured Beldi olives swimming in olive oil, and three glasses of ice water.

"Really," Destiny said. "How do you know Lisi's still not connected?" She took a whiff of the garlic bread and picked up a piece.

"The way my father told it to me—" I used my folk to spar an olive—"Lisi had just gotten out of the Marines Corps and needed a job. He had an elderly mother at home. Three sisters. He had just gotten married. He took the police and fire-department tests with my father, passed with flying colors. But an entry-level job with the Gambino crime family came up first. He was a gofer—ran errands, delivered messages, even had to babysit some of the mob guys' kids on occasion." I put the olive in my mouth; chewed, swallowed. "After a while they had him collecting overdue gambling debts."

"So he was a leg breaker," Destiny said.

"Not exactly," I responded. "Tough as Lisi was, he didn't have it in him to hurt anyone—which was a problem. And then some of the mob guys found out Lisi had taken the police test with my father; they thought he could be an undercover cop." I sipped some water. "Then there were the don's enemies, the ones who wanted to take over. They saw Lisi as a weak link, an opportunity to be exploited. They nicknamed him Sweet Tommy—it wasn't meant as a compliment. But the name stuck." I reached for a bread stick, broke it in half, laid it on my bread plate. "Then one day the regular driver for the Gambinos' don—by that time he was La Cosa Nostra's *capo di tutti capi*—calls in sick. The don's enemies made sure Lisi got the job filling in for the sick driver. They figured when they made their move, and the shooting started, Sweet Tommy would fall apart."

"Like Fredo did in the first *Godfather* movie?" Destiny said.

"Exactly."

Destiny nibbled at the garlic bread. "Okay, so Lisi fills in for the sick driver. And?"

"Right. Now keep in mind Lisi was in the Marine Corps, did two combat tours. He was a battle-hardened veteran, still edgy, alert as a Doberman."

The sommelier stepped up to the table, showed us the bottle of wine, opened it. I did the dumb tasting thing—I couldn't tell the difference between a 10-dollar bottle of wine and a 500-dollar bottle of wine—and nodded my approval. The sommelier poured three glasses.

"So Lisi pulls up in front of this steak house on East Forty-sixth Street," I continued once the sommelier was out of earshot. "He gets out of the car, comes around to open the don's door, and recognizes the assassins coming down the street—the rest you know."

"Lisi kills the two hit men," Destiny said. "Saves the don's life. But takes a bullet to the chest. Almost dies."

"Not almost," I said. "He was clinically dead for fifteen minutes. Literally came back from the dead—a bona fide, fourteen-karat miracle. And the tabloids made a celebrity out of Sweet Tommy Lisi—end of story."

We picked up our wineglasses, clinked, and drank.

"So dying was Lisi's way out of the mob?"

"Sort of," I said. "Lisi was still in the hospital. He tells the don he wants out. That he already gave his life for 'this thing of ours.' Now the don's between a rock and a hard place. Sure, he owes Lisi his life, but he can't just let him quit."

"Yeah? So? What happened?"

I sipped more wine. "The family simply stopped communicating with Lisi. He stopped communicating with the family. When my father was promoted to lieutenant, he and Lisi decided to take advantage of Lisi's celebrity status. They started Lisi and Beckett Protective Services. They were the 'it' bodyguard agency for years. Had a long roster of A-list clients. Until my father retired from the PD. That's when his mental faculties began to fade. And then Lisi's wife died... he had a heart attack and other health issues—you know the rest."

"So, technically," Destiny said, "Lisi's still in the mob."

"Technically?" I thought about it. "Yeah. I guess you could say he is."

Loud voices. Everyone in the restaurant turned to look.

"Yeah?" Lisi barked from across the room. He pushed back from the table, shot to his feet, stuck his index finger in Ice Pick Martucci's face. "You fuck with me, I'll stab you inna throat, you piece a' gahbidge."

The other wiseguys got to their feet. The blondes (*goumadas*) cowered.

Ice Pick remained seated. "Lower your voice," he said calmly.

"Fuck you," Lisi said. "Fuck all of youse guinea cocksuckers."

The six bodyguards at the bar slid off of their stools, converged toward the commotion.

"Don't," I called out, and held up my shield, my hand on the butt of my weapon, obviously willing to draw and fire. The bodyguards stopped, sized up Destiny and me. One short, twitchy thug looked ready to pull his weapon. The problem for me was there were civilians sitting at tables between us and them—not that the thugs would care. The tallest of the thugs grabbed the twitchy one's gun arm and told him to cool it. Then he looked to Ice Pick for instructions. Ice Pick signaled for them to stand down.

"Drop dead," Lisi said, threw a cloth napkin in Ice Pick's face, then stormed away from the table. The bodyguards returned to the bar. The other wiseguys sat back down and comforted their *goumadas*. Ice Pick Martucci, face flushed with embarrassment and rage, continued to glare at Lisi.

Lisi sat across from us and took a deep breath. "Well," he said with a smile. "That coulda gone better."

"Nice move, Tommy," I said. "Embarrassing a psycho killer in public. You have a death wish or something?"

"What can I say?" Lisi shrugged. "The mook has delusions of adequacy."

"What was that all about?" Destiny said.

Lisi picked up his glass of wine. "*Salud.*" He took a healthy swallow, and I noticed his hands were shaking from the adrenaline rush. "Old business." The waiter came over to the table, handed out menus, and moved away, a little faster than before.

"We're listening," I said.

Lisi took a moment, sighed. "Ice Pick's second cousin was one of the scump-bags that tried ta whack the don years ago. Some people don't subscribe to the notion of forgive and forget." Lisi forced a laugh.

"So, you killed his second cousin?" Destiny said.

"Yeah—hey," Lisi said, finally noticing. "What happened to your lip?"

I dabbed it with my napkin, wiped off a smidgen of blood. "Must've bit it."

Destiny shot me a quizzical look.

"I do it alla the time." Lisi opened his menu, flipped a page. "So, youse guys hungry, or what?"

CHAPTER 12

"SO, VICTORIA'S NOT as paranoid as I think?" I said, steering the conversation away from my love-bitten lip.

"You tell me." Lisi put down the bread stick, closed his menu. "The Angel a' Death sent her another letter." He looked at Destiny. "You know who I'm talking about?"

"The stalker who killed Audra Gardner."

"According to my father," I said.

As I mentioned earlier, there had been six "suspicious" celebrity deaths during the past ten years. All had been officially ruled accidental drug intoxication overdoses. Since all of the celebrities were receiving death threats from someone calling himself the Angel of Death, and all were drug addicts, and all had died from tainted heroin, my father was convinced they were murdered. So began his Angel of Death odyssey.

"We still don't know his identity," Lisi said. "Just his, whatchamacallit—nom de plume?" He plucked a stack of letters from his jacket pocket, handed one to me. "Read."

I scrutinized the first piece of paper: common 20-pound stock, white, letter size. The message was typed, italicized. The font looked to be a size 12, Times New Roman. I guessed it was printed on a commonplace ink-jet printer.

You continue to flaunt His commandants. You continue to live in sin. Your immoral existence sets an aberrant example to others. This is your last warning. Repent sinner, or the Angel of Death will be upon you.

"Where'd you get these?" I handed it to Destiny.

"Victoria," Lisi said, placing the rest of the dozen letters on the table. "That one came yesterday afternoon." He patted the stack. "All of 'em say basically the same thing: Repent, sinner, or else."

Destiny handed the letter back to Lisi. "You agree with Beckett's father's theory?"

"Truthfully?" Lisi said. "Not till I read Shamus's files."

"What files?" Destiny said.

"Yeah," I echoed. "What files?" I was embarrassed to admit I had no idea what Lisi was talking about. But then again, my father never told me much.

As a kid, there was always tension in the house when my father was home. Since he "worked the clock," varying his work schedule, days, evenings, and nights, he was home for dinner one week out of every three. And on those evenings my sister and I did our best to avoid him—he was always pissed off about something. I got the occasional ass-kicking, which I usually deserved. He never laid a hand on my sister, though. Fact was, my father and I never had a real conversation. Never communicated in the way a father and son should. He was at no time a friend or a confidant. He was a disciplinarian, and that was that. Though he never told me, I assume—because I was his son—he must have loved me. But I don't think he ever liked me. And I guess I didn't like him much, either.

"Your father reinvestigated alla the celebrity deaths," Lisi said.

"He did?"

"Concluded that the original case detective had profiled alla the victims, including our former client Audra Gardner." Lisi addressed Destiny. "Understand, alla the celebs had histories of depression, drug and alcohol abuse. A few attempted suicide. Problem was, your father wasn't all there mentally by then, so no one took his theory seriously. Some thought he was still grieving, reacting to your sister's death—I suppose he was in a way. Besides, he had absolutely no proof. He was playing one of his hunches."

"As I recall," I said, "his hunches were usually good."

"Yeah. They were."

"You're saying—what're you saying?" Destiny asked.

Lisi leaned forward, elbows on the table. "Only that six celebrities receiving death threats from the Angel a' Death injected heroin mixed with fentanyl."

"Well, from what I've read, fentanyl overdoses are common. Besides, some dealers sell some junkies hot loads." Destiny shrugged. "You're talking criminally- neglect homicide. Not serial murder."

"Maybe," Lisi said. "If it was different dealers. But Beckett's father was convinced the dealer was the Angel a' Death in all six cases." Lisi reached for a slice of garlic bread, spread extra butter on it, then dipped it in the olive oil. "If he was right, that means that there's someone out there who ain't just another star-struck, drug-dealing, scump-bag looking to get close to celebrities by supplying them with grade-A smack. Show business is fulla those hard-ons." Lisi took a bite of bread, spoke with his mouth full. "This guy is targeting and stalking his victims. Supplying them heroin spiked with fentanyl. These were six premeditated murders—and it looks Victoria Carrington's the Angel a' Death's next target."

Destiny addressed me: "Shamus spoke to Manhattan Narcotics?"

"Ask Lisi."

"And the DEA." Lisi used his napkin to dab the olive oil that was running down his chin. "Twice. First time was after Audra Gardner's death. Shamus told them about the Angel a' Death letters. They blew him off. Said Audra was a notorious junky and nutcase who probably had no idea what the hell she was inject-ing—tough shit."

"I can see their point," Destiny said.

"Second time was after he reinvestigated alla the other celebrity deaths. He told them his Angel a' Death theory—again they didn't believe him. They told him junkies overdose all the time. That's what junkies do." Lisi forked a black olive, popped it into his mouth. "Honestly, I don't think some a' those detec-tives appreciated Shamus poking around, second-guessing their investigation. Can't say as I blame 'em."

"I never bothered to mention this before," Destiny said, "but I always thought..."

"What?" I said.

"That the name *Angel of Death* itself could be a clue to the sicko's motive."

"How's that?" I said.

"Well, half-a-dozen modern-day serial killers—nurses, hospi-tal orderlies, and physicians—were called Angels of Death."

"So was a Nazi concentration-camp officer," I said.

"True, but the killers in the medical field all had the same motive. They decided their victims would be better off if they no longer suffered from whatever severe illness was plaguing them. They saw themselves as angels of mercy."

"You're saying that this Angel a' Death thinks he's saving his victims?" Lisi said. "From what?"

Destiny shrugged. "Depression? Drug addiction? Who knows?"

"At least it's something to consider," I pointed out.

"Would be interesting if some, or all of the six victims had a doctor, a shrink, or someone in the medical profession in com-mon," Destiny said.

"They don't," Lisi said. "Beckett's father already checked."

We all thought about alternate possibilities, although noth-ing seemed as solid to me as my father's hunch.

Destiny said, "Did you tell Victoria and her mother what you just told us?"

"I tried." Lisi smirked. "Her mother didn't wanna hear it. Victoria's had stalkers before. Thinks they're no big deal, except for PR purposes. But here's the kicker: Lynn was hiding the letters from Victoria. Said she didn't want to upset here. Claims her daughter's a drama queen." Lisi sipped some wine. "When Victoria found out, read a couple of the letters, she freaked out, big-time. Had a couple a fights with her mother. She's scared out of her mind. So onna the things I suggested was she stop Tweeting her whereabouts. It's like laying a trail for any crazy to follow. She said she'd think about it."

My cell phone vibrated. Ex-cops and former Rockers Serria and McKee sent a text, in code, to my personal cell phone, asking to meet in two hours. I texted back, *10-4.*

"You have any suspects?" Destiny said.

"Yeah, anyone and everyone with access to celebrities," Lisi said.

"So the answer is no."

"Right. But I've been poking around, making a lot a' noise, asking a lot of questions, generally pissing people off like Shamus did. You know, your father got his share of death threats—obviously he scared someone."

"He never told me," I said. "He never told me any of this."

"Well, you know how he was. Kept things to himself—typical mick." Lisi sipped more wine. "I got one death threat already on my answering machine." He grinned, nodding obliquely across the room. "Two if you count the one that mook Ice Pick just made."

"Way to go," I said.

"Lissena me," Lisi said. "If anything should happen to me, everything you need to know, all of your father's Angel a' Death files're in my apartment."

"Now you're starting to freak me out," Destiny said.

"Don't worry about me, kiddo." Lisi winked. "Only the good die young."

"What about Victoria Carrington?" Destiny said.

"She's safe enough for tonight," Lisi said.

"What about after tonight?" Destiny looked at me. "You going to bodyguard her, or what?"

"I'll think about it."

"Think fast, fucko," Lisi said. "She gets outta the hospital inna morning." He reopened his menu again. "So, what looks good heah?"

CHAPTER 13

THE DISCREET DOOR on busy East Fifty-fifth Street just east of Third Avenue shielded a long set of steep wooden steps to a members-only, moodily lit, intimate bar and dining room.

Sidecar, on the second floor above the renowned P. J. Clarke's bar, was a welcome throwback to the late 1800s. The ceiling was original tin, the walls exposed brick, and the overall ambiance was warm, exuding Old World charm.

An attractive twentysomething woman manning the hostess stand at the top of the stairs greeted us with a smile. "Welcome back, Mr. Beckett, Ms. Jones."

"We're meeting someone." I returned the smile as I checked out the small bar and the mostly occupied tables. Saw Serria and McKee across the room, huddled at a table by a window overlooking Third Avenue.

Retired police officer and gunslinger Ernie Serria had killed two armed robbers in two separate shootings. One part Julio Iglesias, two parts Bronx Puerto Rican, he was the diminutive, bitterly divorced father of a troubled twenty-three-year-old son who, after years in and out of drug rehab, had actually turned his life around. His son earned a degree from a community college, got married, and was now employed as a drug counselor. An empty nester, Serria now spent much of his time singing—off- key—in a swing band and mumbling an unfunny stand-up comedy routine in open-mike clubs.

Serria's longtime partner, retired police officer Thomas McKee, was a chain-smoking, wheezing, couch-potato-fat candidate for a quadruple bypass and, since the love of his life perished, the saddest man I knew. Soon after disbanding my Rockers, McKee's fiancée, April, fell to her death in a tragic accident. While smoking a cigarette on the terrace of a San Diego high-rise hotel, April leaned against a guardrail that gave way.

When they saw Destiny and me approaching, McKee and Serria shot to their feet, bro-hugged me, then took turns bear-hugging Destiny. I gotta admit I barely recognized McKee. He had lost a lot of weight. Looked fit. But his hair was dyed a bizarre reddish-brown. His teeth, which were either caps or veneers, were too big for his mouth, not to mention ridiculously white.

"Christ, McKee," I said. "You living in the gym?"

"Look who's talking," McKee said as we all took seats.

"You guys sure you weren't followed?" I added.

"Positive," McKee said.

"I took the liberty," Serria said as we all settled in, "of ordering your drinks." He handed Destiny a glass of white wine. Handed me a cold bottle of Stella.

"Stella?" I said. "Stella? Really?"

"I told you, he drinks Coors Light," McKee said. "You dumb spic."

"Bite me," Serria shot back. "You drunkin' Irish faggot."

McKee flexed his newly developed pecs and blew Serria a kiss.

Serria wiggled his eyebrows, blew a kiss back.

And Destiny wondered why I loved those guys.

"To us," Destiny toasted. "It's good to see everyone."

We all clicked glasses and drank.

"Potty time." Destiny put down her glass, shouldered her handbag. "Excuse me."

McKee had to move so Destiny could pass.

"How're you two doing?" McKee said when Destiny was out of earshot.

"Good."

"I mean, you two still aren't..." McKee pumped his fist. "Doing the nasty?"

"No," I said. "We're just friends."

McKee chuckled. "You're a pisser, you are. The way you can stay friends with all of your exes."

"Hey," Serria said. "Remember when he was dating three airline stewardesses at the same time? They all lived in the same building but flew for three different airlines on different schedules?"

"That was almost twenty years ago," I said, though I was pleased to be reminded of a more adventurous time in my life.

"You still friends with them?" Serria asked.

"Two of them," I said. "The other one hates me."

"No wonder," Serria said. "Remember you bought them all the same negligee for Christmas. Only in three different colors?" Serria and McKee guffawed at that.

"I hope I've matured since then."

"Well, one can hope." McKee drank some beer.

That's when I noticed a new tattoo on McKee's right hand: a teardrop heart with *APRIL* in the center. "How about you?" I said. "How're you doing?"

"Me?" McKee flashed a brittle smile. "I'm good. Gave up smoking. Cut back on the hard stuff." He gestured with the glass of Miller Light. "I'm at the gym five days a week. Lost fifty pounds. I joined a couple of those online dating sites. I've got a young hottie can't keep her hands off of me."

"That's what hookers get paid to do," Serria snickered.

"She's not a hooker," McKee said, mock outraged. "She's a Russian countess."

"Countess, my ass," Serria said. "She's six foot, got hands she could palm a basketball with. And an Adam's."

"That's an Eve's pear," McKee said.

"And what's with the white boots she always wears?" Serria said. "What're they, size fourteen?"

"Same as me," McKee said. "We share our shoes."

I broke out laughing. A waitress stopped by, asking if we'd like anything to eat. Serria and McKee, P.J. Clarke's regulars, went ahead and ordered their usual appetizers. I said that Destiny and I had just eaten, and ordered another round of drinks.

"I miss anything?" Destiny asked as she retook her seat alongside McKee.

"Just the usual," I said.

"Oh, before I forget…" Destiny reached into her shoulder bag, handed out the prepaid cell phones, and saw McKee's new *APRIL* tattoo. "Nice tat."

Former police-academy classmates, Destiny and McKee had always been close—flirtatious even—back in the day, but had never dated. Although we all knew April, Destiny was the one who'd truly bonded with her. McKee had yet to open up to Destiny, or any of us, about how his fiancée's accidental death had affected him.

"How are things, Thomas?" Destiny said.

"Good." McKee forced a smile, his eyes on the table.

"I'm glad." She squeezed his hand.

"Okay. Question," Serria said. "Why's the FBI coming around, asking us about Rockers? What in the hell is going on?"

"We don't think they're regular feds," Destiny said. "They might be Joint Terrorist Task Force."

Serria and McKee exchanged glances.

"They're also investigating the German Hotel explosion," Destiny said. "And the Lochlainn O'Brian homicide."

The husband-and-wife owners of the German Hotel—the wife was another ex-girlfriend of mine named Enia, yet another long story—were the catalyst that caused me to organize my gang of Rockers. Lochlainn O'Brian, an IRA-connected terrorist and drug dealer, and his vicious gang, the Belfast Boys, had squatted in the hotel and had seized control. Enia and her husband wanted their hotel back. We negotiated a price, and early one morning my Rockers and I forcibly—as in shock-and-awe—evicted O'Brian and his gang.

"Sounds like you're the feds' main target," Serria said.

At first I didn't respond. Everyone at that table assumed that I'd killed Lochlainn O'Brian because he'd sold the drugs that killed my sister, among other things. Not that I blamed them. "The feds are fishing," I said casually. "If they had anything, I'd be in handcuffs."

A group of six businessmen entered Sidecar. We all eyeballed them suspiciously as the hostess sat them at a table on the other side of the room. All at once I recognized a couple of them. One had been a professional hockey player. Another was a sports newscaster. The others looked just as familiar, but I couldn't place them. Not that I cared, as long as they weren't spying on me.

"You know," McKee said, "the feds might have another agenda, besides the obvious." He sipped his beer. "The bastards could be making a move against the department, like they did in L.A."

"The feds take over the NYPD?" Destiny said.

"Never happen," Serria said.

"That's what they said in L.A.," Destiny said. "And Pittsburgh. And Detroit. And New Orleans. And Phoenix. And about twenty other cities."

"Just think about it," McKee said. "If they could prove the existence of a gang of vigilante cops? Add that to all the other allegations of police misconduct—the shootings of unarmed civilians. The rape cops scandal. Ticket-fixing scandal."

"So, you're saying: we're the linchpins in this scenario of yours?" Destiny asked. "We could be the cause of the feds taking over the NYPD?"

"We could be," McKee said. "I'm just saying."

We were all quiet for a long moment. The scenario seemed extremely unlikely to me.

"At least this cat-and-mouse game with the feds gives me something to think about," Serria said. "What I mean is, I'm bored shitless." He sipped his beer. "And I'll tell you another thing: I enjoyed Rocking. The action, I mean."

"Agreed," McKee said. "I'm either working on my house, in the gym, or—"

"Watching midget porn," Serria said, grinning.

Destiny nearly spit up her wine laughing.

"Point is," McKee said, "I'm climbing the freaking walls."

"At least when we were Rocking," Serria said, "we were having fun—and doing the world some good."

I had to agree. Forcibly evicting predatory drug gangs from their lairs, disrupting their lives and wrecking their businesses, had been a rewarding experience.

"Aren't you the guys who voted to disband?" I said.

"We got tired," Serria said. "That's all."

"You were tired too." McKee tapped his index finger to his temple. "I remember."

"Yeah," I said. "I was tired too."

"I guess what I'm trying to say..." Serria said, "I miss working with all of you."

"Gotta admit," I said, "I feel the same."

"Well," Destiny said, "why don't we all do something together?"

"Like what?" I said. "We're not going back to Rocking."

"Like starting our own security company," she said with more enthusiasm than usual. "How about we form our own PI agency?"

McKee shook his head. "The PI business sucks."

Serria said, "Every retired cop and his grandmother has a PI license."

"And they undercut each other's rates," McKee said. "Some schmucks are actually working for twenty-five dollars an hour."

"Well, we could do bodyguard work," Destiny gushed, and I gave her a look. Where was all this coming from?

"It's the same," McKee said. "Too many ex-cops. Too little work."

I focused on Destiny. She was fidgeting. Clenching and unclenching her jaw. Perspiration glistened on her forehead—she was high on something. *Shit*.

"But you could work for Sweet Tommy Lisi," Destiny said.

I shot her a sharp look. I wish she hadn't said that. No matter how good a cop was on the street, no matter how tough, resourceful, or diplomatic, some became positively goofy when in the presence of a star. And no matter how many times Lisi recited his rules about not speaking to a client unless spoken to, he'd had to fire quite a few veteran cops, FBI agents, and even Secret Service agents who were simply incapable of controlling themselves around celebrities. Years ago I'd personally witnessed a former FBI special agent who found himself in the same room as the actress Gwyneth Paltrow morph into embarrassingly silly, gushing fool. I glanced at my two friends. Serria would work out. He'd listen to Lisi's Rules and know how to behave. But McKee? I had my doubts. Not that I was one to talk. I tongued my slightly swollen lip.

"Lisi?" McKee said. "Your father's former business partner?"

"The old gangster?" Serria said.

"The same," I answered.

"His business is picking up," Destiny said.

I immediately countered with, "Well, I'm not so sure signing one A-list client makes much of a difference."

The waitress brought the next round, along with the appetizers.

"It's Victoria Carrington," Destiny volunteered after the waitress had left.

"That psycho?" McKee snickered.

"One A-list client might lead to more," Destiny said

reasonably. "And Michael gets to choose his own team." She put me on the spot. "Isn't that what you told me?"

Destiny high again: What a delightful change. "That's right."

"Okay, wait," McKee said. "I just thought of something. What're the feds gonna think of us all working together again? Huh? Maybe they'll use our association as proof of some ongoing criminal conspiracy. Use the RICO statute to prosecute us."

Destiny said, "That's a possibility."

"I'm just saying," McKee said.

"Screw the feds," I said angrily, going against my previous position. "They're not gonna dictate what I do, or when I do it. You guys wanna try bodyguarding? No problem."

"I'm in," Serria said.

"I'm with the spic," McKee said.

"All right, then," Destiny said.

Serria raised his beer in a toast. "To Beckett's Rockers."

"Back together again," Destiny said, and chugged down her entire glass of wine.

CHAPTER 14

"**A**LL I'M SAYING," Serria said as McKee steered his silver Dodge Charger SRT8 Super Bee off the Bruckner Expressway and merged onto I-295 south, "is that a lot of people wanted Lochlainn O'Brian dead. I mean, the guy was a drug dealer *and* terrorist, for chrissake."

"Can't argue with that," McKee said as he got off at exit 9.

They had stayed at Sidecar for another couple of hours. Ordered more drinks, exchanged prepaid cell- phone numbers, and toasted their plan of going into business together over and over again. Before the evening ended, Beckett had reiterated his theory that the feds were just fishing, that they were attempting to shake one of his Rocker team up, panic him or her into cooperating. In the end, Beckett had picked up the entire tab—in McKee's mind, showing off as usual. He also needlessly reminded everyone to check their homes and vehicles constantly for federal listening devices, and said he'd contact them as soon as any body-guard work came up.

"There's no way his suppliers believed O'Brian's 'I got robbed by a gang of masked men' story," Serria continued. "Would you? Close to twenty-eight thousand in cash? Maybe fifty grand worth of coke? Gimme a break. I'll bet he was killed by his suppliers."

"I don't agree." McKee turned left on 177th Street and right onto Harding Avenue. "For one thing, Beckett never hid the fact he wanted to kill O'Brian. But even if we disregard the fact that O'Brian sold the drugs that killed Beckett's sister, there's still the eyewitness who said that the guy who shot O'Brian fit Beckett's physical description."

"You know as well as I do, eyewitness testimony is unreliable," Serria said. "Besides, the gunman wore a mask."

"Correct. A kelly-green mask." McKee turned left on Pennyfield Avenue, slowed to allow a kid on a bicycle to cross the road. "Who always wore a kelly-green ski mask?"

Serria sighed. "Beckett."

"See, you're not so stupid." McKee turned right onto Chaffee Avenue into the Silver Beach section of the Bronx—a little-known fairy-tale neighborhood of white picket fences and single-family homes that always reminded Serria of the coast of Maine. They drove past a guard booth, traveled along the rustic country roads, then turned onto Sunset Trail and stopped in front of McKee's waterfront brick home. McKee parked behind Serria's old Toyota alongside manicured hedges, on a quiet path on a bluff fifty feet above the East River.

"Hard to believe," Serria said as he took in the spectacular water and Manhattan skyline views, "that we're in the city."

"Come in for a minute?" McKee said as he killed the engine. "You haven't seen the landscaping or what I did inside."

"Sure." They alighted from the car and walked up a new cobblestone path, dodging the misty spray from McKee's new automated lawn-sprinkler system.

"Gotta admit," Serria said as they leaped over puddles of runoff water. "Your landscaper did a great job—place looks like the Botanical Gardens."

"Wait till you see inside." McKee fished out his house key, kicked off his shoes and left them on an outdoor welcome mat. "Take your shoes off or you'll track mud in the place."

"Wow," Serria said as they walked across recently laid wall-to-wall beige carpet; he loved the new smell, plus the feel of the thick pile under his stockinged feet. They passed an elegant, masculine living room—very Ralph Lauren—with a new, custom limestone fireplace. On its mantel sat an array of framed photos: Pictures of McKee with his deceased fiancée April and her two young daughters.

"Hey, babe," McKee said to one of April's pictures. He kissed his index finger and pressed it to the photo.

"You miss San Diego?" Serria had always wondered why his old partner had continued the eight-year long- distance relationship, why he didn't find romance closer to home.

"I miss the bicoastal lifestyle," McKee said. "Loved spending three or four months at a time in San Diego. Three months here."

"You still keep in contact with April's daughters?"

"Not as much as I'd like," McKee said. "They live with their father now. Besides, everyone's moved on."

Have you? Serria wanted to say, but didn't.

Once, when McKee was drunk, he confided in Serria that he sometimes received twilight visits from April. That she'd appear to him in the wee hours of the morning, that the visions and conversations were so real that he would forget she was dead. Serria wondered—and worried—if that was still the case.

They entered a custom-built modern kitchen. Antique French pavers held handmade Italian pottery on the counters. Old English bar stools surrounded the center, granite-topped cooking aisle. The open shelves displayed more photos of April and McKee.

Serria walked across the gleaming tile floor, gazed out the backyard's sliding glass doors at the new combination three-tiered waterfall and Jacuzzi. "Nice. Must have cost a fortune." His alarm scale had reached ten by the time he turned and faced his old partner. "Let me ask you something: Are you out of your mind?

"What?"

"How're you gonna explain where you got the money?"

"Explain to who?"

"What if one of your neighbors calls the IRS?"

"Relax," McKee said. "No one gives a shit. Besides, I can account for the new car, the landscaping, maybe even the hot tub."

"And the inside?"

"There's no way anyone's gonna know about the inside—you thirsty?"

Serria took a deep, calming breath; decided to drop it. "What've you got?" He took a seat at the kitchen counter.

"I've got all kinds of booze." McKee opened his top-of-the-line stainless-steel subzero refrigerator. "Cold beer. Cola if you'd like. Oh, and cold white wine."

"Beer," Serria said. McKee tossed him a can of Beck's.

"Speaking of white wine…" Serria popped his top, took a swallow. "What's up with Destiny? See the way she was knocking back her wine?"

"Yeah. Something's not right."

"She looks unhealthy," Serria said. "Maybe that's why she's pounding them down."

"Maybe it's the only way she can tolerate Beckett," McKee said. "He's a control freak. Probably why she dumped him."

Serria stopped mid-sip. "Where'd that come from?"

McKee made a face and shrugged.

Serria swallowed some more beer and mused, not for the first time, about the changes that had come over his ex-partner since April's death. McKee reminded him of one of his cousins, a churchgoing, mousy, conservative young woman who morphed into a promiscuous, out-of-control sexpot after breast-augmentation surgery. Serria soon realized that the breast implants had not actually *changed* his cousin, but instilled in her the self-confidence to be herself—in her case, not a good thing.

Nor in McKee's.

The quiet, grounded, reserved McKee dealt with his crippling grief by regressing into an adolescent Romeo. He lost weight, got in pretty good shape, began dressing younger, coloring his hair a tacky reddish-brown. He capped his teeth, purchased the Dodge

Charger—a younger man's muscle car. He came on strong to practically anything in a skirt; he wasn't even remotely choosy. Serria felt that, in many ways, McKee was attempting to emulate Beckett, of whom he had always been jealous. Especially after Beckett landed the recurring role on *Law & Order*. Not that he didn't understand why. Beckett was one of those guys who seemed to have it all: good looks, a warm, likable—but take-no-shit-from-anyone personality—and always a beautiful woman on his arm.

"I mean," McKee said, "Beckett's an opinionated alpha male. Always has been. Maybe she was tired of it." He picked up a prescription-pill bottle, opened it, shook out a pill, and swallowed it with some beer.

"What's that?" Serria said.

"Prozac," McKee said. "For depression."

"Since when do you get depressed?" Serria said.

McKee smiled. "Every time I look at you."

"Ouch," Serria said. His gaze drifted to the hallway. "Hell is that?" He put his beer down, headed across the kitchen, and flipped on a light to reveal two fresh sets of muddy footprints.

McKee shot to his feet, drew his weapon. "Someone's in here."

"You have a housekeeper?" Serria whispered.

Shaking his head, McKee pointed to faint wet footprints that led to the basement, then pointed to the prints on the stairs to the second floor.

"I'll take the basement." Serria pulled his weapon, opened the basement door. Descended into the darkness.

McKee crept up to the second floor, into the guest bedrooms—not that he ever had guests anymore—at the front of the house. He flipped on lights, looked in the closets, lavatories, under beds. Then he followed the footprints into the master bedroom.

The bedside photo of April had been moved ever so slightly. A dresser drawer was cracked open. McKee walked into his closet, bent down and examined a cheap Sentry Safe. He dialed the combination and pulled the door open. The 18K gold Piaget wristwatch and 18K gold cuff links were where he'd left them. But the envelope that contained $20,000 in cash was open; he'd left it sealed.

He met Serria at the bottom of the stairs.

"Nothing in the basement," Serria said.

McKee shushed him. Pointed to the footprints that led into his home office. They eased down the hall. McKee used a foot to push the door open. Serria went in first, weapon at the ready.

"Clear," Serria said.

"My computer chair," McKee said, coming into the room. "That's not how I left it. And the mouse has been moved." He sat at his desk and noticed immediately that the 8-by-10 photo of April taken at a New Year's eve party was now facing to the right. McKee hit the space bar and the computer screen lit up. He toggled through a series of screens, then checked his browser's history and then which programs were recently opened and when. "Looks like they went through my bank accounts," McKee said. "Brokerage accounts. Financial statements. They checked out my bookmarks, all the Web sites I visit."

"Who?" Serria said.

"Think about it." McKee got to his feet, paced the room. "Whoever broke in wasn't looking to steal. They were looking for information. And who's been poking around, asking questions?"

"The feds," Serria said.

"Has to be." McKee stopped to consider the consequences of such a visit. "Wonder if they planted bugs." He pulled a book from a bookshelf, reached behind it, and removed a listening detection device. They spent the next twenty minutes scanning for bugs. Didn't find any.

"You'd better get back to your place, see if they broke in." McKee picked up his house phone. "I'll tip off Beckett and Destiny."

"Hold it." Serria gestured at McKee's computer. "Was there anything incriminating on your hard drive?"

McKee took a moment too long before he answered, "No."

CHAPTER 15

EARLY THE FOLLOWING morning I worked out in the
New York Sports Club, located in the basement of my building. I hit the heavy-bag for about twenty minutes, throwing
flurries of lefts and rights, pounding away with a series of rib-
cracking uppercuts: my best punch. I had a lot on my mind.

Destiny and Lisi had finally convinced me to take on the
Victoria Carrington gig. I still didn't feel right about it. I'd be
taking advantage of a thoroughly neurotic, paranoid girl—which
in a way, by succumbing to her charms, I already had. But Lisi's
assertion that it was our job to supply clients with security service
and not question their motives made sense. Plus, if I turned down
the gig, Lisi might very well lose Victoria as a client. I couldn't
allow that to happen.

Last night's call from McKee had opened a whole other can
of worms. He said that the feds—had to be the feds because they
hadn't stolen anything—had broken into his home. Then he con-
fessed sheepishly to having spent much of his share of our illicit
Rocker proceeds on home improvements with cash that he could
not possibly account for.

"Didn't we all agree not to flash money around?" I said angrily.

"I didn't," McKee said.

"What about the new car?"

"I took out a car loan," McKee said. "I'm making payments."

"And the landscaping and hot tub you told me about? What were you thinking?"

"Who the hell could predict that the feds would break in?"

Angry as I was, I had to admit, he had a point.

After hanging up with McKee, I immediately examined my own residence for telltale signs of a break-in. Didn't see any. But then again, my front-door lock was a pick-proof Abloy dead bolt. But just to err on the safe side, I checked my apartment for listening devices—didn't find any—then examined my heavy-duty Acme floor safe. I always left the combination dial on number 7. It was now set at 0. Had I been careless last time I opened the safe and forgot to leave it on 7? Or had the feds managed to break in?

With these thoughts giving me heartburn, I finished working out. Spent fifteen minutes in the steam room, took a quick cold shower, chatted a bit with a few other gym regulars, and headed back to my apartment.

At my door, I picked up my delivered copies of the *Times* and the *Post*. I glanced at the *Post*'s front page: There were "exclusive" color photos of Victoria Carrington tumbling down her townhouse steps. "Shit," I muttered.

I entered my apartment and double-locked the door behind me. I poured myself a cup of coffee I'd brewed earlier and gazed absently at the rising sun and the beehive of activity over LaGuardia Airport. I sipped the black coffee and opened the *Post*.

Pages two through four carried photos of Victoria, from her beginnings as a Mouseketeer, through her Grammy Award–winning singing career, up to her more recent Emmy Award–winning performance in a popular HBO movie. Pages five and six covered her friendships and sexcapades with other wild-child A-listers, along with her two DUIs; the mug shots were not flattering. The articles recounted her meteoric rise to stardom, her descent into alcohol and substance abuse. Her stints in rehab and mental-health clinics. And then her dramatic, rocky comeback, as well as her brief involvement with Kabbalah and the Church of

Scientology. The last article speculated about how Victoria's latest debacle would affect her career.

Destiny came out of my second bedroom/home office looking incredibly sexy in one of my white dress shirts. But she was pale, perspiring—she'd stayed over last night, because she'd drank far too much wine and could not drive home.

"How you feeling?"

Destiny flopped down and curled up on the couch. "My head hurts," she said. "I must've dropped it."

"Would you like me to make breakfast? Or do you need to throw up?" I recalled that, when we were a couple, I usually made us breakfast.

"How much did I drink last night?"

"You don't want to know."

"That much?"

I thought briefly about rubbing her feet—she had sexy, manicured feet—like I used to do, but I didn't want her to snap at me. "Want some dry toast?"

"I can't even think of food," Destiny moaned.

"Well, how about the latest news?" I spread open the *Post* for Destiny to see. "They're doing one hell of a hatchet job on Victoria."

"Stop yelling," Destiny said.

My cell phone vibrated. I checked the caller ID. "Hello, Tommy."

"We got a whatchamacallit, a situation," Lisi said. "We've gotta come up with a plan to sneak Victoria Carrington outta the hospital. But there's gotta be two- dozen reporters staking out the place."

Destiny bolted upright. "Oh, god." She covered her mouth with her hands and raced to the bathroom.

"How about a private ambulance?" I could hear Destiny retch behind the closed door. "Have Victoria's press agent, Meg, distract the reporters. Do an impromptu press conference outside the hospital's main entrance. Then sneak Victoria out the emergency entrance."

"Good idea. When can you get there?"

"Soon." I strolled over to the window and gazed down at the street: no idling Crown Vics. "I'll bring Destiny. And I've got a couple of retired NYPD guys standing by if we need them."

"We need them," Lisi said. "Meet me at the hospital ASAP."

CHAPTER 16

"TOMMY," I SAID, "meet Ernie Serria and Thomas McKee." We were standing in the hallway outside of Victoria Carrington's private suite at NYU Langone Medical Center, having just relieved the overnight security detail.

"Good meeting youse." Lisi shook hands. I could tell by the way he gave them a smiling once-over that he was happy with their squared-away business apparel.

An elderly Asian nurse pushed a stainless-steel cart down the hall and knocked on Victoria's door. Meg Dvoretz opened the door from the inside, allowing the nurse to enter.

Lisi handed Serria and McKee the usual confidentially agreements. Told them to read them and sign at the bottom, then he recited Lisi's Rules: "Lissena me, botha yuhs. You don't speak to the client unless spoken to…" Yada-yada-yada. "I dunno if Beckett told youse guys about Victoria's stalker—"

"I filled them in," I said.

"Good. Okay, lookit." Lisi checked his wristwatch. "I gave Victoria a long rain slicker with a hood. I got the hospital security guy standing by with an elevator. I got a private ambulance waiting at the emergency entrance." Lisi paused as several chattering hospital orderlies moved by. "Destiny, you drive."

He handed her the keys. If he or anyone else noticed she was wearing the same clothes she had on last night, they didn't comment. "There's a uniform jacket and hat onna front seat," he continued. "Serria, McKee, youse guys're gonna be the chase car. Watch for a tail. Do whatever it takes to block them. The press can't know where we're takin' Victoria."

"Where *are* we taking her?" I said.

"A rehab center out on Long Island, called Promises. An hour east of the city." Lisi recited the address. "It's onena those ultra-private facilities."

"Where Victoria's mother?" Destiny said.

Lisi shook his head. "I dunno."

The elderly Asian nurse pushed the cart out of Victoria's room. A moment later Meg opened the door, held it open. "She's ready when you are."

Lisi addressed Serria and McKee. "Youse guys get going."

Lisi, Destiny, and I stepped into Victoria's room. She was sitting in a wheelchair wearing a green full-length rain slicker over her street clothes.

Destiny whispered to Meg, "Where's her mother?"

"She's doing her cougar thing. Flew off to Bermuda with some boy toy she met last night at a party." Meg made a face. "Typical Lynn."

"Hi, everyone." Victoria flashed a rueful smile. "Sorry to be such a bother."

"Lissena me, Victoria," Lisi said. "I'm goin' with Meg while she distracts the press. Beckett and Destiny're taking you out the emergency-room entrance."

Victoria flipped the slicker's hood up. It came down low over her head and covered most of her face—perfect. "I'm ready."

Destiny led the way, taking the point. I pushed Victoria's chair at an unremarkable pace. We moved down the corridor, into the waiting "out of service" elevator manned by Mark Chin, the hospital's security director. We rode down to the main floor.

"Bitch!" I saw the gleam of a blade as the assailant charged. Victoria screamed. I lurched around the wheelchair into the guy's path. Caught his thrusting hand. Locked it under my arm. Pulled him in close. Head-butted. The guy's nose broke with an audible *crack*. Blood gushed down over his mouth and chin. I threw one short uppercut to the guy's throat, caving in his windpipe. The guy went down. The knife skittered across the floor.

"My god," Victoria said, her hands to her mouth.

I picked up the knife, handed it to Mark Chin. "You'd better call in a code blue." I gestured to the gasping attacker. "He doesn't have much time."

I heard Chin speaking into his portable radio as I pushed Victoria down the hall.

The private ambulance was backed up to the entrance, as expected, with its rear doors open. I helped the violently trembling Victoria out of the wheelchair up into the back of the ambulance, and climbed in with her. Destiny closed the ambulance door. I locked us in.

"Know that guy?" I asked as I got Victoria settled in a seat and fastened her seat belt for her.

"He used to be my personal assistant," Victoria said.

"For how long?"

"Maybe six months," she said.

"He quit or get fired?"

"Fired," Victoria said, visibly horrified by what had just happened. "He was great in the beginning, but then he became, I don't know, too familiar. Possessive. He started to scare me."

"So you had to fire him. It happens."

"My mother did the firing," Victoria explained, as though that made any difference.

"How'd he react to that?"

"Not well. Last I heard, he wasn't able to get work. He blamed me for blackballing him. Said he'd get even. But that was two years ago. I haven't heard from him since." Victoria grabbed my hand as a new realization came to her. "You saved my life."

"I told you I wouldn't let anyone hurt you. I meant it."

"Hey." Destiny was speaking though the driver's partition. "You two all set back there?" She was wearing the white jacket and hat that Lisi had mentioned.

"Ready." I let go of Victoria's hand, fastened my seat belt.

Destiny adjusted the ambulance's mirrors, slipped on sunglasses, and pulled the hat down low. She eased out of the driveway. Stopped at the sidewalk to allow pedestrians to pass. I glanced out of the ambulance's side window and spotted Meg standing outside the hospital entrance, surrounded by reporters. Lisi stood beside her. And beside Lisi stood Solana Ortiz; she was looking in our direction.

Destiny pulled out onto First Avenue, then immediately onto Thirty-fourth Street and stopped at a red light. I peered out of the ambulance's rear and saw that McKee and Serria had fallen in behind us. Destiny's cell phone rang. She put it on speaker. "Speak."

"You've got a tail," Serria said. "A black Volvo. It's Solana."

"I see her," Destiny said.

"Hold it," Serria said. "You've got another tail. A black Crown Vic."

"I see them too." Agents Sobel and Englund were three car lengths behind.

The light changed and traffic started to inch forward.

"Hey." I leaned through the partition and spoke into Destiny's phone. "The entrance to FDR Drive becomes a single lane a block or two north. Stay right behind us. When Destiny gives the signal, stop your car like the engine died. Take your time getting started."

"Ten-four." Serria hung up.

Destiny made the left onto the lower level of the FDR Drive north. As the road merged into a single lane, she rolled down her window, stuck her arm out, and gave McKee the thumbs-up sign.

McKee's car rolled to a halt. blocking the single-lane ramp. He opened his door, feigning a New Yorker's exasperation, popped open the car hood. Horns honked. Drivers yelled obscenities. Destiny switched on the ambulance's lights and siren, touched the gas, and began to merge onto the three-lane highway.

"Anyone behind us?" Destiny said as she accelerated.

Way behind us, Solana and Englund had jumped out of their cars. They appeared to be yelling at Serria, their hands working overtime. "No." I sat back and noticed that Victoria was staring at me again. She was a strange girl, hard to read. "How do you feel?" I said.

She shook her head. "I need to lay down for a while."

I helped her onto the gurney.

Even with GPS we had difficulty locating the rehab center. And when we did, we detoured, made several lefts and rights, all the while checking for a tail.

We passed through a manned gate, where Destiny's ID and the purpose of our visit was verified by an armed guard. He directed Destiny up a mile-long, tree-lined road. The dry-out center's driveway alone was impressive. As she crested a steep hill, an enormous Georgian mansion came into view.

Destiny parked at the main entrance. Walking around back, she opened the rear doors. I stepped out first and helped Victoria. She was still shaken, so I put my arm around her and assisted her to the rehab center's front door.

A ramrod-straight uniformed nurse was waiting for us. She buzzed us through a heavy, steel-framed door and ushered us into a two-story, rosewood-paneled library with floor-to-ceiling bookshelves.

"Ms. Carrington," a short, meticulously groomed gentleman in a jacket and tie said as he entered the library. "I'm Dr. Pullano." He shook Victoria's hand. "Will you come with me, please?"

Victoria looked imploringly at me.

"I'll be here waiting," I said. "Promise."

She nodded, fighting back tears. The doctor and nurse escorted her across the hall into one of several small conference rooms. They closed the door behind them.

"We were supposed to bodyguard Victoria," Destiny informed me. "Make sure she got to rehab safely. Nothing more. We're not supposed to get involved in her personal life—Lisi's number-one rule. So why are we waiting exactly?"

I wasn't in the mood for misplaced jealousy. "She asked me to."

Destiny shook her head. "Something going on between you two?"

"Hey," I said blandly. "She's our only A-list client. She rates special treatment."

"Sure," Destiny said. "That's what it is."

I needed to change the subject. Fast. I glanced up at the library mezzanine; the room reminded me of the old Scribner Fifth Avenue bookstore. "This place is a little different than the joint you were in," I joked, referring to the bare-bones, institutional lower Manhattan rehab center Destiny had checked herself into.

"That's an understatement," Destiny said. "Wonder how much a stay here costs?" She crossed the library to a large, wide window, fingered a heavy curtain aside. "Iron bars—thought commitment here was voluntary."

"Maybe not for everyone," I said. "Then again, maybe it's designed to keep enablers out." The library by now had captivated my attention. I browsed the bookshelves, saw what looked like first editions: Henry Miller's *Tropic of Cancer*, F. Scott Fitzgerald's *The Beautiful and Dammed*, J. D. Salinger's *The Catcher in the Rye*, Ernest Hemingway's *A Farewell to Arms*. I plucked a copy of Ralph Ellison's *Invisible Man* from a shelf. Flipped it open, but saw that it was not a first edition. Oh, well. Whoever stocked the library still had great taste.

Noticing another steel-framed door at the rear of the room, I peered through a small window into what must have been the rehab center's inner sanctum—the contrast was startling.

In the center of a stark white corridor was a large, round white Formica desk staffed by a ruddy-faced woman attired in a crisp nurse uniform. Several other nurses were milling about, attending to bathrobe-clad patients. Some of them were pacing in circles. Some were talking to themselves. A couple of them glared balefully in my general direction. What appeared to be sparsely furnished private rooms lined the far wall.

The door buzzed open, startling me. I stepped back. A nurse excused herself as she strode past me, through the library to the main entrance. She buzzed it open. An older man practically carried a young man into the foyer.

"I'm an alcoholic. I'm an alcoholic," the young man sobbed as the nurse led them into a second conference room and closed the door behind them.

"I don't believe it," Destiny said. "Know who that is?"

"No idea."

Destiny sighed, disbelieving my ignorance of pop culture. "You're hopeless."

A few minutes later, Victoria's conference-room door opened. She stepped out, wiping tears from her eyes. The doctor and nurse emerged next. "This way," the nurse said.

Victoria pleaded, "Walk with me?"

"Of course," I said.

"I'll wait here," Destiny said.

The doctor entered the second conference room, where the somebody I had somehow failed to recognize waited. The nurse led Victoria and me to the rear of the library, and buzzed the other door open. We passed the large Formica desk, heading down a long hallway to Victoria's assigned room: a bare chamber with a single bed, bureau, reading lamp, and a view of a lush garden courtyard. Several patients were sitting at the far end of the courtyard, chatting and smoking cigarettes.

"Cell phone?" the nurse said to Victoria. "Or iPad?"

Victoria dumped the contents of her purse onto the bed; she'd been though the routine before. The nurse picked up her cell phone and confiscated it. She then turned her headlights on me, waiting for me to leave.

"Well…" Tears filled Victoria's eyes. "I guess this is it." She waited awkwardly for a long moment, one eye on the nurse. "Please," she said. "Can you give us a moment alone?"

"Sorry," the nurse said. "It's against the rules."

Victoria shot her an angry look, then hugged me, and planted a quick kiss on my lips. "Thank you," she said. "For everything."

"Have someone call if you need me." I handed her my business card, gave her a squeeze, then walked out, leaving her looking sad, vulnerable, and very alone.

As Destiny and I approached the ambulance outside, a newish black Nissan pulled up the drive and parked in front of the rehab center. A guy built like a highland gorilla alighted, rushed around to open the car's rear doors, and assisted a middle-aged man in carrying a young woman into the rehab center.

"Holy shit," I said.

"Yeah," Destiny said. "Tata Andolini."

CHAPTER 17

"WHASSAT?" LISI SAID. "Victoria Carrington and Tata Andolini inna same rehab center? *Marrone.* No good can come of that. I mean, Victoria's never been accused a' being, whaddyacallit, 'picky' when it comes to choosing friends."

"Oh, pleeze," Destiny said, displaying her insider's knowledge. "Why would Victoria Carrington associate with that—that vapid twit?"

"Excuse me," Lisi said. "But Victoria would associate with the Taliban if they could supply her with drugs." He turned to me. "How'd you leave it with her?"

"She'll call after treatment."

"Should be at least thirty days," Destiny said.

"Try two," Lisi said.

"Programs are for at least thirty days."

"Yeah. But last time she entered rehab she stayed two days."

Destiny's phone chirped, and she toggled to Twitter. "Get this. Victoria's mother Lynn just Tweeted. Now she's on her way to Turks and Caicos with Fernando. She's calling him the love of her life." Destiny shook her head, incredulous. "What's wrong with her?"

"She's a whatchamacallit?" Lisi wrinkled his face in thought, then snapped his fingers. "A narcissist. She don't give a rat's ass about anyone but herself. Her father's worse, if you can believe that."

Destiny, Lisi, and I were standing at our usual spot at Rathbones bar. Bobby G, the former racketeer, was sitting at the other end with a very lovely blonde they called the Striking Viking. Charlie the bartender had refilled Destiny's glass of club soda three times in five minutes. Lisi and I were drinking our usual. Some eighties classic rock was playing on the bar's formidable sound system.

"You gotta understand." Lisi took a swallow of his vodka on the rocks, twist, and used a bar napkin to wipe his mouth. "Most celebrity families ain't what one would refer to as *traditional*. The parents don't change diapers. Or get up inna middle a' the night at feeding time. They have baby nurses for that. Then nannies. And everyone, and I mean *everyone*, wants something from them. Distant relatives come outta the woodwork with their hands out. That's why someone like Victoria ain't got no real friends—she can't trust anyone. Combine that with an entertainer's inherent insecurities, and it's a wonder some celebrities function at all."

Charlie the bartender interjected: "I remember reading somewhere that the actor Larry Hagman was raised by his grandmother. His mother was a superstar who had no time for him." We all looked at him, puzzled by his arcane knowledge. "What?" Charlie said. "That's what I read."

A waitress called out and Charlie limped painfully to the opposite end of the bar to fill a drink order—the injuries that had forced him out of the FDNY were acting up.

"There's no excuse for deserting your only child," Destiny said.

"Lissena me," Lisi said. "Lynn Carrington's a worse fuckup than her daughter. Now, tell me about the rehab center."

"It's something out of *The Great Gatsby*," I said, remembering the library.

"But is it secure?"

"Very," Destiny answered.

"What difference does it make?" I said. "Victoria's there voluntarily."

Lisi plucked a swivel stick out of his glass and stuck it in his mouth. "If she's serious for once, and stays, she's gonna be inna same place for the next four weeks, at least. If the Angel a' Death finds out…"

I shook my head. "Be really tough to get at her."

Destiny swallowed more of her club soda. "What about the garden?"

"What about it?" I said.

"Well, it's outdoors," Destiny said. "Patients were out there smoking. There're dense woods out back."

"She's right," I said. "I guess if someone knew the area well enough, they could approach the place from the woods, get to whomever they wanted."

"Easy shot for a sniper too," Destiny said.

"*Marrone,*" Lisi groaned. "Don't tell me that."

"What's the problem?" I asked. "The Angel of Death's not a sniper."

Lisi made a face.

"Or is he?"

"I dunno what he's capable of," Lisi said. "But why take chances?" He signaled Charlie for another drink. "Think I'll take a drive up to the rehab center. Take a look for myself."

"There's no hurry," Destiny said. "Victoria will be going through withdrawal."

Charlie served the next drink. "Just the same," Lisi said. "I'm gonna drive up tonight. See what there's to see."

Just then Rathbones' front door swung opened.

Federal agents Sobel and Englund walked in.

Bobby G was the first to hightail it out the door.

CHAPTER 18

"MISS JONES. MR. Beckett," Sobel said as he and Englund bellied up to the bar.

"I'm done." Destiny pushed her glass away and slid off the bar stool. "Gonna go home." She looked at the feds. "See if any spooks broke in and left me with bugs."

"I'll walk you to the garage," Lisi said, and tossed some money on the bar.

"What's this, a Mexican fire drill?" Sobel said as Destiny and Lisi walked out of Rathbones. "We're not here to ruin anyone's good time—say, wasn't that Sweet Tommy Lisi?"

"It was." I sipped my beer, not sure why I hadn't walked out on them too.

"That old man?" Englund said. "Who's he?"

Sobel rolled his eyes. "Don't you kids read the papers?"

"Name sounds familiar," Englund said. "Wasn't he a ballplayer?"

"He was driving Big Paul Scognamillo the night they tried to eliminate him," Sobel grouched. "That 'old guy' shot it out with two Mafia hit men, killed them both. Foiled an assassination plot. Saved the don's life."

"Right. Now I remember," Englund said. "Took a bullet to the chest. Thought he died—too bad he didn't."

"Fuck you, asshole," I said to Englund, outraged by his stupid comment.

Sobel stepped between me and his partner. "Relax, Beckett." He turned to Englund. "You don't behave, you'll have to wait in the car." Englund huffed and puffed, but didn't say anything more.

Charlie asked the feds what they were having. Sobel ordered a pint of Guinness. Englund ordered a bottle of craft beer.

"So," Sobel said. "I take it Lisi's a friend of yours?"

"You know he is."

"Cops hanging out with mobsters," Englund said. "A disgrace, if you ask me."

"No one asked you," I said. "Besides, Lisi's not connected anymore."

Sobel snickered. "There's only one way out of that life, and you know it."

"That why you're here?" I said sharply. "To talk about my association with Lisi?"

Charlie served the drinks. Both feds took healthy swallows.

"How about we sit down?" Sobel said, and gestured to a row of empty tables.

"I'm not answering any questions."

"No problem," Sobel said. "How about I talk. You listen?"

"All right." With beer in hand, I led the way across the room, chose a seat with my back to the wall. The feds set their drinks down on the table and sat facing me.

Sobel leaned forward, hands folded in front of him, elbows on the table. "We know you led a gang of armed robbers," he said. "Vigilante cops known throughout the NYPD as Rockers."

"You do?"

I noted Sobel's suit sort of hung on him. His necktie was loose. His face and hands were deeply tanned, the hands nicked and callused from some sort of physically demanding pasttime. I recognized the sunglass outline—raccoon eyes—that meant Sobel spent countless hours outdoors.

"And we know you gunned down Lochlainn O'Brian," Englund said. The hard look he was trying for was belied by the fact that his eyelashes were long, like a woman's. His suit was freshly pressed and perfectly tailored. Perfect getup for an uptight asshole.

"You don't know shit."

"We're not here for a debate," Sobel said. "We're here to offer you a deal."

"You guys are unbelievable."

"Blanket immunity," Sobel said.

"In exchange for...?"

"Your testimony before a federal grand jury."

"What would I be testifying to?"

"All you know about vigilante cops. Every robbery you and your gang participated in. Every name of every officer who participated. Dates. Locations. Times."

"So the rumors are true," I said. "The feds are trying to take over the NYPD."

"That is not your concern," Englund said.

I regarded Sobel. There was something "street" about him: reasonable, down-to-earth. "Where'd you work? I mean, before joining the feds?"

"Chicago PD."

"It shows." I drank some of my beer. "So, you're offering blanket immunity for all of the Rocker raids...."

"Some people think you were doing a public service," Sobel said.

"And the Lochlainn O'Brian homicide?"

"Lochlainn O'Brian was scum," Sobel said. "Besides, we know what he did to your younger sister. The government is not aggressively pursuing charges. They concede there were extenuating circumstances."

"And let's face it," Englund said. "The world's a far less dangerous place without the likes of Lochlainn O'Brian."

"No argument there."

"What's it gonna be?" Sobel said.

"Honestly." I guzzled the rest of my beer, letting the time

string out as long as I could. "I don't know what in hell you're talking about." I got to my feet.

"Just remember," Sobel said, "we offered you the deal first."

"I appreciate that." I turned to walk back to the bar.

"You know a woman named Enia?" Englund called from behind me.

That name stopped me in my tracks. I turned back to face the feds, fought to maintain my composure—it didn't work. "Who?"

"Yeah." Englund smiled for the first time. "I thought so."

Sobel got to his feet, took out a business card, handed it to me. "Call me," he said, "when you're ready to deal."

CHAPTER 19

"ENIA?" DESTINY SAID as I closed the door and followed her into her Hastings-on-Hudson apartment kitchen. "The feds asked if you knew anyone named Enia?" She slammed her wineglass down on the counter. "That Romanian slut?"

I took a deep breath, let it out. *Here we go again.* I slipped off my sports jacket and opened Destiny's refrigerator. When we were a couple, she stocked my brand of beer. No longer. I lifted out a bottle of some sort of designer stout. At least it wasn't all wheat beer.

"We're fucked." Destiny paced the kitchen. "Boy, are we ever fucked."

"Look," I said, "Enia collected five million in insurance money when her husband was killed. Went back to Romania—I thought." I took a swallow of the heavy, bitter brew. Maybe not better than wheat. "Honestly, I never thought we'd hear her name again."

"Yeah. Well, you were wrong," Destiny said accusingly. "I can't believe this. Another one of your psycho ex-girlfriends—and you've had plenty—coming back to bite us in the ass."

"Don't start." I knew she'd react this way. Which was why I'd yet to tell her about Solana Ortiz threatening me. She'd *really* flip out when she heard about that.

"I'm gonna make a call." I went out into Destiny's well-appointed living room. She'd made a few changes since I'd been there over six months ago. The 48-inch HD-TV was new, as was the stand. The throw rug under the coffee table was new, as was a New York cityscape painting on the wall.

Slightly annoyed by the changes, I sat on the leather couch, pulled out one of the prepaid cell phones, and dialed a friend of mine who worked as a clerk in the federal court system. "I need a favor."

"It's the only time you call, pally," my friend said.

"I need you to search all active cases that list the defendant as Enia Vladimirescu, or Enia Petrescu, Enia Schultz, or any variation."

"Spell those names for me."

I did.

"Hold on," my friend said.

Enia, I thought, the woman with the face of an angel and the heart of the Marquis de Sade. The pathological, manipulative deviant who'd rocked my world was back in my life.

I had been alone at the now-defunct Elaine's restaurant on Second Avenue early that summer evening when Enia breezed in: scented in lilac, dressed in tasteful business attire that did little to hide her hourglass figure. She took a seat at the near-empty bar, ordered a glass of champagne from the bartender. I smiled at her. She smiled back. And then she announced that it was her birthday—the first of countless lies.

I offered to buy her a birthday drink. She wanted champagne, of course. Then I asked her to join me for dinner. We ordered the porterhouse for two. Drank more champagne. Afterward, I coaxed her back to my apartment. And for the first time in my life experienced life-altering, soul-penetrating sex. Enia soon became an obsession.

During the next few months she proceeded to dazzle me with her sense of style, humor, and shrewd intellect. I saw her seven days a week, neglected my job, family, friends, even myself. Became jealous of everyone and everything that kept us apart; I couldn't get enough of her. The fact that she performed fellatio on me at every possible opportunity—in men's rooms, restaurant coatrooms, the backseat of taxicabs—caused me to ignore the fact that she never did go to work. I also paid almost no attention to my credit-card statements.

"Must be a mistake," Enia said when I finally came out of the sex-induced fog and saw all the bogus charges on my credit cards. "Maybe identity theft." I called the banks and disputed every unauthorized charge. After a brief investigation, I realized that someone very close to me was using my credit cards.

It was time to confront my obsession.

I met Enia for dinner at the now defunct Bruno's restaurant on East Fifty-eighth Street. We ordered a four-star dinner along with a couple of bottles of red wine. Over dessert and after-dinner drinks I confronted her. Enia, of course, denied any wrongdoing. I called her a liar. We fought. Broke up.

A long time would pass before I saw her again. She married a poor schnook named Alex Schultz, a hardworking, meek sort and owner of the doomed German Hotel. Both Enia and Alex begged me to help rid their hotel of a squatter: the drug-dealing terrorist Lochlainn O'Brian, along with his youth gang, the Belfast Boys—which I gladly did. For a price. Later, when Lochlainn blew up the hotel, killing Enia's husband among others, she became a wealthy woman. I couldn't prove it, but I suspected that she had something to do with her husband's death. Her motive? Five million dollars in insurance money. That made my credit-card charges look like chump change.

"You still there, pally?" my friend said.

"I'm here."

"Okay. Enia Schultz. Indicted for insurance fraud. Conspiracy to commit insurance fraud. Grand larceny. You want the details?"

I said I did.

"Okay, apparently she collected five million illegally when a guy named Alex Schultz died."

"Illegally? But Schultz was her husband."

"Not according to the indictment."

"They weren't married?" I said. Another lie.

"She was already married to someone else."

"She was a bigamist?"

"Looks that way."

Another surprise. At least now I knew what the feds had on Enia. I also knew that if she was guilty, she'd cooperate with the feds, say and do anything to save herself.

"Pally? You still there?"

"Yeah. Anything else you can tell me?"

"No. That's about it."

I thanked my friend, told him that I owed him dinner, and hung up.

So, Enia had defrauded Schultz, then the insurance company. The insurance company found out. Had her prosecuted. And now she must be using me as a bargaining chip with the feds. Typical Enia.

Destiny walked over and handed me the purposely neglected bottle of stout. "What're we gonna do?"

"Depends." I set the bottle down on the coffee table. "Think about it. I never told Enia who was on our Rocker team."

"She can guess," Destiny said. "And lie about it."

Destiny was right. However, the only Rocker raid Enia knew about was the one we'd executed for her and her husband: the German Hotel, Lochlainn O'Brian eviction.

"And don't forget," Destiny said. "Enia's husband referred you to all the other landlords. What if he told her about the referrals: names, dates?"

Again, Destiny was right. We had evicted other drug dealers from other tenements at the request of the building owners, all referred to us by Enia's husband. Yet that obviously wasn't the link. "Then the feds would have already questioned the other landlords, and I'd be in handcuffs."

Destiny considered that. "So, it boils down to your word against Enia's."

"And she hasn't much credibility."

"Says who?" Destiny asked.

I tapped the phone meaningfully. "I just found out she's under federal indictment."

"Oh, goody," Destiny said.

My cell phone chirped. I checked the caller ID: Brookhaven Memorial Hospital. What the hell? "Hello?"

"This is Brookhaven Memorial Hospital admissions calling," a woman's voice said. "Is this Michael Beckett?"

"Yes." I sat forward. "This is Beckett."

"Gaetano Lisi asked us to phone you."

"Tommy Lisi?" I tensed. "Why? What happened?"

"Mr. Lisi was involved in an automobile accident."

Was this a coincidence? "How serious?"

"What is your connection to Mr. Lisi?"

"I'm his...er...nephew," I lied.

"Any other next of kin?"

"His wife passed away. He has a stepson somewhere, estranged. Last I heard he was living somewhere in Montana. I've no idea how to contact him."

Destiny said, "What is it?"

I used a hand to shush her. "Where's he now?"

"Intensive care," she said.

"Thank you," I said and hung up.

CHAPTER 20

MCKEE SAW THE feds' Crown Victoria the moment he turned onto Sunset Trail. He rolled down the tree-lined street and parked his Charger in his usual spot, along the manicured hedges across from his residence. As he stepped out of the vehicle, he saw that Agents Sobel and Englund were speaking to his next-door neighbor. The old woman was standing on her front lawn, watering her impressive rose garden. She spotted McKee, then said something he would bet money was unkind to the feds, who upon seeing him, spun on their heel and headed his way. McKee never did like the hatchet-faced Irish biddy. Over the years she'd complained countless times to the Silver Beach home-owners' association about where or how he parked his car, about his music or TV being too loud.

"What'd my girlfriend have to say?" McKee said as the feds approached.

"That's a Charger SRT8 Super Bee," Sobel said. "Isn't it?"

"Yeah."

"I read that it can go zero to sixty in just four-point-six seconds."

"You know your cars," McKee said, playing along.

"They've gottta go for what, about forty-five thousand?"

"Like I said, you know your cars."

Englund took up the charge. "Awesome place you have here."

"Thanks," McKee said. "I work at it."

"Did the work yourself," Sobel said. "Did you?"

"Some," McKee said.

"Not many people can afford to plant mature trees and bushes like you did." Englund gestured at a line of colorful, manicured shrubs. "The landscaping must have set you back a good thirty thousand. And your neighbor—" He indicated the old Irish bat. "Told us you installed an outdoor waterfall and Jacuzzi out back. That had to cost another—what? Forty, fifty-thousand dollars. Am I right?"

"I have a friend in the business," McKee said, knowing where this was going.

"You have a friend in the jewelry business too?" Sobel said.

McKee knew he was referring to the Piaget wristwatch and gold cuff links that were in his Sentry floor safe. "Look, why don't you get to the point?"

"Actually," Sobel said, "I'd like to ask you a question."

"I'm not answering any questions."

"You'll have to answer me here, now, or later in front of a grand jury."

McKee heaved a sigh. "Go ahead. Ask."

Sobel spread out his hands to indicate all the improvements around the house. "Where'd you get the money?"

CHAPTER 21

"I'M SORRY," A salon-perfect, blue-haired Brookhaven Memorial Hospital receptionist said as she slipped off the Prada bifocals that hung from a decorative gold chain around her turkey neck; the scent of her heavy perfume almost made me sneeze. A tag that read *Volunteer* was affixed to the pocket of her starched white hospital smock. "Only immediate family members are allowed in ICU. No exceptions." She smiled apologetically, revealing a set of dazzling dentures.

"I'm his nephew," I offered. "His only living relative."

"Well, in that case…" She made an entry in a computer, then handed Destiny and me two peel-and- stick visitors passes. "Affix them to your outer garments, please."

We affixed as instructed and headed to the elevators.

ICU was dark and quiet except for the faint beep of medical equipment, whose status lights cast a soft, eerie glow. Inside a glass booth a young doctor and a duty nurse were watching a bank of monitors.

Lisi was lying on the first bed in the twelve-bed unit. His face was almost completely obscured by bandages and an oxygen mask. Several IV drips hung from metal poles, and their tubes snaked into his arms. That didn't look good at all.

"Tommy?" Destiny took Lisi's hand in hers and squeezed.

I breathed in the strong hospital scents as I opened the

bedside-table drawer. Saw a few of Lisi's personal effects: wallet, wristwatch, lighter, pack of unfiltered Lucky Strikes, a set of keys, cell phone. But no gun—shit!

I picked up the wallet and counted $231. At least they were honest out here. In a New York City hospital, the cash and watch would have already been stolen. I fingered the set of keys, looked around to make sure no one was watching, and slipped them into my pocket.

"Help you?"

We both turned to face the square-headed, lantern-jawed face of a uniformed Suffolk County police lieutenant. His name tag read *SHAW*.

I closed the bedside drawer. "I'm his"—I gestured to Lisi—"nephew. My name's Beckett. This is Destiny Jones."

"Call me Shaw."

We shook hands. I told Shaw that Destiny and I were both recently retired NYPD.

Showed him our ID cards.

"Anything I can do for you?" Shaw said.

"I was wondering, what happened to his weapon?"

"We vouchered it," Shaw said.

"Everything all right?" a young doctor said as he approached. He was adolescently thin with soft, fine facial features. Dark brown eyes were framed by flawless brown skin.

"How's he doing, doc?" I said.

The doctor's report was grim. "No bones are broken." His voice was just above a whisper. "The cuts are superficial. But I'm afraid Mr. Lisi has suffered a severe concussion. We have placed him in a medically induced coma."

That was worse than I thought. "What're his chances?"

The doctor shook his head. "We'll know more as soon as the swelling around the brain goes down." He checked Lisi's vitals and told us not to stay long before he walked off.

"Would you like to see the accident report?" Shaw asked.

I said we would.

Shaw led us out of ICU and back downstairs into an office with *Hospital Security* stenciled in gold letters on the heavy wooden door. A heavyset hospital guard was walking out as we entered. A lanky female Suffolk County cop whose name tag read *OLIVE* was sitting at one of three unoccupied desks, in front of a laptop computer, speaking on a phone. She ended the call when she saw Shaw.

"Lieutenant." Olive shot to her feet—she was over six feet tall. "The Accident Investigation Squad just uploaded the accident-scene video and photos."

"Let's see them," Shaw said. Olive pushed the laptop over to the lieutenant, who spun it around and positioned it so we could see.

"Near as we can tell…" Shaw said, clicking on an icon that started the video: a wide, sweeping shot of an accident scene. "He must have been going at least seventy-five in a sixty-five zone— not an unusual or necessarily reckless rate of speed. Witnesses said he turned into a van, like he was trying to cut him off. Then he lost control, crashed through a guardrail, then tumbled down the embankment." The video ended. "Here're the stills," Shaw said. He clicked on another icon, and a slide show of wide shots and close-ups of the SUV appeared.

"Hold it," I said, spotting something. "Can you go back a few frames?"

Shaw toggled back.

"Stop there." I leaned forward, studied a close-up of the SUV's exterior. "Where's this vehicle now?"

Shaw looked at Olive. "Where's the vehicle?"

She checked the time. "At the station by now."

"Mind if we take a look?" I said.

"No problem."

Destiny and I climbed into Lisi's Jaguar, and followed Shaw and Olive to the rear of the 5th Precinct house in Patchogue—a squat, modern box—and into a large parking lot, alongside a five-vehicle-wide, open-bayed garage.

AIS (Accident Investigation Squad) officers in greasy coveralls were working on two burned-out car hulks. Shaw pointed the way to the far end of the garage, where Lisi's SUV was parked over an open bay. An AIS investigator was standing beneath the car, taking additional photos, a toothpick stuck in his mouth.

It was obvious that the SUV had tumbled down an embankment. Scratches and dents were everywhere. Small tree limbs were embedded in the door frames, trunk, and tire wells. Three of the four tires were blown. I walked slowly around the car until I saw what I was looking for. "Foreign paint." I pointed at the driver's door.

"From the van he hit," Olive said.

"Could he have been run off the road?" Destiny said.

The lieutenant shook his head. "Not according to the witnesses."

"Why would someone run Mr. Lisi off the road?" Olive said.

"What color would you say that foreign paint is?" I said.

Shaw took a closer look. "Blue."

"Would you call it metallic blue?"

"Yes." Shaw nodded. "Why?"

"Lieutenant?" The AIS investigator wiped his hands on a greasy rag, took the toothpick out of his mouth. "Looks like the windshield was shot out."

"What?" I said. "You sure?"

The investigator produced a small piece of glass and handed it to Shaw, who held it up for us to see. Sure enough, there was a bullet hole cut into it.

"Judging by the size of the hole, it could be a 7.62x66mm sniper round," the AIS guy said. "In civilian terms, a three-hundred Winchester Magnum."

"I hope we don't have another Beltway copycat on our hands," Shaw mused.

"I don't think the shooting was random," I said.

"Really?" Shaw handed the piece of glass back to the investigator. "Suppose I buy you two a cup of coffee. In my office."

Shaw escorted us into the main building. We forded through a hallway maze, then entered a military-bare corner office with a terrific view of the parking lot. Shaw sat us across from his good-sized tin desk as Officer Olive poured us coffees in porcelain cups adorned with the Suffolk County Police logo.

"Tell me," Shaw said once we were settled in. "Who would want to harm Mr. Lisi?"

I told Shaw about Lisi's connection to the mob. The forty-year-old shoot-out that saved the life of La Cosa Nostra's Boss of Bosses. The recent death threat by the mobster Ice Pick Martucci.

"Martucci?" Shaw rose an eyebrow. "That lowlife piece of shit. I know him from my days in our organized-crime bureau. He's involved in extortion. Drugs. They say he has forty homicides to his credit. Maybe more." Shaw leaned forward, elbows on his desk. "I remember hearing about the attempted mob assassination when I was a kid. It was front page for weeks—Gaetano Lisi is *that* Lisi?"

I nodded. "Sweet Tommy Lisi."

"I'll be dammed." Shaw thought that over. "You actually hear Martucci make the threat?"

I shook my head. "Lisi told us about it."

"He say why?"

"Ice Pick's a cousin of one of the hit men Lisi gunned down."

"So it was an attempted mob hit?" Shaw said, incredulous. "After all these years?"

"Lisi insulted Ice Pick," I said, "in public, two nights ago."

"In front of his mob associates," Destiny said, "and girlfriends."

"Your friend Lisi have a death wish or something?" Shaw drank some coffee, then made a disgusted face and glared at Officer Olive.

"I'll make a fresh pot," Olive said and hurried out of the room.

"Okay," Shaw said. "A mob hit is one possibility. Now tell me: What's with the metallic-blue paint?"

"One of our celebrity clients, Tata Andolini—"

"Who?"

"She's on the D-list," Destiny put in.

"—is being stalked by a convicted felon, Matthew Gluck, aka, Matt the Hat. The Hat served time for stalking another celebrity, Audra Gardner, now deceased."

"Her I heard of," Shaw said.

"The Hat drives a van with the same ugly, blue metallic paint we found on Lisi's SUV. My guess—and I'm just spitballing here—the Hat found out where Tata was."

"Which was where?"

"Promises Rehabilitation Center," Destiny said.

"He probably followed her father out from the city when he checked her in. Lisi probably stumbled on him when he was checking out the rehab center. Gave chase—"

"Got shot at in the process?" Shaw said.

"Which caused the accident," I said. "Maybe."

"Couldn't the Hat be the sniper?" Destiny said.

"He'd have to be able to drive and handle a rifle at the same time," I pointed out.

"Or have an accomplice," Shaw said.

We all thought about that.

Shaw said. "Anyone else have it in for Lisi?"

"The Angel of Death," Destiny blurted out.

"Come again?"

I sighed. "A serial celebrity stalker, been around for years."

"Real name?" Shaw said.

"No one knows," I said. "But all he does is make threats. There's absolutely no evidence that he's ever harmed anyone."

"Some of the celebrities he stalked have died," Destiny said, "from tainted heroin."

"And some haven't," I stressed to Shaw. "It's just a theory, a long story."

Shaw was clearly out of his depths with all the histories coming at him. "Well...ah...we've got a fresh pot of coffee on the way."

I retold my father's Angel of Death theory. The six suspicious A-list celebrity deaths. The fact they were all drug addicts, receiving death threats from someone who identified himself as the Angel of Death. "Who my father thought killed by supplying his victims with fentanyl-laced heroin."

"The NYPD investigate any of this?"

"They did," I said. "Didn't think there was anything to it."

"So why's this Angel of Death have it in for Lisi?"

"He stalking another drug-addict client of ours who happens to be at the same rehab center as Tata Andolini. Victoria Carrington."

Shaw perked up at that name. "My daughter idolizes her."

"Lisi received a telephone death threat," I said.

"He thinks it was from the Angel of Death," Destiny said.

"Why threaten Lisi?"

"According to Lisi, the stalker thinks he's getting close to exposing him."

"Is he?"

"I don't know."

"So this Angel of Death character is another possibility."

"If you believe my father's theory," I said.

Officer Olive entered carrying clean cups and a fresh pot of coffee. She poured for everyone and left the room.

"Let's recap." Shaw sipped some coffee. "We've got two crazies stalking two celebrities at the same rehab center at the same time."

"Correct."

"Couldn't this Matt the Hat character be the Angel of Death? I mean, you *know* he stalked Audra Gardner. You *know* he's actively stalking the Andolini woman. Only makes sense that he's the one stalking Victoria Carrington."

"Yeah," I said. "Except Lisi's says it's not the Hat."

Shaw was still floundering, as I could tell. The possibilities were complicated if you didn't know them. "You were both law," he said. "What's your gut feeling? Who shot at Lisi?"

Destiny deferred to me.

"A notorious mob enforcer with a strong motive made a death threat. Next thing you know, there's an attempt on Lisi's life. A gunshot to the windshield. To me it's a no-brainer. Ice Pick Martucci's your man."

CHAPTER 22

THE MECHANIC AT Breen Brothers' Body & Fender, a short, squat, grease-coated ex-convict, used a rusty steel crowbar to force Matt the Hat's van's front driver's-side wheel panel away from its tire. Then he plopped the crowbar down on the motor oil–soaked earth, squatted down, used a penlight to inspect the damage.

"You ain't gonna believe what happened to me," the Hat croaked.

"Please," his former cell mate said. "I don't wanna hear any more of your bullshit stories."

Feeling slighted, the Hat contented himself by sticking an index finger into his nose, hooking a booger, and wiping it on his black jeans. Then he took a pull on a longneck bottle of Budweiser, let out a stomach-purging belch. "I'm telling you, some crazy asshole tried to run me off the road out on four-ninety-five."

The evening before, the Hat had grown concerned when Tata, a notorious serial Tweeter, had stopped Tweeting—everything from her wild mood swings, frequent erotic dreams, to the regularity and consistency of her bowel movements. He'd driven to the Four Seasons Hotel where she'd been staying, and came upon Tata's father and a thuggish character—Tata's brother?—carrying her out and placing her in the rear of a four-door Nissan—what the hell? The Hat followed the Nissan across town and through the Midtown Tunnel, about seventy miles on 495 to a fenced-off wooded area in the middle of nowhere. The Nissan stopped at what appeared to be a main guard gate. Tata's brother powered down the driver's window, spoke to a guard. After a moment, an iron gate swung open and the Nissan drove through—where the hell was Tata's father taking her? The Hat scanned the area. But no signage indicated what lay beyond the guard booth. There were no homes or businesses of any sort where he could make inquiries.

The Hat decided to hang out, see what happened next. But he couldn't just park in front of the guard gate. He spotted an overgrown dirt path just up the road, leading into the woods. He backed into the thicket until he was almost completely hidden. He was reaching behind the passenger seat into a Styrofoam cooler to pull out a bottle of beer when he thought he heard the faint sound of a motor. He cocked an ear; it was coming closer. The Hat leaned forward, peering through the flora, and saw a black Harley-Davidson, its rider clad head to toe in black leather, blond hair spilling out from under his black helmet, slow to a stop in front of the guard gate. The very stalker who'd murdered Audra Gardner had dressed in black leather and rode a black Harley. The rider spun around, gunned the engine, and drove back the way he came.

The Hat leapt from his van and made sure the Harley was leaving. If he was indeed the same stalker who'd murdered Audra Gardner, what was he doing here? Could he be stalking Tata?

Four beers and five cigarettes later, Tata's father's Nissan drove back out through the guard gate and turned left toward the interstate. Her brother was in the front seat. Tata's father was in the passenger seat—no Tata. What the hell was going on?

Well toasted by now, the Hat decided to investigate. He placed his beer in a center-console cup holder, wove and staggered from the bushes onto the main road. He was about to climb the fence and search for Tata when he heard the motorcycle engine again. He saw a single headlight coming his way. The Hat ducked behind a nearby bush. Sure as shit, a black Harley came into view.

The rider slowed as he came abreast of the guard gate, then eased out his clutch and rode slowly away. The Hat dashed back to his vehicle, tripped, and timbered face-first to the ground. Growling a string of curses, he struggled to his feet, climbed into his van, and hit the gas. His spinning tires threw up grass, twigs, and dirt as he fishtailed from his hiding place in hot pursuit of the Harley.

A horn honked from behind. Headlights flashed.

The Hat looked into his review mirror; a large vehicle was tailgating him. He stuck his arm out of the window, waved for the driver to pass. "Go around, asshole." But the driver kept flashing his headlights, waving that the Hat should pull over. *What the hell?*

The Hat eased off of the gas and looked over his shoulder. The vehicle was a black SUV. There were no police markings of any kind. No emergency lights. Whoever it was, most probably not a cop. Yet the driver *had* to be security of some type.

The Hat was not about to pull over and be accused of stalking Tata. "Fuck you, asshole." The Hat threw the wheel to the left, made a sudden U-turn, and mashed the pedal toward the interstate. The SUV followed. Chased him onto 495. Easily overtook him. Pulled up alongside. And then the SUV suddenly veered into him. Rammed him. The Hat fought to keep control as the SUV crashed through a guardrail and rolled down a ravine.

"Hey, Hat." The mechanic pointed at the van. "Looks like your front axle's cracked."

"Can you fix it?" the Hat said.

"Sure." The mechanic hacked up a wad of green phlegm, wiped the sticky residue from his mouth with a dirty shirtsleeve. "But I have to order parts."

"How long will that take?"

"Maybe a week."

"No way," the Hat said, agitated. "I can't wait that long."

The mechanic gestured toward an old green Toyota. "You can borrow that until I get your van fixed. Tires are a little bald, but it runs okay." He reached into his pocket and handed over the keys. "Just bring it back with a full tank."

The Hat growled a thanks, executed a prison handshake. He opened his van's rear-bay doors, lifted out the Styrofoam cooler and a carton of cigarettes, transferred them to the Toyota's backseat. On his van's driver's side, he removed two photos affixed by rubber bands to the overhead sun visor. One was of himself when he was an art director, with his arm around Audra Gardner, taken at a photo shoot for a fragrance she was endorsing. The other was a photo he'd snapped of Tata Andolini a few days ago, coming out of her father's restaurant, Andolini's of Little Italy.

The Hat climbed into the Toyota's driver's seat, adjusted the mirrors, buckled his seat belt. It took a couple of churning and popping attempts before the engine started, and then it idled, wet and lumpy. The best ride he'd ever had. As he affixed the two photos to the overhead sun visor, he vowed to Tata's photo that if the blond-haired demon on the black Harley was stalking her, he would protect her. He would save her from the man who'd murdered Audra Gardner——no matter what it took.

CHAPTER 23

"**Y**OU THINKING WHAT I'm thinking?" Destiny said.

"I dunno." We had just left the Suffolk County Police Department, not before checking the Jaguar for bugs, and were heading to the Long Island Expressway. "What're you thinking?"

"That it's time we looked at your father's files."

"Oh. Yeah. I was thinking that too." I merged onto the highway. Pulled into the center lane. Set the Jag's cruise control to 70.

Destiny's personal cell phone rang. She checked the caller ID, answered. "Yes? This is Destiny Jones speaking. Okay. Eight tomorrow morning? I'll be there." She ended the call.

I glanced at her expectantly. "You'll be where?"

"Sloan Kettering." Destiny put her cell phone away. "I have an appointment at eight a.m."

"What? Why?"

Destiny admitted, "My headaches are back."

"That's why you've been taking Vicodin?"

"You knew?" Destiny said. "I was afraid to tell you about that."

I had to admit that I felt an odd, fleeting wave of relief knowing she had a good reason for ingesting painkillers, that she hadn't actually relapsed. But then the horrid implications of her situation struck me: Headaches could mean her brain tumor was back. Was that even possible? If so, would it be operable this time?

The original brain-tumor diagnosis had been a complete shock. The doctors had said the operation was risky and the odds of success—of Destiny not becoming a drooling vegetable—was low. And so she decided against the operation. She chose to face death, but face it her way, which did not entail suffering the slow, painful physical and mental deterioration she'd been told to expect. She devised a plan that would allow her to die quickly, with dignity, and help her indigent parents in the process.

Crazy as it sounds, her plan was for me to masquerade as a criminal and gun her down in broad daylight, in public, in the line of duty. That way her poverty-stricken parents, her beneficiaries, would collect her lucrative NYPD death-pension benefits. Of course, I had refused to even consider such an insane scheme. But as I watched her grow weaker day by day, I realized I couldn't stand by and watch her suffer. I reluctantly agreed to her scheme.

I showed up at the agreed place and time in a stolen vehicle, the death weapon loaded with hollow points, my kelly-green ski mask at the ready. But when I saw Destiny in full uniform, walking a Second Avenue foot post, heading in my direction, my heart sank. I put the mask and weapon away; I simply could not kill the woman I loved. I had stepped out of the vehicle, fully prepared to face Destiny's wrath, when fate played a hand.

A jealous husband intent on killing his cheating wife stepped out of Rathbones bar, pulled a gun, and fired several shots across Second Avenue. Destiny took police action, stepped directly into the line of fire, never drawing her weapon, and a bullet struck her in the head. I pumped a single bullet into the would-be killer's brain.

"Are the headaches same as before?" I said.

Destiny shook her head. "They're different."

I wove in and out of traffic. "How?"

Destiny seemed glad to be telling someone. "Last time they radiated down my spine, were at the back of my head, you know?

It was like my skull was being ripped off. This time it's like someone is stabbing me between the eyes."

"Could it be a blood-sugar thing?" I said. "Hormones? Stress?"

"From your lips," Destiny said, "to God's ears."

I hit the gas in order to pass a line of sixteen-wheeler trucks. "Would you like me to go with you to your doctor's appointment?"

"No," Destiny said. "I'll be fine."

I pulled back into the center lane. "Look, Sloan Kettering's down on Sixty-seventh Street," I said. "There's no parking. Stay at my place tonight. I'll drive you down. Wait for you. Then we'll head back out to see Lisi."

"You sure?" Destiny said. "I don't want you to go out of your way."

Go out of my way? "It's not a problem," I said. "Really."

"We'll have to stop by my place first," she said. "Get a change of clothes."

We drove to Destiny's apartment. I waited in the car until she reappeared carrying an overnight bag. Next we drove back to the city, arrived at Tommy Lisi's Ninetieth Street tenement. I parked in a no-parking zone and placed the NYPD plaque on the dashboard. A hag-of-a-woman dog walker, attired in a bathrobe and matted fuzzy slippers, was leaning against a parked car, smoking a cigarette, eyeballing us disdainfully as we stepped from the Jag and climbed the tenement steps.

Lisi was one of those lucky guys who was still living in the same railroad flat where his immigrant parents—his father was Italian, mother German—had lived. As a rent-controlled tenant, he paid somewhere in the neighborhood of $96 a month—the market rate was closer to $4,000. Lisi's deceased Irish wife, an amateur interior decorator, had restored the apartment, filled it with early twentieth-century period pieces and expensive antiques.

As always, I noted how clean and well maintained the five-story walk-up was as we ascended to the second floor. The ancient black-and-white floor tiles sparkled, new paint gleamed on the walls, the light fixtures were high-end period pieces. The building owner obviously cared.

I took out Lisi's keys as we arrived at apartment 2A. He had an old Mul-T-Lock installed in the door—a good lock. Pick-resistant, but not pick-proof. Inside, Destiny felt around for a wall light switch and flicked it on. Decorative lamps and overhead recessed lights came to life. The apartment was messy but elegantly appointed. Waterford crystal lined the dusty shelves and the mantel of the working fireplace, over which hung two antique, custom-framed maps: one of Ireland, one of Germany. Plush Oriental rugs and runners covered parts of the parquet floor. I recalled a Christmas cocktail party I'd attended when Lisi's wife was still alive; the apartment had been neat, organized, sparklingly clean, a holiday showcase.

Destiny walked into Lisi's kitchen and opened the refrigerator. "Fridge is almost empty. There's bottled water." She took one, held it up. "You want?"

"No, thanks."

She opened a kitchen cabinet, picked out an empty plastic grocery-store bag. "Let's take Lisi some essentials for when he wakes up: toothbrush, shaving kit. Can you think of anything else?"

"Phone charger?"

Destiny spotted one plugged into an outlet in the kitchen and placed it in the bag.

Lisi's stepson's former bedroom was now Lisi's office. On the wall above a closed cherrywood rolltop desk was a photo montage of Lisi, his wife, and her son. On the other walls hung pictures of him with many of the old A-list celebrities that he and my father once protected.

I picked up a worn Little Italy sweatshirt that was lying in a pile on the floor and used it to dust his office chair and desk; the air filled with the thick dust and made me sneeze. After the air cleared, I pushed up the desk's rolltop; it was locked. I opened a drawer, located a letter opener and jimmied the lock. Revealed by the rolling top, a disorganized pile of paperwork greeted me. As did a framed photo of Lisi with a seventy-year-old Frank Sinatra. Next to it was a photo of Destiny and me, our arms around each other. My stomach flip-flopped as I remembered the exact day it was taken: a summer Saturday-afternoon brunch in P.J. Clarke's—pre-cancer, pre–gunshot wound. I sighed and laid the photo on the desk, facedown.

I began to sort through the mess and uncovered a laptop computer. "Well, hello." I switched it on. While waiting for it to boot, I lifted out the contents of the drawers, found a checkbook, credit-card statements, electric bills; this was going to take a while.

"Answering machine," Destiny said as she came into the room. She sat on the small futon-type couch and lifted a pile of old magazines off the machine. "There're messages." She pressed *play*.

The first few were robocalls from a car-insurance company, a credit-repair firm, along with several calls from the usual scam police charities—legitimate police charities don't solicit donations over the phone. The next few messages sounded like they were business- related. The last call was enhanced by an eerie voice synthesizer.

"*I thought you would have learned your lesson,*" a cyborg's voice said. "*Back off, or you too will die.*"

"Creepy." Destiny rolled the message back. Played it again. "Learned his lesson?" she said. "You too will die? Who else died? He referring to one of the celebrities?"

"Beats me."

CHAPTER 24

"*THEY TRIED TO make me go to rehab...*"

Victoria Carrington, dealing with the familiar, almost crippling cold-turkey withdrawal symptoms, watched as Tata Andolini belted out the Amy Winehouse hit song, "Rehab," danced around the small coed meeting room, and shook her cartoon curves. Tata had introduced herself to Victoria the day after they'd both signed into Promises Rehabilitation Center, but Victoria had no clue who she was. Had never heard of Tata, never even seen a clip of her reality show, or read her apparently commercially successful autobiography, *Confessions of a Guidette,* or read about her off-the-wall antics in the gossip columns. But Victoria knew that for someone to act like that—Victoria gasped as Tata leaped onto a chair, pulled down her tunic, screamed "Ohhfahhh!" and flashed her tits; several of the male patients cheered—meant she had to be stoned on something. And Victoria was desperate to get high.

Tata finished the song, shouted "Rehab is for quitters!" just as two male orderlies rushed into the room. They grabbed Tata, wrestled her down from the chair, forced her into her room, and closed the door. They'd probably restrain her, then search her room thoroughly to discover where she was hiding her stash. Victoria hoped and prayed they would not find the drugs. Since Tata was a fawning sycophant who would gladly share her drugs with an A-list superstar, Victoria planned to lead her on, pretend to be her friend—anything to get at her drugs.

A drug counselor entered and called the small group- therapy session to order. As in other rehab centers, Victoria had started her day at 6:30. She walked to the facility café for breakfast, but she was too sick to eat. Next she began a boring day of process groups, lectures, 12-step meetings, and other recovery-related activities. Which would be followed by educational lectures that focused on teaching patients about the disease of addiction, thinking errors, dual diagnosis, and other issues related to chemical dependency. The day would end with a chronic-relapse focus group that would address relapse-prevention skills and strategies among those, like Victoria, who'd had multiple prior-treatment attempts.

Victoria chose a seat away from the other patients, by an open window that overlooked the lush garden. She gazed out across the vast lawn toward the thick woods, breathed in the scent of freshly-cut grass and pine trees. She picked and bit her nails down to ragged, bleeding cuticles, and zoned out as the drug counselor delivered the day's 12-step reading. No one—not her many former boyfriends, agents, managers, assistants, or even her mother—understood how difficult it was for her to get out of bed every day; to live in a bubble, besieged by suck-ups, isolated by the inescapable trappings of celebrity. The unrelenting pressure to be successful, to support every phony, thankless, bloodsuck-ing member of the ever-expanding cottage industry that was Victoria Carrington.

The counselor raised his voice as he began to speak about an addict's low self-esteem. Victoria tuned him out. She didn't need to be constantly reminded that she despised herself, which was why she drank and drugged, and why, beginning with her father, every man she ever loved had left her. But her mother was a self-absorbed, drugged-up sex addict who had treated her as a cash cow to be pimped out and abused for profit. So what did the world expect of her?

"You have to learn to move on. Get over it," the counselors always told her. But they didn't understand the relentless anxiety, the fear of failure and of desertion, the reality that she was utterly alone, and insecure with her so-called talents. She feared if the world discovered the truth—that she was an incredibly lucky, marginally talented fraud—her superstar status would disappear. Then where would she be? Where would she go? How would she live? Who would love her?

Victoria saw a sudden movement outside, in the distant woods, and snapped out of her reverie. She focused on a patch of thicket—there! Someone or something had moved. The hair on the back of her neck stood on end as a man stepped from behind a tree, a pair of binoculars to his eyes.

CHAPTER 25

"**A**LL OF HIS invoices are on his computer." I walked into Lisi's bedroom. His king-sized bed was an unmade mess. Clothing was piled atop of a bureau and dirty laundry buried the only chair. "He hasn't checked his e-mail in months, not that it matters," I continued. "It's mostly spam. The ones he sent to his stepson bounced back." I held up a folded document. "Only thing of interest is a copy of his last will and testament. You and I are not in the will."

"Go figure." Destiny was sitting on the edge of the bed, reading from a folder. A small stack of files lay beside her. "I found these folders in a box under the bed." She patted the first small stack of files. "These are the celebrity deaths that your father investigated." She patted another pile. "These are Lisi's files."

I glanced at the first pile. *Angel of Death Investigation* was handwritten across each folder. "You read any of them?"

"I did."

"What do you think?"

"The files are thorough, well organized..."

"I hear a *but* in there somewhere."

"But your father's theory is based on a supposition and coincidences. There's no way to prove any of it, especially the older cases. Still, it all makes sense."

"So we're right back where we started from."

"Not quite." Destiny closed the file in her hand. "You'd better have a seat."

I could hear an alarm bell go off in my head. "I'm okay."

"Trust me on this, sit down."

Because of the clutter, I sat alongside her. Our legs touched, and I breathed in her scent and couldn't help but appreciate the way her back arched, her butt, and breasts jutted out; I found myself entertaining erotic thoughts. I mean, we were totally alone, sitting on a strange bed…

"Lisi was keeping a file on you father," Destiny said. "He thinks he was murdered."

"What?" I said, my fantasy evaporating. "Murdered?"

"That's what he wrote."

"But that's crazy."

"Maybe you should read the file," Destiny said.

"My father suffered a heart attack on Route Eighty-seven. Crashed his car into a propane truck." I rose angrily to my feet and began pacing the room. "He had heart problems for years. A quadruple-bypass the year before he died. His heart attack was no surprise to anyone."

"Let me tell you something—now don't get angry, just consider what I'm about to say. Remember what the caller on Lisi's machine said, about him not learning a lesson? Lisi thinks your father's death was supposed to be the lesson."

"Maybe it was a crank call," I said, not wanting to admit this possibility. I had put my father's tragic death to rest in my mind a long time ago. "Or a wrong number."

"I'm not going to argue with you about this," Destiny said. "But according to Lisi's file, your father received several death threats. Then he received a phone call from someone claiming to know the identity of the Angel of Death. Your father drove up to Westchester to meet the informant."

"And?"

"There's no way to know if the informant showed," Destiny

said. "But Lisi thinks that the meeting was a ruse, that your father was set up."

An old ache was starting up in my heart. "Isn't it convenient that there's nothing left of my father or his car? There's no way to prove any of this." I sat back down on the bed. "Know what I think? My father was a sick man both mentally and physically who blamed himself for my sister's death. An ailing, broken-hearted, frustrated old cop looking to rescue someone, save them from drugs. When Audra Gardner died, he realized he couldn't. So he invented the case to end all cases. A serial killer murdering Tinseltown's A-list. And Lisi's just as bad as my father. Another old-timer looking to recapture his youth. If this was a movie, it'd be a Hollywood docudrama. I mean, let's face it: the Angel of Death's an updated, deranged version of Bigfoot, for chrissake."

I snatched my father's file, opened it, and read. "Lisi's saying my father's brakes might have been tampered with." I closed the file. "*Might have.* Supposition."

"Lisi's windshield was shot out. Maybe the same thing happened to your father?"

I tossed the file on the bed. "I say my father had a heart attack that caused him to crash. The Angel of Death had nothing to do with it."

"But no one knows for sure," Destiny said. "Do they?"

"I'm not gonna drive myself crazy blaming my father's death on a boogeyman."

"Answer me this, then," Destiny said. "Who tried to kill Sweet Tommy Lisi?"

"Ice Pick Martucci," I said. "I thought we settled that."

Destiny gathered the files, placed them back in the box.

"What?" I said. "You don't agree?"

"Let's just say that after reading these files, I'm not so sure."

CHAPTER 26

ESTINY AND I arrived at Sloan Kettering on East Sixty-seventh Street at 7:45 the following morning. I parked Lisi's Jaguar in a no-parking zone, alongside a street vendor's large breakfast food cart. Placed the NYPD parking permit on the dashboard, and breathed in the aroma of freshly brewed coffee as we exited the vehicle.

A uniformed Sloan Kettering doorman greeted us pleasantly as we entered the large modern structure—the same building where my father had taken my mother when we feared she had contracted stomach cancer.

We rode the elevator to the appropriate floor and entered a bland waiting area. Destiny checked in with a receptionist, and then we found two adjoining seats in the crowded waiting room. Destiny chose a dog-eared woman's magazine from a pile that was fanned out haphazardly on a coffee table. As she flipped through it, I could tell she was nervous as hell, although she was working hard not to show it.

From what I understood, she was scheduled to undergo a standard neurological exam—checking her vision, hearing, balance, coordination, and reflexes—administered by Dr. Goldsamp, the same oncologist who'd removed her brain tumor and the bullet. Depending on the outcome, Dr. Goldsamp might direct that she endure yet more PET scans, CAT scans, or an MRI.

"You call your parents?" I said.

Destiny shook her head tightly. "They have enough problems."

The receptionist called out, "Destiny Jones?"

Destiny startled. She took a deep breath and rose to her feet. "Well, here we go again."

"Relax," I said with more confidence then I felt. "I'll bet it's nothing."

As she was led past the reception desk through a set of swinging doors, I recalled watching my mother disappear behind a similar set of doors. I also recalled the big smile on her face after her follow-up visit, when she announced that she was cancer-free. It was a stroke that would eventually end her life.

I took out my cell, dialed Brookhaven Memorial Hospital, and checked on Lisi. There was no change in his condition. Putting my phone away, I decided I needed some of that sidewalk food cart's coffee and took the elevator down to the lobby.

Special Agent Sobel was sitting in the passenger seat of a Crown Vic, smiling at me as I exited the building. "Why don't you get in the back?" he suggested.

"I don't think so."

"C'mon," Sobel said, much too nicely. "We brought a surprise guest, someone you should speak to." The back door opened. I saw the long, shapely legs first. Then the short black leather skirt. Then the tight white sweater over eye-popping cleavage.

"Hello, Michael," Enia said.

"I know what you must think of me." Enia made sure that I got a long, lingering look as she slithered from the car; her black leather skirt rode up, revealing flawless thighs.

"No, you don't, " I said. "Coffee?"

"No, thank you."

I walked up to the street vendor and ordered a medium coffee, black, no sugar.

Enia came up behind me. "You must hate me."

"*Hate* doesn't quite describe it," I said.

"I'm here to help you, Michael."

"Of course you are." I paid for the coffee, took a cautious sip, and drifted over to a set of benches alongside Sloan Kettering's entrance, where the feds could not overhear our conversation— not that it mattered. The self-serving, amoral sociopath would most likely be wearing a wire. Enia sat beside me.

I had to admire the fact that, even though she was facing substantial prison time for insurance fraud, grand larceny, and bigamy, Enia still exuded a sultry confidence. Of course, the salon-perfect hair, makeup, understated jewelry, and the distract-ing dress-to-mesmerize designer outfit alerted me to the fact that Enia was not being held in the federal lockup. Which meant they were sequestering her in some hotel at taxpayers' expense. Which only served to underscore her importance to them.

"I suppose I should have known you'd turn up in my life again someday."

"Don't judge me." Enia bent down to pet a leashed bull ter-rier that was sniffing around us; her breasts nearly spilled out of her cashmere sweater. "I did what anyone else would do under the circumstances."

"Attempt to destroy other people's lives in order to avoid the consequences of your own actions?" I forced a laugh; the harsh sound made the dog skitter away. "You're a piece of work."

"I haven't destroyed your life, Michael." She tossed her long blond hair back

"You're giving it one hell of a try."

"I told them, if they didn't make you a deal, I won't cooperate."

I felt my jaw drop at her gall. "If you're so concerned about my well-being, why bring me into your mess in the first place?"

"There is no mess," Enia said. "You do what they want and you go free."

"As do you," I said. "Right?"

"Maybe we can walk away together." Enia did her best to hold eye contact. "Remember how it used to be?"

I had to admit that I remembered all too well—the life-altering sex, my destructive obsession with the amoral Romanian viper. I recalled how I felt when I came out of the sex-induced fog and realized that she'd betrayed my trust in every way possible. Which was why I was avoiding eye contact; I was not about to gaze into to those bottomless baby blues, revel in the scent of her subtly intoxicating perfume, inhale her sweet, enticing breath.

Agent Englund honked the horn. Sobel called out the window: "Let's go."

"That's your cue," I said.

"I don't want to send you to jail, Michael."

"You won't," I bluffed.

"I'll have to tell them everything."

"Go ahead. Way I see it, you have a credibility issue."

"What about the other landlords?"

I took a sip of coffee, doing my best to maintain my composure.

"My husband referred you to other landlords," Enia said. "I doubt they *all* have credibility issues."

"I don't know what you're talking about." I stood, turned to head back into Sloan Kettering. "Good-bye, Enia. Enjoy prison."

"You still don't understand," Enia said. "You don't have a choice."

"Yeah?" I stopped. "Why is that?"

"Someone close to you," she said, "is already cooperating."

CHAPTER 27

"**W**ELL?" I SAID as Destiny came back into the waiting room. "How'd it go?"

"I'm not sure."

I rose to my feet, ready to comfort her, but she seemed pretty prickly.

"Dr. Goldsamp ran the same tests we did before. Plus a few new ones. He said someone would call with the results. But…" She shook her head, still trying to work out something.

"What?" I said.

"I don't know." Destiny shrugged. "Maybe it's just me, but he didn't seem worried this time. Know what I mean?"

We headed down the hall, had to hurry to catch a nearly full waiting elevator. The *lobby* button was already lit as we fitted in, noses nearly on the closed doors.

"So that's good," I said. "Right?"

"Yeah." Destiny's smile was brittle. "I think so."

We passed through the lobby to the street and climbed into the Jag. I started the engine, pulled into traffic.

"Any news on Lisi?" Destiny said.

"No change." I checked my wristwatch. "Rush hour's over. We should make it to the hospital in good time." I turned right on First Avenue, heading to the East Ninety-sixth Street entrance to the FDR Drive.

"You hungry?" I said as we forged our way up First Avenue. "We could pick up some burgers." I gestured at a McDonald's on the east side of the street. "Or how about a couple of Italian heroes from Milano up on Third? Or pastrami sandwiches from the Second Avenue Deli? Of course, we could always eat at the hospital cafeteria. That's if you're hungry. You hungry?" I looked at Destiny. "What?"

"All right. What's going on?" she said.

"What are you talking about?"

"You're babbling. And you've got that look."

"What look?"

"The look you get when you're hiding something."

I shook my head. "You're imagining things."

"Don't even try that routine on me," Destiny said. "Let's have it."

"Okay." I gathered my thoughts, trying not to set off the inevitable explosion. "While you were being examined, I went downstairs for a cup of coffee. The feds were waiting."

"Keep talking."

"They brought Enia."

"Bingo!" Destiny cried.

"Bottom line is, she said someone close to me was cooperating with the feds. She's bluffing, of course." Since Destiny disliked "the Romanian slut" Enia almost as much as "the crazy bitch" Solana, I left out the fact that she looked positively amazing.

"How'd the slut look?" Destiny said.

Read my mind. "Whaddya mean?"

"Which word didn't you understand?" Destiny said. "*How. Did. The. Slut. Look?*"

"I dunno," I said weakly. "The same."

"That good, uh?" Destiny said. "She come on to you?"

"No."

"Liar."

I made the right onto East Ninety-sixth Street. As long as I was taking a beating, I figured maybe now was a good time to tell her about Solana. "Oh," I said. "Did I mention that Solana showed up at the hospital yesterday?"

"So? She's a reporter. No surprise there."

I merged onto the FDR Drive, headed for the Triborough Bridge. "She said the feds had contacted her, asked her about Rockers."

"What?"

"She tried to blackmail me. Said if I didn't give her an exclusive with Victoria, she'd tell the feds what she knows."

A hard edge entered Destiny's voice. "And you waited till now to tell me?"

"What's the big deal? She doesn't know anything. I mean, okay, we sometimes went back to my apartment after Rocker raids. But Solana was always asleep, or in the shower getting ready for work."

Destiny shook her head. "I can't believe how naive you are. Women listen to everything when it concerns the man in their life. They eavesdrop, snoop. There's no telling what she knows."

"Believe me," I said. "She's bluffing."

"Enia's bluffing. Solana's bluffing. You seeing a pattern here?"

I merged onto the Triborough Bridge.

"What about the Rocker money?" Destiny said. "Solana had to know you were bringing home extra cash. How'd you explain that?"

That part I was sure about. "I didn't. I put my share in my safe. By the time I was ready to spend any of it, Solana and I had broken up."

Plus, when I did spend my cut, I did it slowly, methodically, paying cash in high-end restaurants, getaways with Destiny at first-class, upstate Hudson River hotels and spas—there were no records to speak of.

I knew for a fact that Destiny had funneled her entire share to her indigent parents. Employed FedEx to overnight them a couple of thousand at a time. Serria had used his share to send his son to drug rehab, twice. Borrowed the money from relatives, then paid them back from his Rocker proceeds in cash, under the table. As for McKee—well, we all now knew how he spent his share.

"Maybe I should contact Solana?" I said. "Tell her I've reconsidered giving her a Victoria Carrington exclusive? Find out what she thinks she knows?"

Destiny eyeballed me. "That the only reason you want to contact her?"

"Why else?"

"Maybe you still have feelings for her."

I knew that was coming. "Don't be ridiculous."

CHAPTER 28

TURNED INTO THE Brookhaven Memorial Hospital Medical Center's parking lot about an hour later. Had to drive around for a good five minutes before finding a spot. Not that the appalling traffic and lack of parking seemed to affect Destiny. She had her eyes glued to her iPhone, checking her various social-media feeds.

I noted the security cameras that were mounted in the corners of the parking facility as we exited the Jaguar and walked toward the main building. We joined a crowd entering the hospital, surfed to the elevator. In the ICU we were told that Lisi had stabilized enough to be moved to a regular room: great news.

Officer Olive was sitting outside Lisi's private room, fiddling with her cell phone when we came down the hall. She got to her feet, smiled warmly.

"Armed guard," I said. "Shaw's not taking any chances."

"He's seeing Mafia thugs in his coffee," Olive said.

I gestured into the room. "How's he doing?"

"Better," Olive said. "So I'm told."

I looked through the open door into the small, but sunny room. Lisi was lying in bed surrounded by life-support monitors and IV bags. A rotund nurse was attending to him. "He regain consciousness?"

"Not that I know of," Olive said.

"Anyone been to see him?"

"Yeah," Olive said. "About an hour ago. A guy wearing a funny-looking suit, carrying flowers." Olive referred to a memo pad. "Sid Schulsky."

"He's one of our clients," I said. "A press agent."

The nurse was adjusting Lisi's oxygen mask when we entered. She acknowledged us with a nod, checked an IV drip, wrote something on a clipboard that hung on the bottom of the bed frame, and waddled out the door. We approached the bed. I took Lisi's hand in mine. "Tommy!" I squeezed. "Wake up."

Nothing.

Destiny placed the grocery bag containing Lisi's essentials on the bedside table. Then she smelled the vase of flowers on the windowsill, read the get-well card from Sid Schulsky. She and I pulled up chairs and sat alongside the bed. Listened to the *blip* of life-support monitors, the hospital intercom, and Lisi's steady breathing.

"He was good to my sister and me when we were kids," I said. "Always at our house. Always with gifts for me and my sister. Flowers and Italian pastries for my mother. He'd slip me a twenty on a Saturday night, then slip me a condom—things my father never did." I chuckled. "You know I never could relate to my father. He couldn't relate to me—I was a disappointment to him. He wanted me to go to law school. He wasn't happy when I followed in his footsteps, became a cop.

"Lisi was the go-between. Whenever my old man went on a rampage, Lisi'd be the one to take me aside, explain what my father was thinking, why he acted the way he usually did—angry."

"Why was your father angry?" Destiny said.

The question made me uncomfortable. I'd never discussed my father with anyone. "My father killed an undercover cop in the line of duty."

Destiny looked surprised. "I didn't know."

"It was a long time ago." I leaned forward, elbows on my knees. "Bronx anticrime—plainclothes in his day—was shooting it out with a stickup crew. The undercover, a black guy, was dressed like a flamboyant pimp, brandished a silver-plated automatic—not department issue. The shield he hung around his neck had caught in his frilly clothes and wasn't visible. My father shot him once. Through the heart." Destiny was cringing by this time. She knew how easily possible this was.

"A grand jury refused to indict. The department cleared him of any wrongdoing. Everyone agreed that it wasn't his fault, that it could have happened to anyone. But he never got over it. It ate away at him." I was leaning back stiffly, could feel the edge of the chair biting into my thighs.

"My mother told me it changed him, and not for the better. He took a desk job as soon as he could. When he retired, he didn't bother to put in for a gun-carry license. Never carried again, even when bodyguarding celebrities. 'There are no erasers on guns,' he used to say. And then my sister died…"

I stopped talking when Lisi unexpectedly took a deep breath. Let out a sigh. Then nothing. His life-support monitors beeped steadily. Out in the hall the hospital intercom summoned a trauma team to the emergency room. "Stat." A succession of visitors and nurses moved past Lisi's room. Patients roamed the hall.

"You mind if we hang out?"

"Mind?" Destiny said. "I insist. He wakes up, I want him to see a familiar face."

I got to my feet. "I'll go down to the cafeteria, get us some sandwiches."

Destiny made a face. "Get me a salad. Any kind. Diet Italian dressing if they have it. And tea with lemon."

"Anything else?"

"Get me a black coffee," Lisi said. "Lots of sugar."

I froze.

Destiny shot to her feet. "He spoke."

Officer Olive raced into the room. "He spoke?"

"Yeah," I said. "I'll go get the nurse."

CHAPTER 29

"**H**EY." LISI POINTED across the room. "Youse guys bring flowers?"

I shook my head. "Sid Schulsky was here earlier."

"Yeah?" Lisi looked pleased. "Bring them over heah."

I got to my feet, moved past Lieutenant Shaw, and retrieved the vase. Destiny cleared a spot on the bedside table.

"Would you like me to repeat the question, Mr. Lisi?" Lieutenant Shaw said.

"I heard you." Lisi put down the get-well card. "I was checking out the rehab center. You know we got a client there?"

Shaw said he did.

"When I saw Matt the Hat—he's a convicted stalker, you know—I was sure he was stalking my client. I tried to get him to pull over, tell him he'd better knock it off before I had him arrested. That's when someone took a shot at me."

"The Hat?"

"The Hat wasn't the shooter."

The same rotund nurse was examining Lisi as he spoke. She shone a penlight into his eyes, asked Lisi to follow the beam left, right, up, down.

"Was he alone in the van?" Shaw said.

Lisi thought about it. "Yeah."

"You sure?"s

"Look, Inspector…?"

"Lieutenant."

"Whatever. Lissena me: The Hat's *oobatz*. You know, crazy inna head. But he ain't—whatchamacallit—calculating." The color had returned to Lisi's face and his energy level seemed to be growing by the minute.

"What about Ice Pick Martucci?" I said.

"Not Ice Pick's style."

"What *is* his style?" Destiny said.

"If the organization wanted me whacked, they'd a' made an example outta me—you know, like they tried with Big Paul Scognamillo." Lisi seemed to notice the grocery bag for the first time. He hoisted it over beside him and looked in. He pulled out the cell-phone charger. "Youse were in my apartment?"

Nodding, Destiny took the charger and plugged his cell phone into a wall outlet.

I reached into my jacket pocket, plucked out Lisi's apartment keys, held them up for him to see. "We read your files." I placed them on the bedside table. "Why didn't you tell me you think my father was murdered?"

Lieutenant Shaw perked up.

The nurse unrolled a blood-pressure unit and wrapped it around Lisi's arm.

"'Cause I knew you wouldn't believe me. No one does."

"How could they?" I got to my feet as the nurse pumped up the blood-pressure cuff. "My father and his car were incinerated. There's no way that you, or anyone, could know what happened."

"Yeah?" Lisi said. "Well, *I* know."

"How?"

"Who the hell you think just shot at me?" Lisi asked.

"Who?" Shaw said.

"The Angel a' Death."

"You saw him?" Shaw said.

Lisi made a face. Shook his head.

"It was Ice Pick ordered the hit," I said. "Has to be."

"Hey, fucko," Lisi grouched. "Ever hear the saying: *The devil's best trick* is to *persuade everyone that he don't exist?*"

The nurse ripped off the blood-pressure strap.

"The Angel a' Death is a killer hiding in plain sight," Lisi continued. "But you've got your mind made up, just like the cops."

My cell phone vibrated. I pulled it out of my pocket, didn't recognize the number. I hit the *speaker* button. "Hello?"

"It's Victoria," Victoria Carrington said in that little- girl voice.

Lisi, Destiny, and I exchanged looks. "Everything all right?"

"I'm scared," she said. "There was a man in the woods. He was watching me."

There it was, the paranoia. "I'll be there in an hour."

"No," she said. "I'm not staying here—hold on."

I could hear her talking to someone about a boyfriend and a car. "Victoria?"

"I'll text you where to meet me," Victoria told me and hung up.

I put away my phone. "Well, you all heard."

"She's fulla gahbidge," Lisi said. "Ain't no guy in no woods. But that ain't our problem. We go by what she says."

Destiny's cell phone chirped. She glanced at the screen. "Oh, boy."

"Now what?" I said.

"Tata sending Tweets. You're not gonna believe this."

"Whassat?" Lisi said.

"Tata and Victoria checked out of rehab together," Destiny said.

"*Marrone*," Lisi said. "Youse two better head back to the city. Fast."

"We're on it," I said.

"And Beckett," Lisi said. "Lissena me for once."

"Yeah?"

"Watch your back. The Angel of Death ain't just another douche bag making death threats. He's for real." Lisi pointed a finger at me. "You find him, you'll find the psychotic son of a bitch that murdered your father."

CHAPTER 30

"**H**ELLO?" AGENT SOBEL knocked on the frosted-glass panel of a partially open office door. Stacked cardboard boxes, each a clearly marked criminal case, crowded the walls around the room. "Mrs. Butcher?" He pushed the door open. "Hello?"

Melody Butcher peeked over the top of the file in her hand. "Yes?"

"I'm Special Agent Sobel. This is Englund."

"Oh. Y'all c'mon in. Find a seat." Butcher pushed a stack of files aside. "Sorry about the mess."

Sobel and Englund stepped into the cubicle on the twelfth floor of the Federal Building at 26 Federal Plaza. They lifted cardboard boxes off a couple of chairs and took seats across from Butcher's desk. The fifty-five-year-old veteran assistant U.S. attorney, originally from Texas, was dressed in an all-business charcoal-gray pantsuit. A pair of horned-rimmed reading glasses balanced on the end of her dainty nose.

"Well, I declare," Butcher said, referring to the file in her hand. "Enia Vladimirescu, Enia Petrescu, Enia Schultz. Ex-girlfriend of our target, former police officer Michael Beckett. She's a Romanian national. Been arrested for, but never convicted of: credit-card fraud, mail fraud, insurance fraud. She was married three times—that we know of—all at the same time." Butcher turned to the next page. "Two husbands confirmed dead. One missing and presumed dead." She flipped several pages before she closed the file. "This black widow is our star witness? Good gawd."

"Funny," Englund said. "*Black widow*. I like that."

"If the shoe fits…" Butcher tossed the file on her desk. "What I don't understand is how a seasoned police officer like Michael Beckett allowed himself to get mixed up with an obvious sociopath."

"She's beautiful." Sobel shrugged. "The flesh is weak."

"I hear ya." Butcher got to her feet and gazed out the office window at a sliver of green called Thomas Paine Park. The Dallas native, nearly six feet tall, was fashion- model thin. Her brown hair was cut short, accentuating her large green eyes that were as alert and vibrant as a cat's.

"Be candid with me," Butcher said. "Both y'all" She sized up the two agents: one a rumpled, world-weary veteran, the other a squared-away, wide-eyed recruit. "Did Michael Beckett lead a gang of vigilante cops known as Rockers, or didn't he?"

"Yes," Sobel said. "He did."

"Did he gun down the terrorist Lochlainn O'Brian?"

"Yes, again," Sobel said.

"Can y'all prove it?"

"Not yet," Sobel said.

"That's what I figured."

"So far," Englund said, "only thing concrete we have on any of Beckett's Rockers is on Thomas McKee. He has a problem with undeclared income."

Butcher waved a dismissive hand. "Tax-evasion charges at most." She looked back down at the street. The park benches were occupied by people eating, reading newspapers or their handheld devices. Across the park, on Foley Square, a film crew was shooting a group of actors as they legged down the broad, steep steps of 60 Centre Street. "Are you even sure who was part of Beckett's gang?"

"Pretty sure," Sobel said. "Beckett was living with a woman, Solana Ortiz, about the time he formed his team. He never told her what he was up to, but she heard Beckett refer to ex-cops Ernie Serria, McKee, and Destiny Jones as his Rockers."

"So the Ortiz woman was, what, a roommate," Butcher said, "or another of Beckett's ex-girlfriends?"

"Girlfriend," Sobel said.

"Their breakup amicable?"

"What breakup is?" Sobel said.

"Tell me why Beckett killed Lochlainn O'Brian."

"O'Brian sold the drugs that killed his younger sister."

"So we have motive, at least." Butcher was clearly unhappy about what she had to work with. "I wish we weren't targeting four highly decorated former police officers solely on the word of Beckett's two ex-girlfriends. This Solana Ortiz? She might have an ax to grind. We all know that Enia—whatever her real name is—will do anything, say anything to save herself." Butcher rested her elbow on a file cabinet and heaved a resigned sigh. "Sometimes I hate this job."

"We have more than the two ex-girlfriends," Sobel said.

"Really?" Butcher looked more interested. "Talk to me."

"We have an informer," Sobel said. "Claims Beckett's involved with organized crime."

Butcher's cat eyes sparkled. She sat on the edge of her desk. "Let's hear it."

"First a little background." Sobel gestured to Englund.

Englund referred to a notebook. "A Mafioso, Gaetano Lisi, supposedly did the unheard of and quit the Gambino crime family."

"He didn't actually quit," Sobel said. "He was shot. Pronounced dead. Revived. He claims he told the don that he wanted out. That he'd already given one life to the mob. It appears that the family simply left him alone after that."

"I remember the case." Butcher nodded. "Sweet Tommy Lisi.

The don's bodyguard. Saved his life. Tabloid fodder for weeks. They made a TV movie about him. Go on."

"Lisi used his celebrity, partnered up with his childhood friend, police lieutenant Shamus Beckett, Michael Beckett's father, now deceased, and opened a legitimate, successful bodyguard business."

Sobel picked up from there. "Beckett just retired from the NYPD and assumed his father's position in the firm. Destiny Jones, ex-cops Ernie Serria and McKee are all working for him."

"Beckett's Rockers ride again," Englund sniggered.

"If you can link Lisi to organized crime, and Beckett to Lisi, we'll have the elements of a conspiracy," Butcher said.

"It gets better," Englund said.

"The informer claims that not only is Lisi still a member of La Cosa Nostra," Sobel said, "but that he's actively involved in extortion."

"Who's he extorting?"

"His celebrity clients," Sobel said. "Bodyguards are privy to a celebrity's darkest secrets."

"Example?" Butcher asked.

"Audra Gardner."

"The singer," Butcher said. "I loved her."

"Her father was a neo-Nazi," Englund said. "Apparently, there are videos of Audra, before she made it big, wearing a swastika armband, calling for..." He referred to his notes. "The extermination of all mud people: Jews, Blacks, Hispanics, Muslims. Chinese." He closed the notebook. "Basically everybody except the Irish." He put the notebook away. "Lisi threatened to release those videos."

"According to her bank records," Sobel said, "Audra made large, monthly cash withdrawals for years. The NYPD detectives said the cash was used to party: buy booze, drugs, among other things. But the informer swears the cash went to Lisi."

"Apparently, Audra grew tired of being blackmailed," Englund said. "Threatened to go to the police. The informer claims her overdose was no suicide."

"He provide proof?"

Sobel's confident tone died away as he admitted, "No."

"Beckett's father Shamus?" Butcher said. "He in on the extortions?"

Sobel shook his head. "Matter of fact, he went to his own department and the DEA. Told them a serial killer was targeting celebrities, killing them with hot loads of heroin. That the serial killer was responsible for the death of the Gardner woman."

"Something doesn't fit," Butcher said skeptically. "I mean, how'd Lisi go about pulling the wool over the eyes of Beckett's father? You did say he was a retired police lieutenant."

"We don't know that he did," Sobel said. "Shamus was killed in a car accident. Witnesses say he crashed into a propane truck at over seventy miles an hour."

"My god," Butcher said.

"Shamus had a touch of dementia, plus a heart condition," Englund said. "The official accident report states that he 'probably' suffered a massive heart attack and lost control."

"You don't believe that?" Butcher said.

"Well, for one thing," Sobel said, "the victim and the car were incinerated. There's no way anyone could know that he suffered a heart attack."

"And?" Butcher said.

"And our informer swears that Shamus was assassinated by a sniper," Sobel said, smirking, "who was a former United States Marine combat veteran. I'll give you one guess who."

"Sweet Tommy Lisi." Butcher sat back, thought over this new twist. "So Beckett's father discovers that Lisi murdered Audra Gardner. And Lisi kills him?"

"That's what the informer claims," Sobel said.

"And Beckett's now partners with the man who killed his

father." Butcher shook her head, bewildered. "You can't make this stuff up." Her eyes clouded with suspicion. "Who's this informer?"

"That's the catch," Sobel said. "He, or she, is anonymous."

Butcher's mouth started to grow firmer.

"Whoever it is calls from an untraceable cell phone," Sobel said. "He won't ID himself. Say he's afraid of reprisals—can't say I blame him. Even uses some sort of a voice-synthesizer app."

"Not good," Butcher said, starting to tap her fingers.

"What the informer says makes sense," Englund tried to explain.

"Why?" Butcher said. "Because he's saying what we want to hear?"

"He's the best lead we have," Sobel said. "Hell, besides the two ex-girlfriends, he's the only real lead we have."

Butcher was back to skeptical and dissatisfied. "You do financials on Lisi yet?"

Sobel nodded. "On the surface, Lisi's finances seem in order. But mob guys know how to hide income. My guess is, we'll find what we're looking for when we search his apartment—which is why we need a search warrant."

"You'll have it in an hour," Butcher said. "In the meantime, I'll schedule Beckett's two ex-girlfriends to testify before a grand jury—I want to get them both on record." Butcher had another thought and grinned. "Hell, let's kick-start things. Let's subpoena Thomas McKee as well. Hold his feet to the fire."

"Good idea," Sobel said. "See you in an hour." The two feds got to their feet.

"One more thing," Butcher said.

"Yes?" Sobel said.

"What's his name?" Butcher asked.

"I told you," Sobel said. "Anonymous."

Butcher shook her head. "Beckett's father's supposed serial killer."

"Oh," Sobel said. "He calls himself the Angel of Death."

CHAPTER 31

VICTORIA CARRINGTON HAD been a nervous wreck since seeing the man with the binoculars in the rehab-center woods; she was sure he'd been watching her. And so she had stayed away from those windows. Didn't dare go into the garden. She was about to demand that the duty nurse summon her new bodyguard, Michael Beckett, tell him that she feared the Angel of Death had located her. Since seducing him at the hospital, she was certain that Beckett would drop whatever he was doing and charge to her rescue.

But then her new pal Tata Andolini had said: "I'm outta heah. You're welcome to come if you want."

"Say what?" Victoria was loath to admit that Tata was actually growing on her. And not just because she'd shared the Oxycodone that she'd snuck into rehab by inserting a dozen of them into her vagina, although that was a B-I-G plus. But once she had gotten past Tata's odd physical appearance—the woman was all hair, lips, and tits—and her rough-around-the-edges manner, she realized what a resourceful and deviously single-minded party girl she was. And then there was the fact that Tata was Victoria's polar opposite: utterly talentless and yet supremely confident. Tata made Victoria feel good about herself by comparison.

"I'm gonna call my boyfriend, Nicky. Ask him to pick us up."

Victoria popped four of Tata's Oxycodones into her mouth.

Washed them down with water. "Wait," she said. "You have a phone?"

Tata produced a cell phone and gestured across the room at a repulsive, portly male orderly with a pockmarked face and bad teeth who was mopping the floors. "He lets me use it whenever I want to."

"Him?" Victoria was incredulous.

Tata grinned. "He loves to play with my tatas."

Oh, gross. "May I borrow the phone?"

Tata handed it over.

And Victoria called Michael Beckett.

The Hat couldn't believe his bloodshot eyes when he saw Tata Andolini sitting in the passenger seat of a shiny black Cadillac as it passed through the drug and alcohol rehabilitation center's—he now knew from Google Earth—front gate. The Hat's cell phone chirped. He pulled his finger out of his ear, raking out a glob of wax, wiped it on his pants. He heard a beep, then checked the cell-phone feed. Tata had just Tweeted that she was heading to the Soho House—wherever the hell that was.

The Hat started the engine, fishtailed from his hiding place, and raced to catch up to the Caddy as it merged onto westbound 495. He gave it some gas in order to come abreast of the speeding vehicle. Tata was in an animated conversation with another woman sitting in the backseat.

The Hat dropped back and hung in the Caddy's wake. He popped open a beer and thought about his next move. He decided he'd follow Tata. If the man who'd killed Audra Gardner and rode the black Harley was stalking her, he was sure to make an appearance.

Only this time the Hat would be ready for him.

CHAPTER 32

"**Y**OU DRIVE," DESTINY said as we dashed through Brookhaven Memorial Hospital's parking lot. She used the remote to beep open the Jaguar's doors, then tossed me the keys.

"You okay?"

"Just tired." Destiny slipped into the passenger seat, powered her seat to the recline position, and closed her eyes. "Wake me," she said, "if there's a fire."

"Ha-ha." I slid into the driver's seat and dropped my cell phone on the center console. As I drove out of the parking lot, my cell phone vibrated "Get that, please?"

Destiny groaned. "It's a text from Victoria. She'll be at Soho House in the Meatpacking District." She put my phone down, and her iPhone chirped. "Now Tata's Tweeting. Posting selfies. Okay, now she's downloading a video of her and Victoria, making a big deal out of her new BFF and her going to the Soho House." Destiny had the resigned tone of a cop looking at an accident. "That place will be a zoo."

Soho House was an exclusive private club and hotel that catered to those in the arts, media, and fashion industries. Located on the beginning of Ninth Avenue just below Fourteenth Street, its reputation had been recently tarnished when a trust-fund playboy strangled and drowned his swimsuit-designer girlfriend in one of its suite's bathtubs.

I merged onto the Sunrise Highway and filtered into stop-and-go traffic; our one-and-a-half-hour trip was going to take much longer. "Do me a favor," I said. "Text Serria and McKee. Tell them to get over to the Soho House ASAP—they're a lot closer than we are." Destiny groaned in protest. "Oh, and ask them to reach out to whoever runs security. Anything happens, we're gonna need to look at the club's security tapes."

I crawled past a road-construction crew and monster earth-mover at ten miles an hour. Got off at Exit 52, cut north across the narrow width of Long Island, and merged onto the Expressway. Traffic was light. I put the pedal to the metal, raced to get ahead of a row of sixteen-wheeler tractor trailers that were jockeying perilously in the right two lanes.

Destiny's cell chirped again. "Serria can be at Soho House in twenty minutes. Nothing yet from McKee." She put her phone away, closed her eyes once again.

"Thank you," I said.

"You're welcome," she said, then added with a grin, "you ferret-faced geek."

Now that was my old Destiny speaking.

I allowed Destiny her sleep. Kept my eyes on the road and tried not to think of anything for the next hour. I realized that I was all wound up, my stomach in knots. The irony being that I was one of those calm individuals who compartmentalized the complications in my life. Stick them in a box. Close the box. Lock the box. Not think about the problem until I was ready.

But now everything was coming at me at once: Take the alleged serial killer Angel of Death—had he in fact murdered my father, and attempted to murder Lisi? Then there were Agents Sobel and Englund, who were hell-bent on forcing me, or one of my Rockers, to turn rat. And how about the women in my past— Enia and Solana—cooperating with the feds; no matter what they knew, no good would come from that. Destiny's headaches were back, and I was worried that her brain cancer had returned. And last but not least, I had become Victoria Carrington's white knight.

The more I thought about what happened at the hospital, the more chagrined I was over my behavior. Sure, Victoria was incredibly desirable, and she had seduced me—and I hadn't been with a woman in months. But she was a paying client, placing her trust in me, her life in my hands, and I had let her down. I had taken advantage of a thoroughly neurotic girl. As I wove in and around slower-moving traffic I vowed that, no matter how strong she came onto me, whatever her nutty behavior, I would not be intimate with her again.

An air horn shattered the usual road hum and scared the bejesus out of me. I looked into the rearview mirror. "What's that asshole doing?" A tailgating Mack truck's gleaming chrome grille filled the Jaguar's rear window. Huge headlights flashed. I flicked on my right directional, moved into the far right lane. It's not like I was going slow, I grumbled.

Suddenly the Jag's windshield blew apart. I covered my eyes with one hand as glass shards cut into my face. I swerved. Fought to control the car. I jammed down on the brakes, tried to pull over to the shoulder. A car struck us from behind. Propelled us back onto the highway.

"Michael!" Destiny screamed. The Jag bounced off of a Petco delivery van and into the path of a UPS truck. The truck skidded, crashed into the Petco van. Then wiped out a MINI Cooper.

Blindly, I threw the wheel to the right. The Jag slewed ahead and to the left. Struck a BMW. The Jag's air bags deployed, engulfing me. A Toyota T-boned us. Forced us into the path of another monster sixteen-wheeler. The truck sounded its air horn. Hit its air brakes. Jackknifed. Toppled onto its side, releasing a spectacular surge of sparks as it skidded in our direction.

"Hold on!" I screamed.

CHAPTER 33

MATT THE HAT executed a boozy, looping right turn off West Fourteenth Street onto Hudson Street. He followed the Caddy onto a slanting Thirteenth Street and then onto Ninth Avenue. The Caddy pulled to the curb. The Hat screeched to a skidding stop behind them. He scrunched down so as not to be seen as Tata Andolini and a skinny young guy with spiked hair stepped out; that was Nicky Bada-bing from Tata's TV show. Nicky paused to help the other woman climb out of the backseat —she looked familiar—as a horde of paparazzi rushed them. Flashbulbs flashed as they cleaved their way through the shutterbugs. The three of them pushed through a door that had *Soho House* printed on its canopy.

The Hat sat up, drained his very last beer, belched, and tossed the empty over his shoulder. He stepped out of the vehicle and scanned the area for the guy on the black Harley-Davidson. There were no motorcycles of any kind on the street.

The Hat took a position outside the entrance to the Soho House. The paparazzi were wirelessly uploading their photos to various tabloid-news organizations; the photos would be on the Web within minutes. He checked his watch and lit a Marlboro red. A succession of people entered the building. He had no way of knowing that the brash middle-aged woman with the kinky red hair was Meg Dvoretz, Victoria Carrington's PR agent. Or that the goofy-looking guy with the horrendous comb-over and loud polyester suit was Tata's PR agent, Sid Schulsky.

The Hat had more pressing matters on his mind: (A) he had to take a wicked piss, and (B) he was thirsty. He took a look-see in his well-worn wallet, found a crinkled $20 bill. Now, where to spend it? Everywhere he looked, a new upscale bar or restaurant had cropped up. What happened to the old neighborhood? Across the street, he spotted a run-down corner building with a dive called Bill's Bar—that was more his price range. The Hat took one last look around for the Harley and legged down the street to Bill's.

The checker-tablecloth place was a lot nicer on the inside. The Hat spied the men's room in back and headed in that direction.

"Hey," a gruff bartender said. "Restrooms for customers only."

"Gimme a shot of Irish whiskey and a bottle of Bud," the Hat called and sped down the hallway. A few moments later, he bellied up to the bar. His whiskey and beer were waiting.

"Fifteen dollars," the bartender said.

"What?" The Hat's smile was lopsided. "I break something, or what?"

The bartender didn't get the joke.

The Hat put his money down.

The bartender made change, laid down five one-dollar bills.

The Hat downed the shot. Drank some of the beer. Looked out the window. Still no Harley. He looked at his money. Looked at the bartender. Looked at his empty shot glass. Looked back at the bartender. "How much is a shot?"

"Nine dollars."

"Half a shot?"

The bartender shook his head and turned his back.

"Asshole," the Hat groused. Only one table was occupied. They should be grateful he was there spending his money instead of giving him attitude. The Hat finished his beer, slammed the empty down on the bar to make a point. He swept his $5 off the bar—no tip for the asshole—and made for the exit.

The Hat held the door open for a hip-looking young couple who were entering as he stepped onto the sidewalk. As he headed toward the Soho House and lit a cigarette, a black Harley-Davidson pulled between two recently arrived network-news vans and parked. The rider killed the engine, stepped off the bike, pulled off his helmet—his blond locks fell to his shoulders—and disappeared into the Soho House. The Hat freaked. The sound he made was a combination shriek, roar, and bark. He dumped his cigarette, dashed across Ninth Avenue, slipping and sliding on the old cobblestone street. He barged into the Soho House lobby and slammed into two monstrous security guards.

"Can we help you?" the larger of the two guards said.

The Hat flailed his arms, yelled that Tata Andolini was inside. "Who?" the guards asked in unison. The Hat protested that Tata was in mortal danger from a stalker who had killed Audra Gardner. "She be dead?" the smaller guard asked his partner. "No shit?"

"Now, get the hell out of my way, you dumb fucks," the Hat demanded. "Or I swear to god, I'll fucking kill you both."

The Hat woke up in a rat-infested, garbage-strewn alley behind the Soho House about ten minutes later.

CHAPTER 34

TATA ANDOLINI, FASCINATED by what she'd read over the years about the glamour and exclusivity of the Soho House, and wishing to show off to her guido and guidette friends, suggested that, immediately after leaving rehab, she and Victoria Carrington throw a tequila party at the New York venue. Victoria, a Soho House member in New York, Hollywood, as well as East London and Miami, said, "Fuckin' A," called ahead, and rented a suite. Told Tata to invite whomever she wished and said she'd pay for everything—as long as Tata supplied the "party favors." Tata agreed and then shot a selfie with Victoria, plus a short video clip, and posted their plans on Twitter, Snapchat, Facebook, Google+, Instagram, and Vine.

After checking into the suite and ingesting the last six Oxycodone—three apiece, none for Nicky—Victoria called room service. Tata called several key members of her *Jersey Shore Confidential* posse, told them to spread the word. Then she phoned her PR guy, Sid Schulsky, told him to get his polyester ass over there. Next she sent Nicky out on an errand, told him to go score some H, and to make sure he brought the best China white, or black tar, or mother pearl, or whatever was the rage for her new superstar BFF; she intended to see to it that— since associating with Victoria would no doubt fast-track her up to the A-list—she cemented their friendship by getting Victoria whacked out of her fucking mind.

Within fifteen minutes, two Soho House staffers entered the suite though the kitchen service entrance. They rolled in a portable bar stocked with Cabo Uno tequila—$250 a bottle retail—an assortment of Mexican beers, and positioned it by a window overlooking bustling Ninth Avenue. A handsome young Latin bartender arrived next, carrying a box of fresh limes. He flashed an eye-crinkling, devilishly sexy smile, introduced himself as Miguel, and proceeded to organize the bar. Tata decided she'd jump his bones later.

The Soho House restaurant waiters came through the kitchen service entrance next. They wheeled in several carts of food, unloaded, and got to work preparing hors d'oeuvres.

Not five minutes later Victoria left Tata at the bar flirting with Miguel, answered the front door, and greeted a hair stylist—from across the room Tata would swear it was Serge Normandu—and a makeup artist—could it be Dick Cage?—and their haughty assistants, who were pulling kits on wheels containing the tools of their trade. Tata was both astounded and touched by Victoria's thoughtfulness and generosity—I mean, paying for a party *and* supplying A-list hair and makeup was almost too much! In celebration, Tata threw back her first shot of tequila, chased it with a Corona beer.

"Bring what I asked for?" Victoria whispered to Serge.

"Right here." He opened his shoulder bag. Victoria peeked in at a *Jersey Shore Confidential, Season Four Highlights* DVD.

"We'll be awhile," Victoria called out to Tata, then directed the fawning beauty team into the master bedroom, followed them in, and closed the door behind her.

Tata sat there, stunned, staring at the closed door. She felt like she'd been slapped in the face. This was like grade school: the cool, mean girl and her adoring minions snubbing her. Tata felt like punching someone's lights out.

The suite's doorbell rang. Bottle of Corona in hand, Tata got off the bar stool and answered it. A flamboyantly dressed, adolescently thin young black guy was standing there.

"Whaddyawant?" Tata said.

"Victoria sent for me," the guy said as he swished in. He paused to look at Tata. "And you are...?"

"Tata Andolini."

"I mean, *what* is your function?"

"I'm a friend of Victoria's."

The guy snickered. "Sure you are, sweetie. Where *is* Victoria?"

"In there." Tata gestured to the master suite. The guy sashayed across the room, knocked, entered, and closed the door behind him.

Tata fumed. She thought about barging into the master suite, act like she hadn't just been snubbed, had her feelings hurt. She'd sit down, join or start a conversation, and wait for her turn with hair and makeup. And if that faggot or anyone else gave her a hard time, she'd punch them in the face.

Tata instead drank some beer and counted to twenty like she'd learned to do in a court-ordered anger-management course. She told herself to relax, not come on too strong, not to force herself on the superstar. After all, she and Victoria barely knew each other. Friendships took time to grow. And she needed Victoria. Victoria didn't need her.

The master-suite door flew open and the young black guy came racing out. He slowed a moment to check Tata out from head to toe, and headed out the front door.

"Hell're you looking at?" Tata said as the guy disappeared into the hall. She checked her appearance in a wall mirror. On balance, she liked what she saw, although she could use a change of clothes. She thought about dashing out to Ninth Avenue and buying a new outfit. But she didn't want to miss anything. Tata picked up her shoulder bag, entered the foyer lavatory, dumped the vast assortment of makeup and hair products she always carried on the vanity. It took around thirty minutes to freshen up.

Tata was chatting up Miguel, drinking shots of tequila, when the young black guy returned, carrying an armload of shopping bags. He ignored Tata completely as he floated across the room and entered the master suite. Tata could hear snippets of howling laughter as the guy closed the door behind him.

Tata downed another shot, had to count to fifty this time. Then she leaned forward, made sure Miguel got a good, long look at her cleavage, and decided to busy herself by updating all of her social-media feeds. She took another selfie, and short video clip of her and Miguel, and then posted how "awesome" it was to be at the Soho House as the guest of her good friend, Victoria Carrington. Next she located an iPhone doc that connected her to the suite's high-end stereo system. She chose one of her custom mixes, the one with some of Victoria's platinum-selling singles, hit *play*, and wiggled around the room.

Tata was on her forth shot of tequila and Corona beer chaser, debating whether she should give Miguel a blow job before or after the party got started, when Sid Schulsky and Meg Dorvitz, followed by several of her TV-show posse, arrived. Tata greeted everyone and pumped up the music.

Before she knew it, the suite was crowded with guidos and guidettes of every size and shape. The booze was flowing. Joints were lit and passed around. Soho House waiters were serving the delicious finger food. People were dancing and the party was in full swing. Tata noticed the hair and makeup team slip quietly out of the master bedroom, and out the service entrance. She assumed that meant that Victoria would be joining the party soon. Nicky Bada-bing arrived next, accompanied by a scary-looking red-bearded guy: his drug connection, Tata assumed. Nicky spied Tata, gestured thumbs up! Which meant he'd scored the heroin. Suddenly the master-bedroom suite's door swung wide open. All at once everyone stopped what they were doing.

The entire party turned to look.

Victoria Carrington, now the A-list version of a guidette, had entered the room.

*

Victoria, tired of waiting for her new bodyguard Michael Beckett to arrive, paused in the doorway. Her hair was a professionally coiffed facsimile of Tata's crudely styled pouf. Her temporarily henna-tattooed boobs were popping out of a tight black Prada strapless bustier top—she was not stupid enough to self-mutilate with a *real* tattoo. Her perfect A-list ass filled out her Saint Laurent distressed skinny blue jeans as she balanced on a pair of Christian Louboutin Ombré Crystal Leather 4.75-inch-high pumps.

Victoria scanned the freak show of big dyed hair, heavy dark makeup, orange-bronzer skin, boobs bursting out of tight clothes, and acrylic nails. But instead of being beset by the dreaded social anxiety she experienced whenever she met new people—anxiousness, weak knees, dry mouth, palpitating heart—she felt relaxed, absolutely safe and secure. Which was why she'd decided not to wait for Michael Beckett. After watching most of *Jersey Shore Confidential, Season Four Highlights*, Victoria was certain she had nothing to fear from the reality-TV crowd. She had at long last found a group of lowlifes that she felt truly, utterly, and completely superior to. She had Tata Andolini to thank for that.

Victoria, Serge, and Dick had all found *Jersey Shore Confidential* to be an inane, pretentious, fist-pumping buffet of self-absorption, inanity, and depravity. The show's faux-tanned stars—aimless trailer-park knuckleheads, oblivious to their own deficits, and delusional about their attractiveness and their importance in the world—did nothing except sleep, and party, and drink, and puke, and hook up, and spend quality time with their hair. It made *Keeping Up with the Kardashians* look like Shakespeare, the Hugh Hefner reality show *The Girls Next Door* look like *The Brady Bunch*. And made Victoria appreciate her miserable life as never before.

The crowd parted as Victoria strode into the room and flashed her superstar smile. She said hello to a few of the dolts she now recognized from the show. "Hello, Monkey Man. Hey, Hood Rat. What up, Big Gina? How's it hanging, Sleepy Joe?" And there was Nicky Bada-bing—who she now knew was not only Tata's dim-witted boyfriend, but her love interest on the show—standing with a thuggish guy in a red beard.

"Yo, Nicky," Victoria said. "What up?"

"Nada," Nicky said. "Say hi to Keating."

Victoria reached out to shake, but something about Keating's bearded, ruddy face gave her pause. His eyes were very cold, and very gray, and very hard. All at once she felt anxious and vulnerable. Keating reached out with a catcher's mitt–sized hand and shook, squeezed a little too hard. He liked to hurt people, she could tell.

"Hey," Keating said. "I'm a big fan, ya know."

"Thanks." Victoria yanked her hand away and looked around the room, hoping to see Michael Beckett walk in—where the hell was he?

"Victoria!" Tata gushed. She wrapped her arms around the A-lister and whispered in her ear: "Ready to get high?"

"Fuckin' A," Victoria said.

"Will you take some selfies with me first?"

"Of course," Victoria said. "I'd love to!"

Tata was so thrilled that she peed her pants.

CHAPTER 35

SEARCH WARRANT IN hand, Sobel and Englund led a team of six federal agents into Sweet Tommy Lisi's East Ninetieth Street apartment building.

"FBI!" Sobel said as he knocked on Lisi's steel-framed door. He leaned on the doorbell. "We have a warrant to search the premises." He waited for a response. Pounded the door. Paused and listened for any sound from inside. He turned to his team of agents. "Open it."

A female agent got down on one knee and opened a small black burglar's tool kit. She chose a set of picks, inserted them into Lisi's deadbolt lock. Thirty seconds later there was a distinct metallic *click*.

"Got it." Still on her knees, the agent pushed the door open.

Everyone pulled weapons.

Flashlights in hand, the agents entered the dark apartment in standard single-file attack formation. "Clear," an agent shouted from the living room. "Clear," another agent shouted from the bedroom. "Clear," came from the kitchen.

Sobel switched on the overhead lights, illuminating the stuffy apartment. He headed to the windows that faced Ninetieth Street and rolled up the shades. He cracked open the windows and breathed in the fresh air.

"Let's get to it," Sobel said.

As the agents deployed, Sobel roamed Lisi's apartment. Scrutinized the living room, dining room, and lavatory. He paused in the small kitchen, checked out the worn refrigerator, stove, and other appliances. In his considerable experience with organized-crime figures, he'd found that mobsters usually splurged within the confines of their private living quarters: expensive décor, high-end electronics and kitchen appliances. But although Lisi's apartment was tastefully appointed, the old Mafioso was not living large.

Sobel continued to wander through the railroad flat—a layout similar to that of a passenger-train car—and watched as his team gutted Lisi's life. Besides seizing all paperwork and files, the entire apartment would be dismantled in the search for evidence. A handheld Doppler sensor would scan the walls, ceiling, and floors for inconsistencies indicating possible hiding places; they were searching for accounting ledgers, CDs, DVDs, or USB drives containing local or offshore banking records.

Sobel walked into the bedroom at the rear of the apartment. He opened a closet door, checked out Lisi's wardrobe: a dozen somewhat dated off-the-rack suits, inexpensive shoes, shirts and ties. He stepped aside as a couple of agents lifted a king-size mattress and cut it open. He spied a cardboard box under the bed, stepped closer and saw that *Angel of Death Investigation* was inscribed on its side.

Sobel lifted out a small stack of files and fanned them out. The name of a deceased celebrity was written across each file. He scanned the files, found he was familiar with every incident. All the superstar victims were infamous drug addicts. All had died from tainted heroin. Sobel paused when he came to the last file. Beckett's father's name, Shamus Beckett, was written in neat block letters across the cover. He opened the file.

He found a couple of transcribed phone messages: Death threats from the Angel of Death. There were handwritten notes concerning a call Shamus had received from an anonymous informant claiming to know the identity of the Angel of Death, which he would divulge for a price. The caller had requested that Shamus meet him at the Cross County Shopping Center in Westchester. Shamus had died on Route 87 not far from the shopping center.

Sobel flipped to a copy of the police accident report, which speculated that Shamus's fatal crash was most likely caused by an acute myocardial infarction—a heart attack. Glued to the back of the file was a yellow, neatly handwritten Post-it note stating that Shamus's brakes might have been tampered with. But there was no mention of who had done the tampering. And no mention of proof.

Sobel closed the file. He had to admire Lisi's cunning. Leaving the Angel of Death files where they would be easily discovered was an obvious attempt at planting a false trail. Not that it would do him any good. Sobel was certain that it was only a matter of time before they uncovered evidence that would incriminate the old mobster and in turn Beckett and his Rockers.

Sobel re-boxed the files, handed them over to a passing agent, walked out of the bedroom and into Lisi's home office. Photos of the old mobster with a slew of former and contemporary celebrities lined the walls. Englund was sitting in front of a cluttered rolltop desk. "Anything?" Sobel said.

"Someone's tossed this place recently," Englund said over his shoulder.

A couple of agents crowded into the room and began to box its contents.

"This desk has been jimmied open." Englund produced a letter opener. "They used this." Then he ran a finger though some thick dust. "This area was recently dusted." He held up the Little Italy sweatshirt, smeared with dust. "Whoever searched the place searched the drawers, probably got into the computer. We're checking for prints."

On the desk, alongside a photo of Lisi with Frank Sinatra, was another framed photo that lay facedown. Sobel turned it over; Beckett and Destiny Jones were smiling ear to ear. They looked like a couple of professional models, Sobel mused, instead of what they actually were: violent criminals.

"Excuse me." One of the agents squeezed past, disconnected an answering machine and began to place it in a box.

"Hold it," Sobel said, and placed the photo back on the desk. "Plug it back in. Give it here."

The agent did as instructed. Sobel pushed the *play* button. Fast-forwarded through until the last call, enhanced by a voice synthesizer. Sobel pressed *stop*. Then *replay*. "*I thought you would have learned your lesson. Back off, or you too will die.*"

Sobel and Englund straightened. They recognized that cyborg voice.

"What the hell?" Englund said.

"Sounds like our anonymous informant is threatening Lisi," Sobel said, and gestured to the agent that it was okay to disconnect the answering machine and box it.

"Could be a coincidence," Englund said. "Anyone can access a voice synthesizer."

"And choose the same cyborg voice?" Sobel said, bewildered by this turn of events. "Some coincidence." He walked to the office window and gazed absently across the alley into a tenement flat. An old woman wearing a housedress was leaning out a window, using a teapot to water some scraggly plants on her fire escape. "So what's our guy's connection to Lisi?" Sobel turned away from the window. "And why the death threat—back off of what?"

"A guy like Lisi," Englund said, shrugging, "has to have a long list of enemies."

"Granted." Sobel shoved his hands in his pocket, still dissatisfied.

"Bingo!" someone shouted from the living room. A smiling junior agent strode into the room, holding a key in his outstretched hand. "Found this," he said, "beneath a floorboard."

Sobel accepted the key and broke into a Cheshire-cat grin. "Looks like a safety deposit-box key."

CHAPTER 36

"**Y**OUR WINDSHIELD JUST shattered?" a uniformed cop from Highway Unit 3 said.

"That's right." I was standing on the roadway amid a surreal multi-vehicle accident scene. I was leaning against what was left of Lisi's Jaguar, dabbing a tissue on a couple of tiny, superficial glass cuts on my cheek, while the officer finished filling out an accident report. Destiny was rummaging around in the Jag's front seat, searching the tangled wreckage for her purse and both our cell phones. The fact that she'd been lying down when the windshield shattered had probably saved her life.

Past a line of parked police cruisers, several ambulances had arrived on the scene to attend to the injured. By some miracle no one was killed. Firefighters had pulled hose from a tanker truck and were washing away small rivers of leaked gas. Large and small tow trucks were arriving and hooking up the damaged vehicles.

"Where'd you work?" the highway cop asked.

I stopped dabbing my cheek and checked the damage on the tissue. What little bleeding there was had stopped. "Both of us worked the Bronx mostly," I said. "I retired out of the Nineteenth."

"Fort Hook," the cop said, a reference to the fact that in order to get assigned to the 19th you needed a "hook" or "rabbi."

He walked around the totaled Jaguar. "A tractor trailer must've kicked up a rock," the highway cop said. "Happens all the time."

"That must be it," I said, knowing that although our own Accident Investigation Squad, (AIS), would probably discover it eventually, if I told the officer that a sniper had tried to kill us, Destiny and I would be in for hours of questions.

"You've got one hell of a lawsuit, you know," the officer said.

"What do you mean?"

"I've never seen safety glass shatter like that. It must be defective."

"Oh. Right." A sharp pain in my midsection caused me to double over.

"You okay?" the officer said.

I took a few deep breaths and straightened up. "Just a muscle spasm."

The officer handed me back my license and insurance information. Then he held a clipboard out for me to sign the accident report. "You should go to the hospital," he said. "Both of you. I'll take you if you want. No problem."

I signed. "No, thanks. But I appreciate the offer."

"You need anything," the officer said as he handed me a copy of the report and walked away, "I'll be in my car."

Destiny came up and tossed me my cell phone. "The Angel of Death just tried to kill us," she said. "You know that, don't you?"

I nodded, dealing with that new reality. "You. My father. Lisi. You were all right. I was wrong." The spasm gripped me again. I winced in pain, starting to think that maybe we should go to the hospital. McKee and Serria could keep an eye on Victoria.

I glanced at my cell phone and saw that Serria had tried to call several times. I didn't brother to check his messages. I returned the call and put the phone on speaker; it was difficult to hear above the whining tow- truck winches and blasting fire hose. "Where are you?"

"At the Soho House," Serria said. "Where are you?"

"We got delayed," Destiny said.

"You lay eyes on Victoria?" I asked.

"No. But the cops were here when I got here. Someone in the Soho House overdosed. I don't know who."

"Shit," I said. "We're on the way." I ended the call, looked around for the highway cop. I was gonna ask him for a ride back into Manhattan. We had to get to the Soho House, and fast.

CHAPTER 37

"**S**TOP HERE," I said. The highway cop pulled the marked vehicle to the curb across the street from a mob scene outside the Soho House. As expected, Tata's social-media posts had alerted the world to her and Victoria's whereabouts. A half-dozen news vans were adding to the horrendous traffic jam along Ninth Avenue by double- and triple-parking, their microwave antennas stretching into the sky. A dozen uniformed cops were dealing with the flash mob of autograph hounds, fans, tabloid reporters, and the stalkerazzi that clogged the cobblestone streets and sidewalk.

We thanked the highway cop, promised him some off-duty bodyguard work in the near future as we slid out. I glanced at the surrounding rooftops. That wasn't an issue, I decided. Even if a sniper was after us, there's no way he'd make a try with all the cops and media in the area.

I looked for Serria and McKee. Couldn't pick them out in the crowd. Traffic began to crawl up the avenue, exposing a medical examiner's black van parked among the news vans. I took out my cell phone. "Serria, we're out front."

"I'm upstairs with the guys from narcotics," Serria said. "I'll be right down."

"Wait. Who OD'd?"

"Two people."

"No," I said. "Don't tell me."

"Victoria Carrington's DOA."

"Shit! We're too late." I shoved my phone back in my pocket. Jacked up with emotion, I paced mindlessly in a circle. I hardly knew the young superstar, yet her death hit me hard. "I told her that I'd protect her," I said. "I promised."

"Yeah," Destiny said. "But you couldn't protect her from herself."

Another muscle spasm struck. I was forced to lean against a parked car. My head was starting to throb. My neck was stiffening up. Destiny reached into her purse, took out a bottle of Vicodin, shook out two pills.

"Take these."

I waved her off. "No, thanks."

"Victoria Carrington is dead!" someone shouted.

Chaos. Fans screamed. One fainted. Several young men and women broke into theatrical tears. The media ranks, feeling quite the opposite, started swelling with anticipation and excitement; this would be the entertainment story of the year.

I saw Serria and waved as he came out of the Soho House.

"See McKee?" Serria said. "He's not answering his phone."

"Haven't seen him," I said. "What gives upstairs?"

"The homicide dicks came and went," Serria said. "They're calling it an accidental overdose. I mean, the needle was still in her arm."

"It was the exact same with Audra Gardner," I said, startled by the similarity.

"Who's the other DOA?" Destiny said.

"A guido from Staten Island."

"Where'd this happen?"

"Victoria rented a suite," Serria said. "Near as I can tell, about twenty people were present when she and the guy overdosed; then everyone scattered like roaches. All except her PR agent. Meg Dvoretz."

"What about Tata Andolini?" Destiny asked.

"Who?" Serria said.

"Short. Big boobs. She was with Victoria."

Serria shrugged. "There was nobody else up there."

"You ask if we can we see the security tapes?" I said.

"Anytime we want," Serria said.

A roar from the crowd. The uniforms shoved everyone aside as two glum-faced morgue attendants, escorted by additional uniform cops, pushed two gurneys, on which lay two black body bags, across the sidewalk. Cameras flashed and video whirled as the bodies were placed in the rear of the morgue wagon. The attendants closed and locked the rear doors, stepped into their vehicle and drove away.

"There's that hunky Fabio guy," Destiny said.

Fabio, dressed head to toe in tight black leather, came strolling out of the Soho House. Women, including Destiny, swooned—Lord, how I hated that guy.

Fabio smiled tolerantly at his admirers, paused to speak briefly to several people in the media. Suddenly, Matt the Hat sprang from behind a network-news van. Cracked Fabio on the head with a longneck beer bottle. "Murderer!"

The uniformed cops swarmed the Hat. They twisted his hands behind his back and handcuffed him. A young black cop helped Fabio up off the ground and sat him on the curb; he was bleeding from a gash on his scalp.

"What's this all about?" the cop said.

"No idea," Fabio said unsteadily. "Never saw him before."

"You gonna need stitches." The cop radioed for an ambulance.

"He's a murderer!" the Hat squawked, glaring at Fabio. "A murderer!"

"Yeah?" an Asian cop said. "Who'd he murder?"

"Audra Gardner."

"Who?"

The Hat rolled his bloodshot eyes. "What the hell do you mean, *who*? Audra Gardner the superstar, for chrissake!"

"Oh," the Asian cop said. "She's dead?"

"Now he's trying to kill Tata Andolini—"

"Who?" the Asian cop said.

"He's gotta get through me first. You hear me, you piece of shit?" The Hat tried to kick Fabio, but the cops held him back. "You want Tata, you gotta get though me first."

"Wait a minute." Fabio focused on the Hat. "I *do* know him." He addressed the cops. "That guy's crazy. He went to prison for stalking Audra Gardner."

"I wasn't stalking her." The Hat fumed and stomped his feet like a petulant child. "I was stalking you! You killed her!"

"Okay," the Asian cop said to the Hat. "Relax." He reached into the Hat's rear pants pocket, picked out a wallet, and checked the ID. "Matthew Gluck. Dobbs Ferry, New York." He looked at Fabio. "You too. Let's see some ID."

Fabio took out his wallet and handed over his driver's license.

"Daniel Caruso," the Asian cop read. "Los Angeles, California."

"They call me Fabio," he said, "for obvious reasons."

"Yeah?" The cop handed him back his license. "What're you doing here?"

"Working." Fabio produced a press pass from the TMZ.

Destiny turned to Serria and me. "So he's a reporter."

"Yeah," I said. "Which would account for his following Audra Gardner, Victoria Carrington, Tata Andolini, or anyone else, for that matter."

The black cop said to Fabio, "You wanna press charges?"

"Goddamned right. The guy's out of his mind, a menace."

"I'll kill you!" the Hat screamed and tried to kick Fabio again. "You stay away from Tata or I'll kill you!"

"You're under arrest, Matt," the Asian cop said. "You have the right to remain silent. And if I were you, I'd shut the fuck up."

"Oh, yeah?" The Hat spit at the cop. Sick of this crap, the cop seized him by the scruff of the neck, twisted the cuffs, causing him to shriek in pain. He dragged the Hat kicking and cursing to a police car. "Accidently" banged his head into the doorframe as he shoved him into the caged rear.

An ambulance pulled onto the scene and attended to Fabio.

"Okay, we've gotta find out what the Hat's talking about," I said, knowing that since he'd gone to the 19th Precinct in an attempt to have me arrested after our little, uh, "altercation" at the Beacon Theatre, I couldn't interview him. "Destiny, talk to him?"

Destiny showed her ID to the Asian cop and asked if she could speak to the Hat. The cop said it was okay. Serria and I took a position at the rear of the blue and white, out of the Hat's sight, so we could overhear the conversation. Destiny sat in the car's front-passenger seat, left the door opened, and spoke through the cage. "Hello, Matt."

"I know you," the Hat croaked. "You were with that asshole that hit me."

"You frightened Tata," Destiny said, reeling from the Hat's rancid beer and cigarette breath. "What do you expect?"

"I would never hurt Tata. I just wanted a picture."

Destiny gestured at Fabio. "Why do you say he killed Audra Gardner?"

"'Cause he did. And now he's after Tata."

"How do you know that?"

"I'm not telling you shit," the Hat said, and glared out the window.

"You do realize we're on the same side, Matt?" Destiny said. "I mean, you say you want to protect Tata. I get paid to protect her. Besides, I can help you."

"Yeah? How?"

"I'll put in a good word with the DA. Tell him you cooperated."

The Hat thought about that. "You'll tell the DA I'm not stalking Tata? That I'm protecting her?"

"I'll tell him," Destiny said.

The Hat seemed content with that. "Tata was in the Promises

rehab center out on Long Island. I saw that prick out there." He gestured toward Fabio. "Twice."

"That doesn't prove anything," Destiny said. "The guy's an entertainment reporter. It's his job to dig up scoops on celebrities. Besides, there are bigger stars than Tata in Promises. Why do you think he's after Tata?"

"You don't believe me," the Hat shouted and kicked the back of Destiny's car seat. "No one ever believes me!"

"Take it easy, Matt," Destiny said, annoyed by the thump. "You'll have a stroke." She peered harder at him. "What happened to you anyway? You're all banged up."

"Those security guards," he indicated the Soho House, "beat the shit out of me. I tried to tell them that prick was stalking Tata. But they wouldn't listen to me. No one ever listens to me."

"I thought maybe you were hurt in the car accident," Destiny said, "out at the rehab center?"

"That wasn't my fault!" the Hat hollered. "I swear. Some crazy bastard tried to run me off the road."

"Why would he do that?"

"He probably thought I was stalking Tata. But I wasn't. I was protecting her. You'll remember to tell the DA, right? I'm not stalking Tata. I'm protecting her."

"I'll tell him." Destiny exited the RMP. She twirled her finger around her ear as she approached us.

"You heard," Destiny said. "He's a nutcase."

"Just for the hell of it," I said. "Contact your friend in the credit agency. Let's check Fabio's whereabouts against all the Angel of Death murders. And do a background check on him while you're at it?"

"My pleasure." Destiny smiled.

I scowled. "Now, let's go look at the security tapes."

CHAPTER 38

SERRIA LED US through the police lines into the main entrance of the Soho House. The two beefy security guards, probably the same ones who'd clobbered the Hat, nodded to Serria and waved us through. We moved down a first-floor hall and entered an impressive modern security office, where the metallic scent of electronics mixed with the aroma of fresh coffee.

We were greeted by a couple of ex-cops that Serria knew from who knows where. I told the guy in charge, a retired sergeant, that we were investigating the two overdose deaths. Trying to determine who'd sold the victims the drugs. He suggested that we'd better hurry and review the lobby and penthouse elevator video before the guys from narcotics confiscated them.

While Serria and I settled in front of a series of computer screens, each with a different feed from different locations—rooftop pool, bar, restaurant, etc.—Destiny worked her phone. She called a friend, the director of security at one of the big-three credit agencies. She'd supply Destiny with Fabio's credit-card charge history, which could very well pinpoint his locations on specific dates and times. Then she'd phone one of our contacts in the NYPD detective division, run Fabio's name though the system.

"Watch the center screen," the guy at the controls said. "Rolling tape."

A succession of individuals—Sid Schulsky, Meg Dorvitz,

followed by some of the crowd from *Jersey Shore Confidential*—entered the lobby. Elevator load by elevator load, familiar faces moved across the computer screen. I remembered Tata calling them: Monkey Man, Hood Rat, Sleepy Joe, just to name a few. The guidos and guidettes all appeared to be in their early twenties—too young by far to be the Angel of Death. Bringing up the rear was Nicky Bada-bing and the felon Sean Keating, the red-bearded punk that Destiny had once arrested. So that explained why the Teamster Keating was associating with the talent. He was Nicky's friend.

The traffic entering the penthouse elevator slowed to a trickle. We fast-forwarded until everyone began leaving, jamming into the elevator. Tata, obviously stoned, had to be practically carried by Nicky Bada-bing and Sid Schulsky.

"Can we see the exterior tape?" I said. "Same time frame?"

The guy at the controls keyed the exterior tape and let it roll; it was a wide shot that took in the entire sidewalk in front of the building. The milling press, stalkerazzi, and fans filled the frame. "There's the Hat," I said, pointing at the screen; he was lurking between two parked news vans, focused on the Soho House entrance. After a few moments Tata, supported by Sid Schulsky, came weaving out. They crossed the sidewalk, out of frame, I assumed to hail a taxi. But the Hat did not follow. "See that?" I said. "He had to have seen Tata, but he didn't follow her."

"That's because he knows Fabio is still in Soho House," Destiny said. "Sort of gives credibility to his claim that he was not stalking Tata, but stalking Fabio."

We switched back to the interior elevator tapes, fast-forwarded as uniforms, ambulance attendants, and detectives came and went. We were about to stop watching when Serria and one surprise visitor stepped into the elevator.

"Freeze frame," Destiny said from over our shoulders. She pointed at the computer screen. "Solana Ortiz." She addressed Serria: "How'd she get in?"

"She begged me to let her take a picture of Victoria's body. Said it meant her keeping her job at the *Post*. But the guys from narcotics wouldn't allow it. Why? Is there a problem?"

"No, no problem," Destiny said, her expression blank.

Serria and all my Rockers had gotten to know Solana pretty well when she and I were living together. We double- and triple-dated often. We spent holidays together. Trips to Atlantic City and the Florida Keys. Being Bronx-born Hispanics, Serria and Solana shared a special bond. I recalled that they sometimes spoke Spanish to each other, laughed at private jokes. Now I found myself worrying, if during one of their many booze-fueled, private conversations, if Serria had ever been loose-lipped about my Rockers and our activities. If so, Solana's threats about cooperating with the feds took on a whole new meaning.

"I didn't see Fabio in the penthouse," Destiny said.

"You're right."

I asked the console guy, "Can we check the other feeds?"

"Sure." He rolled back each camera, and then let them play at once.

"There he is," Destiny said.

"That's the bar," the console guy said.

"Any way to determine when he arrived, when he left?"

The guy rewound several tapes. Then hit *play*. We saw Fabio enter the lobby, step into an elevator, and then the bar. He sat on a stool, ordered a beer; I noted the time. We fast-forwarded; Fabio did not leave the bar until after Victoria's body was removed from the suite. And then he entered an elevator, rode down alone to the street where the Hat was lying in wait. The fact that Fabio had no interaction of any kind with Tata or Victoria—or anyone else, for that matter— belied the Hat's claims that Fabio was trying to kill anyone. No surprise there.

I nervously scanned the rooftops as we stepped out onto Ninth Avenue. The stalkerazzi were gone, as were most of the news vans, fans, and cops. Destiny's phone rang. She took out a pad, took notes, ended that call, and then fielded another.

"Okay," Destiny said to me after she'd ended the second call. "Daniel Caruso, aka, Fabio, has an eight-hundred and thirty FICO score. I think eight-fifty is the highest, so he's in good financial shape. According to his credit-card receipts"—she referred to her notes—"he was around when all of the six celebs died. And he was in town when your father had his accident—interesting. But it still doesn't prove anything." She flipped to the second page. "One DUI out in California five years ago. Divorced. Two kids. His ex has custody. Been with TMZ five years. Was with the *National Enquirer* before that."

"Military record?"

"Army," Destiny said. "Second lieutenant. One tour in Iraq." She closed the notepad. "Dishonorable discharge."

"No. Really?" I said.

"That's nothing," Serria said. "He could've been caught doing drugs."

"Maybe he was openly gay," I said.

"I'll bet he was fraternizing with female subordinates," Destiny said, a twinkle in her eye.

"We need to see his records," I said quickly, annoyed by her allusion.

"Won't be easy," Destiny said.

That was when my phone rang. "Beckett."

"Hey, pally." It was my friend who worked as a clerk in the federal court system, the one who'd told me about Enia's legal problems.

"Whaddya got?"

"The woman you asked me about, Enia Petrescu, was just served with a federal grand-jury subpoena."

"No surprise there," I said. "Thanks for letting me know. I owe you one."

"Three," he said. "You owe me three."

I didn't know where this was going. "Okay."

"A woman, Solana Ortiz, is also set to testify."

Shit.

"And your old pal, Thomas McKee?"

I straightened. "What about him?"

"He is also being subpoenaed."

CHAPTER 39

THOMAS MCKEE WAS dozing on his living-room couch when his doorbell rang.

He startled awake, used a remote to mute the sound on his 65-inch Ultra HDTV. Walking barefoot across the carpet to his front door, he peered out a window and saw a male, white, dressed in nondescript clothing, lurking on his doorstep. *What the hell?* Silver Beach was not the type of community that cold-calling door-to-door salesmen, Jehovah's Witnesses, or con men frequented—Girl Scouts selling cookies, maybe.

McKee opened a coat-closet door, and underneath a neat pile of assorted, cashmere winter scarves on the top shelf, he retrieved an S&W .38 with a 2-inch barrel. He opened the cylinder, checked that the gun was loaded, and flipped it closed.

"Mr. McKee?" The guy rang the doorbell again, then knocked impatiently.

McKee held the gun to his side, cracked the door open, and barked, "What the fuck do you want?"

The guy raised his hands in surrender. "I'm only serving pro-cess." He reached into a pocket and pitched a blue document into McKee's foyer. "You've been served," he said, and hurried away.

McKee slammed the door. He picked up the document—he knew what it was before he opened it. A federal grand-jury sub-poena. He walked into this home office, sat at his desk, and read.

He was to testify the day after tomorrow at 11:00. "Shit!" McKee tossed the subpoena aside, looked at April's 8-by-10; as always, her smile touched his heart. "It's like the whole goddamned world is against me," he said to the photo. "Why can't I catch a break?

You know the reason why, April responded in McKee's mind. She was right.

He had acted carelessly, spent his cut of the Rocker booty on over-the-top home improvements, TVs, and ostentatious vanity jewelry; money he could not possibly account for. And he'd kept records of all those transactions on his computer. Records, he was pretty sure, the feds had in their possession.

He picked up April's photo. "It's just… it's so hard living without you."

I know, my love, April said.

McKee reached into a desk drawer, took out a glass and a bottle of Irish whiskey, along with another bottle of Prozac. He poured himself a three-finger shot, tossed it down. Poured himself another and drank that too. He knew that if he refused to testify or took the Fifth, at the very least he'd be handed over to the U.S. Department of Justice, and be prosecuted for criminal income-tax evasion. He could be sentenced to five years in prison plus a hefty fine.

If they granted him immunity and he refused to testify, he'd go to prison until he did. Bottom line: There was no way he could appear before the grand jury. His testimony would undoubtedly destroy Serria, Destiny, and Beckett. Sure, he resented Beckett, always had. After April's death, he'd even begun to despise him. Still, there was no way he'd turn rat. He was not about to be remembered as just another bad cop who'd turned rat to save his own ass, like grandstanding self-promoter Frank Serpico.

McKee got up. Sat down. Got up. Sat down. He downed another shot, and thought about disappearing. Yeah, that might work. He could fake his own death. Drive to a bridge somewhere, abandon his car, pretend to jump, leave a suicide note at home for the authorities to find. Or he could make a run for it, create some false ID. Head south, melt into the freak show that was the Florida Keys. Become a struggling artist. Maybe sell seashells by the seashore.

His phone rang. It was Destiny. He let it go to voice mail.

McKee poured himself another shot. Thought about the fact that the world was against him. He drank and paced and did his best to deal with the fact that he had painted himself into a corner; he had no options. He opened the bottle of Prozac, shook out two. He looked at April's photo. "God, how I miss you." He popped the pills into his mouth and swallowed them with the whiskey.

CHAPTER 40

"TALK TO ME, y'all," Assistant U.S. Attorney Melody Butcher said as she hurried along Duane Street, late for a meeting at the federal courthouse. "Make it quick. I've a dirtbag defendant ready to take a plea."

"We no longer have confidence in our anonymous informant," Sobel said, buttoning up his trench coat against a crosstown chill.

"That's just great," Butcher said, juggling her briefcase and laptop. "What changed your mind?"

"We're pretty sure he left a threatening message on Lisi's answering machine."

They paused as traffic raced south on Lafayette Street, then they crossed to Centre Street. "So he's informing on Lisi," she said, "while threatening him. Playing both sides."

"Apparently," Sobel said.

"No. Not apparently," Butcher said. "Look, I don't care what your informer's motives are. I believe him. No one retires from the mob. Lisi's involved somehow. Find the connection."

"That's what we're trying to do."

"Try harder." They continued north on Centre Street. "I've already stuck my neck out with the director. What about the safety-deposit key you found in Lisi's apartment?"

"There were no identifying marks, other than a serial number.

We're trying to match the key to a bank. Oh, there's one more thing—two more, actually."

Butcher sighed. "Are you going to ruin my day?"

"Someone tried to kill Lisi," Sobel said.

Butcher stopped in her tracks. "How?"

"He was driving," Sobel said. "A sniper took a shot. Missed Lisi, but caused a crash. He's in stable condition."

"Isn't that what allegedly happened to Beckett's father?" Butcher asked.

"It gets better," Englund said. "A sniper took a shot at Beckett and Jones too."

"What the hell's going on?" Butcher said. "Who's responsible?"

"My guess," Sobel said. "Our anonymous informer."

A fire truck raced north, sirens blaring.

"We've been going over Lisi's files," Sobel said. "It's starting to look like Beckett's father was on to something. A serial killer called the Angel of Death could very well be targeting, stalking, and killing celebrities—and anyone who gets in his way."

"That's the NYPD's problem," Butcher said. "Ours is the big picture."

Which Sobel and Englund knew that meant finding a way to link Beckett to the mob, and/or find a way to indict him and his Rockers for armed robbery, and Beckett for the murder of the IRA-connected terrorist, Lochlainn O'Brian. That, along with all the other allegations of police misconduct, would allow the U.S. attorney to take over the NYPD.

"Link Lisi to the mob," Butcher said. "Lisi to Beckett. And do it quickly. If you don't, I can promise that the two of you will be reassigned. I'm told Bismarck, North Dakota is nice this time of year."

"If there's a link, we'll find it," Sobel said, sounding beleaguered.

"And find that safety-deposit box. I'm afraid we'll need more than Enia Petrescu and Thomas McKee to sustain an indict-ment—that's if McKee will cooperate."

"He'll talk," Sobel said.

"From your lips," Butcher said, "to God's ears."

They turned onto Pearl Street, and Sobel's cell phone rang. He fished it out of his coat pocket.

"Sobel." He listened for a moment, then gave Butcher the thumbs-up sign. "Address?" He checked his wristwatch. "We'll be there in ten minutes," he said, hung up, and smiled.

"What?" Butcher said.

"We located Lisi's safety-deposit box."

Sobel and Englund walked into the bank and were greeted by a junior agent who introduced them to the bank manager. The manager escorted them to the rear of the bank, down a steep set of stairs and into an open vault containing over 750 safety-deposit boxes.

"When was last time someone accessed Lisi's safety- deposit box?" Sobel said.

"It's been twenty years," the manager said as he led them to the rear of the vault. He stopped in front of a row of medium-sized boxes. The manager inserted his key into one keyhole. The junior agent inserted the key found in Lisi's apartment. They both turned their keys at the same time. The manager slipped the box out, handed it to the junior agent, who carried it over to a small conference table.

"That will be all," Sobel said to the bank manager.

"This way," the junior agent said as he escorted the manger from the vault.

Sobel lifted the safety-deposit box lid. Inside was a stack of old voice cassettes along with some paperwork; it looked like an index of the cassettes. Sobel handed the list to Englund. Under the tapes was a stack of sealed envelopes addressed to the FBI,

Manhattan DA's office, and various news and media outlets. Below the envelopes was a single manila envelope. Sobel opened it and an old leather folio slipped out onto the table. Sobel flipped it open. "Holy shit," he said, and showed the folio to Englund.

"Holy shit," Englund said.

CHAPTER 41

"I HAVE TO ASK you, Ernie," I said as we walked up Ninth Avenue, away from the Soho House. I was speaking behind my hand just in case the feds were video-recording us. "You ever talk to Solana about our Rocking, you know, when we were all partying?"

Serria considered that before replying behind his hand. "I don't think so."

I continued to scan the rooftops. "She ever ask any questions about what we were doing?" I said. "Try to remember. It's important."

Serria shook his head. "No, she didn't. Why?"

"The feds subpoenaed her to testify at the grand jury."

"Her and Enia," Destiny said.

"Enia?" Serria said, and his face filled with pleasure. "Now, there's a name from the past."

"They subpoenaed McKee too," I said.

Serria didn't like that. "I haven't been able to reach McKee."

"I just tried," Destiny said.

"That unusual these days?" I said.

"No," Serria said. "Not really."

"I have to wonder," Destiny said behind her hand, "how McKee will handle being subpoenaed. He could be looking at jail time." She looked at Serria. "Ernie?"

"Then he'll do the time," Serria said decisively. "He won't talk. No way."

"You can't be sure," I said. "I mean, we all know he hasn't been himself lately."

Serria was shaking his head in absolute denial. "McKee would rather die than turn rat."

Destiny knew how tight they were, which didn't really help us at this point. She turned to me. "We have a plan?"

I voiced an idea that had been slowly developing in my mind. "The Angel of Death is trying to kill us. Why?"

"Same reason he killed your father," Destiny said, "and tried to kill Lisi. Because he thinks we know more than we know."

"Right," I said. "He's panicking."

"Yeah," Destiny said. "So?"

"What if we give him something to panic about?"

"Go on," Destiny said, always in favor of action.

"We flush him out. Use the media," I said. "Plant a story, maybe a blurb on Page Six, exposing the Angel of Death. List every celebrity homicide. Say we know who he is and that we're building a case. Say it's a matter of days before he's arrested."

"What if he sees the story and goes underground?" Serria asked.

"You have any better ideas?" I said. "Because I'm all ears."

"No responsible news organization would publish a story like that without some evidence," Destiny said. "All we really have is coincidence, speculation, uncorroborated facts. A theory—a thin one at that."

"Who said anything about a responsible news organization?" I said. "We go to the tabloids."

"Bob Kappstatter," Destiny said, "at the *Daily News*?"

I shook my head. "Kappy's a pro. He'd never fall for it. I was thinking the *Post*. And who do we know that's working at the *Post* and is desperate for a story?"

"Don't tell me," Destiny said with a shake of her head. "No. No way."

"Solana Ortiz?" Serria said.

"Solana Ortiz."

CHAPTER 42

"COME AND GET me before I smack someone," Lisi told me over the phone. "They use ketchup for marinara sauce. Can you believe it? I'm telling you, they're trying ta poison me in heah."

"We're on the way," I said, and hung up.

"You go," Destiny said as she slid into her Mazda MX-5. We were at Lisi's Ninetieth Street garage, where Serria had dropped us off before heading home to feed his dogs. "I'm gonna drive up to McKee's place." She started the engine. "See if I can find out what the hell's going on."

"Keep me posted," I said as Destiny drove off. I checked out Lisi's last working vehicle, an older SUV. I also noticed that the usual garage attendants were working again. I conducted the now-habitual search for listening and tracking devices, then headed out to Brookhaven Memorial Hospital.

A nurse, escorted by Officer Olive, pushed the former mafioso's wheelchair to the curb. Lisi's hair was a mess, his appearance disheveled, but his color was good and he was obviously anxious to leave the hospital. The nurse helped me load him into the passenger side of the SUV. Then Olive handed me a large white envelope; it was heavy. "It's his weapon," Olive said.

"Thank your boss for me."

"Hey, fucko," Lisi said as he strapped on his seat belt.

"When were you mooks planning on telling me about Victoria Carrington?"

"We didn't want to upset you," I said as I shifted into *drive*.

"Yeah? Well, I saw it onna TV. There goes our only A-list client." Lisi powered down the window, stuck a cigarette in his mouth and lit it.

"That the only thing bothering you?"

"Don't be a smart-ass," Lisi said. "Anything else youse haven't told me?"

"Someone took a shot at us last time we were out here." I drove out of the parking lot. "We wrecked your Jaguar."

"*Marrone.*" Lisi took a long pull on his smoke. "The killer thinks youse two know what he thinks I know."

I made a turn onto Sunrise Highway. "I have a plan to flush this guy out," I said. "Figure I'd recruit Solana to plant a story in the *Post*. Say that Lisi and Beckett knows the identity of the Angel of Death, that it's only a matter of time before he's arrested."

"Can't hurt," Lisi said, pleased with this idea. "I mean, he's shooting at us anyway. A story like that just might force him to expose himself, do something stupid. Besides, it could be good PR. God knows we need it after the Carrington fiasco."

Lisi switched on the radio and was snoring loudly a few minutes later. I woke him up as I parked in front of his building. Upstairs, as we approached his apartment, we saw something was taped to his front door. Lisi opened the document, glanced at it, then handed it to me.

It was a copy of an executed federal search warrant.

Lisi used his key to open the door. The place was a total mess. We stepped over piles of debris as we entered. Lisi walked into the dining room-living room area. I checked out the bedroom.

Lisi's bed and box spring were standing on end; they had been cut open and their guts ripped out. The closet was open, its contents strewn around the floor. All the bureau drawers had been pulled out and the contents dumped.

"They didn't have to be this destructive," I called out.

"They're sending a message," Lisi replied.

Then I noticed that the box containing the Angel of Death files were not where we'd left them. I looked behind the mattress. Searched under the debris on the floor. Double-checked the closet. The files were nowhere to be found.

"Oh, no," Lisi said from the living room.

"What?" I came up behind him. He was down on one knee, alongside a rolled-up area rug, fiddling with a floorboard that had been pried up and was lying askew.

"What'd they get?" I asked.

"You wouldn't believe me," Lisi said, "if I told you."

CHAPTER 43

"**E**XCUSE ME?" ASSISTANT U.S. Attorney Melody Butcher said to Sobel and Englund as she stepped out of an official government car in front of the Hotel Wales on Madison Avenue and East Ninety-second Street. The two feds had been spending the evening standing under the out-of-the-way boutique hotel's awning, watching the girls go by, waiting for Butcher to arrive. The three were on their way to prep Enia Petrescu on her grand- jury testimony in the morning. "Say that again?"

Sobel handed over the worn, cracked leather folio they'd discovered in Lisi's safety-deposit box. Butcher flipped it open, scrutinized a yellowed ID card and photo. "Well, I declare." She handed back the ID. "Lisi was FBI?"

"Thirty years ago," Englund said.

They walked through the stuffy, sparse European-style lobby to the elevators in the rear. Englund pressed the *up* button. "Lisi was recruited while he was still in the Marine Corps," Englund said. "He was an undercover military cop. Made some good arrests. Got the Bureau's attention."

"After training," Sobel said, "he was assigned to a deep-cover organized-crime investigation called Operation Godfather. Lisi was supposed to be another Donnie Brasco." They stepped inside an arriving elevator and Englund pressed the *PH* button. The doors swished closed.

"Growing up, he hung around in the Italian section of East Harlem," Englund said, "with guys who were born into the mob. He was the perfect undercover agent. Everyone already knew him." The elevator door opened and the three proceeded down the hall.

"We located a retired agent who supervised him," Sobel said. "He told us that after Lisi was shot, he abruptly resigned from the Bureau."

"That's when he quit the mob too, right?"

"Turns out he didn't just quit," Sobel said. "He threatened Big Paul. Told him he knew where bodies were buried. Literally. That he'd written everything down, had secret tape recordings—he wasn't bluffing."

Opening a briefcase, Englund showed Butcher the tapes and the stack of envelopes addressed to various law-enforcement entities and media outlets.

"He told Big Paul that if anything should happen to him—if he was hit by a car, killed during a street mugging, or struck by a bolt of lightning—that the authorities and the media would automatically get copies of his notes and tapes."

"Good stuff," Butcher said. "Give what you've got to our organized-crime people. Dismantling the Mafia, even the old guard, is always good PR."

"The old guard is the problem," Sobel said. "Most of the mobsters Lisi incriminates are either dead or infirm."

That brought up another question for Butcher. She paused outside the penthouse and turned to face the two feds. "You think Beckett's father knew about Lisi?"

"The way deep undercovers operate?" Sobel shook his head. "No. I doubt anyone outside of his Bureau handlers and their supervisors knew."

"So Lisi withheld this incriminating evidence from the Bureau?" Butcher said.

"Far as we can determine," Englund said. "Yes."

"But we can't touch him," Sobel said. "The statute of limitations."

"Unless he's still involved with organized crime," Butcher said. "Which would constitute an ongoing criminal conspiracy. Is he?"

Sobel shook his head. "There's no evidence. We've done everything but a rectal examine. Far as we can tell, Lisi's clean."

Butcher rang the penthouse doorbell with a sharp tap. "That leaves us with two of Beckett's ex-girlfriends and Officer McKee to present before the grand jury." She rang the bell again. Knocked impatiently. "Hello?" She turned back to the two feds. "I want you to focus on McKee. Pressure him. Do whatever you have to do to flip him."

"Will do," Sobel said.

"Hello in there." Again Butcher knocked, leaned on the bell. "What the hell's going on?" She checked her wristwatch. "I told them to expect us."

Sobel eased Butcher out of the way. He pounded on the door. Put his ear to it. "Something's not right." He spotted a maid down the hall.

"Miss?" Sobel called out. "Come here, please."

The maid complied. "Yes, sir?"

Sobel flashed his identification and told her to open the penthouse door. The maid swiped a master key card. The door popped open. Sobel and Englund pulled their weapons, eased into the suite combat-ready.

They saw the female special agent first. She was lying on her side on a sofa, eyes closed. An overturned cup of coffee and sterling-silver coffee urn lay on the carpet. Sobel rushed to check her pulse.

"Mother of God," Butcher said. "Is she—?"

"She's okay," Sobel said. He picked up the cup of coffee, sniffed.

"In here," Englund said.

Sobel and Butcher rushed into a bedroom. The male agent was laying prone on the floor, snoring loudly; a broken coffee cup lay beside him.

"Where's Enia Petrescu?" Butcher said.

The two agents searched the penthouse.

"Not here," Englund said, coming out of a bedroom, holstering his weapon.

"Not in here either," Sobel said, exiting another room, carrying a small prescription bottle in his hand. He read the label. "Lormetazepam. They were drugged."

"Shit," Butcher said. "She has to be found."

Sobel spied a room-service receipt lying on the floor beside the coffee urn. He used a napkin to dab it dry; the coffee had been delivered at 6:05 that evening. He checked his wristwatch. "She has a four-hour head start." Sobel addressed Englund. "Call it in. Lock everything down. The airports. Bus and train stations. Rental-car companies, the usual."

"But she's got a four-hour head start."

"Just do it!" Sobel snapped, knowing in his gut that they'd never see Enia Petrescu again.

CHAPTER 44

ESTINY PARKED BEHIND McKee's car on the bluff overlooking the East River and the Long Island Sound. She noticed that the tree-lined neighborhood was country-quiet, and realized that she hadn't been to McKee's home in years. His house was dark, so she dialed McKee's home number. No answer. She tried McKee's cell. Straight to voice mail.

As Destiny stepped out of her car, she was swathed in a pleasant, cool saltwater breeze. She checked McKee's Dodge by placing her hand on the engine hood: cold. She scanned the area for federal surveillance. Didn't see any. She walked up McKee's newly paved footpath and took in the lavish landscaping. Why, she wondered, would her police academy classmate call attention to himself like that? He'd made himself vulnerable to any jealous neighbor.

After he didn't answer his door, Destiny peeked in a window, but the drapes were drawn. She was about to give up, figured McKee had gone off somewhere and left his car, when she thought she heard music.

Destiny walked around to the side of the house, her feet sinking into the lush turf—more ostentatious money. The music grew louder and she heard voices. A faint scent of chlorine filled the air as she rounded the corner into the backyard. McKee was alone in his bubbling Jacuzzi, a glass of champagne in his hand.

"Thomas!" Destiny called out over the sound of the Jacuzzi jets.

McKee startled. "Destiny." He broke into a wide smile. "Get yourself something to drink and join us."

Us? Destiny looked around. "You have company?"

"Not really." McKee grinned stupidly.

Destiny walked into the house, worried about that piece of weirdness. She'd definitely heard him talking to someone— who wasn't there. McKee's kitchen was completely redone, a showpiece that could very well be featured in *Better Homes and Gardens.* Feeling an increasing dread, she found a glass, opened the Sub-Zero refrigerator, and poured some white wine. She saw the federal subpoena lying on the granite counter. She carried her drink out to the Jacuzzi. "Cheers."

"Work is the curse of the drinking class," McKee toasted.

Destiny pulled up a patio chair and saw that an open bottle of champagne along with a full flute glass were set in front of an 8-by-10 framed photo of April. That explained the missing someone.

"So, what brings you to Château McKee?" McKee said.

"Where you been?" she said, starting off neutral.

"Here and there."

McKee switched the Jacuzzi jests to low, gestured with his glass to April's photo. "Tomorrow is April's birthday."

Is. The present tense. "I saw the subpoena," Destiny said.

"Yeah?"

"When were you planning to tell me about it?"

"There's nothing much to tell," McKee said. "I'm to testify before a federal grand jury tomorrow at eleven. It's not a problem."

"Really?" Destiny said. "They give you immunity?"

"No," McKee said. "But I wouldn't be surprised if they offer it."

"Why you?" Destiny said. "And not the rest of us?"

"Because, my friend, I screwed up. Big-time." McKee waved his hand, encompassing his spiffy new place. "If they saw what was on my computer, they've got me for income-tax evasion."

"You kept records?" Destiny asked, her stomach sinking.

McKee refilled his glass. "I kept records."

"What're you gonna do?"

"What can I do?" McKee broke into a lopsided grin. "I'm gonna be a man, and take it like a woman."

"Hell does that mean?"

"Seriously?" McKee said. "I'm gonna ignore the subpoena."

"Yeah." Destiny sniggered. "Right." She drank more wine.

McKee said, "So, what's going on with you and Beckett?"

"What do you mean?"

"He's still in love with you, you know that?"

Destiny wasn't surprised her old Rocker buddy had noticed. "I know."

"You still in love with him?"

"You writing a book or something?"

"You date anyone since you two broke up?" McKee asked.

Destiny shook her head. "No."

"Why not?"

"I'm waiting for Denzel Washington to call."

McKee ignored her sarcasm. "Beckett hasn't dated anyone either." He sipped some champagne. "Wanna know what I think?"

"Not in the least."

"You're too good for him."

Destiny laughed a little. McKee always was a romantic. "You don't know what you're talking about."

"If you say so."

"I say so." Destiny thought of all the stuff she'd put Beckett through. No, no question who was better. By now he could be nominated for sainthood. "So, you've got a lawyer, I assume."

McKee shook his head. "No, I don't."

Another very bad sign. "You trying to be a comedian, or are you out of your mind?"

McKee laughed. "Opinions vary."

"You know as well as I do," Destiny said. "You don't show at the grand jury, they'll come get you."

"What's your problem, my sister? You think I'd betray you? That I'd turn rat?"

Honestly, she didn't know what to think. "No."

"There's one of April's old bathing suits up in my room. Go change"—he switched the Jacuzzi jets back to high, raised his glass, then his voice—"and get your pretty little ass into the hot tub."

CHAPTER 45

"I STOPPED BY MCKEE'S place," Destiny said over the phone.

"He there?"

"Yeah."

"Hell's his problem?"

"I'm not sure," Destiny said. "He said he's going to ignore the grand-jury subpoena."

"Yeah," I said. "Right—he serious?"

"I think he's gonna run."

"Run? Run where?"

"Hell do I know? Honestly, I'm worried about his mental state."

"You're not the only one." I was standing in the midst of a jovial happy-hour crowd, at the far end of Rathbones bar, waiting for Solana Ortiz to arrive. Charlie the bartender had just served me a beer. Amazingly, there was no sporting event of any consequence on TV. Every one of the bar's eight 60-inch plasmas were tuned to the entertainment news: Victoria Carrington's death was on every screen.

"McKee won't rat," Destiny said. "But there's no way he'll go to jail. No way."

"He runs, he'll be caught," I said.

"Wish I knew what he was thinking."

"If you don't know, no one does."

"Where're you?" Destiny said.

"Rathbones. Waiting for Solana."

"That bitch is nothing but trouble," Destiny said. "A user."

"Hey," I said. "We're using her this time."

"That's what you think." Destiny hung up.

Rathbones's door swung open and Solana breezed in. Every guy in the bar stopped to look. Her eyes swept the room, and several inebriated Romeos—goofballs dressed like tackling dummies—made their play. I waved and she brushed past the riffraff.

"Before you say a word," Solana said as she approached, "I apologize. I know it sounded like I was threatening you at the hospital, but I was frustrated, desperate. I need this job." Her face was flushed and she was short of breath.

"I know," I said. "That's why I called—you okay?"

"No," she said, "I'm not." She reached into her purse. "They're making me testify before a grand jury tomorrow." She produced the subpoena. "I already answered their questions. I'm scared to death."

I glanced at the subpoena and handed it back. "There's nothing to be afraid of." I choose my next words carefully, just in case the feds had forced her to wear a wire. "All you can do is tell the truth as you remember it—after, what? Three years?"

"Yeah." Solana put the subpoena back in her purse. "I guess you're right. But I need for you to understand, I'd never do anything to hurt you. And you know how I feel about Ernie Serria."

"He said to say hi." A party of four excused themselves as they squeezed past us, heading out the door. I lowered my voice, leaned close to Solana. "You ready to hear about the hot story I mentioned?"

Her clouded expression cleared immediately. "Yes!"

"Let's get a table."

We walked into the back room, slid into a booth. I sat facing front where I could see who came and went. A waitress appeared and Solana ordered white wine. We both glanced at the Victoria Carrington coverage.

"She had everything," Solana said. "Youth. Beauty. Talent." A waitress walked past, carrying a large plate of pungent, mouthwatering chicken wings.

"There's more to her death than meets the eye, you know," I said.

"Really?"

Our waitress brought our drinks. We lifted our glasses, clinked and drank.

Solana blurted out, "I'm sorry we broke up the way we did."

That took me by surprise.

"Did you know that you were my first real love?" she said.

That touched me, sort of. Until I remembered how she dumped me. "No, I didn't."

"You saved my life. Took care of me, treated me better than any man has before, or since. You were my knight in shining armor."

I bit back a couple of spiteful remarks and forced a smile. "We shared something special."

"Yes," Solana said. "It really was."

The waitress laid menus down on the table and walked away.

"You hungry?" I said.

"Not very."

"Well, are you ready to hear the scoop of a lifetime?"

"Am I ever." She took out a notepad and a pen.

I leaned forward. "It all began about ten years ago...."

Solana listened, rapt, took copious notes as I laid out the entire Angel of Death conspiracy, leaving out only my father's murder and murder attempts on Lisi, me, and Destiny—I didn't wish to confuse her. I started with the first A-list celebrity death from fentanyl-laced heroin, onto the Audra Gardner death, which had piqued my father's interest, and exposed the conspiracy, and ended with Victoria Carrington.

"From what I hear, the feds and the NYPD have formed a joint task force." I lied with a straight face, knowing that, if I told her the truth—that no one in law enforcement believed in the Angel of Death conspiracy—the story would never see publication. "But it's an ongoing, hush-hush investigation."

"I understand," Solana said breathlessly.

"So I can't let you have the names of the investigators who are involved," I said. "Not yet, anyway." I figured the specifics wouldn't bother her too much. Only cops had to have their facts straight.

"This story is sensational!"

"Right? The crime story of the decade," I said. "There's a book here, a TV movie, maybe even a feature film."

"You know the identity of the Angel of Death?"

"We think we do." I sipped my beer to help hide the lie. "But we've no way to prove it—that's where you come in." I leaned in closer, like a conspirator. "A small article, maybe a mention on Page Six. You know, one of those: 'Bodyguard to the stars, Lisi and Beckett Protective Services, Inc., is close to reveling the identity of a serial killer called the Angel of Death, who stalks and murders A-list celebrities.' Something like that might flush him out. Cause him to expose himself, make a fatal mistake."

"I could write this up as an exposé," Solana said, her eyes wide with enthusiasm. "Push the glamour angle, the celebrity victims."

"That's it," I said. "But like I said, I'll be happy with a blurb on Page Six."

"I'll do my best," Solana said. "No promises." She put her pad and pen away. "Can I ask you for a favor?"

"Sure." I had a pretty good idea what she wanted.

"I'm embarrassed."

Now I was sure. "Don't be."

"I need two hundred and fifty dollars. I can pay you back in two weeks. As soon as I get my paycheck."

"Of course." I reached for my wallet. By a miracle, I just happened to have the cash on me.

I'd always paid our bills and supplemented Solana's paltry *Law & Order* apprenticeship writer's income. Which only seemed fair since I'd been receiving two paychecks: one from the NYPD, the other as an actor for portraying the doomed Detective Eric Stone for two seasons. (The actor salary was more than ten times what the NYPD paid me.) Not that Solana had ever shown any appreciation for my generosity.

"No hurry paying me back," I said as I handed her the cash, knowing I'd never see the money again anyway.

Solana slipped the money into her purse. Effusively, she reached across the table and squeezed my hand. "You're saving me. Again. Seems you're always saving me." There were phony-baloney tears in her eyes. "If you ever need me for anything, anything at all—"

"All I have to do is whistle?" I said, a line from an old Humphrey Bogart and Lauren Bacall movie and a running gag of ours.

"You know how to whistle, don't you?" Solana said, playing her part. "You just put your lips together and blow...."

CHAPTER 46

"THAT CRAZY BITCH gone yet?" Destiny said over the phone.

"Just put her in a cab," I said, smiling.

"Be right there," Destiny said and hung up.

I had now taken a perch on my favorite stool at the head of the bar. Charlie served me a beer, and I noticed that the TVs were no longer turned to the Victoria Carrington debacle—finally—but to a pregame show. The usual bouncer, Danny Noonan—a six-foot-three, off-duty firefighter and old friend—was stationed at the entrance, checking customer IDs. A line was forming out front. The place would soon be crowded with young sports fans.

Destiny hugged Noonan as she walked in. She fended off come-ons from the same drunken goofballs who'd hit on Solana. "Give me a break, douche bag." Destiny shoved them aside and sat on the stool next to me. She hung her purse on a handbag hook under the bar and her phone chirped as a text came in. "There's another one."

"Another what?"

"Guys from the old four-one and the nineteenth are bugging me."

"I know," I said. "I've been getting messages."

"So, you gonna have a retirement party, or not?"

"Not."

Charlie came smiling over, handed Destiny a glass of white wine, and blew her a kiss.

"So, the crazy bitch bite?" Destiny took a nonchalant sip of her wine.

"Big-time," I said. "She's hot for the story."

"I'll bet. What else she hot for?"

I decided to stick it to her a little. "You wouldn't believe me," I said, "if I told you."

"Try me."

"Okay." I turned to face Destiny full on. "Solana told me that she's sorry we broke up. That I was her knight in shining armor: the best, most generous, kindest man she'd ever known."

"As if." Destiny snickered. "C'mon. What'd she say, really?"

I was not about to tell her that Solana had asked for the $250 loan, plus another $20 for cab fare; she'd only berate me for being conned. "Where's Lisi?"

Destiny gestured outside.

Alarmed, I got off my stool, stepped over to a large window that overlooked Second Avenue, saw Lisi through the growing queue of Rathbones customers. He was standing by the curb, smoking a cigarette, talking on his cell phone. "What's he doing?" I said. "He knows there could be a sniper out there."

"He knows." Destiny joined me at the window. "He's still hurting, should be home in bed." She gave me a slight elbow in the ribs. I flinched. "Touchy. How're you feeling?"

"Banged up. You?"

"A little sore." She careened her neck. "The dammed air bags did more damage than the crash. At least my headaches are gone."

I'd forgotten all about Destiny's headaches. I studied her surreptitiously, didn't see any evidence of her ingesting drugs. I can't express how happy I was about that.

"What?" she said.

"I was thinking."

"How refreshing."

"If McKee runs," I said, "Enia's their whole case."

"What about Solana?"

"From what she just told me, I don't think she'll be a problem."

Lisi walked in stinking of cigarettes and saddled up to the bar. "Just talking to Vincenzo Andolini, Tata's father," Lisi said. "Cops from narcotics showed up at his restaurant. Wanted to question Tata; he wouldn't let them." Lisi settled on a stool. "But that ain't what's worrying him. He's worried about her stalker."

"Matt the Hat?" I said.

"That's what I want youse two to find out." Lisi handed me a piece of paper. "That's the address a' the restaurant." Lisi asked Charlie for his usual. "I feel like shit, so I told Vincenzo to expect youse two."

"Want us to walk you home first?" I said.

Lisi gave me a long look. "Hey, fucko," he said, picking up his drink. "I just got heah."

CHAPTER 47

TWENTY MINUTES LATER, we were driving south on Lafayette Street. We passed a small triangular park named in honor of Lieutenant Giuseppe "Joseph" Petrosino, a decorated NYPD officer from the early years of the last century who put hundreds of Mafia members behind bars. Destiny turned left onto Grand Street, pulled to the curb and parked just east of Mulberry Street. She tossed the NYPD parking plaque on the dashboard as we exited the vehicle and walked into Andolini's of Little Italy.

The birthplace and former stronghold of the American Mafia, Little Italy conjured up romantic images of Hollywood movies and TV shows filmed on its streets: the three *Godfather* movies, *Donnie Brasco*, *The Sopranos*, just to name a few. But in reality, life in Little Italy, once described as "the foul core of New York's slums," was anything but romantic. The Mafia had ruled the neighborhood, one of the poorest and most densely populated slums, until the end of the twentieth century. That's when John Gotti, at the time La Cosa Nostra's *capo di tutti capi*, was sent away to prison.

Today, because of gentrification, skyrocketing rents, and a yuppie invasion, traditional Little Italy had been driven to the verge of extinction. Once a teeming neighborhood stretching fifty square blocks and populated by over 10,000 Italians, it barely covered three blocks of Mulberry Street—and even that strip was under threat.

We breathed in Andolini's mouthwatering aromas as we stepped through the door. The authentic Old World eatery was not an elegant, high-end café, but—with its checkered table-cloths, brick walls, and large Italian landscape paintings—a warm and cozy neighborhood bistro.

The same gorilla we'd seen help Tata's father carry her into rehab greeted us from behind a tall wooden hostess stand. The name tag on his starched white shirt read. *BRUNO* "Table for two?"

"We're here to see Vincenzo," I said. "Tommy Lisi sent us."

"*Onea momento*," Bruno said with a New York accent. He picked up a phone, lowered his voice, turned his back to us as he spoke. After a moment Bruno hung up. "This way."

We followed him out of the restaurant and took an immediate left into what appeared to be a residential entrance. Bruno used a key to unlock the front door, another key for a foyer door, then led us up a set of carpeted wooden stairs into a large living room.

"Have a seat. My father will be with you in a moment," Bruno said.

We sat on a couch that was covered with thick, clear plastic. Besides the elaborate, heavy Victorian furnishings, I counted five—no, six—ancient-looking religious oil paintings: three of the Madonna, three of the Crucifixion. I recalled watching an *Antiques Roadshow* episode with Destiny where similar paintings were referred to as the proto-Renaissance style, or something like that.

All at once the air was thick with an astringent eye-burning scent. Bug spray?

"What's that smell?" Destiny wrinkled her nose.

"My father," Bruno said.

"*Buon giorno*," Vincenzo Andolini said as he waddled into the room. "*Mi chiamo* Signor Vincenzo Andolini—I mean, I'ma Vincenzo Andolini." Vincenzo spoke pretty good broken English. His short hair was dyed jet-black and greased back.

His Cheshire-cat, white-on-white smile was set in a creepy-dark sun-bed tan. The velour leisure suit he wore was too small for his roly-poly frame—the man had more chins then a Chinatown phone book. Large diamond-encrusted rings sparkled from both pinky fingers.

"I'm Michael Beckett."

"And whosa thisa lovely lady?" Vincenzo said, brushing me aside.

"I'm Destiny Jones. Nice to meet you, Mr. Andolini."

Vincenzo made a show of looking Destiny over from head to toe. "*Bella.*" He took Destiny's hand, bowed and kissed it. "Pleasea, calla me Vincenzo."

"Thank you, Vincenzo," Destiny said. She took back her hand and wiped it on her slacks.

"Woulda you care for any refresh-a-ments?"

We said we didn't.

Vincenzo said to his son, "Bruno, *una bottiglia di vino.*" Bruno left the room.

"Is Tata staying here with you?" Destiny said.

Vincenzo stiffened. "We don't usea that name here!" His face flushed with anger. "Her name isa *Francine*, after my sainteda mother." Vincenzo blessed himself. "May she resta in peace."

I blessed myself. "May she rest in peace."

"I'm sorry," Destiny said. "I didn't mean to—"

"Yeah. Yeah. It'sa okay." Vincenzo dropped onto an easy chair. "Justa so you know."

"Vincenzo," I said. "Lisi told us Francine is being stalked?"

"That'sa whata she says." Vincenzo sat back, crossed his pudgy legs. "Buta before we geta started, answer somethinga for me?"

"We'll try," I said.

Vincenzo made a visible show of gathering his thoughts. "You ever seea Francine'sa TV show?"

We both lied, said we seen an episode or two.

"Thena maybe you cana tella me: What's her appeal? I meana,

she'sa my daughter, I love her. She'sa beautiful to me, but come on. She'sa not conventionally attractive. I see her onna TV. I see her jumping up ona tables, hooting and hollering, anda I'll saya to someone, 'What drawsa you to my daughter? Be honest.' Because it's very harda for me to seea what it is. She doesn't singa. Dance. Act. She'sa not especially intelligent. I'ma not saying she hasa no talent, but let'sa be honest…"

"I think," Destiny said, "that people can relate to her."

"That's it?" Vincenzo said. "Simple asa that?"

Destiny was in her element, explaining about stars. "That would be my guess."

Vincenzo thought that over. "I stilla don't get it." He leaned forward, elbows on knees. "Lisi tella you, the cops were here?"

I nodded. "They question Francine?"

"She'sa not in any condition to bea questioned," Vincenzo said. "What'sa going on?"

I filled Vincenzo in on his daughter leaving rehab with the superstar Victoria Carrington, then the events that led to Victoria's overdose death at the Soho House.

"Christ," Vincenzo said. "I'ma lucky she'sa alive." Bruno reappeared with a sterling-silver tray on which sat a bottle of red wine and glass. Bruno poured a glass for his father and disappeared again. Vincenzo took a sip, put the glass on the coffee table. "You know, I puta Francine ina rehab half-a-dozen timesa." He shrugged. "She breaks outa every time. This timea her press agent, this stupido idiota named Sid Schulsky, drops her offa here after this Soho House incidente. She'sa stoneda outa her mind. I screamed ata the guy, threw him out—why I'ma paying gooda money for her to have a press agent, I'vea no idea. Then I calla my doctor. He sedated her. I'vea got her locked upa here, ina bedroom. A psychiatric nurse isa with her." Vincenzo scrubbed his face with both hands. "I'ma telling you, I'ma ata my wit's end."

"The cops are trying to find out who supplied the tainted heroin. They'll be back."

Destiny said, "About Francine's stalker: She receive threats?"

"You tella me." With a helpless look, Vincenzo reached into his leisure-suit pocket, picked out a cell phone and handed it to Destiny. "That'sa Francine's phone."

"How about her computer?" Destiny said.

Vincenzo gestured with his big head. "Over there. Ona dining-rooma table. That'sa her lap-a-top. I tolda her not to leave it there." Again Vincenzo shrugged. "She don'ta listen to me."

We walked over to a dining-room area, pulled up chairs, and sat down. I was curious to see if the dingbat actually had some actionable information.

"I feel like I'm in a time warp," Destiny whispered, scrutinizing our surroundings. "Very retro—1950s."

"What do you think of Vincenzo?"

Destiny thought a moment. "There's something endearing about him."

Destiny began to checka Tata's—er, I mean, *check Francine's* cell phone. I flipped open the laptop. Going back one year, it took us twenty minutes to scan Tata's e-mails, texts, and instant messages. The D-list reality star had her fair share of bizarre fans, but we couldn't find anything we considered threatening, nothing from Matt the Hat. Nothing from the Angel of Death.

"Lisi's right," I said. "Tata probably made up the cyber-threats."

"Or erased them."

My cell phone vibrated. Destiny's rang at the same time.

We both checked our caller IDs: *Unknown.*

"A Skype conference call?" Destiny said.

"For both of us?" I said.

"Would Dr. Goldsamp call on Skype?" Destiny asked.

"Maybe," I said. "But why call me?"

We both toggled to speaker and waited for the caller's image to appear on our screens. All at once we were looking at McKee.

"You can all stop worrying," he slurred.

Destiny said, "You okay?"

"I mean about the grand jury."

I said, "We know what you mean."

"I'm no rat."

"We know," Destiny said.

"Just so you know," McKee said, and our screens went blank.

.

CHAPTER 48

MY DOORBELL WOKE me the following morning. I
glanced at my bedside clock: 9:54. I wasn't expecting
anyone. I rolled over, pulled the covers over my head.
But then I remembered with a start that the grand jury would
convene in six minutes. My eyes popped open. I was suddenly
wide awake. I wondered who'd testify first. Not that it mattered.

Solana wouldn't have anything incriminating to say, I hoped.
Enia would do her best to bury me. And McKee... well, we'd
have to see how that turned out.

My bell rang again. "It's me!" I heard Destiny shout.

"I'm coming!" I threw the covers aside and padded to the
front door, my back and shoulders still sore from the accident. I
looked out the peephole: Sure enough, Destiny was standing on
the other side.

"Open up," she said.

I unlocked the door. Destiny walked in carrying two con-
tainers of coffee, a newspaper, and a bag that I assumed contained breakfast.

"Hell you making me stand out there for?"

"I just got up," I said. "Be right back." I hurried to the back
bathroom, did my business. I slipped on a ball cap, a pair of
worn jeans, a sweatshirt, a pair of boat shoes and walked into

my sun-drenched living room. Destiny, a scowl on her face, was sitting on my leather couch.

"What's got your panties in a bunch?" I picked up a container of coffee from the coffee table. I flipped off the top, blew on the steaming beverage, took a cautious sip.

"This." Destiny held up a copy of the *New York Post*.

VICTORIA CARRINGTON MURDERED—Angel of Death Targets A-list Celebrities read the front-page headline. "Holy shit," I said and grabbed the paper.

A SERIAL KILLER'S TRAIL OF DEATH— *Exclusive by Solana Ortiz*. I read the article and realized that the *Post* had gone overboard, embellishing what I'd told Solana as only a tabloid would dare.

Destiny unwrapped two bagels. She picked up my remote and switched on the TV. For the next twenty minutes we ate in silence, watching the TV news, flipping stations every few minutes. Destiny checked the Internet news feeds; Victoria Carrington's murder had gone viral.

"Looks like every news station has a serial-killer 'consultant,'" Destiny said wryly.

Some of the so-called experts—mental-health professionals and academics with no law-enforcement experience—discussed a variety of topics related to serial murders, including common myths, definitions, typologies, pathology and causality, and forensics. I found at least a few of them interesting because they had retained actual experts.

"There is no generic profile of a serial murderer," a gray-haired guy who I knew was a retired supervisory FBI special agent from the Bureau's forensic-science division said on FOX. "Serial killers differ in many ways, including their motivations for killing and their behavior at the crime scene. The majority of serial killers are not reclusive, social misfits who live alone. They are not monsters and may not appear strange."

I switched to CNN. A woman who was a FBI crime analyst

was saying, "—many serial killers hide in plain sight within their communities. Serial murderers often have families and homes, are gainfully employed, and appear to be normal members of the community. Because many serial murderers can blend in so effortlessly, they are oftentimes overlooked by law enforcement and the public."

I surfed to ABC News. A retired NYPD detective and Harvard graduate we knew was saying: "However, not all serial killers are psychopaths and not all psychopaths are serial killers. If serial killers are psychopathic, they are able to assault, rape, and murder without concern for legal, moral, or social consequences. This allows them to do what they want, whenever they want."

My cell phone rang. "It's Lisi," I said.

Destiny killed the sound on the TV.

I activated the speakerphone. "I know what you're going to say, Tommy."

"What happened to the blurb on Page Six?" Lisi groused.

"That's what I'd like to know," I said.

"I mean, tryin' to con the killer is one thing, but this is like waving a red flag in front of a bull. And did yuhs hafa use our company name?"

"You're the one who wanted publicity," I said. "Remember?"

"Publicity is one thing, but this? *Marrone!*"

"Obviously, it's a slow news day," I said. "Whoever Solana pitched the story to decided to run with it."

"I'll bet the Angel a' Death is running too," Lisi said. "Outta the country."

"Maybe not," Destiny said.

"Whassat?" Lisi said.

"We all read the letters," Destiny said. "This guy's a psychopath who thinks he's doing God's work. He's not about to let us stop him. I think he'll come after us."

We were all silent for a moment. She was right, especially if he had killed my father. I'd be a natural target for him.

"None of us takes any unnecessary chances for the next few days," I said.

"How much more careful can we be?" Destiny asked. "We're already sneaking around, looking over our shoulders."

"From now on no one goes anywhere alone. Tommy, you need to go out," I said, "call and I'll come get you."

"What're you, *oobatz*?" Lisi said. "I ain't going anywhere. I'm locking myself innee apartment. The Angel a' Death wants me, he's gonna hafta come through my front door. *Capeesh*?"

CHAPTER 49

MCKEE HAD OFTEN thought about seeking help in order to deal with April's death— talking to a grief counselor, attending support groups, maybe speaking to a priest. He never did. As a matter of fact, he'd never spoken to anyone.

What he did do was invent a story. He told everyone that April's death was a tragic accident. While smoking a cigarette on the terrace of a San Diego high rise, she had leaned against a guardrail that gave way. To this day he'd never told anyone, even Destiny, the truth. Which was that April's death was a suicide.

No one knew why she had rented a room at a San Diego airport hotel. McKee liked to think she was on her way east for a surprise visit. According to the police, she had stayed up all night, mixed the antianxiety drug Xanax with booze. Early the next morning she wrote a suicide note—*I can no longer deal with being a burden to my children*—whatever that meant. Then she got dressed, walked out onto the terrace, built herself a platform with the outdoor furniture. She stepped up on to the makeshift dais, stepped over the railing, and jumped into the abyss, leaving McKee, her ex-husband, and her two daughters that she loved more than anything in the world to wonder why.

It just didn't make sense.

The eight-year long-distance relationship was the happiest time in his life. He and April had met at a birthday party in

Manhattan soon after he'd retired from the NYPD—not exactly love at first sight, but pretty close. He began to travel to April's home in Del Mar, north San Diego County, every chance he got. Rented short-term apartments on the ocean. (April wouldn't allow him to spend the nights with her when her daughters were home. Didn't wish to set a bad example.) Their connection grew to the point of distraction; McKee couldn't bear being separated from her. After two years they rented a beautiful four-bedroom home in San Diego's Carmel Valley together. Still keeping up appearances, McKee slept in his own room on the first floor. April and her daughters took the three bedrooms on the second floor. They all loved the house on Torrey View Court in the upscale gated community: the assortment of roses that lined their property fences, the small, narrow swimming pool—shaped like a penis!—and Jacuzzi. McKee built himself a first-class gym in the two-car garage.

While April toiled away in the three very successful, Southwestern-style restaurants she and her ex-husband owned, McKee volunteered to play Mr. Mom. He drove the girls to school, picked them up, drove them to dance classes, soccer practices, sleepovers, whatever was required. He'd had no idea that he'd enjoy the family life the way he did; he felt truly needed and useful for the first time in his life. But then April's ex-husband's longtime gambling addiction and serial philandering affected their business. Incredibly, in the course of five years, they lost all of their restaurants.

The business failures didn't appear to affect April—not outwardly anyway. She had mood swings—melancholy followed by high anxiety—but McKee presumed that all women had mood swings. Maybe it was the long distance, or maybe McKee was just plain thick, but he did not recognize the signs of clinical depression.

He checked the time. The grand jury would be in session soon. When he didn't appear, the U.S. Attorney would issue a warrant for his arrest. He estimated that the feds would be pounding on his door, arrest warrant in hand, by around noon at the latest.

A *ping* alerted McKee to an incoming e-mail. He walked into his home office and found that the youngest of April's daughters had written to thank him for the twenty-first birthday present he'd give her—a string of Tiffany pearls. That was the oddest experience. When he'd gone shopping for the present, he'd felt April's presence stronger than he ever had before. He felt like her spirit led him past dozens of stores, into Tiffany's, directly to a necklace display. McKee found himself pointing at the beautiful string of pearls. He was about to tell the saleslady to wrap it for a birthday gift when a voice in his head, April's voice, said, "You don't need wrapping paper, silly. Tiffany's blue box and bag are all that's necessary." As usual, she was right.

McKee wrote back that he loved and missed her and her sister, and hit *send*. He pushed to his feet and walked into his kitchen. A glance at the wall clock told him the grand jury was now in session.

He sat at the counter, popped another Prozac, washed it down with whiskey, looked at a photo of April, and mumbled, "It won't be long now, my love."

CHAPTER 50

MATT THE HAT was frantic after his release from police custody; he'd lost track of Tata Andolini. He'd driven to the Four Seasons Hotel, where she had spent last night. When he saw the group of autograph hounds staking out the hotel, his hopes soared. But then he realized that since stars like Jennifer Aniston, Katie Holmes, and Kanye West had stayed there, the fans could be swarming for anyone. So he inquired with the doorman and found out that Tata had checked out. And so he'd driven to her family residence, located on Grand Street above Andolini's of Little Italy.

The Hat steered the rattle-bang Toyota in front of a fire hydrant, where he had a clear view of both the residential and the restaurant's entrances. He powered down the window and was promptly greeted with the exhaust fumes from the chronically gridlocked traffic on Grand Street. He lit a Marlboro red, blew the smoke out the open window. The belching exhaust from a passing derelict Little Italy tour bus blew the smoke right back in; the Hat coughed his brains out.

Hurriedly, he powered the window back up and killed the engine. From the Styrofoam cooler in back he pulled out a long-neck beer, opened it and took several grateful, throat-cleansing gulps. The Hat checked Tata's Twitter feed for the umpteenth time. Still nothing.

The Hat was starting to think it was a mistake not to follow Tata when he saw her staggering out of the Soho House. But
he knew that Audra Gardner's killer, and Tata's stalker, was still
inside, which meant Tata was safe for the time being. And he
couldn't resist the opportunity to finally get his hands on Daniel
Caruso, or Fabio, or whatever the killer's real name was. But when
the opportunity did present itself, the dammed cops interfered.

The cops had taken the Hat to a station house and, after
questioning him, charged him with simple assault for bash-
ing Audra's killer over the head with a beer bottle. At first he
thought they were going to hold him pending yet another psych
evaluation, remand him to the mental ward at Bellevue Hospital.
Again. Instead, since he had served his full jail sentence and was
not on parole, they issued him a desk appearance ticket (DAT)
and allowed him to go free. His court date was in two weeks.
"So much for getting me out of the way, Fabio," the Hat said to
the car interior. Then he glanced at the photo of Tata that he had
affixed to the sun visor. "He comes around you again," the Hat
said, "he's a dead man."

As the Hat waited, he thought about, after he'd avenged
Audra Gardner, what he'd do with the rest of his life. Maybe he'd
return to the advertising business. Start fresh in L.A., Chicago, or
San Francisco, although London, Italy, and Spain were also attractive alternatives. His BFA from New York's School of Visual Arts
practically guaranteed him employment, and worldwide cosmetic
giants like Coty, Inc. and Estée Lauder were always hiring. He
wasn't worried about his criminal history. Advertising agencies,
even the mega-shops, rarely took the time to verify resumes, and
practically never performed criminal-background checks.

The Hat saw the familiar black Cadillac stop in front of the
restaurant. The same young, skinny guy with spiked hair he'd
seen at the Soho House stepped out. Yes, that was Tata's love
interest on *Jersey Shore Confidential*. Nicky Bada-bing. Great! Tata
was home.

Nicky advanced to the restaurant's display window, cupped his hands over his eyes, and peered inside for a long moment. Then he pulled open the door, allowed an elderly couple to exit before entering. The Hat sat back, sipped some beer, and felt a wave of relief. At least now he could continue to protect Tata from Fabio, or any other psycho with a problem. And the Hat knew firsthand that the world was full of psychos with problems.

A middle-aged waitress in Andolini's of Little Italy stopped Nicky Bada-bing at the door. "You stupido, ora something?" The waitress's eyes darted to the street. "You'da better get outta here before her father getsa back."

Nicky didn't have to ask why. Tata's father had made it perfectly clear the night he had Bruno punch his lights out that he thought Nicky was a bad influence on his "little bambina."

"Where is she?"

"Upa-stairs."

"You're sure her old man ain't heah?"

"I'ma sure."

"Bruno with him?"

"Bruno's always witha him."

"So, she's alone?"

"No," the waitress said. "Some woman's witha her. A biga blacka lady. She's a nurse of somea sort, I think."

Nicky thanked the waitress, walked out of the restaurant, and into the building's residential entrance. He used the keys Tata had given him to open the front, then foyer doors. Nicky moved quickly and quietly up the stairs into the apartment. He crept down the hall, peeked around a corner, saw a heavyset black woman sitting in the kitchen, eating hungrily. He backed away, headed for the other end of the apartment. Nicky approached Tata's room, eased it open, stepped inside the darkened room, and closed the door behind him. "Tata?" he whispered.

"Nicky?" A bedside lamp clicked on. Tata propped herself up on one elbow. "Nicky?" She wiped sleep from her eyes. "Hell're you doing heah?"

"Come to see how ya doin'—how ya doin'?"

"Lousy—wait a minute." Tata was blinking her eyes, like that would jog her brain into gear. "Where's the nurse?"

"Inna kitchen. Eating."

"We gotta hurry." Tata threw off her covers and reached out a hand. "Help me." Nicky put his arms around her waist, supported her as she staggered to a closet, lifted out some clothes.

"You stoned?" Nicky said, remarking on her sluggishness.

"They gave me a sedative," Tata said. "Knocked the shit outta me." She pulled on a pair of jeans, a blouse, slipped on shoes, picked out a purse.

"What're we doin'?" Nicky said.

"Getting outta heah."

"Sure that's a good idea?" Nicky said. "I mean, your father—"

She pinned him with her adorable eyes. "You love me, Nicky?"

"Ya know I do."

"Then you'll help me get outta heah."

Tata and Nicky crept out of the bedroom. Tiptoed down the hallway. Tata spied her cell phone on the dining-room table alongside her laptop. She retrieved the phone and dropped it in her purse. Soon all the world would know she was a free woman.

The Hat's phone chirped. It was a Tweet from Tata. Finally.

On the move! the Tweet read.

Within minutes Tata and Nicky Bada-bing emerged from the residential entrance door. They hurried to the curb and got into Nicky's Caddie.

The Hat hurried to turn the ignition key. Pumped the gas. The engine cranked… and cranked… and cranked. "C'mon!"

The Hat took a deep, calming breath and tried again. The cranks became slower and slower until there was a clicking sound. "Fuck!" The Hat pounded on the steering wheel as he watched the Caddie pull away.

CHAPTER 51

DESTINY DIDN'T KNOW what caused the sudden head-ache—which reminded her, yet again, that her oncologist, Dr. Goldsamp, had yet to call with her test results. Not that she was concerned at this point. She was convinced that if he'd found something, he would have contacted her immediately.

Destiny cleared the coffee table of breakfast and left Beckett watching the ongoing Victoria Carrington–Angel of Death coverage on TV. Although his growing outrage at the news organiza-tions for capitalizing on Victoria's death for the sake of ratings was vintage Beckett, he was more emotional, in her opinion, than he should have been. Destiny's feminine intuition told her that it wasn't just his stated inability to save their A-list client's life as he'd promised that was causing his over-the-top angst. She recalled that he had been in Victoria's hospital room, alone, for an inordinate amount of time. Then he'd come out with a bleeding lower lip. It was not bleeding before he'd entered Victoria's room. She was sure of it.

Destiny shrugged those thoughts from her mind—telling herself it was none of her business—and carried her purse into the guest bathroom. She regarded herself in the mirror; she looked tired, worn. She ran the cold water, splashed some on her face. Combed her hair. Dabbed some makeup on here and there. Then a touch of lipstick. She found a bottle of Vicodin in her purse, swallowed a couple. She left the bathroom, glanced into Beckett's bedroom at the waist-high, four-poster bed. Recalled the drunken night four months ago when he'd bent her over that bed, took her from behind—the act passionate, primeval, almost violent. Their relationship had changed over the years from partners and best friends to being lovers, and now they were best friends again. A sense of loss washed over her.

Destiny wandered into Beckett's bedroom and glanced around. Nothing had changed. All the furnishings were cherrywood, the lamps brass, everything very nautical, and squared away. Pictures of the warships Beckett had served on while in the Navy—two destroyers, a destroyer escort, and a guided-missile cruiser—covered the walls. A huge, frightening color photo of a three-masted schooner in rough seas hung over the bed—the bed.

She knew Solana's plan was to screw Beckett's brains out on that bed. Solana, who'd waltzed back onto their lives with her little black dress and needy ways. A damsel in distress, begging Beckett to help her. And when Beckett balked, she threatened him, said she'd tell whatever she knew—and insinuated she knew plenty—about Beckett's Rockers during her grand-jury testimony. But Beckett went ahead and involved her in the Victoria Carrington's death, and Angel of Death investigations anyway. In Destiny's opinion a dumb move. His justification being that he/ we had nothing to fear from Solana, that this time *he* was using *her*. Men were so clueless.

Destiny could overhear Beckett's cutting remarks directed at the clueless talking heads on TV. His rants bathed her in a comfortable, warm glow. All at once she felt a sense of nostalgia. She didn't understand why she felt that way.

Destiny walked back into the living room, sat beside Beckett, and asked herself: If the improbable happened and Beckett rekindled his relationship with Solana, could they still be friends? Not if Solana had anything to say about it.

"Goddammed vultures," Beckett huffed. "The way they're

picking over Victoria's bones." He used the remote to channel surf. On every news station appeared glamorous photos of the serial killer's prior "alleged" A-list victims, everyone from Audra Gardner to Victoria, at various red-carpet events. Another channel was broadcasting excerpts of a tearful Lynn Carrington—the phony bitch—doing an *Entertainment Tonight* interview, along with a montage of family photos: Victoria's childhood to adulthood. Yet another station was airing a video of Victoria arriving with Tata Andolini at the Soho House for her date with death. Cut to: Tata's *Jersey Shore Confidential* posse moving across the screen. Matt the Hat standing by the entrance. Cut to: the newscaster identified Victoria's press agent, Meg Dvoretz, who, along with Sid Schulsky, entered the private club—Sid Schulsky? Destiny straightened. Why hadn't she thought of that before?

"Who else knew Lisi was in the hospital?" Destiny said.

"Huh?"

She picked up the remote and muted the TV. "Who knew Lisi was in the hospital besides us?"

Beckett, having to shift his thought processes, shrugged. "I don't know."

"Did you tell anyone?"

Beckett finally looked away from the TV. "No."

"You sure?"

"I'm sure."

"So how did Sid Schulsky know?" Destiny asked.

Beckett was perplexed by this question. "I don't know."

"I mean, Lisi's in a medically induced coma, in a hospital sixty miles out on Long Island. Who told Sid?"

"The hospital admissions people?" Beckett said. "Had to be."

"Better ask Lisi," Destiny said.

Beckett dialed Lisi and activated the speaker.

"So?" Lisi grouched. "Say something."

"After your accident," Beckett said, "you told the hospital to call me?"

"That's right."

"Tell them to call anyone else?"

"No."

"Sid Schulsky?" Beckett said.

"What about him?"

"Did you tell the hospital to call him too?"

"No," Lisi said. "We ain't that close."

"So, how'd he know you were in a hospital sixty miles away?"
Silence filled the line. "I dunno."

"He was at the Soho House," Destiny said.

"And he's an industry insider," Beckett said.

"With unfettered access," Destiny said, "to celebrities."

"What're youse two saying?" Lisi said.

"That the only way Sid could've known where you were,"
Destiny said, "is that he put you there."

Everyone was stunned for a moment.

"So, Sid takes a shot at me," Lisi said, "then he comes to the
hospital with flowers as a cover. But he's really there to finish me off?"

"He sees you're being guarded," Destiny said, "leaves the
flowers and bolts."

"Makes sense," Beckett said.

"Yeah," Lisi said. "It does."

"How much do you really know about him?" Beckett asked.

"He was one of our first clients," Lisi said. "Put us onna
the map."

"His personal life," Destiny said.

"Married. Kids."

"He in the military?" Beckett said.

"Yeah, come to think of it. He was a Marine."

"So, he knows weapons."

Destiny heard her cell phone chirp. She reached into her
purse and retrieved it. "Tata just Tweeted. She and Nicky-Bada-
bing are at Reif's Tavern."

"The dive bar down the street?" Beckett said.

"If there's even a chance that Sid Schulsky is the Angel a' Death…" Lisi said.

"But he's not after Tata," Beckett said. "We checked her cell, e-mail, computer. You told me yourself her stalker claims were 'gahbidge.'"

"What if I'm wrong?" Lisi said. "What if he threatened her in real time, onna phone? Dontcha understand? We can't take a chance."

"He's right," Destiny said.

"I want youse two to get over there. Fast. Keep an eye on Tata. And fer Christ's sake, don't let her shoot any dope. I'm gonna call her father."

CHAPTER 52

THE FEDS RANG McKee's doorbell around one in the afternoon. They had come, he knew, to arrest him for ignoring the grand-jury subpoena. McKee couldn't explain why, but he was happy that they had finally arrived, relieved somehow. He leaned back in his home- office chair and decided to make them wait.

He had only recently come to terms with the fact that he was wasting his life, merely taking up space on Earth, counting down the days. Since April's death he'd had no real interests. He no longer enjoyed sunrises, or sunsets, holidays, dating, socializing, even sports, eating or drinking. And during those rare occasions when he forgot that the love of his life was dead, and had a good time, he felt guilty. Guilty that he was enjoying life without her.

April had come to him in a vision only a month ago. They laughed. Argued about her smoking habit as always. Then they made love; it was all so incredibly real. He woke up, swore he smelled her perfume. He'd reach across to her side of the bed, sure that he would touch her. Certain that her suicide had been a horrific nightmare. But then reality would set in and his stomach would clench; dread would fill his heart.

The feds pounded their fists on the door. "Federal agents!" a man called out. "We have a warrant for your arrest. Open the door. Now!"

McKee heard footsteps running along the side of his house, then heard someone trying to open the backyard's sliding glass doors; the feds had surrounded the house. "It's time," he said to April's picture. He pushed to his feet, headed to the front door, and called out, "Just a minute!"

McKee reached into his closet and grabbed the S&W .38 with a two-inch barrel. He raised the weapon. Aimed. Fired. A single shot ripped through the top of the front door, well over the head of the feds. He didn't want to harm anyone, especially not someone in law enforcement.

CHAPTER 53

WE HURRIED DOWN the steep hill that is East Ninety-second Street and saw what looked like *Jersey Shore Confidential* fans—teenage guidos and guidettes—gathering outside Rief's Tavern. Several news vans from competing networks pulled to a stop at the southeast corner. Their doors flew open, and the occupants raced to be the first to set up a live-feed.

"Look at them," Destiny said. "They're like locusts."

I was more amused. "What's Tata planning to do? Hold a press conference?"

"Wouldn't surprise me if she did," Destiny said. "The little twit knows she's part of a major news story. She'll play up her brief relationship with Victoria Carrington for all it's worth—it's her way off the D-list."

"So you're thinking Sid Schulsky will show?"

"He's her press agent." Destiny shrugged. "What do you think?"

We waited for the green light before crossing busy Second Avenue. By habit we scanned the tenement rooftops and parked cars for anything suspicious. Just then, three stalkerazzi cars made a screeching left off of Second Avenue. They double-parked in front of Reif's and piled out, their cameras at the ready. We crossed Second and cleaved through the gathering swarm.

"God," Destiny said as we were about to enter Rief's Tavern, "I hate this place."

"After you," I said and held the door open.

The smell of stale beer hit us like a slap to the face.

Still owned and operated by the Reif family, the foreboding storefront dive bar had opened in 1942 and looked it. The dark, depressing joint that served no food attracted affable local retirees by day. At night it became a destination for a younger, hipper crowd looking to rub and bend elbows with the neighborhood's denizens. Why? What was the attraction? I had no idea.

Our shoes nearly adhered to the sticky floor as we bellied up to the bar and checked out the crowd, surprised that the place was crowded at that time of day. Two sinister-looking characters sporting ponytails and prison tattoos were standing to my right, huddled in conversation. At the far end of the bar, the sheer girth of two regulars nearly concealed the entrance to the back room, where I caught a glimpse of Tata playing a game of pool with Nicky Bada-bing.

"Destiny! Beckett!" Ray, the bartender said. Now I knew why the bar was crowded. A popular neighborhood resident with a quick smile and sunny disposition, Ray attracted a large, consistent bar following.

"Long time no see," Ray said.

He kissed Destiny on the cheek and shook my hand. We ordered drinks, our eyes alert for suspicious characters—a redundant task since the bar was full of them. Soon Tata's posse began arriving, making their way through to the back room. The red-bearded Teamster Keating came in last with his arm around a leather-clad guidette.

"Keating," Destiny noted. "Again."

"How many you count?" I said.

"Fifteen," Destiny said. "Looks like the same group from the Soho House." She checked that her glass was clean before sipping her wine. "Anyone of those bozos could've supplied the drugs that killed Victoria. They could be holding now."

Two guidos approached the bar and ordered six glasses of white wine and two buckets of beer. Ray asked them both for ID, then filled their order. The guidos paid with cash, then carried their order into the back room and passed out the drinks.

"Let's toss them," Destiny said.

"Good idea." I put down my beer. "We'll be right back, Ray."

We were forced to kibitz with the bar crowd as we drifted to the back room. Bobby G, the former racketeer, sold me a couple of raffle tickets: a fund-raiser for a local, Irish waitress who was disabled and out of work.

"Do me a favor," I said to Bobby G. "We're gonna roust the kids in the back room. If there's a stampede, don't let anyone leave."

"You got it," he said.

"Freeze," Destiny said as we entered the back room, her shield held up for all to see. "Nobody move."

"Oh, shit," Keating said.

"Hello, Sean." Destiny headed straight across the room to get into his face. "How're the teeth?"

Keating's face flushed, but to his credit he kept his cool. He backed up until he banged into a wall under an overused dartboard.

"Everyone, empty your pockets on the pool table," I ordered. "Then step back against the wall by the dartboard. "Do it. Now."

Reluctantly, the crowd began to comply.

I looked around. "Where's Tata?"

Destiny hurried into the ladies' room, but came out shaking her head. I bolted out back to the cluttered patio area that passed for a beer garden, saw Tata sitting in a corner, her back to Reif's.

"Hey," I said.

Tata turned to me, trying to cancel the hypodermic needle

that she was about to stick into her arm. I rushed forward and said, "Hand it over."

"Fuck you," Tata screamed. "You asshole!"

I wrestled the needle away from her. Then I picked up her purse and pulled her to her feet. "C'mon. Inside."

"Lemme alone!"

I manhandled Tata back into Reif's, handed the needle and purse over to Destiny. "She was about to shoot up."

Destiny placed the needle on the pool table, opened Tata's purse, dumped out the contents, spread it out.

"You can't do that," Tata said.

Besides a drugstore counter's assortment of hair and makeup products, there was cash, credit cards, keys, breath mints, and one glassine envelope of heroin.

Destiny picked up the heroin. "Where'd you get this?"

"Pulled it outta my ass," Tata said.

Thwack! Destiny slapped Tata. Hard.

There was a hush around the room.

Tata's hand went to her face, tears filled her eyes. "I'm tellin' my father."

Destiny shoved Tata into a corner, got into her face. "Now, you listen to me. Your friend Victoria injected heroin spiked with fentanyl. It was given to her on purpose. Which means she was murdered. The same guy who murdered her could be after you." Destiny gestured to the hypodermic needle. "Now, you wanna inject that shit, be my guest."

Tata looked at the needle in horror, didn't move.

"Where'd you get it?" Destiny said.

Tata crossed her arms across her chest. "I'm no rat."

Destiny leaned into Tata, whispered in her ear. "Think about it: You help find Victoria Carrington's killer, you'll be international news. Front page of every newspaper."

That brought about a startling change. "You think?" Tata's eyes went wide with wonder.

Destiny stepped back to give Tata room. "Say hello to the A-list."

A series of revelations crossed Tata's blotchy face as Destiny's words sank in: This was her shot at the big time. Tata stepped around Destiny to the pool table, raked the contents back into her purse. She left the hypodermic needle and bag of heroin where they lay.

"Who gave you the drugs?" Destiny said.

"Nicky."

"You bitch!" Nicky Bada-bing said.

"Shut the fuck up," I said.

"Good," Destiny said. "Now. Who supplied the drugs at the Soho House?"

Tata lowered her voice. "It was Nicky."

"Liar!" Nicky raged. Yet he spun around and made a run for the front door. Bobby G shot to his feet and effortlessly blocked him. "Where you think you're going, fuckhead?" He grabbed Nicky by the shirt. "I'll kick your fucking ass!" Bounced him off the bar and shoved him back into the poolroom.

Nicky retreated into a corner, frantic, looking for a way out: a deer in headlights. "You." He pointed a finger at me. "You keep away from me."

"Relax, Nicky," I said.

But Nicky reached into his waistband and pulled a gun. And Destiny cracked him over the head with the business end of a pool cue. Nicky bounced off the pool table and toppled to the ground

Destiny picked up Nicky's weapon. "Beretta twenty-two long. Six in the clip. One in the pipe." She sneered down at the prone Nicky. "A ladies' gun." She slipped it into her pocket.

Nicky groaned and he rolled over. Felt the back of his head. "Hey," he whined. "I'm bleedin'."

"You're lucky you're breathing." I dragged the punk to his feet and slammed him onto a plastic chair. "You have a license for the gun?"

"I got a target permit," he said belligerently. "Belong to a gun club."

"Dummy." I smacked him on the back of the head. "You're looking at a mandatory year in jail."

"Which is the least of your problems." Destiny made a show of picking up the bag of heroin from the pool table. "You supplied the heroin that killed Victoria Carrington. You're looking at two counts of murder one."

"Murder?" Nicky freaked. "Fuck you talkin' about?"

"I'm thinking you knew the heroin you sold to Victoria Carrington was poison," Destiny said. "Convince me otherwise."

He was way out of his league, I could tell. "I swear I didn't know. I wouldn't poison anyone."

"Where'd you get the heroin?" I said.

Nicky looked around; everyone was watching, listening. He shook his head.

"Then you're the fall guy." I pulled Nicky to his feet, slammed him face-first against a grimy, cheaply paneled wall, and roughly searched him.

"I didn't know," Nicky pleaded. "You gotta believe me."

"I believe him." Tata came forward. "There's no way he knew." She approached Nicky, tenderly examined the back of his bleeding head. "He's a two-timing, lying piece a' dog shit. But he'd never harm anyone on purpose."

"She's right," Nicky cried. "Ya gotta believe her."

"No, I don't." I twisted Nicky around. "Unless you give up your supplier."

Again Nicky looked at the guidos, guidettes, and the Teamster Keating. I could see it on his face, in his eyes—Nicky was afraid of someone in that crowd.

Then Tata's father and his son Bruno barreled angrily into Reif's back room with Sid Schulsky in tow. "Francine!" Vincenzo said, his face red with rage. "What the hell'sa wronga with you?"

He glared at Tata's posse, and then his gaze settled on Nicky. "You—" he snarled. "*Ti ammazzo. Tu piezza di merda!*"

I had no idea what Vincenzo said or how much Italian Nicky knew, but he freaked. He shoved Tata into Bruno and bounded over the pool table. Before I could stop him, he dashed out to Rief's beer garden, scaled a rickety wooden fence and was gone.

"Nicky!" Tata shrieked. "You piece a' dog shit!"

I ran after Nicky. Across Rief's backyard. Over the fence. Came down hard. Stumbled on broken concrete. Tweaked my ankle. I looked around a garbage-strewn courtyard, then looked down a city-block valley of courtyards. Laundry hung from dozens of clotheslines that were strung from mature trees to fire escapes. Overgrown shrubs and fences of differing heights and designs obstructed my view. I didn't see Nicky. Suddenly I heard an old tin garbage can being knocked over off to my left. I scaled another fence. Limped painfully down an alley that led back to Ninety-second Street, twenty yards east of Reif's front door. Nicky was nowhere to be seen.

Reif's door flew open. Bruno dragged Tata out, across the sidewalk toward their father's Nissan. The stalkerazzi and fans rushed them. Cameras flashed. Reporters shouted questions. "Were you with Victoria when she died?" "Did you inject Victoria with the heroin?" "Where did you get the heroin?" Bruno knocked everyone aside, shoved Tata into the back of the car, and stood guard. Vincenzo came out of the dive bar next, screaming at Sid Schulsky about who knows what. Across the street I spotted Matt the Hat leaning against a news van, smoking.

"Michael," Destiny said excitedly as she came out of Reif's. "We have to go."

"Nicky's hiding on the block somewhere. I know he is. He couldn't get away that fast."

Just to make the confusion complete, Fabio made the turn off of Second Avenue and rolled by on his Harley. Matt the

Hat dumped his cigarette, stepped into the street, and glared after Fabio.

"Looks like your boyfriend's here."

"Michael!" Destiny grabbed my arm. She was pale, face tight, her hand that held her cell phone was shaking. Uh-oh. I braced myself, feared that her oncologist had called with devastating news. "What is it?"

"McKee just shot at the feds who came to his house."

CHAPTER 54

"**M**CKEE TOOK A shot at the feds?" I said. "I don't believe it."

"That's what Serria said." We had left the Tata mess behind at Reif's Tavern without saying a word. We raced across First Avenue against the light, dodged speeding cars, truck, busses, and bikes on our way to Lisi's Ninetieth Street garage. Destiny had called ahead and told the attendant to have the vehicle ready.

I called Serria and put him on speakerphone. "What's going on?"

"McKee blew off the grand jury like he said he would," Serria said. "When the feds came to take him into custody, they claim he fired a shot at them."

"McKee wouldn't shoot at cops," Destiny said.

"Maybe he shot into the ground or into the air," Serria said. "But the feds aren't taking any chances."

"Where are you now?" I asked.

"Just got to McKee's block. Came as soon as I saw the news bulletin on TV. Looks like the entire neighborhood's on lockdown. They've got a forced evacuation in progress. Emergency Service is here. They've got snipers scoping out the house. There's an NYPD negotiator trying to get McKee talking. He won't answer his goddamned phones."

The regular, blushing knuckleheaded garage attendant pulled

the old SUV into the driveway as we arrived. He held the door open for Destiny, who slid behind the wheel.

"You said the area's in lockdown," I said, climbing in the passenger side. "How do we get in?" We roared out of the garage.

"I parked on Linden Avenue," Serria said. "Came in that way."

"We'll be there soon," I said and ended the call.

Destiny slowed at a red light, looked both ways before proceeding. She made a left onto York Avenue heading north. "I don't like this. McKee's forcing a confrontation." She merged onto the FDR Drive at East Ninety-sixth Street and put the pedal to the metal. "You thinking what I'm thinking?"

"I hope not."

Linden Avenue was blocked by police cars from the local 45thth Precinct. Two female uniforms, one tall and rangy, one shot and fat—the modern female version of Toody and Muldoon from the old *Car 54* TV show—were standing guard, blocking access to Sunset Trail.

We approached the officers and showed our NYPD ID cards. The tall one scrutinized our IDs. "Retired, huh?"

"Yeah," I said. "Look, we need to go up Sunset Trail."

"Sorry," the fat one said. "No one's allowed in this way."

"Don't say we told you," the tall one said, jabbing her thumb. "You could walk down a couple of blocks, cut through someone's backyard—but be careful. This neighborhood's populated by lots of active and retired cops. Lots of staunch conservatives. Everyone's got a gun."

We hurried down two blocks and cut through a backyard. Several dogs barked, but since most of the neighborhood had been evacuated, no one challenged us.

Sunset Trail looked like a war zone. Dozens of police vehicles were parked end to end, serving as barriers for the cops in body armor who squatted behind them—their assault rifles pointing at McKee's house. As we moved toward a van that appeared to be serving as a command post, several people shouted, "Get down!" "Take cover!" We ignored them.

Serria stepped from behind a van and waved us over.

"What's the latest?" I asked.

"No movement," Serria said. "He still won't pick up his god-damned phone." He pointed at McKee's house. "All the shades on the ground floor are down, curtains pulled tight."

"You sure he's in there?" Destiny said. "Couldn't he have gone out the back before reinforcements arrived?"

Serria shook his head. "The feds had the place surrounded before the gunshot. Besides, they have an infrared sensor that detects body heat. McKee's in there, all right. Sitting in his living room. Probably watching us all on TV."

Over our heads, six TV helicopters were hovering offshore. Down the street several news vans, their satellite disks reaching into the sky, had set up shop. Their talking heads held micro-phones in their hands and were speaking into cameras, broadcast-ing the live standoff with police.

Serria said, "The feds let me try to talk to him on the mega-phone." He shrugged. "Nothing. No response. I don't know what he's thinking."

Agent Sobel stepped around the vehicle with a worried look on his face. "Any ideas?"

Serria said to Destiny, "He might pick up for you."

Destiny whipped out her cell and speed-dialed McKee.

He answered on the third ring. "Hello, Destiny."

"Thomas." Destiny gave us the thumbs-up. "Are you all right?"

"Never better."

"Want to tell me what's going on?"

"You know what's going on."

"No," Destiny said. "I don't."

A fed manning an infrared scope said, "He's at the front door." All eyes turned to McKee's house. "He's holding something in his hand. Could be a weapon."

"What are you planning to do?" Destiny said.

"What I should have done a long time ago."

"Thomas?" Destiny said. More desperately, she repeated: "Thomas?" She put her phone down. "He hung up."

McKee's front door swung open. He stepped out onto his front stoop. The .38 dangled from his right hand. Assault rifles were aimed. Handguns cocked.

"Hell's he doing?" Serria said.

"Federal agents. Drop the gun!" Englund shouted into a megaphone. "Put the gun down! Do it now! Drop the gun!"

McKee stepped down his newly renovated concrete and brick stoop, walked the manicured path, passed the lush landscaping toward the line of cops.

"Stop where you are!" Englund shouted.

McKee stopped.

"Drop the gun. Now!"

But McKee raised the .38. Pointed it directly at Englund. Cocked the hammer.

There was a fusillade of shots.

Destiny screamed.

Gun smoke clung in the air as ESU quickly—but warily—approached McKee's prone body, their weapons at the ready. An NYPD sergeant in body armor lowered himself to one knee and checked for signs of life. The sergeant looked at Sobel and shook his head.

"Shit," Sobel said.

Destiny turned away, tears in her eyes.

The sergeant retrieved McKee's .38 and flipped open the cylinder. He held it up for everyone to see. "Empty."

Destiny pounded her fist on the hood of a police car. "What the hell just happened?"

"Suicide by cop," I said quietly.

"Well," Englund said, coming up behind us. "That's one less dirty cop."

Thwack! The punch Destiny threw broke Englund's nose.

He staggered back and fell against a police car. "You're under arrest," Englund said, bleeding into his hands, "for assaulting a federal agent."

"No, she's not." Sobel stepped in between them and checked Englund's injuries. "Nice punch," he told Destiny. He turned back to Englund and gestured to a waiting ambulance. "Go. You and your big mouth, get out of my sight. You're bleeding all over the place."

Englund, furious, huffed and puffed, and stormed off.

"As for you," Sobel addressed Destiny, Serria, and me. "The whole lot of you, get the hell out of here."

CHAPTER 55

"**I** SHOULD HAVE SEEN this coming," Destiny sobbed. I placed a consoling arm around her shoulder as we walked down Sunset Trail, heading back to our vehicles. Residents were coming our way, streaming back to their houses.

"Don't do that to yourself." I squeezed her reassuringly. "No one can know what's on someone's mind."

News reporters began to chase after us. One idiot blocked our path and stuck a microphone in Destiny's face. "How well did you know the deceased?"

Destiny savagely knocked the microphone away, lunged, both hands reaching for the reporter's throat. I caught her around the waist, dragged her backward.

"Keep away from me, asshole!" Destiny screamed. The reporter cowered, stunned by her ferocity, and the others wisely backed off.

We wove though a squad of grim-faced ESU personnel who were taking off their body armor, storing sniper rifles, etc. Ahead, the team from the Hostage Negotiating Unit was stepping into their van, their deflated posture and tight facial expressions a testament to their failure.

We arrived at Linden Avenue, where the two female uniforms manning the road were directing the crime- scene lab van and a morgue wagon to McKee's place.

"McKee have any family?" I said.

"A brother up in New Hampshire somewhere," Destiny said.

"They weren't on speaking terms," Serria put in.

"April's two daughters out in San Diego," Destiny said. "I'll notify them. Track down his brother." She turned to Serria, bewildered. "He ever talk about suicide to you?"

"No." Serria hung his head. His voice was a whisper. His chest was impossibly concave, like he'd folded in on himself. "But ever since April died…"

"You think that's what this was about?" I said. "April?"

"Yes," Serria said.

"So do I," Destiny said.

A news helicopter swooped in and hovered noisily overhead.

"You wanna grab a beer somewhere, Ernie?" I said, loud enough to be heard. "Hang out a while?"

"No," Serria said, looking like he was on the verge of tears. "Hey, I gotta go take care of my dogs." He hugged us both clumsily before climbing into his vehicle. He started the engine, put the car in gear; I could swear he was crying as he drove past us. The news helicopter moved down the shoreline.

We legged down the block and climbed into the SUV.

"I read somewhere," Destiny said, "that guilt is the one emotion that seems to be universal to all survivors of suicide."

"It's not just suicide survivors who feel guilt," I said.

Destiny started the engine. "You talking about your sister?"

"Yeah." We headed back to the city.

When my sister Shannon died of a drug overdose, I was consumed by guilt. I was her big brother. Her protector. I should have known she was in trouble, done whatever it took to save her. But I was too busy with my own life. I'd neglected her, ignored the obvious signs—if I had bothered looking—of drug addiction. In retrospect, I knew that if I'd been a better brother, I would have saved Shannon. As it was, I—and my Rockers—managed to avenge her death.

Ten minutes later, we crossed the Third Avenue Bridge and merged onto the FDR Drive. Soon we were driving down Second Avenue past Reif's Tavern. The stalkerazzi, media trucks, and fans were long gone, replaced by the usual regulars who were milling about outside, smoking. We made the left onto Ninetieth Street—and saw a line of police cars out front of Lisi's apartment. Pedestrians crowded the sidewalk, pointed up at Lisi's windows. A news van was setting up across the street.

"Oh, no," Destiny said.

My mind raced. Had the Angel of Death gotten to Lisi?

We double-parked behind a police car and hurried through the crowd into Lisi's building. The lobby door hung by its hinges; it had been forced open. That sight set a shiver through me. We climbed the stairs. A uniformed officer we both knew was standing guard outside Lisi's front door, which was wide open.

"Hey, we just heard about McKee," the uniform said as we approached. "Never thought a guy like him would crack up."

"Join the club." I saw a gaping hole in Lisi's front door. "Hell happened?"

"Shotgun blast," the uniform said. "The guy lives here a friend of yours?"

"Yeah, he is."

"Someone tried to kill him." He stepped aside. "He's in the living room."

We entered the apartment, said hello to a couple of busy crime-scene techs we also knew. Lisi was sitting on his couch, legs crossed, a lit cigarette in his right hand, a glass of vodka, rocks, in his left, looking none the worse for wear.

"I already told yuhs," Lisi said to a young female detective who was hovering over him, taking notes. "There's a knock onna door. I ask, whossit. But no one answers, so I get suspicious. See? So I stand off to the side of the door, reach out my hand, flick the peephole guard up—you know, so the mook thinks I'm standing onnee other side. And bam! Some cocksucker fires a shotgun through the door. Pardon my French."

"You see who shot at you?" the detective asked.

"No. I don't have X-ray eyes."

"You having trouble with anyone?" she asked.

I figured Lisi would tell her about the recent and nearly successful attempt on his life, along with the telephone death threats. Tell the young detective about the Angel of Death, but instead he said, "Ice Pick Martucci ordered the hit."

I exchanged looks with Destiny. The detective exchanged looks with her partner; everyone knew Ice Pick was a notorious La Cosa Nostra enforcer. "Why would a mob assassin target you?"

"That's Sweet Tommy Lisi you're talking to," I informed the detective.

For the first time she noticed me and Destiny. Nodded a greeting. "Really." I could tell she had no idea who I was talking about.

"He was bodyguard to the Mafia's boss of bosses," I said, "when they tried to assassinate him. He killed the two hit men."

If that impressed the detective, she didn't show it. "I'll ask again," she said to Lisi. "Why would Ice Pick target you?"

"Vendetta."

"Explain."

"I killet his second cousin when they tried to whack the don."

"But wasn't that a long time ago?" the detective said.

"Yeah," Lisi said, a little impatience in his voice. "A long time ago."

"So why come after you now?"

"'Cause he embarrassed Ice Pick," I interjected, "two days ago. In public."

"That right, Mr. Lisi?"

Lisi shrugged. "He was being whatchamacallit—condescending. I told him and his crew a' mooks to fuck off."

"That when he threatened you?" the detective asked.

"That's right."

"What did he say? Exactly?"

"He said he was gonna cut my balls off," Lisi said, "and shove them down my throat."

"Anyone else you're having a problem with?"

"Yeah," Lisi said. "But no one who'd pull a stunt like this."

"How do you know?"

Lisi sipped his drink. "Look, lady—"

"Detective."

"Whatever. A button man comin' ta my home in broad daylight. A shotgun which makes a hell of a noise. The hit was meanta make a statement. That's Ice Pick's style. *Capeesh?*"

"Okay," the detective said, putting her notebook away. "We'll canvas the neighborhood for witnesses. Check if there are any security cameras on the block."

"Don't bother," Lisi said, waving off that idea. "Ice Pick don't leave loose ends."

"What's that mean?" the detective said.

"The hit man missed. Whoever he is, he's as good as dead."

We waited for the uniforms and detectives to leave, then for Lisi's building handyman to begin patching his front door, before we filled Lisi in on the events at Reif's Tavern—catching Tata with heroin and finding out that Nicky was the one who sold the tainted drugs to Victoria. About the arrival of Tata's father with Sid Schulsky and Nicky's hasty escape. Seeing Matt the Hat and Fabio. We didn't mention McKee's standoff with the feds at that time. No reason to muddy the waters, since Lisi barely knew him.

"We didn't get the chance to speak to Schulsky," I said, "but we will."

"Fuhgeddabout Schulsky," Lisi said. "His niece is an emergency-room nurse at the hospital. She recognized me, and called him."

"You found this out how?" I said.

"Hey, I don't hafta tell youse two everything." Lisi puffed his cigarette. Sipped his drink. "So, youse're gonna snatch Nicky?"

"Right after we leave here," I said. "Take him somewhere quiet. Sweat him for as long as it takes. Follow the chain of dealers until we get to the source."

The handyman interrupted: "Done, Mr. Lisi." He stood there, toolbox in hand, obviously waiting for a tip.

"Oh," Lisi said. "Yeah." He patted his pockets as if looking for his wallet, something I remembered my father doing before he stiffed someone. "Lookit, I'll take care a' you later."

"Yeah. Sure." The handyman made a sour face as he let himself out.

"So," I said to Lisi. "Next order of business. What're we gonna do about Ice Pick Martucci?"

"Youse guys do nothing. I'll take care a' that mook in my own way."

"How?" Destiny said. "You're not well. What if he tries again?"

"He won't. I know how these guys think."

"You should," Destiny said, an edge to her voice.

"I know what yuhs are thinking," Lisi said defensively. "But what youse don't know is that I was never one of them. Not the way you think."

"C'mon, Tommy," I said. "It's common knowledge. Public record. You were involved. There are some in the Organized Crime Control Bureau that think you still are."

"I know." Lisi lit another cigarette, blew the smoke out. "The bitch of it is, I was one of the good guys. Undercover FBI."

Destiny and I exchanged wry glances, snickered.

"I ain't bullshitting."

I didn't believe him for a moment. But there was something in the old man's eyes that told me maybe there was more to the story. "Care to explain?"

"Youse two think you know everything? You don't know shit."

"Educate us."

Lisi took his time. I could almost see his mind work, recalling his past, his thoughts turning inward.

"I was a military cop. Worked undercover," Lisi said. "Broke up a smuggling ring. Then took down a black-market arms dealer. The arrests got the attention of some big muckety-mucks in Washington. Next thing I know, I'm a fed. But I wasn't trained at Quantico. They flew me out ta Coronado. I trained with class-A special-ops volunteers. Only a handful a higher-ups even knew a' my existence. I was deep undercover from the get-go."

"Why you?" Destiny asked.

"Seems the Bureau had a problem. Some of their agents were onna take. They needed someone imbedded inna mob, someone who could ferret out the crooked feds from the inside. They chose me because I was raised inna hood. Grew up with most of the players."

"You still with the Bureau?"

"Naw." Lisi shook his head. "I hated the work. Don't get me wrong, the guys inna mob I took down deserved prison, maybe worse. But I grew up with those guys. They were my friends. Once I knew which feds were onna the mob's payroll, I turned them in. Then quit. Walked away. From the feds and the mob."

"Why you telling us this?" I asked. "Why now?"

"When the feds tossed my place, they found a key to a safety-deposit box. My federal ID was in there, among other things. I have the feeling my background is gonna be public record. And soon."

My cell phone rang. "Beckett."

"Can you believe all the exposure?" Solana said breathlessly. "The story's gone viral."

"Oh, hi, Solana."

Destiny made a disgusted face, stood and strode out of the room.

"So," I said. "Everything worked out?"

"All thanks to you. I owe you, Michael. Which is why I'm calling."

I head Lisi's front door slam shut; a picture fell off of a wall and shattered.

"*Marrone*," Lisi said.

"I'll have the money I borrowed sooner than I expected," Solana said. "Let me buy you dinner sometime?"

"Sure," I said, glancing at the fallen painting. "I'd like that."

CHAPTER 56

"ANYTHING ELSE YOU wanna tell me?" I said after I hung up with Solana.

"Yeah," Lisi said. "But first I gotta ask—you trying to piss off Destiny? Or are you just an ordinary idiot? And don't gimme that innocent look."

"What?"

"Didn't you notice how she stormed outta heah?"

"She hates Solana," I said. "That's all."

"Unfuckingbelievable," Lisi said. "Youse young guys today, youse don't know shit about women."

"First off," I said, "it's none of Destiny's business what I do. She's the one who broke off with me. Besides, Solana's paying me back a loan, that's all."

"You lent Solana money?" Lisi sniggered. "Destiny know?"

"No," I said. "And I'd appreciate if you kept it to yourself."

"Yeah?" Lisi put on a gangster vibe. "It's gonna cost ya."

"Don't fuck around, Tommy."

Lisi laughed. "Only kidding."

I sat down. "Now, what else?"

"Okay. After the shot came through the door, I heard someone double-timing it downa stairs. I got to the front window, saw a guy running outta my building—the shooter."

"You recognize him?"

"No," Lisi said. "But by the way he moved, he was young. He was wearing a long black trench coat; the shotgun hadda be under that. He hadda hood over his head, you know, the way kids do these days. I couldn't see his face, but he had a shaggy red beard."

"Red beard?" I could almost see a cartoon lightbulb pop on over my head. I pulled out my cell phone, called a detective I knew in the NYPD's Organized Crime Control Bureau, put the call on speaker. "Mario, this is Beckett."

"Hey, you having a retirement party," Mario said, "or what?"

"What do you have on a Sean Keating? Male. White. Around six-foot-two. I'd guess twenty-three years old. Red hair with a beard."

"Hold on." Mario tapped some computer keys. "Okay, fourteen misdemeanor arrests. Four felonies: armed robbery, gun possession, possession of crack cocaine, resisting arrest. He was doing a nickel at Dannemora, but his conviction got overturned on appeal. Now he's out on bail on an assault charge. He slapped his mother around—another prize, that one. She's been arrested a dozen times for prostitution. But that was a long time ago."

"You have a current address?"

"Sure. He lives with his mother." Mario recited an address in Hell's Kitchen on Manhattan's west side—no surprise there.

Lisi said, "Have him check Nicky?"

"Mario, how about Nicky…?"

"Nicholas Genovese," Lisi said.

"Nicholas Genovese," I said. "He goes by Nicky Bada-bing."

"Give me a minute," Mario said. "Okay, here he is: two counts of simple drug possession. First arrest was three years ago. Since then, arrested for petty larceny six times; looks like he's a career shoplifter. He did thirty days out on Rikers Island."

"Thanks, Mario," I said. "Now tell me about Ice Pick Martucci."

"Mob enforcer," Mario said. "He's a suspect in at least forty homicides."

"He into drugs?"

"He's a top narcotics man."

"Is Keating listed as a known associate?"

Mario hit more computer keys. "No."

"Keating's a member of Teamster Local three-two-one."

"Then he's an associate," Mario said definitely.

"So Ice Pick's involved in the union?"

"Involved?" Mario chuckled. "Ice Pick's sister's the treasurer. We can't prove it yet, but I'll pay for your retirement party if that prick doesn't run that union. Say, when is the party?"

"There is no party," I said and ended the call.

Lisi had been listening, and he took his time putting all the puzzle pieces together.

"So let's assume Keating's one of Ice Picks dealers," I said, thinking aloud. "Which means Ice Pick could be the source of the tainted heroin. Which means Ice Pick could be the Angel of Death. I mean, with forty homicides to his credit, he's already a serial killer of sorts."

"*Marrone*," Lisi said. "This is getting confusing."

"The three-two-one union deals with celebrities all the time. Right?" I said. "So the mob has access—"

"Wait a minute." Lisi snapped his fingers. "You just gave me an idea."

"Yeah?" I waited expectantly.

"Maybe the Angel a' Death isn't your everyday serial killer, after all. Maybe it's a lot simpler than that."

"Meaning?"

"Could be the old protection racket," Lisi said. "Organized crime one-oh-one, like they did onna the docks, and innee Meatpacking District, and construction. They invent a threat, in this instance the Angel a' Death. Then they force the victim ta pay protection."

I paced the living room, thinking over this new scheme.

"Which could mean all of the celerity deaths," I said, "even my father's murder, were mob hits?"

"Yeah, it's possible," Lisi said. "But that's only if Ice Pick's actions were sanctioned. I mean, he could be operatin' on his own—which means he'd be pocketing all the proceeds from his scheme and not kicking back to one of the Five Families. Which would earn him a one-way trip to a New Jersey swamp."

"Any way you can find that out?"

"Lemme think about it."

My phone rang. Mario from the Organized Crime Control Bureau was calling back. "No," I said before Mario got a word out. "I'm not having a retirement party."

"That guy Nicky Bada-bing you asked about?" Mario said.

"What about him?"

"Someone just stuck an ice pick in his brain."

"*Marrone*," I said.

CHAPTER 57

"**W**HAT HAPPENED TO you?" Melody Butcher said. The assistant United States attorney was sitting at her desk, poring over a pile of files, a container of steaming Dunkin' Donuts coffee in her hand.

Agent Englund was sitting across from her, a piece of medical gauze taped to his broken nose. Both eyes were black, watery, swollen. Englund squirmed in his seat, glanced at Sobel. "I walked into a door."

"I'll bet," Butcher said.

"What's the status on Beckett?" Sobel asked.

"With Enia Petrescu gone, McKee dead?" Butcher sipped the coffee. "Have you heard anything more from your anonymous source?"

"No," Sobel said. "He's probably in the wind."

"You still can't link Lisi to the mob?"

Sobel shook his head. "Not only can't we link him, but we think they just tried to have him killed. The NYPD is looking at Ice Pick Martucci for the attempted hit."

"Martucci," Butcher said. "Now, there's a serial killer for you." She looked displeased, like she'd been let down once again by the FBI. "Have you given the contents of Lisi's safety-deposit box to our Organized Crime Bureau like I asked?"

"Yes," Sobel said.

"Let them deal with it," Butcher said. "As for Beckett?" She shrugged. "We move on."

"So Beckett and his vigilantes get away with a dozen home invasions," Englund said. "Armed robberies, assaults, one killing that we know of?"

Sobel also wasn't willing to give up so fast. "What about Solana Ortiz?"

"Haven't you seen the papers?" Butcher lifted a copy of the *Post* off her desk. The Angel of Death story was plastered across the front page. "Check the byline."

"Reported by Solana Ortiz," Sobel said.

"She had to have gotten that story from Beckett," Butcher said, "or someone in his camp. My guess? There's a quid pro quo. I bring her before the grand jury, she'll hedge her words. Clarify her statements."

"Prosecute her for perjury," Englund barked.

Butcher dismissed the young agent's suggestion out of hand. "Unless you bring me something substantial, our case against Michael Beckett and his Rockers is, for the time being, closed."

CHAPTER 58

"**W**E'VE GOT A new Angel of Death suspect," I said excitedly as I walked into Rathbones. Destiny was sitting at our favorite spot at the bar, checking social- media feeds on her cell phone. Charlie picked a bottle of beer off the ice and set it on the bar. I took a big swallow, then waved to Bobby G, who was sitting alone at the other end.

"Who?" Destiny said, putting her phone away.

"Ice Pick, along with your old pal Keating," I said.

That got her attention. "No way."

"I'm pretty sure Keating's the one tried to shotgun Lisi."

"So, it's an organized-crime thing?"

"Lisi's gonna check if one of the Five Families are involved. If they sanctioned the Angel of Death killings, or if Ice Pick was acting on his own, but here's the way they work." I touched on the mob's basic protection racket, then speculated on the roles of Ice Pick and his underling Sean Keating, who I figured had probably sold drugs to Nicky Bada-bing. "By the way, they just found Nicky DOA. Someone stabbed him in the brain with an ice pick."

"Keating was in Rief's Tavern," Destiny chimed in. "That's why Nicky wouldn't talk."

"Ice Pick killed him anyway—no loose ends. Which means Keating's probably dead already."

"Not that slippery bastard," Destiny said.

"You think so?" I downed the rest of my beer, threw some money on the bar. "C'mon," I said. "I know where Keating lives."

We exited Rathbones and headed to Lisi's garage.

"I was able to locate McKee's brother up in Portsmouth, New Hampshire." Destiny said as she buckled her seat belt and shifted to *drive*. "He seemed genuinely upset when I told him."

"Tell him everything?"

Destiny shook her head. "He'll get the details when he comes to claim the body."

Five minutes later, we were still traveling south on York Avenue. I checked the side mirror and glanced over my shoulder. No one appeared to be following.

"So," Destiny said. "You haven't said anything about the phone call from Solana. She tell you how wonderful you are? Again?"

"She thanked me for the story," I said. "Said she wanted to buy me dinner—you know, as a thank-you."

"What did you say?

I shrugged. "I didn't commit."

"She's after you," Destiny said. "You know that."

"No," I said. "I don't know that."

"Are you really that clueless?" Destiny said. "Or stuck on stupid?"

"For the sake of argument," I said. "Let's say you're right, and Solana wants to get back together with me. Why do you care?"

"You're my best friend." Destiny negotiated around a line of double-parked cars. "I care about your happiness."

"Right," I said. "You care because you love me. But you're no longer *in love* with me." I checked across the seat, caught her lovely profile. "Isn't that what you told me?"

Destiny didn't answer. She didn't have to.

With that subject put to bed, I turned around and scrutinized the line of vehicles behind us. In the distance I thought I spotted a black Crown Victoria, a scooter, and a motorcycle weaving around a double-long city bus. Destiny made the right on East Fifty-fifth Street. The double-long city bus also made the turn, blocking our view of any other vehicles behind us.

"Maybe," Destiny said, "when this Angel of Death case is over, we should take a break from one another. Give each other some space."

"You want more space?" I felt like I'd just been kicked in the stomach. "Whatever you say."

We drove into the heart of gentrifying Hell's Kitchen. New construction was everywhere. Gone were entire city blocks of crumbling rodent- and crime-infested tenements. In their place were fully occupied, mammoth residential and commercial real-estate developments. Trendy high-end restaurants and designer boutiques dotted every block.

We parked at a hydrant in front of Keating's crumbling tenement. Destiny tossed the NYPD parking plaque on the dashboard as we exited the vehicle. Then we climbed the crumbling steps into a urine-scented foyer. I noticed that Destiny was doing her almost sexually aggressive strut; moving with purpose, jaw jutted out, shoulders back, eyes alert. No indication that she knew, or cared, that she'd just hurt me. Again. Well, I was not about to clue her in. And I wasn't going to chase her—like the male goofballs do in so many sappy chick flicks—try to convince her to give "us" another chance. I knew from past experience that a woman is into a man, or she's not. Things work or they don't. You can't make someone love you. If Destiny wished to end our relationship as it was, walk away from all we had together, and move on, I wouldn't object. I'd make no move to stop her. If it was space she wanted, space was what she'd get.

Keating's battered, rusty lobby door was wide open and leaning against a wall, off its hinges. We stepped into the foyer. The building's entire row of mailboxes had been vandalized long ago. We climbed the broken stairs, passed pitted, graffiti-covered walls on our way up to the third floor; a mix of sour odors permeated the stale air. We heard a TV blaring behind Apartment 3C, a game show of some sort. We pulled our weapons, stood to either side of the door. I rang the bell. Knocked. Pounded. The door flew open.

"You gonna beat the fuckin' door down?" Keating's mother squawked angrily. "Or what?!" The whip-thin old whore was dressed in a ragged housedress. She stank of cigarettes and stale booze. Thick red lipstick was smeared comically across her nonexistent lips. The cheap, heavy eye makeup was clumped and carelessly applied. The unmistakable stench of rotting garbage wafted from inside the dark, cluttered dwelling.

"We're looking for Sean," Destiny said, lowering her weapon.

"He ain't heah!" If the old broad was frightened by the sight of two people pointing guns at her, she didn't show it. "Who the fuck're you?"

"When's the last time you saw him?" Destiny showed her shield.

Sean's mother glanced at the ID. Sneered. "I don't have to tell you shit." She stepped back into her apartment and slammed the door in our faces.

"Charming," Destiny said.

"Let's talk to the superintendent," I said. "Then check the neighborhood."

We descended to the first floor, then the basement, couldn't locate a super. We started to exit the building, but hung back in the doorway and scanned the traffic: pedestrians, double-parked cars, and rooftops. Saw nothing out of the ordinary.

We searched for Keating in several gloomy "bloodbath" dive bars, once home to the bygone Hell's Kitchen Irish gang, the Westies, many of whom, like Keating, had been members of Teamster Local 321. We asked surly bartenders, bored waitresses, and customers—suspicious inebriates—if they'd seen Keating. No one had, or so they claimed. For whatever reason, Destiny and I believed them.

Down on a side street, we were about to enter another dingy dive bar when I caught the flash of the sun reflecting off something on a tenement rooftop. "Down!" I grabbed Destiny, pulled her behind a parked car. I was about to shout out a warning to nearby pedestrians, but when I looked down the narrow sidewalk, no one was close enough to be at risk. Destiny and I waited for a few moments. No shots were fired.

"What did you see?" she asked.

"A reflection up on a roof," I said. "Could've been from a rifle scope." Using parked cars as cover, we crabbed half a block west. Then I peeked over the hood of a minivan, searching above the tenements' top overhang for the shooter.

"You sure?" Destiny said.

"No." I stood up. "I saw... something."

"Let's check it out," she suggested.

We dashed across the street, down the block, raced up some stairs. Destiny kicked open a locked tenement foyer door, and we ran up to the roof. Not wanting to be backlit, Destiny used her weapon to smash an overhead hallway lightbulb. Then I eased open the heavy door and, our weapons combat ready, we glided out onto the tar-paper–covered roof like we'd done a hundred times before when we were ghetto cops.

All the tenements were connected to one another, so we could see across the rooftops for half a city block in either direction. But the only movement we saw was laundry fluttering from a dozen clotheslines. We crept across the roofs until we came to the approximate spot where I'd seen the reflection. Nothing.

"I must be getting paranoid," I said, holstering my weapon. We headed to the stairs and saw that the rooftop door had been kicked open. Fresh wood splinters were on the ground. "This is recent," I said, looking around one last time.

Feeling a new scent, we descended the stairs, exited the building to the street, our eyes scanning neighboring rooftops.

We visited a few more local business and dive bars, questioned workers and customers. No one admitted to seeing Keating.

"You thinking what I'm thinking?" I said after we exited a timeworn strip club, worked by third-rate topless dancers who'd seen better days. "Keating's gotta be DOA."

"I won't believe it until I see his body and stick a pin in it."

"Still, we're running out of places to look," I said.

"Let's stake out his building," Destiny said. "Give it a little more time."

I purchased some food—a corned beef on rye and a couple of beers for me, a fruit salad and wine coolers for Destiny. We ate in the car and spent the next few uncomfortable hours watching Keating's tenement, not saying much to each other.

Destiny opened her second wine cooler, and when I saw her furtively reach into a pocket and swallow a painkiller, I decided to intervene.

"Dr. Goldsamp ever call?"

Destiny shook her head. "No news is good news."

"Why don't you call him?" I asked, my voice harder.

"Maybe I will."

We called the stakeout quits a little after midnight and headed back to the garage. As was the norm at that time of night, the steel security gate was down, and most of the overhead fluorescent lights had been turned off. We pulled into the garage driveway. I exited the vehicle, rang the attendant's night bell. The steel gate rattled loudly as it slowly rose, but the overhead lights did not go on. Also, the usual gushing, knucklehead garage attendant didn't rush to greet us. No one did.

I stood to one side as Destiny drove the SUV into the usual spot. She killed the engine, opened her door that illuminated the interior.

Pop!

The first noise-suppressed shot shattered the windshield. I dove. Rolled.

Pop! Pop! Pop! Pop! Pop! The automatic-weapon fire pitted the SUV's doors.

I scrabbled across the concrete floor to the relative safety of a thick support pier, my body screaming in protest. I was still sore from our automobile accident. "Destiny?"

No answer.

Inside the garage office, the knucklehead attendant was lying facedown on the ground, blood pooled beneath him. I heard movement to my right, peeked from behind the stanchion, across the cavernous interior, into the garage's numerous deeply shadowed nooks and crannies. I wished to hell I knew who was shooting at us. Ice Pick Martucci? His henchman Sean Keating? Another mob assassin? Hell, maybe it was Matt the Hat. But since both Destiny and I had received numerous death threats from criminals we'd put in prison over the years, it could be almost anyone.

Something stirred to my left. A shadowy figure moved in the dim light. I took aim, but not knowing Destiny's location, I didn't dare fire. I checked back to Lisi's vehicle. Squatting all the way down, my face on the cold cement, I looked underneath the car to the other side. If Destiny had been shot and badly wounded, that's where she'd be—no Destiny. I was about to call out her name again, but stopped myself. Answering me would only give away her position.

I focused on the area across the garage where I'd seen movement. I decided to force the issue. I dashed and ducked behind a car. Waited a moment. No one fired. I dashed and ducked behind another car. Then a third, fourth, and fifth.

Pop! Pop! Pop! Pop! Pop! The gunfire strafed the cars around me. Glass shattered. Tires were blown. Rounds buzzed past, pitted the walls. I had to cover my eyes to keep the shrapnel from blinding me. The smell of cordite was thick in the air. I could tell that the shooter was moving as he fired. I came to my feet and returned the fire. In one burst I emptied a thirteen-shot clip.

Ducked. Reloaded. Fired off another thirteen rounds. Ducked. Slapped in another clip. And waited.

Bam! Bam!

Those shots were fired from a different weapon.

I peeked over a car hood.

"Hey." Destiny was standing over a prone body dressed in black and wearing a ski mask, her weapon still combat ready. "We got the son of a bitch."

Alert for a backup shooter, I sprang to my feet and advanced cautiously across the garage. Destiny kicked the assassin's automatic weapon away—it looked like a Heckler & Koch HK416 assault rifle, which could shoot around 900 rounds a minute. She used her foot to roll the guy over. The shooter was struck four times. Which meant that Destiny's two shots and two of mine had found their mark. Destiny squatted down to feel the carotid artery for a pulse. She shook her head. "DOA." She holstered her weapon and used two hands to pull off his ski mask.

Fabio.

"I'll be a son of a bitch," I said in disbelief.

"Can you believe it?" Destiny said. "That lunatic Matt the Hat was right all along."

CHAPTER 59

ICE PICK MARTUCCI sat with his back to a wall, in his usual booth in the rear of the nearly empty Greek diner on Cross Bay Boulevard, where he routinely ate breakfast every morning at 6:00. The sun was streaming in through large plate-glass windows, reflecting off the establishment's spotless white floors, gleaming counters, and chrome display cases, casting the restaurant in a cheery yellow glow.

But Ice Pick didn't feel cheery that morning. Across the room his two beefy bodyguards were eating like pigs at the front counter. He fought to deal with his stomach's twisting anger. After insulting him at Bocca al Lupo Ristorante in the presence of his associates—and most embarrassing of all, the evening's *goumadas*—that fucker Sweet Tommy Lisi was still alive.

Ice Pick regarded his breakfast of crispy bacon, scrambled eggs, home fries, a side of heavily buttered rye, and felt nauseous. He reached into his pocket and popped a couple of antacids

He hadn't counted on the brash, young Irishman Sean Keating screwing up a simple hit; I mean, how difficult can whacking a sickly old geezer be? Granted, Keating didn't have the street creds to be trusted with a contract killing. But like the old guard, the new Westies were anxious to ingratiate themselves to the Italian mob, and Keating appeared both capable and hungry. Ice Pick decided to take a chance on the smarmy, ambitious mick mainly because he couldn't assign the contract to anyone in his own crew—or, for that matter, anyone in any of the other crews already closely associated with the Five Families, because Lisi had once been connected. Even though they all knew that Lisi had killed his cousin years ago, and had recently insulted him in public, Ice Pick needed permission before ordering the hit. Breaching mob protocol—killing Lisi without permission and being found out—could result in consequences. Which was precisely why, after the failed hit, he'd promptly tied up all loose ends. He'd disposed of Keating, along with his little greaseball pal, Nicky Bada-bing; the reality star was a disgrace to his Italian ancestors anyway. Now there was no one left to inform on him. Unless Sweet Tommy Lisi figured out who was behind the attempted assassination and made a stink within the mob. That was yet another reason why Lisi had to die.

Ice Pick felt the antacids begin to work. He forked two slices of bacon, some eggs on the rye toast, and made a small sandwich. He bit off a large mouthful, glanced at the counter in front, and noticed that his two bodyguards were no longer stuffing their faces. What the fuck? Ice Pick swore under his breath. He placed his sandwich down on the plate, wiped the crumbs from his hands on a napkin, took out his cell phone and dialed one of them. He did not notice the man in the black trench coat, hat pulled down over his face, who'd come gliding out of the men's room.

Bobby G stepped up to Ice Pick's table, raised a .9mm automatic with a noise suppressor, and said "Sweet Tommy Lisi says hello." Then he pumped six shots into Ice Pick's face.

CHAPTER 60

EVEN UNDER THE cover of darkness, amid the chaos of Midtown traffic, Ernie Serria and I knew at once that we were being followed—the battered blue Chevy passenger van, three car lengths back. But we were careful not to alarm the Jurassic British rock star, Jorden Richards, who was sitting in the rear of the SUV. At his request, his rock band's vintage music was blaring on the vehicle's sound system. He was chain-smoking cigarettes, drinking tequila, and, much to my disgust, swapping spit with the still reigning Queen of the Guidettes, Francine "Tata" Andolini. (Apparently *Jersey Shore Confidential* had been renewed for yet another season.) Serria and I were escorting the two "celebrities" to one of those self-congratulatory music-industry award dinners. This event was being held at Cipriani at Forty-second Street and Lexington Avenue, an Italian Renaissance–inspired catering facility featuring towering marble columns, soaring ceilings, magnificent inlaid floors, and glorious chandeliers.

To lose the tail, Serria hit the gas. Ran a red light. Executed a screeching turn onto Fifth Avenue. The blue van followed.

"I say, Mr. Beckett." Jorden used the rear-seat controls to thankfully lower the music. He leaned forward, belched a squall of tequila and cigarette smoke in my face. "We in a hurry, mate?"

"We're being followed," I said.

Tata glanced out the rear window. "Oh, Babbo"—her pet

name for the cadaverous, drug-ravaged, seventy-five-year-old rock legend—"That's Matt the Hat! See? In the blue van." Tata waved at the Hat. The Hat waved back.

"Who?" Jorden said.

"My very own stalker," Tata gushed. "He follows me everywhere."

"Like I've told you before," I said, "if the Hat's a problem, we'll help you file a restraining order."

"No! I think he's kinda cute," Tata said. "You know, in a deranged, sleazy sort of way."

"Wait a minute. I read about that bloke," Jorden said. "Mr. Beckett, isn't he the individual who assisted you in the capture of that famous serial killer?"

"The Angel of Death," Serria supplied.

"Sort of," I said. Even though I was pretty sure that the Hat had no idea that Fabio actually was a serial killer until he, like Jorden, Tata, and the rest of the world, saw it on the TV news.

The demise of the Angel of Death had dominated the press for weeks. Fabio's crossdressing lifestyle (I knew it!) struggles with manic depression along with a half-a-dozen civil lawsuits filed against him for stalking female co-workers and neighbors, (we never thought to investigate civil suits) stoked the public interest. As a happy consequence, it was slowly helping to return Lisi & Beckett Protective Services, Inc. to profitability. All thanks to the avalanche of positive press produced by the *New York Post* reporter, my "friend" Solana Ortiz. But the story faded fast once the police stated that they could not find any hard evidence linking Fabio to any of the celebrity murders. As far as they were concerned, Victoria Carrington and all of the other celebrities died from tainted heroin, which was readily available and which had killed, and was still killing, hundreds of drug addicts across the country. As a result, they could find no motive for Fabio ambushing Destiny and myself in the Ninetieth Street garage and killing the garage attendant.

That didn't matter to me. I was confident that Destiny and I had killed the Angel of Death. I had avenged my father's and Victoria Carrington's murders. Especially after learning that while in the Army, Fabio had "accidentally" killed an unarmed Iraqi civilian and was a suspect in the death of several others. That's why he'd received a dishonorable discharge.

There were also the bonus deaths of drug dealers Nicky Bada-bing and Sean Keating. (Keating's body was discovered in a Hell's Kitchen dive-bar men's room with an ice-pick puncture to the brain.) Most satisfying of all, the mob-style hit of Ice Pick Martucci.

Interestingly enough, the story about the assassination of the infamous mobster never gained much traction. It was reported on the TV news, written up on their online editions and Twitter feeds. A Mafia buff's blogs speculated that Ice Pick's attempted hit on Sweet Tommy Lisi without permission from the Commission was the reason he was murdered himself. Whatever the motive, in the end no one cared about why Ice Pick died, or who killed him. For my part, I never asked Lisi about the early-morning shooting at the Greek diner. He said he'd take care of Ice Pick in his own way. I assumed that's exactly what he'd done.

Serria made an illegal turn off Fifth Avenue onto East Forty-second Street and into horrific bumper-to-bumper traffic. Three blocks east of us, huge movie spotlights swept the night sky. Flash-camera fusillades lit up the street like July 4th fireworks as limos dropped off their celebrity clients. I used my cell to phone Tommy Lisi, who was awaiting our arrival, along with Sid Schulsky. Thanks to all the recent positive press, Lisi & Beckett Protective Services was not only providing personal security to a few select guests, but also providing all of the event security for the Cipriani gala. Using a list of mine, Lisi had hired an additional two-dozen retired cops.

"We're stuck in traffic about three blocks away," I said to Lisi.

"S'what I figured."

"Sid Schulsky there?"

"Waitin' for Tata at the curb," Lisi said. "Guy's a nervous fuckin' wreck—pardon my French. Can't believe we actually thought he coulda been the Angel a' Death."

"Do me a favor," I said. "Let him know where we are?"

"Will do."

The traffic inched forward.

"Anything you need to tell me?" I asked.

"Oh, yeah," Lisi said. "Victoria Carrington's mother's heah with her boy toy."

"Anything else?"

"Like?"

"Don't fuck with me, Tommy."

"Okay." Lisi giggled, really enjoying himself. "Destiny's working the event. Matter of fact, she's bodyguarding Victoria's mother."

"Didn't I ask you not to call her?"

"Hey, fucko. Whaddya want me to do?" Lisi said. "You try staffing an event this size at the last minute—hell, I'm still shorthanded."

"All right. Calm down," I said. "Solana there?"

"I saw her earlier, interviewing celebrities onna red carpet."

"She and Destiny speak?"

"Hold on." Lisi had obviously seen something. "*Marrone.*"

"What?"

"Solana just walked over ta Destiny. They're talking right now."

"Shit." I put my phone away. Took a deep breath. Tried to rub away the tension headache that was forming behind my eyes. I knew that if Destiny worked the event, Solana would find a way to gloat about the fact that she and I were seeing each other again. Not that I had anything to hide. It was none of Destiny's business who I dated.

Destiny had left for parts unknown three weeks ago, the day after Victoria Carrington's star-studded funeral. (McKee's brother had had his body cremated and his ashes un-ceremonially sprinkled off the cliffs of Silver Beach). Although I have to confess my first instinct was to tell Destiny how much I still loved her and beg her to stay, I didn't. Instead, I told her that she should do what she had to do. After that, I decided that would be a good time for Solana to buy me that thank-you dinner. Long story short: Solana and I ate too much, drank too much, and things sort of took off from there.

"Know what your problem is?" Serria said, keeping his voice low so the two whack-a-doodles in the backseat couldn't hear. "You don't understand women."

"And you do?"

"When a woman breaks up with a guy, especially after a long-term relationship like yours and Destiny's, they go through a mourning period. They get depressed, obsess over what went wrong, agonize over if it was their fault."

"That's dumb."

"'Cause we don't think that way," Serria said. "Men jump on the first babe that comes along—that's how we deal with a breakup. You fall off a horse, you get right back on the horse. Woman aren't like that."

"You trying to tell me something?"

"Yeah. You going back to Solana, of all people, so soon after breaking up with Destiny?" Serria shook his head. "She'll hate you for that."

"So soon? Our romance was kaput over a year ago. Destiny's idea. Not mine."

"She'll still hate you."

"But that doesn't make any sense."

"There you go," Serria said. "Expecting women to makes sense."

Jorden leaned forward. "How much longer, mate?"

We hadn't moved an inch in the past few minutes. "Not long." I pointed ahead. "We're on the queue to drop you off."

"Let's just walk, Babbo," Tata said.

"I wouldn't advise that," I said. An A-list rock star since the sixties, Jorden knew better than anyone alive just how dangerous a mob of crazed fans could be. But before I knew what happened, the rear door opened, and Jorden and Tata bounded out of the SUV.

"We're going to hoof it, mate," Jorden said and closed the door.

"Pull over," I told Serria. I threw my door open and bolted out of the car. I quickstepped and fell in alongside Jorden and Tata. We walked for a full crosstown block, passing pedestrians and tourists of every description. By a miracle no one recognized the legendary rock star—that is, until he began to weave through the massive crowd of fans that totally blocked the sidewalk in front of Cipriani. Jorden sidled forward with purpose, excusing himself politely. I thought that we were actually going to make it without incident when a woman screamed, "Jorden Richards!"

All hell broke loose.

Tata was shoved aside. Jorden was swarmed. Women tore at his clothes and hair, knocked the old geezer to the ground. I shouted to Lisi for help. Lisi and his team of bodyguards—Solana included—and a dozen uniformed cops rushed to our rescue. I dove into the fracas, managed to reach Jorden, pull him to his feet. Lisi and I all but carried him past the red carpet and into the safety of Cipriani.

Someone found a chair and Jorden, thoroughly shaken, sat down. His clothing was in shreds. His nose was bleeding. And he was bleeding from where fans had literally torn out clumps of his long, dyed black hair and scalp.

"I'm okay," Jorden said good-naturedly. "Really." British chin-up and all that.

A waiter appeared with a stack of white dinner napkins. Lisi pressed one to Jorden's head in an attempt to stop the bleeding. Jorden pressed another napkin to his nose and laid his head back. Solana came up behind me. Used me as a shield as she snapped furtive photos of Jorden for the *Post*.

"Where's Tata?" Jorden asked.

"Where's Destiny?" Lisi asked.

I didn't see Tata or Destiny. I dashed back out to the street, where it was still chaos. Lisi's security team was assisting the cops, who were arresting disorderly fans. Those resisting were being pummeled into submission. Several individuals were already sitting on the sidewalk in handcuffs, cursing the cops. I spotted a dazed Tata being helped to her feet by Sid Schulsky. Behind them, a policewoman was attending to a woman lying prone on the pavement—Destiny.

I ran down the sidewalk and squatted down alongside the female cop. "Destiny?" No answer. I looked for signs of blood or broken bones.

The female cop informed me, "She was knocked down. Hit her head." She reached for her radio. "I'll call an ambulance."

"No time," I said. "Where's your car?"

She gestured to the curb.

I picked Destiny up in my arms. When I turned, I found that I was face-to-face with Solana. She was blocking my way.

"Beckett!" The policewoman was holding the car door open. "Let's go!"

"I have to do this," I said to her.

"Do you?" Solana sighed as she stepped aside, resignation in her eyes. "Go. And good luck."

I wondered what Solana meant by that as I rushed to the police car, gently placed Destiny in the backseat, and climbed in beside her. As we raced, lights, and sirens down Forty-second Street and making the right onto Second Avenue heading to Langone Medical Center, I checked Destiny's pulse. She stirred, sat up, a dazed look in her eyes.

"Where... ?"

"Easy," I said. "I've got you."

Destiny's eyes finally focused. "Michael?"

I held her hand. "You're gonna be okay."

"You're an idiot," she said. "You know that, don't you?"

CHAPTER 61

I SPENT THE ENTIRE night at Langone Medical Center pacing the floors, badgering the doctors and nurses with questions about Destiny's status, until Mark Chin, the director of Security, told me to "cool my jets" or he'd kick me the hell out.

Destiny had sustained a slight concussion, cuts, and bruises when she'd been knocked down and trampled during the melee at Cipriani. Because of her past medical history, the doctors had insisted upon keeping her overnight for observation. After an X-ray and other tests, I helped get her settled in a private room.

Lisi arrived at the hospital around 1:00 a.m. after the event at Cipriani ended. He'd seen to it that a replacement bodyguard escorted Victoria Carrington's mother and her boy toy back to her daughter's former town house. Serria showed up a while later, after he'd dropped off Jorden Richards at his hotel and then delivered Tata safely home to her father. But Destiny was sedated and absolutely no visitors were allowed.

And so Lisi and Serria kept me company. We hung around in a waiting area down the hall from Destiny's room. We drank coffee and made small talk about Tata's disturbing affair with Jorden Richards, Lynn Carrington's bizarre celebratory behavior, and speculated about why the feds were no longer harassing us. We all agreed that with Enia gone—which was now common knowledge—their case against my Rockers had fallen apart; it was the only thing that made sense.

Lisi and Serria called it a night around three. I grabbed a catnap on a cot in Mark Chin's office.

Destiny was sitting up in bed the following morning, looking alert, checking her social-media feeds on her iPhone when I walked into her room. No IVs of any kind were hanging around the bed—a good sign. Only an index-finger clamp was recording her heart rate and pulse; the results were visible on the screen suspended above the bed.

"You look tired," Destiny said.

"How do you feel?" I grabbed a chair and pulled it close to the bed. "You had me worried there."

Destiny put her cell phone down and hit me with "the look."

"What?" I said.

"You're an idiot."

"You already told me that."

Destiny crossed her arms across her chest. "I spoke to Solana. Or should I say, Solana spoke to me."

"Okay." I sat back, crossed my legs.

"I told you she was after you."

An orderly wheeling a large cart stacked with food trays paused outside. He extracted a tray, shuffled into the room, said a cheerful "Good morning," and placed it on a high-top, rolling table alongside the bed.

"Thanks," Destiny said as the orderly retreated. She uncovered the plate of food—fresh fruit, oatmeal, orange juice, hot tea, toast—and wrinkled her nose. "Fresh fruit doesn't look bad. You hungry?"

"I'll pass."

She picked up the container of OJ, gave it a good shake. "In case you were wondering, I was in Florida, visiting my parents."

I had been wondering and worrying, but I was not about to tell her that. "How are they?"

"Not great." She opened the OJ and drank.

"So," I said, not going to be deflected. "What did Solana have to say?"

Destiny shrugged. "She told me you two were back together, among other things."

A nurse walked in, checked Destiny's vitals, and placed an assortment of pills in little paper cups on the tray table, alongside the food.

Destiny perused the cups and pointed at one. "What's that?"

"Vitamin A."

"And that?"

"Vicodin."

"I can't take either of them."

I sat up straight. Destiny turning down Vicodin?

"Why not?" the nurse said. "You pregnant?"

"Yes," Destiny said. "I am."

I blinked once. Twice. Three times. "What?"

"I'm pregnant," Destiny said as the nurse picked up the vitamin A and Vicodin and walked out. "You know, with child. Expecting. Knocked up. Got a bun in the oven. Eating for two."

"I got it," I said. "You sure?"

Destiny squeezed a lemon slice into her tea and gave it a stir. "I finally called Dr. Goldsamp. He apologized for no one getting back to me. Apparently, because the cancer tests were negative, his assistant simply forgot. He said my pregnancy was probably causing the headache."

"Holy shit," I said.

"Exactly," Destiny said.

"Is it? I mean. How long—?"

"Four months," Destiny said. "In case you're wondering, it's yours."

I shot to my feet and started pacing. "What're you gonna—I mean, what are we gonna—I mean—"

"Good question." Destiny put down her cup of tea and

pushed the tray of food away. "I've done whole lot of soul-searching the last three weeks. Long walks on the beach, endless talks with my mother and girlfriends. I even spoke to a shrink. Know what I realized?"

"I'm an idiot?"

Destiny smiled. "Besides that, you're the most honest, decent human being I've ever known. I've missed you."

I sat back down. "What do you want me to say to that?"

"You missed me too?"

I crossed my arms across my chest and didn't say anything.

"I know I've given you a hard time the last few years," Destiny said.

"That's an understatement."

"I wouldn't blame you for telling me to go to hell."

"I might," I said, "if you'll tell me what the hell you're trying to say. And please, no roundabout female-eze. Get to the point."

"The point is, I'm still very much in love with you. There's no one on earth that I'd rather have a family with."

"Just like that."

Destiny saw no need to apologize. "Just like that."

Again I shot to my feet. "So this is all about you. What you want. How you feel. Well, how about what *I* want? How *I* feel? Doesn't anyone care about how *I* feel?"

She seemed irritated by this intrusion. "How do you feel?"

"Quiet!" I said. "I'm having a rhetorical conversation." I paced a bit more, sat back down. "So you miss me, realize I'm a great guy, wanna have a family with me. What am I supposed to do now? What do I tell Solana?"

"I wouldn't worry about Solana," Destiny said. "She's gone."

I sat up straight. "Gone? What's that mean? Gone. Gone where?"

"She told me she could tell you didn't love her anymore, that what you two had together was over a long time ago."

"So you're saying... What are you saying? She dumped me? Again?"

"Annoying. Isn't it?"

I whipped out my cell phone. "I wanna hear it from Solana." I began to dial, but saw a text message from her waiting. *Any fool can tell you still love Destiny and not me. Good-bye. Good luck.*

"Well?" Destiny said.

I put my phone away. "I changed my mind." I walked angrily around the room, feeling like a pawn in a game I knew nothing about. Serria was right. I knew squat about women. I mean, How dare Solana dump me. How could I not see that coming? Sure, she was right about me loving Destiny and not her, but it was the principle of the thing.

"C'mere," Destiny said and patted the mattress.

I hesitated, playing hard to get. But five steps later I was sitting on the edge of the bed. Destiny was smiling at me.

"You need a good spanking," I said. "You know that?"

"You going to give me one?"

"Maybe after…" I patted her stomach. I couldn't believe it. There was a little love child in there. "I love you."

"I know."

I bent forward and kissed her lightly on the lips. "You taste like orange juice."

"Shut up." Destiny grabbed my face and kissed me back.

"*Marrone,*" Lisi said.

We both turned to look. He was standing in the doorway, face red with embarrassment, a bouquet of flowers in his hand.

"If youse'll excuse me"—Lisi stepped into the room and laid the flowers on the chair—"I'm outta heah." He hurried back out the door, leaving us alone.

Dear Reader:

If you enjoyed this book, kindly tell your friends about it. And please post a review at amazon.com and/or barnesandnoble. com, or Goodreads. Thoughtful and positive reviews encourage a writer. And they help sales. After all, writers have to live and eat, just like real human beings. ☺

TF

www.thomasfitzsimmons.com

ABOUT THE AUTHOR

THOMAS FITZSIMMONS DIDN'T need to go to the public library, interview participants, or hire a team of high-priced researchers to write gritty stories. For Fitzsimmons, a former New York City police officer, NBC television personality, Ford model, soap-opera/TV commercial actor, private investigator, and bodyguard to numerous A-list celebrities, it was as simple as recalling his life.

Fitzsimmons grew up in an Irish Bronx neighborhood in a family of career cops. After high school, he joined the Navy and pulled sea duty aboard a guided-missile cruiser on its way to Vietnam. The wartime experiences kindled a civic spirit in Fitzsimmons, who, upon being honorably discharged, joined the New York City Police Department. During a career that spanned ten years in the precinct dramatized in Paul Newman's *Fort Apache, The Bronx*, Fitzsimmons notched numerous arrests collaring armed robbers, drug kingpins, and arsonists.

Fitzsimmons's heroics were brought to the attention of talent scout Joey Hunter, who was the president of the men's division for the Ford Modeling Agency. The Ford executive convinced Fitzsimmons that he had a future in the TV/modeling industries. The young cop soon filled his off-duty hours with modeling assignments, which eventually led to an audition with NBC TV for a position as an on-camera personality and cohost for the magazine-format talk show *Now*.

Success in the entertainment industry forced Fitzsimmons to choose between law enforcement or a glamorous, new lifestyle. The decision was tough, but Fitzsimmons never looked back. The actor/writer won the coveted TV assignment with NBC, and although the show was eventually canceled, he soon became a top TV commercial actor and print model. As a rising star with the Ford Agency and the J. Michael Bloom Television Agency, he appeared in such soap operas as *One Life to Live* and *Texas* and served as a principal in more than 150 television commercials.

Fitzsimmons also drew from his law-enforcement experiences with the NYPD, as well as numerous show- business contacts, to become a top security consultant. He has appeared on shows such as *Good Morning America*, *Geraldo Rivera*, and *Montel Williams* as a security expert.

CPSIA information can be obtained at www.ICGtesting.com
Printed in the USA
LVOW11s1839200616

493348LV00009B/1137/P